MW01230166

Joseph DeMark

A Jake Lester Mystery

THE MIXER

Walter, Spots, Spotsman Mysteries

CRISS CROSS

FINDING AARON LAWS

DARKEST TUNNEL

THE ETHOS SYNDROME

DEADLY GAME

BACKDROP

Copyright © 2023 Joseph DeMark

This book is a work of fiction. Names, characters, places, and incidents are products of the Author's imagination or are used fictitiously. Any resemblance to actual events or locales or persons, living or dead is entirely coincidental.

All rights reserved. No part of this book may be reproduced, stored, or transmitted by any means whether auditory, graphic, mechanical, or electronic without written permission of both publisher and author, except in the case of brief excerpts used in critical articles and reviews. Unauthorized reproduction of any part of this work is illegal and punishable by law.

ISBN: 9798868130892

Because the dynamic nature of the internet any web addresses or links contained in this book may have changed since publication and may no longer be valid. The views expressed are solely those of the author and do not necessarily reflect the views of the publisher and the publisher here by disclaims any responsibility for them.

Manufactured in the United States of America: Amazon

Jake Lester Mysteries
PRIME MOTIVE
THE MIXER

1

Jake Lester and his wife, Dr. Maggie Kliener, were on their newly purchased thirty-eight foot power boat making their way to a favorite fishing site with Joan Fetter, a (Lind City Times) reporter, aboard. Joan, twenty-four years old and one year out of college, joined the (Times) six months ago as Human Interest Reporter with her eye on becoming an investigative reporter. The four great lake size fishing poles neatly stowed in metal racks on the inside of the hull proclaimed the owner's genuine enjoyment of the sport. Joan recently asked Jake and Maggie for an exclusive interview for an article about the recently retired Lind City Chief of Homicide Detective. Jake and Maggie agreed to the interview and decided the perfect venue would be on Big Bass Lake, close to their cottage, with a probability of no interruptions. Jake drew the throttles back on the twin engines and the vessel coasted to a stop adjacent to a crop of budding lily pads. He touched a small button on the dashboard and the anchor gently descended into the water. He placed the shift lever into reverse, released the anchor line, slowly backed the boat about twenty feet, and stopped.

"It looks like you've done this before," Joan quipped. She sunk her petite body into the white waterproof seat and thought, "What did I say? Jake's going think I'm immature."

Jake grinned and said, "I've done this many times on our other boats but this is the maiden voyage for this one." He slipped out of the captain's chair and sat next to Maggie. "Why don't we get the business of the interview behind us before we have lunch?"

Joan, relieved from what she thought was a major blunder, replied, "That's a great idea." She turned on her note pad and settled into one of the cushioned seats. "Before we start the interview, would you like me to mention you as Chief or Jake?"

"I'm no longer the Chief, so Jake would work just fine."

"Dr. Kliener, what would you prefer?"

"Dr. Kliener would be fine, thank you. When we are together, please call me Maggie."

"Jake, it looks like you're about five eleven and around one hundred and eighty pounds. How close am I?" Joan asked.

"You're right on and, for the record, I'm forty six years old," Jake replied.

"It's been six months since you retired from the Police Department. I'm going to start by asking you about your daily routine. I mean what keeps you motivated?"

"Joan, that's a great question. I work out two hours a day five days a week at the Police Department gym. Maggie is still the Lind City Medical Examiner and has a hectic schedule. I like to spend my evenings with her, and usually we find something to keep us occupied on Saturdays and Sundays. I know that sounds mundane," Jake replied. He noticed a slight breeze picking up and said, "Hold on for a few minutes, the boat is starting to swing a little. I'm going to drop the stern anchor." Jake firmly held the anchor line, swayed the heavy anchor back and forth, and let the anchor loose. It landed with a big splash twenty feet from the boat. "There, that's much better."

"Jake, can you tell me about your new venture?"

"Right after I retired, I applied for a Private Detective License, and it was approved last month. I guess I'm in the PI business."

"You were at the top of your game with the Police Department, what was the determining factor for your decision to retire?"

"I felt it was time." Jake paused. "I think a PI's life is not as constricted as a law enforcement investigator. That is to say, the law provides more investigative leeway for a Private Detective."

"I see." Joan typed a few notes on her iPad, and nudged her horn rimmed glasses up. "Do you have any clients?"

"No, not at the present time. I haven't tried to look for any clients and, when the right time comes, I want to pick and choose. I know that may sound arrogant, but I'm retired and have that option," Jake replied.

"Maggie, I'm sure you're proud of your husband. I mean he's athletic, keeps himself busy, and he's starting a new career."

"Yes, I am very proud of him. Not only is he all the things you mentioned, Jake is a thoughtful, loving husband."

"Have you ever thought of changing careers and joining Jake in his venture?

"Joan, off the record," Maggie noted.

"Certainly," Joan replied.

"I'm forty years old. Now we can go on the record." Maggie pushed her hair behind her ears and laughed. "I'm not ready to retire." She placed a baseball cap on her head and narrowed the visor.

The interview continued for another two hours before an unexpected downpour interrupted their plans for lunch on the boat. Jake thought the rain was a good excuse to break off the interview for the day and have lunch at their cottage. "I think you ladies would feel more comfortable in the cabin while I weigh the anchors."

"Good idea, Jake. Let me know when you're ready for us to help you," Maggie shouted, as she and Joan disappeared into the cabin.

"Yeah, right. No chance of getting them out of a dry cabin and hot coffee," Jake mumbled. He jiggled the stern anchor line, clearing the line of lake weeds and, hand over hand, he began to haul in the heavy anchor. Jake said to himself, "I must be getting weak. The anchor weighs a ton." He gave the line some slack. "I must have tangled the line around a submerged tree branch." As he leaned over the transom he noticed a large piece of white cloth, about four feet below the surface, clinging to the line. The cloth appeared to be part of a person's shirt. Jake's twenty years of experience dealing with fatalities told him there was something drastically wrong. He needed to get a closer look at the cloth and began to draw in the line. "Holy crap," Jake shouted. He quickly tied the line to one of the boat's cleats.

Maggie came out of the cabin and stepped onto the deck shouting, "Jake, what's wrong?"

"We have a body in the water and it's tangled around the anchor line," Jake responded.

Maggie inched closer to Jake and saw the body. "We're in Lind City Jurisdiction, and we better give your old boss a call."

Joan came scurrying up the cabin stairs asking, "Did I hear there's a body in the water?"

9

Jake forcefully responded, "Yes there is a body in the water and, until we have evidence, we'll consider this a crime scene. You cannot take any pictures or record information about the scene into your news room. Is that clear?"

"Yes, perfectly clear," Joan replied.

"I'll call Robert and tell him about the body and our location," Jake said.

"You're calling Robert? Commissioner Robert Marshal?" Joan asked, excitedly. "This would be my first crime scene report. Can I have an exclusive on the case?"

Maggie replied, "Joan, calm down. Jake told us this may be a crime scene or it may have been a boating accident. We have a deceased person here and this isn't about a news scoop. The Commissioner, or the detective in charge is well aware of the First Amendment and will ask for your cooperation."

"Robert is on his way with police boats. His ETA is twenty minutes and forensics will be here with a diving team forthwith. In the meantime, we're going to sit tight, secure the scene, and above all let's be respectful," Jake said.

Maggie handed Jake a mug of coffee. "Thank you." he sat at the edge of the Captain's chair. For the first time in over twenty years Jake was at a highly probable crime scene and was on the outside looking in.

"I know you feel like a retired race horse, with all the young horses at the starting gate, and all he can do is watch. Robert's new team will handle things just fine. Jake, remember you have a PI License and some of your contacts may be future clients." Maggie gave Jake a peck on the cheek. "That's for being my husband."

Jake's thoughts were interrupted by the sound of power boats, skimming across the lake and heading in their direction. He picked up his binoculars and saw Robert standing alone at the bow of the lead boat. Something didn't seem right. If Roberts's new team could handle the rigors of what appeared to be a crime scene, why wouldn't they be aboard the boat? A larger search and rescue boat with five officers dressed in diving gear sped alongside the Commissioner's boat. The two vessels throttled their engines down and drifted into the investigation scene. Jake was completely puzzled by the lack of detectives.

"Jake, can we tie onto your boat?" Robert asked.

"Certainly," Jake replied. "What is the ETA of your detectives?"

"That's what I would like to talk about," Robert replied, as he climbed aboard Jake's boat. "Dan Zigerfield has his diving team prepared to get into the water. While he's busy with them I'd like a minute."

Dr. Dan Zigerfield, Crammer County Chief of Forensics, aka Zig, has been the Lind City Supervising Forensic Officer for ten years and is a licensed deep sea diver. Jake has the highest regard for Zig's professionalism. Jake shouted, "Hey Zig, good to see you here. I wish it was for a more enjoyable reason. Let me know when you would like me to release the anchor line."

"We're going to take it slow and find out what we're dealing with. I'll give you a shout when we're ready to

11

slack the line." Zig lowered his diving glasses, pushed the oxygen mouth piece into his mouth, leaned backward, over the hull and splashed into the lake. The rest of the diving team immediately followed Zig carrying high powered under water lights and multiple pieces of hardware and forensic instruments.

Robert looked at Joan and whispered, "Jake, I'd like to talk business with you. Who's the young lady?"

"Her name is Joan Fetter and she's a new reporter trying to get herself established with the Lind City Times. She's doing a story about my retirement. Maggie and I thought we could have privacy and an informal venue on the lake. We were here about two hours when a flash storm came up and interrupted the interview. That's when I pulled the anchor line and the body came to the surface. I instructed her that everything she sees or hears is off the record. She's going to ask you for an exclusive when you deem it appropriate."

"What do you think? Is she credible?" Robert asked.

"I advised her what the consequences would be if she screwed up. I'd give her a chance," Jake replied.

"Okay, I'll talk with her later." Robert looked out at the SCUBA diver's location as they dropped off the side of their boat. The air bubbles, from the diver's air tanks, popped to the surface marking their positions. Robert's deliberate pause in his conversation with Jake was his genuine concern for the divers and time to think about how to approach Jake with the police department's personnel situation. He motioned Jake to walk with him to the bow of the boat. "Jake, I'm in a difficult situation. I haven't found people qualified enough to replace the detectives and uniform officers we lost after last year's impropriety debacle. I know you received your Private Investigator's License and, I also know this is short notice, but would you be able to work with the department as a PI Consultant?"

Jake was taken by surprise and, without hesitation, said, "Robert, I don't know what to say. I'm enjoying retirement and…"

"Jake, if it's money, I have the authority to offer you any, within reason, compensation you want."

Zig popped to the surface and shouted, "Commissioner, we have a man's body. We'll get him out of the water as soon as we can. But we're going have a problem doing that."

"What's going on?" Robert asked.

"The man's legs are chained to two large cans filled with cement. We're going to need time to lift him and the cans, in one piece, out of the water."

"How big are the cans?" Jake asked.

"My best estimation, about fifty pounds each, and the body, about two hundred pounds," Zig replied.

"Robert, there's a guy at the marina who has a small flat top barge with a heavy duty hoist. I'm sure if you contact him, he would able to help us," Jake said.

Zig's officers marked the area with several crime scene buoys while Zig contacted the barge owner. Zig swam to Jake's boat, "Permission to come aboard?"

"Certainly, come aboard," Jake replied.

Zig flopped off his swim flippers and placed them neatly next to the transom. "Great to see you, Jake. Are you on this case?"

Maggie smirked, nodded her head, and said, "Well Jake, why are you waiting? You've been like a crazed, caged lion, and looking for something to keep you in the law enforcement profession."

"What do you say, Jake?" Robert held out his hand. "Common let's shake on it."

"Commissioner, I would be happy to have you and Lind City as my first client," Jake replied.

"Commissioner, what about me? Can I have an exclusive?" Joan asked.

"Sure, as a courtesy, I'll run it by the Mayor while we're at the marina, and I'm sure she will be ok it. As far as I'm concerned, you can have an exclusive now," Robert replied.

The old barge maneuvered into the crime scene, swung its boom over two of the divers, and lowered a makeshift gurney to the divers. Everyone at the scene watched nervously as the divers and the gurney disappeared.

Zig stood on the boat's swim platform, "I've got to go to work." He lowered himself into the water with a light splash and was out of sight in seconds.

The boom's motor started to strain, the cable pulled tight, and the barge began to lean. The diver's surfaced maintaining a tight stabilizing hold on the gurney. One of the divers was kneeling in the center of the platform, holding onto the man's body and cement filled cans.

"Holy shit," Joan shouted. "My God that's terrible." She leaned overboard and got sick.

Jake looked at the corps from his boat, shook his head, and called out, "Zig, whatever the victim did, he

14

was deliberately placed in shallow water to be found with little difficulty. We're going to head for the marina and meet you at the public launch dock."

Maggie said, "That will work for me. I have some of my equipment in our car and I can be ready to do some preliminary work as soon as the barge docks. I'm going below to change my clothes."

Joan appeared to be over her sickness when she asked Jake, "Are crime scenes always like this?"

"Not always, some murder scenes are worse than others. He started the engines and eased away from the scene. "You can start your new career now. When we get to the marina, I would like you to subtly take pictures of the crowd at the dock parking lot. Take as many pictures as you can, and we'll have them processed through the Police Department's photo recognition department."

2

The barge started the slow journey to the marina. Zig secured the man's body to the deck and straightened the heavy chain. He knelt close to the seaweed covered cadaver, whispered a brief prayer, and remarked, "By the looks of the deceased's clothing he must have been one of the higher figures in whatever he was involved in. I'm assuming it was drugs." He gently pulled duct tape from the cadaver's lips, eased a packed wad of paper out of his mouth, and read out loud the scribbled note, "This is a message for mixers." He searched through the man's clothing looking for identification. "No ID so we can't notify a next of kin. This is going to be a tough one. Maggie will take care of identifying the body."

"Sir, what do you make of the note?" One of the divers asked.

"The message is very clear to other mixers," Zig replied.

"Dr. Zigerfield, I'm not familiar with the term mixer. Do you know what it means?" The diver asked.

Zig slipped the duct tape and note into separate evidence bags, tightly sealed them, and replied, "The drug Cartel ships hundreds of kilos of pure heroin into the United States every day and the heroin is mixed, in cement mixers, with fentanyl, cocaine, and methamphetamine. The person who actually performs the mixing is so named, "the mixer." The mixer is under close scrutiny for obvious reasons. They are dressed in their underwear and nothing else. If the mixer decides to become a silent partner, by stealing an ounce a week, the drug lord, drug baron, or, king pin will make an example of that person by executing he or she in front of the other mixers. An ounce a week, or point zero two eight kilos, on the streets sells at twenty-one hundred to twenty-eight hundred dollars. We're going to wait until we get to the lab to free him from the chains. After I'm through getting the evidence from the body, I'll get him to Maggie's lab"

As in most small villages similar to Big Bass Lake, the word traveled rapidly about a man with cans of concrete chained to his legs. A small crowd had gathered around the marina parking lot to see the much gossiped about body found in the shallows of the lake. The lake and the marina are the town's center of business. The citizens of Lind City travel a short distance to enjoy the great fishing, the town diner, small businesses for boating, fishing, and camping supplies. The slow and tranquil lifestyle of this little village is about to change.

Gus Highland, the marina manager, pulled the yellow crime scene tape over his stout frame and ambled to the end of the public boat dock. He stood at the end of the dock, with one hand on his hip and the other hand holding a pair of binoculars to his eyes, waiting for the marina barge to appear. "It's about two hundred fifty yards out and it looks like there's something on the deck covered with a tarp." Gus turned and shouted, "Bring the Forensics' pickup truck here and back it up to the dock. The Forensic guy wants to use the barges' crane to hoist the body onto the truck."

Someone from the crowd hollered, "Holy shit. Gus, what's the weight of that body?"

Gus grunted under his breath, "What a nut case. No respect." He made his way back to the end of the dock, waved his arm at the Captain, and barked, "Tie up on your port side and get as close to land as you can." Gus saw Jake and Maggie appearing through the crowd. "Hey Dr. Kliener, Jake, I didn't know you guys were here."

Maggie smiled, "Hi Gus, Jake and I happened to be out on the lake with a friend, putting some legs on our new boat's engines and you know the rest of the story."

Gus, a power boat man all his life, knew more about power boats than the average bear, and one of the town's gossips, was more interested in Jake and Maggie's new boat and asked, "Yah, your new boat is a beauty all right. Jake, how much leg did you give her?"

Jake replied, with a grin, "I gave her about half throttle and she answered smartly. I'll tell you more about the boat when we have a chance."

The barge inched through the marina, maneuvered to the public dock, and stopped a few feet from shore. The captain shut down the engine, tied the lines to the dock's cleats, tugged on his greased stained cap, went to the bow of the barge and shouted, "I have a couple of strong men in the shop. If we can cut the chains from the guy's legs, I know they could get the body on to the truck without using the hoist."

Zig replied, "Thanks, but I don't want to separate the body from the cans. We need to keep the evidence's integrity as much as possible. My team will help you and your crew hoist the body and cement filled cans when you load it onto the truck."

"Zig, before you move the body from the barge, do you mind if Maggie and I take a quick look," Jake asked.

"No problem, be my guest," Zig replied, pleasantly. Jake and Maggie had a long understanding with Zig and, regardless of friendship, they agreed on following crime scene protocol. The Forensics team has charge of the scene until they complete their work. "We've done as much as we can here."

Jake said, "Thank you, Zig. Maggie knelt next to the body and remarked, "I can tell you this, by the lack of decomposition and absent animal activity he was in the water, possibly twenty-four to thirty-six hours. He looks to be approximately twenty-five to thirty years old." Maggie, using a power flashlight, looked deep into his throat and saw what seemed to be, a strand of transparent monofilament fishing line. She gently pulled on the line with no success.

18

"I'll have to wait until I have him on the lab table. Zig, I'm sure the string is attached to evidence and as soon as I extract whatever is attached to the string, I'll get it right over to you."

Jake looked around the barge, and briefly studied the body, "I've seen enough. Maggie, whenever you're through, I think we should cover the body and all other evidence."

"I agree. We don't want someone with a cell phone camera taking pictures of the deceased before we have an ID and contact his next of kin."

Zig drew close to Maggie and mumbled, "I'm very happy for Jake. I mean getting back into the law enforcement gig. If anyone can solve this case Jake would be the man to do it. It will be my pleasure to work with him again."

"Jake, how does it look? I mean, is there much to go on?" Robert asked.

"Commissioner, I kind of lost track of you," Jake replied.

"I thought I would wait behind the crowd and keep out of everyone's way," Robert said.

"You missed Zig by a few minutes. He found some pieces of evidence and Maggie completed some preliminary work. Zig didn't take the chains from the man's legs for fear of losing evidence integrity, so they're transporting the body, covered with a tarp, on the pickup truck. I know it sounds bizarre, however this homicide is bizarre. Bottom line, it looks like a drug related murder," Jake replied.

"Where is that Joan lady? I'd like to talk with her for a few minutes."

"I have Joan roaming around taking pictures of the crowd and hopefully she'll get some favorable results."

Robert noticed a caravan of media vehicles heading their way, "Oh shit, here come the media trucks. Jake, I want to approve Joan's request for an exclusive before the other reporters get here." Robert scanned the crowd. "I don't see her anywhere."

Joan had completed her picture taking assignment and was approaching Robert from his blind side, "Commissioner, who are you looking for?"

"I'm looking for you. The other reporters are in the parking lot and, before they get set up, I want to formally give you an exclusive to this case. I cleared it with the Mayor and a good friend of mine, your Editor-In-Chief. You can start working with Jake, if he agrees."

"I think Joan would make a great investigative reporter." Jake turned to Maggie, "What do you think?"

"Awesome, I'm sure we'll be spending some time together. Joan, welcome to the world of crime," Maggie replied.

"Jake, I'll handle the media. I can respond to their questions with no comment all day long." Robert started to walk away, turned, and said, "Jake, by the way. Your old office is still empty and gathering dust. If you like, it's yours to use." He put his hand on Jake's shoulder, the most demonstrative Robert has ever been with Jake, then said, "Thank you, you took a big load off my shoulders."

3

When Maggie's digital alarm sounded, set with the most irritating sound in the alarm clock's menu, she rolled out of bed and heard singing in the shower. "I don't believe he's out of bed, in the shower before me, and he did it without an alarm clock." She knocked on the bathroom door. Jake, are you going to be in there much longer?"

"I'm drying off now. If you would like to help, the door's unlocked."

Maggie snickered, "I don't think so. No thank you, I can wait out here!" She paused, "Jake, it's five thirty. Why are you out of bed this early?"

"I want to get an early start at the office and get organized." Jake opened the door, gave Maggie a peck on the cheek, and said, "Besides, I don't want to be late for my new job."

The grass on Jake's front yard was wet with the early morning Spring dew as he climbed into his car and, he remembered, "I'm usually on my way to the lake at this time of the morning." The overhead streetlamps were systematically turning off when he arrived at Police Headquarters. He drove past the reserved parking place, which he enjoyed for several years, and the metal placard was covered with a bright yellow cloth. The parking lot was practically full as he pulled into one of the marked, 'visitor only spots.' Jake sat motionless behind the steering wheel thinking, "Will the people who reported to him accept him as a PI? There's only one way to find out."

The first shift desk Sargent, Michael Donavan, was standing behind the bulletproof glass divider concentrating on the nightshift's report, and seemingly ignoring the sound of the front door opening and the person in front of him.

Jake stood in front of the glass shield, "Excuse me, Sargent."

Sargent Donavan, without looking up said, "I'll be with you in a minute, I'm busy right now." He kept his head down, while he picked up the phone and mumbled, "Okay."

Jake was startled when he saw men and women of all police ranks rushing into the room shouting, "Welcome back, Chief."

Sargent Donavan laughed out loud, The Commissioner sent out emails letting everyone know you were going to be here, most likely real early, and working as a PI."

"I don't know what to say. I'm overwhelmed. Thank you, everyone. However, I'm not chief anymore. Please call me Jake."

Sargent Donavan said, "Jake, we're not the only people reporting early this morning. There's a young lady, Joan Fetter, who showed up fifteen minutes ago and she's in the guest waiting room. The Commissioner said he'll be in his office if you need him."

"Thank you, Sarge."

The probability of a person from the press accompanying him in an investigation would be a first for him. The thought of knowing Joan would have the power of the press and, the opportunity to make public the progress of the investigation was somewhat

22

unsettling. He entered the waiting room with a positive attitude.

Joan was sitting in a straight-back wooden chair engrossed in her iPad "Good morning, Joan, you're up early this morning. Did you have a chance to meet some of the officers?"

"Good morning, Jake. Yes, the Commissioner and I came through the door at the same time. I met a few of the officers and, without introducing myself, they knew who I was and why I was here. I must say, I was pleasantly surprised by the friendly welcome they gave me, and Sargent Donavan was a great help filling out the permanent visitors pass paperwork. Jake, I want to thank you for the opportunity to work with you in the transition from reporter to journalist. You have my solemn word I will not file a report without your approval."

Jake was awed by Joan's solemn word and, without a reply, nodded and said, "Let's get to work."

When Jake opened the door to his old office, contrary to Robert's description of a dusty office, it was freshly cleaned and not a spot of dust anywhere. "This is it. This is where we will be headquartered until we have the case solved."

"Is there room enough for two people in this office?" Joan asked.

Jake replied, "This office is merely a place for us to visit. We will be conducting the investigations in the field."

There was a soft tap on the partially open door. A young lady in her thirties, slender form, conservatively dressed, and wearing horn-rimmed glasses said "Good morning, Mr. Lester, Miss Fetter. I'm Penney Grant. The Commissioner temporarily transferred me from the Motor Vehicle Division to be your secretary." She placed a manila folder on Jake's desk. "Here are your computer sign-in ID's and you can use your own passwords. Is there anything more I can do for you?" The room fell silent for a few seconds. Penney's smile became a look of concern. "Mr. Lester, I was an employee at the MVD for two years, with some clerical experience. I was never a secretary, or worked with a Private Investigator in my entire life, however, I'm a very fast learner."

Jake smiled, "Penney, please call me Jake. Your two years with the MVD tells me you're a very detail oriented person. You'll be just fine. Welcome to our team."

"Penney, if it's any comfort to you, this is my first day as an Investigative Journalist. I'm here as a part-time journalist and, as news breaks, I'm the exclusive reporter."

Jake's cell phone rang, "Good morning, Zig."

"Good morning, Jake. We're about three-quarters of the way through the crime scene's hard evidence and have completed the trace evidence. I think you'll find what we discovered in the hard evidence very interesting. When you get here, I'll be in the lab."

"Zig has some information for us," Jake picked up his iPad. "Joan, you're welcome to come along. Penney, you can reach us on our cells."

The forensics' lab and garage were within walking distance from the LCPD building. The garage was tucked into a medium size brick building attached to the labs. Zig refers to the building as his 'man-cave away from home' perhaps since he spends more time at the lab than at home.

When Jake opened the front door to the forensics building, he stepped back to let Joan walk in front of him. She whispered, "Jake, we don't need to be formal."

"Zig will be waiting for us in the lab. I'll give you a heads up. He's pretty persnickety about strangers coming into the lab and he might be a little gruff at first, but don't take it personal."

Jake stepped up to the receptionist's desk. She was deeply engrossed in paper work, and he softly said, "Cindy."

"Oh, Chief, I didn't see you standing there. Dr. Zigerfield is in the lab. He's expecting you. I'll let him know you're here. Chief, does he know you have someone with you?" Cindy asked, sarcastically.

Jake was irritated by Cindy's question. He has brought people into the lab in the past and was never questioned. "No. This is Joan Fetter, she's been cleared by the Commissioner and the Mayor. Zig met her yesterday at a crime scene, and I'm sure he will have no objection to her being with me," he replied.

Zig entered the room, wearing a white smock and looking like he had been up all night. "Hey, Jake, how's it going on your first day?" He glanced in Joan's direction. "I assume Joan's been cleared."

"So far everything is going great and, yes, Joan has been cleared. You said you have evidence I would be interested in."

"Sure, follow me the hard evidence is in the garage." Zig led them into an incredibly spotless room and stopped in front of a black tarp on the floor. He eased the tarp from three neatly assembled varieties of evidence, consisting of sifted cement, two large red metal cans, and two hefty steel chains. Jake, take a look at the cement. That's not ordinary, everyday, do it yourself type cement. The chemical makeup indicates it's a fast curing, high density mixture used in the construction of large commercial buildings such as high-rise offices or apartment buildings." He picked up one of the metal cans and tipped it upside down. "The numbers indented on the bottom of the cans designate the gauge of the metal, where it was manufactured and, one other factor, they were hermetically sealed. We're still analyzing the cement for the possibility of drug residue."

Jake commented, "Fentanyl. China White."

"You might be right." Zig turned one of the red cans on its side, "The scratches you see on this can are also on the other can, which tells me they were using a small metal boat, or a vessel of some kind, and they had difficulty putting the cans and body into the boat."

Joan pointed at the chains, "The chains alone would sink anyone to the bottom of the lake. Why do you think they used such heavy chains?"

Zig replied, "That's a good question. Those chains are made of Arden steel, used to lift tons of weight, possibly a large truck or boats into a repair building. The chains may have been in the building where the crime was

26

committed. The three categories of hard evidence in front of us, we'll cover the trace evidence in a minute, will be crucial in locating the geographic area of the actual murder scene."

"If a small boat, possibly a rowboat, was used, they could have placed the body inside the boat, drive to a remote location on the lake, and dumped the body by the Lilly pads. The one thing they didn't count on, lifting the body over the boats' metal hull," Jake said.

"How are we going to find a metal boat with red paint scratches?" Joan asked.

Jake took another look at the can, "I'll give Gus Highland a shout. He knows every inch of Big Bass Lake and where a small boat could be launched."

"Jake, as usual, the evidence will be locked in the evidence cage, and available to you at any time." Zig replaced the tarp. "Let's go into the lab."

Zig led them into a brightly lit, almost sterile, lab where Forensic Technicians were laboring to discover the secrets of the hard and trace evidence gathered from the crime scene. He stopped at a stainless steel table, where a digital high definition microscope was mounted, and typed evidence codes into a keyboard. The screen next to the microscope came alive. "You folks need to get a glimpse of this. This is the shirt you saw on the man we pulled out of the water, only magnetized with an eighty-X scope."

Jake stepped forward for a closer look at the cloth, and stepped away from the microscope, "Is this what I think it is?"

Joan looked through the microscope, didn't detect anything unusual, and was puzzled by Zig and Jake's remarks, "What did you see, Jake?"

"The man's shirt is made with silky Egyptian cotton and is one of the most expensive white shirts money can buy. They sell for fifteen hundred dollars and higher," Jake replied.

Zig pointed to clothing neatly spread across the table, "Right, and the rest of his wardrobe is equally expensive." He turned off the microscope's screen. "Jake, we're analyzing trace evidence and as soon as I have positive results, I'll give you a shout."

"Would someone tell me why the victim's expensive clothes are so important?" Joan asked.

Jake replied, "The victim's clothes tell us he held a very high position in the drug world. A mixer, no doubt, makes a lot of money, however, is not in the 'Men's Rich and Famous Quarterly' category." He closed his iPad, "Zig, this is beyond me, how on earth did you accomplish all this in such a short period of time?"

"We've been working non-stop from the time we left the crime scene. We know it's imperative for you to have as much information you can get to apprehend whoever is responsible for this heinous crime."

"Thank you, my friend. You and your team have done a great job. If you need us, we'll be at the ME's office."

4

The automatic bi-parting doors glass doors swished open as Jake and Joan approached the M E's Lab. The odor of disinfectant floated into the hall and caught Joan by surprise.

Joan rubbed her nose, "Oh my, what a terrible odor."

Jake grinned and said, "I take it you've never been in an ME lab?"

"I have never been in a ME's lab or the morgue." Joan glanced around the room, homed in on one of the autopsy suites, and remarked, "I'm impressed with the cleanliness of the room and the up-to-date equipment. When will we see the morgue?

Maggie's voice came over the intercom, "Hello, make yourself comfortable. I'm completing an autopsy on the murder victim, and I'll be out in a few minutes."

Joan wandered around the lab for a few minutes and returned to where Jake was standing. "Why can't we go into the operating room and observe Dr. Kliener perform the autopsy?"

Jake replied, "We can't enter the room while she's working, however, we can watch the procedure through the OR window." He led the way through a short hall and stopped in front of a double plate glass window. "Here we are and, like Maggie said, she's completing the procedure."

Joan looked intently at the body and blood on the floor and operating table. She clutched Jake's arm and started to collapse. "Oh shit."

Jake caught her by the waist and carried her to a nearby chair. "I think you've seen enough."

Joan lowered her head between her knees and, after a few minutes, regained her strength. "Jake, I don't think I want to do that ever again."

Jake helped Joan walk to Maggie's office. "There's no reason for you to see it again. Maggie will be finished with the autopsy in a few minutes. We can wait for her here."

Twenty minutes later Maggie entered her office wearing clean scrubs and a white smock. "Good morning. I apologize for the long wait. I thought it would be a good idea if I cleaned up before I came back to my office."

"I messed things up by almost passing out. If it wasn't for Jake, I would be laying on the visitor's floor," Joan said.

"No worries." Maggie opened a folder stacked with chronological pictures of the autopsy. "The first picture was taken with a microscopic lens. If you take a good look you'll see residue from duct tape across his mouth, indicating the assailants wanted to keep him from screaming. I can tell you he wasn't drowned, actually, he was overdosed with fentanyl. His organs were in very good condition confirming he was not an alcohol or drug user. I sent a blood sample to our DNA lab, scanned his face and fingerprints. I should have the ID results in a few minutes. Zig filled me in on his wardrobe and the jewelry he was wearing including the two carat diamond ear pin." She closed the folder. "Jake, this man was no ordinary drug peddler. He must be among the elite of drug dealers."

Their conversation was interrupted by one of Maggie's assistants entering the room. "Dr. Kliener, here are the results of the fingerprint and photo scans from the US Database."

Maggie flipped through the ID results and said, "These results confirm my theory. The victim is Hans Osterfeld, twenty-nine years old son of Carter Osterfeld, aka CO, who is sole owner of Osterfeld Construction Company. His mother is deceased." Maggie placed the folder on her desk. "Jake, the victim is definitely not directly involved in drugs and, in my opinion, this was possibly a Cartel hit."

"The hit was a message. I don't think the message was for Carter Osterfeld. Maggie, was his father notified?" Jake asked.

"Yes. One of the Lind City Detectives went to his home and informed him of his son's demise. He's on his way here to ID his son. Jake, he called me for an appointment time to come to the morgue and, next, he said something that puzzled me. He stated that Hans Osterfeld was his son in name alone. What do you think he meant?"

"I don't know. Do we have the DNA report?" Jake asked.

"No, we haven't received anything from the lab," Maggie replied.

Maggie's interoffice phone rang, "Dr. Kliener, Mr. Osterfeld is here and he has two gentlemen with him. Should I show them into your office?"

"No thank you, I'll see them in the lobby." Maggie hesitated. "Jake, you and Joan can observe the ID from the one way glass in my conference room." She left the office and entered the lab where she was joined by two morgue assistants. "Okay guys, let's get to the lobby."

Three men were standing in the lobby. One of the men was tall well-dressed, in his fifties, with salt and pepper hair, who was flanked by two very muscular men casually dressed, and standing with their hands folded in front of them.

Maggie thought, shit this is a scene straight out of a crime movie, "Mr. Osterfeld, I'm Dr. Kliener, Chief Medical Examiner and these two gentlemen are my assistants.

"You can call me CO." He stood and pointed his finger at the two men. "These two guys are my lawyer and bodyguard. Now let's go see the guy you think is my son."

The whirling sound of small refrigerator compressors, keeping the body compartments at a degree above freezing, echoed in a dismal tone. Maggie's morgue technician opened door number five and pulled back a stainless steel handle. A platform slowly rolled out of the compartment carrying a closed body bag.

Maggie asked, "Mr. Osterfeld, are you ready for this?"

"Ya, sure, if you're ready," CO replied, coldly.

Maggie unzipped the body bag exposing the victim's face. "For the record, Sir. Is this man your son, Hans Osterfeld?"

CO smirked and replied, "What a dumb shit. Yup, he's my wife's son. If you're looking for a DNA match it ain't there. I adopted him when I married his mother, that was twenty years ago. Times were tough when Mary and I started the business, with a fifty-fifty ownership. The business got bigger and bigger and when Mary passed, she left all her stock to this punk. Doc, you can

32

close it up. I don't need to see anymore and, you can tell whoever's behind the one-way glass, I didn't have him whacked. Guys, let's get out of here."

Maggie waited until CO and his bodyguards were out of the building before giving Jake a call to meet in her office. She sat behind her desk with her head in her hands, visibly touched by the experience she had witnessed and whispered, "How could a person be so insensitive to a family member's death?"

Jake and Joan joined Maggie in her office. "Maggie, are you okay? Jake asked. "We can give you some time if you need to catch your breath."

"I'll be fine. What did you gather from CO's attitude?" Maggie asked.

"I think his demeanor was a façade in an effort to conceal the fact he has an incredible motive to have the kid killed. He's, without a doubt, a dangerous man, "Jake replied. "Joan, you can release the victim's identity and, without accusations, mention who made the ID."

"Jake, when I file my report to the editor can I put on the record you are leading the investigation?"

"I sensed CO had the information before he came to the morgue and, by now, the rest of the world knows. Yes, put it in print," Jake replied.

"Maggie, I'll see you later. I'd be interested in the results of Hans Osterfeld's DNA report and who's the biological father. CO didn't name his wife's first husband. It could mean nothing. I have to see Robert before the end of the day."

5

"Jake, come in. It sounds like you had a very busy day. Have a seat." Robert closed his office door.

"You're right, it's been a very busy day and a productive one as well. The small town gossip mill is in full action or you wouldn't know."

"Jake, you're the main buzz in this town today. We at PD1 have heard nothing but good things about you leading the Hans Osterfeld murder investigation. Which brings me to one of the matters we should talk about. The Mayor's city attorneys recommend you should be sworn in as a Warren County Deputy Sheriff. What do you think?"

"I think Carter Osterfeld and the Mayor had lunch at the Lind City Hotel today, where he frequents, and CO whispered into the Mayor's ear. What do you think I should do?"

"Jake, it was the Mayor's idea to have you come into the Lind City PD murder investigation as a consultant and, as far as I know, the Mayor is pretty independent and doesn't always listen to his attorneys. He told me the decision is entirely up to you."

"Robert, you've known me a long time. I think you knew my answer before you asked the question. I like the new Mayor's approach and I think he also knew my answer, but he had to pose the situation and hear it from me. You can tell the Mayor thanks, but no thanks, about being a Deputy Sheriff, and he can let Carter Osterfeld know as well."

Robert burst out laughing. "I have a bet with Mayor Comfort. I told him you would say no. Jake, we had to go through the exercise to cover everyone's butt, including yours."

Jake responded, "How does Carter Osterfeld fit into this equation?"

"CO is a good friend of the Governor and a big contributor to his political party," Robert replied. He knew Jake wasn't satisfied with his answer. "Jake, when I said you have full control of this investigation, I meant it. Please don't let CO's presence intimidate you."

"CO doesn't intimidate me. I like to understand the rules of engagement, and if he's in any way involved in this murder, he'll go down just like any other criminal."

"Jake, I'm happy to say you and I are on the same page. If you need anything give me a shout."

Jake left Robert's office satisfied the new path of law enforcement at the Lind City Police Department was settled, he could continue with his investigation without the Mayor's involvement.

Jake stopped at his secretary's desk. "Penney, please come into my office."

"How can I help you, Mr. Lester?"

"You can start by calling me Jake. You will be answering to me and only me. What we discuss and your duties, are confidential."

"Yes, sir, her Penney replied. She sat in a chair in front of Jake's desk, folded her legs, and turned on her notebook.

"I would like you to discretely dig up as much information as possible on Carter Osterfeld aka CO. I need to know everything about him from the day he was born, who he hangs out with, his companies and where he travels. I also want know about his stepson, Hans Osterfeld and, when we know who his biological father is, process a check on him as well." Jake hesitated. "And run background checks on the Big Bass Marina Manager, August Highland, and his handyman, George Grazer."

"Would you like me to reach into Mrs. Osterfeld and her first husband's backgrounds?"

"Yes, Penny, that's a good idea. It's six o'clock. Why don't you call it a day, and start fresh in the morning."

"Good night, Mr. Lester."

"Jake, am I interrupting anything?"

"Maggie, no you're not interrupting a thing. Penney was about to leave. What a nice surprise."

"I knew you were working late so I was going to pick up some Chinese for us and, as I was leaving my office, the DNA report came back with Hans Osterfeld's biological father's name on the title line. His name is Oscar Gonzales."

Penney said, "Sir, I have his name, and I'll have the information first thing in the morning. Good night."

"Honey, you've had a long day. Why don't we go home, build a fire, open a good bottle of wine, and have our dinner in front of the fireplace. What do you think of that?"

Jake gave Maggie a devilish smile, and replied, "Why do we need the food?"

The smoldering ambers provided a comforting atmosphere for Jake and Maggie as they relaxed and fell into a deep sleep.

It was five thirty a.m. when Jake's cell phone rang. He rolled off the sofa and went into another room. Penney's name was on the caller ID. "Hello, Penney. What's going on?"

"Jake, I have all the information on Oscar Gonzales."

"Penney, its five thirty a.m."

"I know, but I had to call you because Gonzales is getting on a private plane at the Metro Airpark and he's leaving seven at a.m. this morning and heading for Bogotá Columbia."

"That's good information, however; how can I stop him?"

"He has 'wants and warrants' on him from the Narcotics Division, among other things, and he's been hiding from the police for several months. I'm sure if you call a NARCO guy he'd be happy to help you out," Penney replied. "I have a close detective friend who works in Narcotics. His name is John Swift. I'd be happy to call him and you can meet him at the Airpark."

"Yes, by all means. Let him know I'm on my way." Jake shook his head and asked, "Penny, how did you get this information?"

Penney replied, "I have guys."

Maggie sat up from the sofa, "My God it's five forty-five. We slept in the living room all night. Jake, who was on the phone? What's going on?"

"That was Penney and she has information regarding Oscar Gonzales. He's wanted by the Narcotics Division and he's hightailing it out of country on a private jet. If we hurry, we can catch him before he takes off for Bogotá."

"Jake, please tell me you're not going alone."

"John Swift is meeting me at the Metro Airpark." He gave Maggie a kiss on the forehead. "I'll be back before you know it."

Jake turned off his headlights as he approached the entrance to the Airpark, and parked behind a high stack of wooden boxes. He took out his binoculars and scanned the perimeter of the Airpark terminal. There were few security lights outside the terminal and florescent ceiling lights in the lobby. He noticed the building had one main entrance and two back exits. What Jake didn't see was any sign of John Swift. 'Were the hell's Swift?' Jake was startled by a battery of bright runway lights illuminating the entire runway with several color coded lights outlining the tarmac and taxiway. He looked at the aircraft through his binoculars and recognized the Dassault Falcon 7X landing lights in the distance vectoring a final approach to the Airpark. 'Damn, that's a big ass plane for one man going to Columbia.'

Jake drew out his Glock nine millimeter pistol when he saw a man dressed in blue jeans, hunched over, and slowly approaching from the rear of his car.

"Jake, it's John Swift. Penney said you would be here. It's good to have an experienced PI with me," he whispered as he slid into the front seat of Jake's car.

"I'm glad to be here. What's going on?" John asked.

"We have to act fast. Gonzales made a last minute change. My FAA source informed me, an hour ago, that the pilot filed a flight plan to Switzerland, with four passengers aboard a long range aircraft, and they're scheduled to depart in twenty minutes. I didn't have time to muster up a NARCO team, so I guess it's the two of us. There's one little problem, Gonzales knows me." Jake replied.

"Okay, I got it." Jake jumped out of the car. "I have a sniper rifle in the back seat with a scope and laser. I'm assuming two of those passengers are bodyguards, another is Gonzales, and I don't know the fourth person. "I'll get a drop on the two bodyguards and I'll wing it from there. John, as soon as I have Gonzales in the open you put that red laser beam on his chest. Are you good to go?"

"Yes, good luck," John replied.

Jake holstered the Glock, eased himself out of the car, reached into the back seat, hauled out a sniper rife, a twelve gauge pump action shot gun from the car, and handed the sniper rifle to John. "I'll see you later." He used the shadows of the terminal building to conceal his approach to the entrance and waited for the four people to exit the building. He crouched down and remained in the shadows while the aircraft taxied to the passenger ramp, parked, and shut down the engines. The copilot opened the cargo hatch, loaded ten large boxes into the aircraft's hold, started the mandatory aircraft check, and disappeared to the other side of the aircraft.

Jake knew he only had a matter of a few seconds after the people came out of the terminal to have the element of surprise on his side. He quietly jacked a round into the shot gun's chamber, made his way a few feet short of the terminal door, and stopped. The terminal door swung open and four people, three men and a woman, emerged from the building. He waited for them to clear the exit and shouted, "Freeze and put your hands where I can see them." He repeated the order, "Put your hands where I can see them."

One of the bodyguards reached inside his jacket and pulled out a pistol. Jake fired a shot into the air. "The next one's for you."

One of the men, about five foot-nine, slender built, wearing gold chains around his neck, stepped forward. "You gotta be really stupid or very smart. Who the hell do you think you are?" He took a few more steps toward Jake. "I'm Oscar Gonzales. I don't know you but you're going to be dead."

Jake shouted, "I don't care about your bodyguards, or the young lady. I want you to come with me."

"Are you a cop?" Oscar asked.

"No, I'm Jake Lester, a Private Investigator, and I'm investigating your son's murder."

"You're a PI," Oscar laughed. "You should have brought an army. I'm going to shoot your ass right now." He reached inside his jacket, pulled out a pistol, and heard the very intimidating sound of a round being pumped into the shot gun's chamber. He froze. "You don't have the balls."

Jake calmly replied, "Maybe I don't or maybe I do, but you gotta know the sharpshooter pointing the red dot on the left side of your chest has brass balls and he doesn't miss. Now I want all of you on the ground with your legs crossed and your hands folded over your head. Now!"

The sun was rising behind Jake and casting an image of a lone man carrying a sniper rifle over his shoulder. The four people raised their heads from the ground and Gonzales screamed, "Lester, you bastard, you're not a cop and you can't hold me. That's it. There's only two of you?"

"Yup, we were going to bring an army, but what the hell, we didn't need one to apprehend you. I'd like you to meet, NARCO Detective, John Swift, and he sure as hell can hold you."

John swung the rifle off is shoulder, opened the breach, and said, "Good work, Jake. If you were still on the force, Gonzales would be your collar. We can take Gonzales in, interview him together, and his every word will be on the record. If you can't get him for murder, I can get him for possession of Narcotics. Either way, he's going on vacation for a long time."

6

"Penney, where's Jake? I've been looking all over for him, and where is Gonzales?"

"Commissioner, I peeked through the one way glass into interview room five, and I think he and Detective Swift are interviewing Oscar Gonzales at this very moment."

"You can observe the interview with me. Anne Moffitt, the DA is going to meet us in the interview room." Robert quietly closed the door to the observation room, where he and Penney watched and listened while two of the best criminal interviewers on the police force put one of the most notorious drug and arms dealer through the 'by the book' questioning. "Hi Anne, glad you could make it," Robert said.

The two detectives sat across from Gonzales with the video recording turned on while they listened intently to the criminal's every word.

Gonzales wiped the pearls of sweat from his forehead with a handkerchief and, with disgust, threw the soiled hankie on the table. He looked up at the flashing red light on the video camera. "Look," he shouted. "I've been in this room for over an hour with no coffee or water, answered some of the most ridiculous questions I've ever heard and that tells me you got nothing." Gonzales pushed away from the table, stood, and boldly said, "I'm outta here."

"Sit your ass down," Jake shouted.

"I want a lawyer," Gonzales shouted.

"Sure, you can have a lawyer. Think about what you're asking. We got you on possession of enough fentanyl to kill an army, and other drugs you loaded into your charter plane. Here's the big one, suspicion of murdering your son, Hans Osterfeld, and trying to escape prosecution for several other crimes. Sure, you can have your lawyer, but then again, you

said you've been in here over an hour and the entire Cartel will figure you spilled your guts." Jake stepped to the door and placed his hand on the door knob, "I'll get you an outside line. You can call your lawyer, but you're not leaving this room."

"Wait, I didn't kill my son. I didn't kill anyone, and I don't know about any drugs. You gotta believe me. If I tell you anything, I'm a dead man before I leave this building." Oscar sat down and placed his elbows on the table. "Let's talk a deal," he said, frantically.

Jake shook his head, "You lawyered up. We can't have a conversation until your lawyer gets here, and we can't force you to change your mind. It's strictly your decision."

"Okay, okay, scratch the lawyer. What kind of a deal can you give me?" Oscar asked.

Jake replied, "We can't give you a deal, however, we can recommend something to the DA based upon the information you're willing to give us. The DA can offer you the plea bargain."

"I gotta be in the Witness Protection Program. Like I said, I'm a dead man before I leave this building," Oscar said.

Robert, Anne, and Penney watched in amazement while Jake finessed Oscar into testifying. Robert gave Penney and Anne a high five and whispered, "Jake's got him."

Jake returned to the table and said, "Mr. Gonzales, I want to remind you, you're still being recorded and we will read you your rights. For the record give us your name and your refusal of an attorney."

John read Oscar his rights. "Okay, Jake, you're good to go."

"Mr. Gonzales, why did you kill your son, Hans Osterfeld?" Jake asked.

"I swear, I didn't kill my son or anyone else. I didn't really know him because Hans was a little boy when my wife married Carter Osterfeld. On the day CO adopted him I got a message from CO telling me not to ever contact Hans."

"Oscar, really, do you really want us to believe you had no contact with your biological son for almost twenty-nine years?"

"Yeah, it's the truth. I thought about it several times, except I knew if I got caught, I would be a part of the cement in an apartment building. When Mary died, she left Hans her fifty percent share of the Osterfeld Construction Company. CO came unglued when Hans told him he didn't want any part of the construction company and was going to hold on to the stock for investment purposes." Oscar asked, "Can I have a glass of water?"

"Sure," Jake replied. "What kind of investments did Hans have in mind?"

"Hans called me about six months after Mary died and wanted to have dinner to discuss some business. When I asked him what kind business, he said he couldn't say over the phone. We set a time to meet at my restaurant, Carlotta's. I hadn't seen him in a long time and when he came into the restaurant, I could swear it was Mary. I asked him, after we had a couple of drinks, what business did he want to talk about. He looked at me square in the eyes and said, 'I have over one hundred million dollars and I want to invest half of it in drugs.' He wanted me to help him. I told him I couldn't help him. He should keep his money in the construction company and enjoy the dividends. That was the end of

the business conversation. We finished our dinner and
parted ways."

"Oscar, you're telling us, with all the contacts you
have, you couldn't help him. Is that what you want us to
believe?"

"Yes, that's the truth. I could have given him a lot of
names who would've been happy to take his money. I
didn't want the kid to get involved with the Cartel."

Robert grinned and did another high five. Robert said,
"Jake's got him again."

Jake slid a notebook in front of Oscar. "Write the
names, locations of all the Cartel contacts you have, and
who would be their executioner."

"I will give you all the information you want. But first,
I want to talk with the DA. I gotta be in the Witness
Protection Program, and it's gotta be in Switzerland."

Anne walked into the room carrying a large bottle of
water and placed it in front of Oscar. "Here's your
water."

Oscar drank a few gulps of water and asked, "When
can I see the DA? I'm not writing anything until I see the
DA."

Anne declared, "I'm Anne Moffitt, the Lind City
District Attorney. We'll talk about the WPP as soon as
you give me the verifiable information I need for
prosecutions. If your information is true, I'll recommend
your WPP to a Federal Judge. It will be up to the judge
to authorize a trip to Switzerland." She placed a yellow
legal size tablet on the table. "I know this interview is
being recorded, nevertheless I want you to write down
the names, locations, and the crimes committed for each

individual and, know this, if you give me false information you won't see the light of day for a long time. Do you understand?"

Penney grinned, glanced at Robert, and said, "She's tough."

Robert remarked, "I've never seen her in action. Hell, she scared me. I can't wait to get out of this room and commend her on her commanding approach."

Oscar timidly responded, "Yes, Ma'am." He frantically started writing and continued for half an hour, placed the pen on the notebook, spun it around and shoved it in front of Jake. "That's all I have."

Jake perused the information written in the notebook. He marveled at the precise description of every person's function as members of the Cartel, however, Jake noticed the lack of essential information he needed in Oscar's statement. He passed the notebook back to Oscar and asked, "Where are the names of the executioners who killed your son?"

"I don't know who killed Hans. I swear, I don't know who killed my son," Oscar shouted.

"All the evidence we have points to a Cartel hit. Why would they kill a man who wasn't involved with Cartel business?" Jake stood, walked away from the table, and looked into the one way glass window. "Gonzales, you're playing us. We don't have time for your superfluous bullshit. You know we're after a murder conviction. I'm going to ask you one more time. Why would the Cartel kill your son and who did the hit?"

Oscar shouted, "You keep asking if I killed my son and I keep telling you I didn't. I'm going to tell you again, I don't know who killed my son." He picked up his sweat soaked hankie from the table, wiped the perspiration from his forehead, and growled, "Who the hell is on the other side of that window?"

Jake purposefully ignored Oscar's question and continued looking into the window. He knew Oscar desperately needed to disappear from this country and get to his numbered bank accounts in Switzerland, and the longer he remained in the US the more susceptible he was to being murdered by a Cartel hit squad. The room had remained quiet while Jake played out one of the oldest unwritten detective interviewing strategies in the book. Jake turned away from the window, looked at his watch and quietly said, "Oscar, we've been in this room several hours and all we have from you is a list of people we could have gotten on my laptop from an online search of names. You basically played us for hours in hopes you could get a free ride to Switzerland. I've come to the conclusion there is no reason to keep you here. You're free to go. Go on, get outta here."

Oscar cried out, "No, Jake, you can't do this. You don't have the authority to let me go."

John said, "Well I'm a detective and I have the authority. I agree with Jake. You're free to go. Now get out of here."

Oscar became frantic and called out, "No wait, you can't let me out of here. They'll know I've been in here talking to you guys. When I walk out of this building, with no protection, and a place to hide, I'll be dead. What am I gonna do now?"

"We gave you a chance, and you didn't have the answers we needed to apprehend a suspect in your son's murder," Jake replied. He picked up his notebook from the table. "Oscar, unless you have something substantial for us, we don't need you."

Oscar jumped up and screamed, "Consuela Delgado, you need to find her. They call her the Angel de la murte, the Angel of Death. The Cartel gives her the big jobs, like my son. She has an army of people working for her."

"Oscar, sit down." Jake stood, placed both hands on the table, leaned over Oscar, and roared, "No more bullshit. Why did the Cartel consider your son a big job, and why did they want him out of the way?"

"The Cartel kills people for different reasons. Sometimes they kill someone to send a message. Honest, I don't know the real reason, just rumors, why they wanted to kill him. The rumor going around, they didn't care much about the hundred million dollars in cash. They wanted more than cash. They wanted the fifty percent ownership he had in his stepfather's construction company. The kid probably told them to shove it."

"Jake, CO must have known about a deal the Cartel tried to make with Hans, or they wouldn't have sent him a message," Anne commented. "There's no doubt, if the Cartel owned any part of CO's company, eventually the Cartel would own the company and use it for laundering money."

"I agree," Jake said. "Oscar, were does this Consuela Delgado person hang out?"

"I don't know. I only saw her one time for a few seconds. It was in Columbia three years ago at a fiesta. She walked up to some umbrae and stabbed him in the heart with a long needle. They say she hasn't been seen in public since then. I'll never forget her face. She is the most beautiful lady I've ever seen. Now can I have protection?"

"If Delgado disappeared for three years, the person Delgado murdered must have been a very close friend or lover. Assuming you can identify Consuela Delgado, and testify against her in a court of law, I think they, Detective Swift and District Attorney Moffitt, may take it under consideration." Jake replied.

Anne turned off the recorder, grinned at Jake, and said, "The Angel of Death has to be living somewhere. Now all you guys have to do is locate her, prove she was responsible for killing Hans Osterfeld, and arrest the Angel de la murte."

"If Gonzales' statement is true, I would recommend his protection. John, do you agree?" Jake asked.

"I agree," John replied.

7

Jake was looking out his kitchen window while he sipped the last of his coffee, and thought about when the pieces would come together in Hans Osterfeld's murder. Two days have gone by with one, semi reliable informant who may, or may not, live through the investigation. There is one possible suspect, Consuela Delgado, whose identity is sketchy and her whereabouts are unknown.

Maggie stepped behind Jake and said, "You look like you either need another mug of coffee, a workout at the gym, or both."

"I'm thinking about another mug of coffee and scratching the workout. Maggie, basically I have nothing. The pros who murdered Hans knew exactly what they were doing and how they could make a statement by dumping the chained body into the shallow part of the lake. They were strangers who came into a small town, in the middle of the night. Honey, they had to have help from a local resident." Jake's cell phone rang.

"Jake, it's Joan Fetter. I've been doing some background investigating on the individuals in the pictures I took at the Big Base Lake Marina. I wasn't able to find anything on the people at the scene, so I ran George Grazer, the marina's handyman, through local and state criminal files. Jake, he's got a rap sheet from the time he was twelve years old until a year ago. The most significant sentence was six years ago for transporting drugs. The judge gave him ten years, but then a prominent New York City law firm appealed on a technicality and he ended up with a suspended sentence. I tried to ascertain where the money came from to pay the legal fees. The court records indicated the law firm took the case pro bono."

"Thank you; good job, Joan. It sounds like he has some influential friends. You'll be the first to know if he's connected to the murder."

"Maggie, I might be late for dinner. I'm going to the marina and have a chat with Gus Highland."

"Honey, if Joan is onto something, you have no idea what you're getting into at the marina. Don't you think you should have a backup with you?"

"No, fishing season's a week away, and I've known Gus a long time. This should be a walk in the park. I'll call Gus and let him know I'm on the way. How could I possibly get into trouble," Jake replied.

The hour and twenty minute drive to the lake was one of Jake's enjoyments in life. Like most law enforcement professionals, it gave him time to clear his mind of trivial issues and concentrate on serious matters such as the current murder case. The trip to the village was a weekly drive in the summer months. Their cottage was less than five minutes from the village diner and the marina. Jake craved a cup of strong coffee from the diner, but he opted to drive directly to the marina.

Jake approached the Marina Manager's office, knocked, pushed on the door, as he had in the past, and was surprised to find it locked. He knew Gus was planning to meet him and, when Gus is at the marina, the office door is rarely locked. He peeked through the office window and, in the shadows behind Gus' desk, he saw what appeared to be a man's work boot. Jake put his face against the office window, strained his eyes, and saw the lower part of a man's torso. He quickly pulled off his jacket, wrapped it around his hand, shattered the glass, unlocked the door, and saw George Grazer lying behind the desk mortally wounded, his throat cut from ear to ear. "Holy shit, where's Gus?" Jake pulled out his pistol and cautiously moved around the three room office. When he came to the supply room, he saw Gus lying on the floor with a head wound. He shouted, "Gus, Gus, speak to me. Speak to me."

The local police and EMS people arrived three minutes after Jake placed the call. "Gus what the hell happened," Jake shouted. Gus remained unconscious.

"Jake, please, we gotta get Gus to the ER right now," the EMS driver urged.

For the last two hours, the drove of hospital monitors became normal to Jake and filtered out Joan's voice when she whispered, "Jake, Jake."

Jake flinched and asked, "Joan, what are you doing here?"

"Our people in the News Ops room heard a "Code sixty-eight in Big Base Lake," on the police radio. They immediately called me when they heard a murder code at this location, Joan replied. She squatted next to Jake and asked, "What the hell happened?"

"I don't know. I came here to talk with Gus about George Grazer. The short version, I found Grazer lying on the floor, next to a desk, with his throat slashed. The Cartel will do that to people who talk too much. I've been trying to link a connection with Grazer and the Cartel and keep coming up with a blank. The kid, at best, was nothing in the Cartel's chain of command," Jake replied. "Have you seen Maggie?"

"I think Maggie and Zig are still at the crime scene, and John Swift is on his way to the marina," Joan replied. "Jake, this is the second murder in the Village of Big Bass Lake within a week, and I know the Editor and Chief of our newspaper will be on my butt if I hold back. I have to ask you, can I put this in the news?"

"Joan, legally, I can't suppress the news and you've lived up to your word on the first murder. Yes, splash the story on the front page and maybe we'll get some leads, "Jake replied.

"Jake Lester?" A woman dressed in scrubs asked. She pulled her sweat stained surgeon's cap from her head. "I'm Dr. Mason, the ER Doc. I've been working on Augustus Highland."

"I'm Jake Lester. How's Gus doing?"

"He has a large contusion on the back of his head and a brain concussion. Mr. Highland has been conscious for about ten minutes and he's asking for you. He's very fortunate to be alive. You can see him for a few minutes," Dr. Mason replied.

Jake entered the Intensive Care Unit, stood next to Gus's bed, and attempted to act unconcerned at the severity of his wound. He and Gus were the only people in the room and nothing would be recorded. "Gus, how are you doing?"

"I'm alive," Gus replied. "Where is George?"

Jake hesitated for a few seconds, "Gus, I'm afraid George didn't make it."

"Damn." Gus wiped the tears from his eyes. "Why did they kill him?"

"Can you tell me what happened?"

"I don't know. Everything happened so fast. I was in the tool room getting some supplies when I heard some noise in the office. I had a wrench in my hand when I went out to see what was going on, I saw two tall men wearing ski masks. Both had dark completion, and they were beating the hell out of George. One guy was standing behind George with one arm wrapped around his neck. I jumped at the guy who was holding George's arms and swung the wrench at his head. That's when it felt like my head caved in. I woke up in the ambulance." Gus's voice became weak as he passed out.

Jake sat outside of Gus's room and realized there may have been three men, or possibly two men and a women involved in Gus' attack. Jake knew Maggie was either in the process, or had completed the autopsy on George. He needed to know the results.

"Hi Maggie. I'm at the hospital and Gus is going to be okay."

"Jake, it's odd you called. I was about to call you. The cause of death wasn't from the knife wound to the neck. George was murdered by a large dose of Fentanyl. It was large enough to kill a hundred people. There were hand bruises on his arms and on the back of his neck, which indicates there was a third person in the room injecting the lethal poison."

"Your analysis confirms what I thought. There had to be three people in the room, and not necessarily all men," Jake remarked.

"There's one more thing. George put up a hell of a fight. He had a considerable amount of skin under his fingernails, and I'm

53

running a DNA test on it now. I'll get back to you when I have something."

Jake turned off the phone and walked toward the Charge Nurse's desk. He was convinced Consuela Delgado was the third person in the room, injecting George with the lethal dose Fentanyl and disappearing. He had to inform John and the nurses of a possible attempt on Gus's life.

Jake left the hospital, after notifying the Charge Nurse and John of the possible threat to Gus's life. He made his way to the diner for a much needed mug of black coffee. He stared at the half full mug and tried his best to answer the question that had been circling in his mind from the time he assumed Consuela Delgado may have been the third person at the murder scene. 'Why would the highest ranking Cartel assassin risk her life to execute a smalltime punk like George Grazer?' Hopefully, the DNA from the victim's fingernails will ID one of the killers.'

8

It was eight a.m. when an Oriental room service waiter rolled a rattling four wheel table, draped with a white tablecloth, and stacked high with plates covered with stainless steel covers. He stopped at suite number five. He vigorously rapped on one of the double doors and announced, "Room Service. My name is Mùchén Yáng."

The door slowly opened and a man in his mid-thirties, dressed in a gym sweat suit, appeared. "Come in, and you can put the table in the main room next to the windows." He followed Yáng into the main room and shouted, "He's here."

A man and a woman stepped into the room. The woman, Consuela Delgado, wasted no time, and asked, "What do you have for us?"

Yáng methodically removed the stainless steel covers from each of the food dishes and stepped away from the table. "This is the first of many larger shipments of our product."

Consuela looked at the contents of the table and asked, "Diego, is this what you ordered?"

Diego Garcia is the leader of the US Cartel and oversees all the first time suppliers and the large purchases of drugs. Diego pulled a switchblade knife from his pocket, cut open one of the plastic bags of white powder, and dropped a sample of the powder into a small glass container. The half-filled container of clear liquid immediately turned blue. He removed the cover from another dish, revealing a large white brick of Fentanyl. He nodded at Consuela, and said, "Mùchén Yáng, if all the product on the table is as good as these small samples, we have a deal."

"I think you'll be more than satisfied," Yáng said. "Now, let's move on so I can get the hell out of here before anyone knows I'm here."

Diego picked up the hotel's room service menu and quipped, "Yáng, you can relax and stay. We're going to have our breakfast while Marven Padano, our Chemist, inspects all the product. When Marven completes his tests and, if everything is okay, you can leave."

The room became extremely silent. Consuela gave Yáng a terrifying glare, slipped her right hand under her robe, and started to move toward the door.

"As you wish, Diego," Yáng said. "We wish you to be satisfied with your purchase."

Diego took the last bite of his breakfast, sipped the remainder of his coffee, and swiped his lips with his napkin, "Yáng, the last hour has been informative in several ways. You are a man of your word and the product you presented today, according to Marven, is perfect. We will look forward to many more purchases. The money for this product is being transferred into your country's numbered account. Now you may leave." He locked the door after Mùchén Yáng left the room and turned his attention to Consuela.

"Consuela, the Capos talked to me early this morning and asked when you were coming back to him in Columbia. He said he needs you there as soon as possible and, when the Boss says as soon as possible, he means now. Why are you in such a big hurry to leave us?"

Consuela lit a cigarette, walked to the floor length windows, looked down at the street full of people, and said, "Diego, I have to go back to Lind City."

"Are you crazy?" Diego shouted. "You, of all people, knows Pablo Ramirez is the highest of all the Cartel leaders and you don't say no to him. Consuela, what the hell is so important that you would risk your life?"

"I have loose strings in Lind City," Consuela replied. She stubbed out the cigarette on her breakfast dish. "I'll be on a plane to Lind City this afternoon and by tomorrow afternoon the loose strings will be cut, and I will be with Capos for cocktails."

"Consuela, you must take people with you. Please, take the two men who dumped the punk kid's body in the lake."

"Diego, you underestimate me. I'm flying alone to Lind City; however, I will not be alone in that wretched city. I have a very loyal friend who will watch my back and assure my safe return to Columbia."

56

"As you wish. You know how to reach me if you need help," Diego said.

Consuela sped across New York City to JFK Airport in a limousine to a waiting private jet bound for Lind City. She knew Diego, who was loyal to the Capos, would report her actions to Pablo Ramirez. Time was essential for her to complete the extra activity in Lind City and return to Columbia. She had received the information needed from her friend in Lind City to assassinate Jake Lester, the first loose string, and ultimately eliminate her friend who was the last loose string.

It was three thirty Friday afternoon when Consuela checked into a suite at the Lind City Hotel. She quickly unpacked her casual clothes, two hypodermic needles, and four connectable pieces to assemble a long range sniper rifle. Her friend indicated Lester never missed the opening day of bass fishing season on Big Bass Lake. The long range sniper rifle will more than adequately serve the purpose of the first task. She looked at her watch, decided a short catnap was in order, threw herself across the king-sized bed, and fell into a deep sleep. It was eight p.m. when she was awakened by her cell phone. "Hello."

"Consuela, its Diego. Pablo is looking for you. He asked me if you were on your way back to Columbia. I could never lie to him. I told him about your unfinished business in Lind City. He asked me about the unfinished business. I told him I didn't know what it is. Consuela, he's very mad."

"Where are you?"

"I'm in our jet on my way back to Columbia. He should be calling you very soon. I think you better do what you gotta do and get the hell out of there." Diego turned off his cell phone.

Consuela closed the sniper rifle case. She whispered, "I can't wait for tomorrow. I have to get the job done now and without help from my friend." She pulled a piece of paper from her pocket with Jake Lester's home address scribbled in black ink and hurried out of the hotel.

Consuela turned off the vehicle's headlights, parked about fifty yards from Jake's address, and approached the slightly lit home on foot. She found a strategical position in the back of the property, assembled the rifle, attached the night vision scope, and scanned the kitchen and living rooms. "Now I'll wait for the perfect shot." The vibration of her cell phone interrupted her concertation. "Yes."

"It's Pablo. What the hell are you doing? I have important work for you here in Bogotá."

"I have unfinished business here. I'll be back tomorrow evening," Consuela replied.

Pablo screamed, "No. Leave your friend there; he can take care of himself. I have a plane waiting for you at the Lind City private airport. Get your ass on that plane first thing in the morning."

"But, Pablo." Consuela's phone went dead before she could utter another word. She quickly touched the speed dial for her close friend. "It's me. El Capos called. He wants me in Columbia right now and, for now Amigo, I have to leave you here. Trust me, I'll return as soon as possible. It is important you keep me informed of Lester's progress."

9

"Good morning, Jake. It's Bill at the airport's FAA office. Sorry to bother you so early in the morning, but I thought you should know, the pilot of a long range jet filed a flight plan for Bogotá Columbia with one person aboard. The name on the manifest is Mrs. Smith. The plane took off at one a.m. There was no possible legal way for me to delay their flight."

"Good job, Bill. Thank you.

"What was that all about?" Maggie asked.

"Bill, at the FAA, gave me a heads up about an early morning flight from here to Bogotá. I'm going to check with the manager of the Lind City Hotel. Maybe the passenger on the plane stayed at the hotel last night."

Jake arrived at the Lind City Hotel lobby at eight a.m., proceeded directly to the hotel manager's office and knocked on the door.

Carman Cruz, one of Jake's fishing buddies and known for his outgoing personality, shouted, "Come on in, Jake. The door's not locked."

"Thanks Carman. I appreciate your time this morning. I need some help."

"No problem. I'd like you to meet Mary Conner. Mary's our nightshift desk clerk. Help yourself to coffee and Danish. I reviewed last night's registration list and there was a Mrs. Smith registered in one of our rooms. She checked out a couple of hours after she checked in and paid cash for the room at that time. I asked Mary to stay awhile in case you wanted to ask her some questions."

"What time did this woman check in," Jake asked.

"She checked in to the hotel at eleven forty-five."

"Thank you. Mary, can you describe the lady who checked into the hotel last night?

"Yes, she's about five foot five inches, dark completion, long black hair, no lipstick, and she spoke with a Spanish accent. When I asked her for a credit card, she was adamant about paying cash and wouldn't sign a check-in card. One other thing, she wore gloves when she checked in and was wearing the same gloves when she left the hotel."

"Mary, you're very observant. Do you think you would recognize her if you saw her picture?" Jake asked.

"Yes, I'm pretty sure," Mary replied. "I'm free any time."

"Did anything happen while she was checking in? Something that may have stuck in your mind," Jake asked.

"Now that I think about it, there was something unusual. The woman pulled a burn phone from her pocket and started speaking Spanish. I couldn't understand a word she was saying," Mary replied.

"Thank you, I'll set you up with my secretary."

"Carman, do you mind if I have a forensic team take a look in the room?"

"Certainly, but try not to tie the room up very long. We have guests coming in for the Big Bass Lake fishing contest. It seems the hotels are getting booked early this year. I remembered to reserve a bass boat for us."

"Jake, we've been at this for two hours and we have nothing. Mrs. Smith didn't leave anything behind. There are no fingerprints, or hair in the bathroom drain, and no trace evidence indicating she was in the room. Jake, this woman is a pro," Zig said.

"Ya, you're right. Something happened, she got spooked, went to the airport, and took off in a private plane bound for Bogotá. Zig, there has to be a connection between Grazer's and Hans Osterfeld's murders. I'd like to cover all the bases. Maybe she used the restroom at the airport."

"Sure, I'm on it. Jake, what would Grazer and Osterfeld have in common? They sure as hell don't travel in the same social circles."

Jake left the hotel, headed for police headquarters and, as he drove through the city, his mind was fixated on the unusual woman Mary described. He mumbled, "There had to be something missing in Mary's statement. It's humanly impossible for someone not to leave trace evidence. Zig couldn't find evidence of Mrs. Smith's presence in her hotel room. Shit." Jake made a U turn and sped back to the hotel.

Carman was standing in the lobby when Jake walked through the hotel's revolving door. He noticed a sense of urgency on Jake's face, "Jake, let's go to my office."

Carman closed his office door and asked, "Jake, what's going on?"

"Zig couldn't find any evidence, not even trace evidence in the room Mrs. Smith checked into because she was never in the room. There is no woman on this planet who would not shower, bathe, or take care of every day personal hygiene before leaving the room. Did anyone check into the hotel after Mrs. Smith?"

Carman turned on his computer and scanned the guests' check in column. "No, Jake, there was no other guest."

"Okay, Mary stated the woman was using a burn phone and speaking Spanish. She must have a very close friend in Lind City. She called her friend, made arrangements to stay with that person until her plane left the airport, which explains why she paid her hotel bill in cash when she checked in. She had no intention of staying at the hotel, and the entire hotel scene was a distraction from why she was really in Lind City. I was right when I told Zig something or someone spooked her and she rushed out of town.

The questions remain, why was she here, and who is her close Spanish speaking friend?"

"Well, I don't think she was here for the opening day of bass season," Carman chuckled.

"Ya, right. Its two days away. I'll pick you up about five Saturday morning. I'm going to run by the hospital and check on Gus. He probably wishes he could be at the marina Saturday, and I'm sure he's going to miss George."

Jake stepped up to the Charge Nurse's desk. "Hi, Betty. I'm here to see Gus. Is he in his room?"

"You missed Gus by about twenty minutes, Betty replied. "He's a pretty tough guy. He told the doctor he had to get back to work at the marina, and either the doctor released him from the hospital or he was going to walk out without a release. Jake, I think Gus is making a big mistake. He shouldn't perform any physical labor."

"Thank you, Betty." Jake's cell phone rang. "Hey, Zig, have you been able to find anything at the airport?"

"The janitor cleaned the restrooms at eleven last night and the mystery woman arrived here at eleven thirty. I can give one positive note and two negatives. We found hair samples and fingerprints in the restroom sink and commode. I scanned the fingerprints through the International Data Bank and came up with nothing. I haven't received word on the DNA. On a positive note, the airport's lobby security camera has a detailed video of a female entering the lobby. I scanned the picture of her and sent it to the Facial Recognition Data Base and to Interpol. We received a positive recognition from Interpol. Her name is Consuela Delgado, aka, Angel de la muerte or the Angel of Death. Delgado has been on the Interpol top ten list for a couple of years. Her permanent residence is Bogotá, Columbia where she disappears. What do you make of an assassin coming to Lind City?"

"I'm playing a hunch someone was sent here to kill Gus. He's the only witness to George Grazer's murder," Jake replied. "Zig, why would they send a high profile Cartel killer like Delgado?"

"That's a good hunch, however, what if she was sent here to eliminate someone else? Possibly a person who presents a higher risk to the Columbians," Zig replied. "I gotta run. Good luck, Jake."

Jake remembered the interview he, John, DA, Anne Moffitt, had with Oscar Gonzales. Anne stated, "Now, assuming you can identify Consuela Delgado, all you guys have to do is find and arrest the infamous Consuela Delgado." He chuckled as he drove into the police headquarters parking lot, and mumbled, 'We have identified Delgado, and now we can wait until she leaves Columbia. The Angel of Death certainly wasn't in Lind City sightseeing and, whatever it was, she'll be back to accomplish her task. That's when we will arrest her.' Jake was struck with an immediate answer to why there was no trace evidence in the hotel room. 'I'll be damned, we were right, she wasn't in the hotel room she was shacked up somewhere else." Jake was startled by a tap on his window.

John Swift was peeking into Jake's car and asked, "Are you going to your office?"

"Yeah, what's up?"

"Let's wait until we get to your office. I'll meet you there in a few minutes," John replied, as he walked away from Jake's car.

It was close to noon when Jake stopped at the office personnel coffee bar, filled a mug full of black coffee, and found Danish left over from the morning coffee break. He juggled the coffee, Danish, and briefcase to his office where John sat alone with a large manila folder in his hands. "What's going on?"

John closed the office door and placed the folder on Jake's desk. "I was contacted by a friend of mine, from Harvard Law School, who is an undercover agent for Interpol. He told me about a guy they've tracked for quite some time. His name is Mùchén Yáng, he represents the Chinese drug producers for narcotics buyers. A couple of days ago, Yáng had a meeting with Columbian buyers at a hotel in New York City. Yáng allegedly had a small number of various drugs, including fentanyl, for the Columbians to sample. Interpol did not want to interfere with the sampling, they have bigger fish to fry. Everyone is aware the Columbians can produce most of their own drugs except for fentanyl."

"So, what's this got to do with us?" Jake asked.

"Interpol Intel stated they followed four people into the hotel room, Mùchén Yáng, Consuela Delgado, Diego Garcia, and the chemist, Marven Padano; however, five people left the hotel. Two of them left together, Consuela Delgado and an unidentifiable man. Interpol lost the man when he went into the subway. The Interpol agent has a strong suspicion Delgado and the man met in Lind City that evening," John replied.

"How did a fifth person get into the hotel without the Interpol agent's knowledge?"

"We don't know. All the information about this case, compiled by Interpol, is in that folder. Jake, my agent friend has his neck stuck out a mile. No one else, and I mean no one else, has seen this information."

"I understand," Jake said. There was a pause. "You have a Harvard Law Degree. Why are you in law enforcement?"

John replied, "I was a defense attorney and, after defending murderers and drug dealers for a year, I decided arresting the bad guys rather than defending them would the most suitable direction for my life. I'm forty-four years old and a few months away from getting my pension."

"Do you have any plans for retirement?"

"Yes, I'm going fishing, camping, golfing, and whatever my heart desires."

"Please let me know if you ever get tired of doing what your heart desires. I think we would make a good PI team. Think about it."

10

"Hi Jake, I've been trying to reach you all day."

"Hi Maggie, I've been pretty busy. What are we doing for supper tonight?"

"I don't know about supper," Maggie replied, sarcastically. "I finally received the results of the DNA sample George Grazer had under his finger nails. They belong to a local guy, Anthony a.k.a. Bubba, Commons. Have you ever heard of him?"

"Sure, I know the guy. When I was Chief of Detectives, we gave him a break on a couple of small charges and, with his cooperation, we were able to apprehend a heavy hitter in a drug trafficking ring. He's got a history of assaults and car theft. He doesn't strike me as a hardened killer. I remember his address. I'll stop by his place and ask him a few questions."

"Honey, this Bubba guy may have graduated to murder. Don't you think you should bring some backup with you?"

"I'm not on the force anymore and, to ask for back-up, I would need strong probable cause. I'll stop by his place on the way home, ask him a few questions, and I'll be home in a few of hours for dinner."

"You mean you'll meet me at a restaurant for dinner," Maggie snickered.

Jake and Clarence Dobbins, the apartment building manager, carefully walked down a dimly lit hall, wading through trash, smelly garbage, and an occasional rat, on their way to Bubba Commons' apartment.

"It's not much farther to Bubba's place," Clarence said. He pulled up his dirty blue jeans and wiped the sweat from his upper lip. "I wasn't always this heavy, it kinda snuck up on me. Here we are."

"Wait," Jake commanded. "I smell something I don't like."

Clarence took a hardy sniff, and uttered, "That's the garbage you smell."

Jake slowly stepped toward Bubba's apartment door while pulling his pistol from his holster. The odor coming from the apartment became stronger and was too familiar. He tapped on the door and shouted Bubba's name several times. "Clarence, do you have keys to this apartment?"

"Yes."

"Okay, unlock the door and step away."

Jake cautiously opened the door, stepped a few feet into the apartment, and was immediately struck with the overwhelming stench of a decaying human body. He saw Bubba lying on floor and, by the appearance of mixed larvae and maggot activity, he surmised the body had been there for a little more than twenty hours. His first impulse was to escape from the horrific odor.

"What's going on in there?" Clarence shouted. "You, okay?"

"I called the Police Department. The Crime Scene Investigators are on their way. Get down to the front door and make sure it's unlocked. I'll wait for them outside the apartment," Jake shouted. He found a clean place in the hall, leaned his back against it, and waited for the CSI people to arrive. After all the years on the police force and investigating crime scenes, it was extremely difficult for Jake to wait in the hall and do nothing until the crime scene commander cleared the area.

A familiar voice rang out, "Jake, where are you?"

"Hey Zig, I'm on the second floor, just follow the ugly stench," Jake replied.

"Jake, I have to say, you have a knack for finding corpses. Maggie's on her way and my team is behind me, lugging up the equipment. I'll try to release the scene to Maggie ASAP." Zig climbed into a white full-body breathable suit, to prevent synthetic blood penetration while he worked the scene, and paused. "Jake, a heads up. Joan Fetter is at the front door. She must have heard the call over the police scanner at the Times office." He placed a white mask over his mouth and went into the apartment.

"Can I go home now?" Clarence asked.

"Clarence, how many hours do you work in the building?"

"I'm here for as long as it takes to fix whatever needs fixin. It ain't a great job but it helps pay my bills," Clarence replied.

"Did you see, or hear anything coming from this apartment in the last couple of days?"

"Sir, I heard a couple of guys hollering. I couldn't hear what they were saying, but they were both pissed off at some guy. Hollering and screaming goes on all the time in this place. I mind my own business," Clarence replied. "There was one thing I do remember. Two nights ago, I saw two men go into Bubba's apartment and, when I got to work the next morning, the two men were leaving. I think they stayed the night with Bubba."

"Did they mention the guy's name, you know, the one they were hollering about?"

"No, but it sure sounded like they wanted to kill the guy."

"Why is staying the night so unusual?" Jake asked.

"There's only one cot, one chair, and no beds in that place," Clarence replied.

"Have you ever had trouble with Bubba?"

"Sure. We were going to get into a fight the first day he was here. He dumped his garbage in the hall and I got pissed off, but nothing happened. Can I go now?"

"Yes, you can go. Give me your phone number before you leave."

"Hi Honey, it looks like we're going to have a late supper tonight," "Maggie said.

"It looks that way. Zig should be through with his work soon. He has been in the apartment for a couple of hours."

"Yes, and Zig is done," Zig remarked, as he came out of the apartment. "We found nothing of interest in the hall. The scene is clear in the apartment. It's all yours Maggie."

"Were you able to find anything interesting?" Jake asked.

"Well, we were able to pull some fingerprints and DNA samples. He had a cell phone in his pocket. We'll track down as many phone numbers as we can. I haven't sent them through the data system. I'll do it as soon as I'm out of these smelly clothes," Zig replied. "Oh Jake, we received the report on the trace evidence in the Hans Osterfeld murder. The report showed a white talc powder inside the small boat."

"Jake, you're allowed to come with me." Maggie entered the apartment, forewarned of the overwhelming stench. "Whew, they weren't kidding about the smell."

Jake thoroughly examined the position of Bubba's body. "He's exactly the way I found him."

"By the looks of him, and no sign of rigor mortis, he's been dead for about twenty four to forty eight hours. However, I can tell you something you probably surmised, he didn't die from blunt force trauma or gunshot wounds. By the looks of the saliva around his mouth, my guess is this is murder by fentanyl injection similar to Hans Osterfeld and George Grazer. I can give you and John a better analysis after I perform an autopsy. There's one thing for certain, this is not the work of a serial killer," Maggie said.

"Maggie, what I can't wrap my head around, why here, why in a small town like Lind City? This stuff happens in the big cities. Why here?"

"That's a good question," Maggie replied. "You've had a long day. I'll get the body to the morgue and meet you for dinner."

Joan came scurrying toward Jake. "I was tired of waiting downstairs. I heard the call over the radio and came right over. What's going on?"

"I'll see you later," Maggie said.

"Did I interrupt something?" Joan asked.

"No, we're finished," Jake replied. "To answer your question, we don't have much. We have to wait for Zig and Maggie's results. A man was murdered a couple of days ago. There was no visible sign of blunt force trauma, and..."

Joan interrupted Jake, "Fentanyl, right?"

"We don't know. Maggie will let us know the cause of death as soon as she can. I don't want to assume anything, and we're certain this is not the work of a serial killer."

"Hi, Jake, Joan. I was about a hundred miles from here when the call came over the scanner. Curiosity got to me," John panted.

"Hey, John, no problem. The victim's name is Anthony a.k.a. Bubba Commons. He's got a record of minor arrests. Zig was here and came up with some latent prints and DNA samples and Maggie is with the victim."

"I have enough for a 'murder is under investigation' story. I'll see you guys later," Joan said.

"Jake, I'm not here as an investigator. The word came from the top down, the Mayor, Commissioner, Chief, and me, this is your baby. I stopped by because I was curious and no other reason," John said, reassuringly."

Jake said, "I appreciate everyone's vote of confidence."

"Make some room you guys, we're moving the victim to the morgue," Maggie barked.

Jake stood silently in the hall as the body was taken down the stairs, followed by Maggie and John. He ducked under the apartment crime scene tape to take another look and asked himself, 'What the hell happened in this city. Three people, who apparently had no ties to one another, murdered in a matter of two weeks, and the weapon used was fentanyl by injection. We have the means, opportunity, except we don't have the motive. Jake left the apartment and drove home. The odor in the apartment had permeated his clothes. The thought of a shower, fresh clothes, and time to clear his head before meeting Maggie seemed like a great idea. When he entered his home, there was a dim light on in the family room. Maggie and he never left a light turned on in the room while they were away. He tip toed across the living room and cautiously peeked into the family room. He saw a bottle of champagne in an ice bucket, two glasses on the coffee table, and Maggie sitting on the sofa wearing a very sexy negligee.

She smiled and sensually asked, "What took you so long?"

Jake stammered before he replied, "I thought we were going out for dinner tonight."

"We are in a sense." She poured some champagne into the two glasses. "I ordered a delivery from the restaurant, and it will be here in about three hours. What do you think we should do for the next three hours?"

11

"Jake, CO here."

Jake closed his office door, and touched the record app on his cell phone. "Carter Osterfeld, how did you get my private cell phone number?"

"Never mind that. I need to meet with you alone. I won't bring any of my people, and you do the same. You're a Private Investigator, and I can tell you anything without incriminating myself."

"What do you want to talk about?" Jake said, hesitating. "You understand the Lind City PD is my client."

"I know they're your one and only client. You have to understand where I'm coming from. I can't tell you, not even on your cell, because if I were in your shoes, I would be recording this conversation. Trust me, I wouldn't call you if this wasn't big."

Jake wanted to discourage a client relationship with CO. "So why me? You have the resources to hire any PI company in the world. Why would you hire a startup PI in a small city? CO, even if I agreed to meet with you, I can't fly to New York City on a moment's notice. If it's as insignificant as you say it is, why don't you get the FBI involved? I can recommend an agent I know."

"I can't contact any law enforcement people. I need to give you the information anonymously. Jake, you don't have to come to New York. I'm alone, without bodyguards, somewhere in Lind City."

Jake's curiosity got the better of him and he said, "I'll meet with you; however, I pick the time and place. We can meet this afternoon at the water fountain in Liberty Park at two p.m. The park is on the Southside of the city."

"Done. Jake, don't screw with me, wherever we meet, no recordings, people, wires, or weapons."

"You have my word."

Jake sat back in his chair and began to reminisce when he was a detective in the Big Apple. The unwritten rule was, 'use your gut feeling when you're meeting with a known criminal, and be alert to ulterior motives.' He thought CO's extreme sense of urgency was genuine and, the fact he took the time out of his busy schedule to travel here, tells me he's in deep shit.

"Penney, I'm stopping by the ME's Lab and then I'll be out of the office for the rest of the day. You can reach me on my cell phone."

"Don't forget tomorrow is Saturday and it's the first day of bass season, so don't get into any trouble," Penney giggled.

"Hi Jake, I was thinking about you," Maggie smirked. "I meant about the autopsy I performed on   Anthony Commons."

"I was thinking about you too, but it wasn't about an autopsy." Jake looked around to see if anyone was nearby and gave Maggie a peck on the lips.

"The time and date of death would be approximately nine p.m. Wednesday, and the cause of death was an over dose of fentanyl by injection. Jake, this man had enough fentanyl in him to kill a hundred people. This is the same MO as the other two victims in the last two weeks. I hope these homicides are not the beginning of a drug war in our beautiful city."

"I don't think there's going to be a drug war here. I know drugs are involved, however I don't think the motive is over a drug dealer's territory," Jake commented. "Honey, I have to run. I have a meeting with CO at two p.m."

"Jake be careful. CO's an extremely dangerous man, and wouldn't hesitate to make you disappear."

"Honey, I'm going to be very careful. The park has one entrance and exit. If I see any sign of CO's men, or if I feel uncomfortable for any reason, I'm out of there. I think we're jumping to conclusions. The man who called me this morning wasn't the cantankerous man we saw at the morgue. The CO I talked with this morning was nervous, stressed-out and, frankly, he sounded frightened."

"How are you going to prepare for this meeting?"

"I have two hours before the meeting. The park is twenty five minutes from here. I'm going to drive to the park, scope out the surroundings, and grab a quick lunch."

"Jake, don't get into any trouble, tomorrow's the first day of bass season."

"Yes, Penney reminded me when I left the office. What can happen? We're meeting alone in Liberty Park."

Liberty Park is a nondescript, parcel of secluded land, far enough out of the city limits to have a clandestine meeting. Jake circled the park a few times mentally noting the surroundings, and stopped at the dried out fountain. He thought, 'The fountain isn't making the splashing sounds fountains usually make. This is perfect, I can hear a fly hiccup here.'

When Jake returned from lunch, he stood at the side of the fountain, where he could run for cover in case this was a setup.

It was precisely two p.m. when a black, midsize sedan, drove slowly to the fountain and parked. CO wiggled his tall frame from behind the wheel and said, "I don't think my body will ever be the same. Jake, thanks for meeting with me on such short notice."

"No problem."

"Is there some place we can sit?"

"I have two folding chairs in my trunk," Jake replied. "Would you like to watch while I take them out of the trunk?"

"No, we're here on our honor."

Jake methodically positioned the chairs in front of the fountain, and facing the entrance. "CO, please tell me why we're here?"

"You don't waste any time. What I'm about to tell you cannot go any further than this fountain. If you repeat any our conversation I will deny every word, and you will vanish. You can use what I'm going to tell you to your own advantage. I'm sure you will understand my situation when we're through here."

"Okay, you've got my attention," Jake said, earnestly.

"When we were at the morgue, identifying my son Hans, I mentioned at the top of my lungs Hans inherited fifty percent of my company. I thought, perhaps, he would join me in the operation of the construction company and I would handle the sales and financial part of the entire International Corporation. I

74

also told you how the stock agreement with Mary and me came about. When Mary and I started the business, times were tough and we agreed to a fifty-fifty stock ownership. The business got bigger and bigger, and when Mary passed, she left all of her stock to Hans. There was no 'right of first refusal' for me to purchase the stock in our bylaws. I was upset over the fact Hans did nothing to earn the position. Nevertheless, I was forced to recognize Hans as half owner in the company. I tried to be pleasant and told him what I thought we should achieve going forward."

"How much is the stock worth?"

"Jake, it's worth one hundred million dollars, and he gets a piece of the monthly revenue from the construction business. I'm going explain the rest of it in a minute," CO replied. He ran his hand over his partly bald head. "What do you think the kid said? The little shit told me he was going to take some time to see the world and working with me wasn't in his future. I went totally ballistic, grabbed him by the neck, and started choking him. I was going to kill that son of a bitch right in my office."

"Did you kill Hans?"

"No, I swear, I didn't kill him, and I didn't put a hit on him. I regained my composure, I let go of his neck, and told him to get the hell out of my sight. That was six months ago," CO shouted. He shook his head and smirked. "Hypothetically, if I wanted to off someone, I wouldn't put oversized, heavy chains on him, use metal cans full of cement to sink him in a local lake, and dump the body where would easily be found."

"Was that the last time you saw Hans?"

"No. He showed up about two weeks ago, without calling me first, at the top floor of the corporate office building. He walked past my secretary, opened the doors to my private office, and demanded I talk with him about a business deal he was going to make. I told him I was too busy and didn't have time for him. I called security and had his ass kicked out of the building. Little did I know, kicking him out of the building was what finally broke us apart?" CO slumped down in his chair.

"Did Hans ever tell you what the big deal was?"

"He told me he met with a man named, Diego something or other, he was going to make millions of dollars, and he was going to live in Bogotá Columbia. What a dumb shit."

"CO, what you're telling me sounds like a personal problem. Now that Hans is out of the picture, you own one hundred percent of the stock. You have full control of your businesses and you answer to no one. I'm going repeat myself, why are we here?"

CO became silent, as if Jake's question was contemptible. He glanced at Jake with rage in his eyes. The rage was not aimed at Jake, but was for what he was about to divulge. "Okay, I'll tell you why we're here," CO replied, mockingly. "About two weeks ago, just after my argument with Hans, I received a call from a man named Diego Garcia on my private office landline. The line is for private only to my immediate circle. I asked him how he acquired the phone number and he replied, "Hans Osterfeld gave me the number." He then told me, he didn't ask me, we had to meet immediately in my office to discuss a large business proposition. I told him to piss off and hung up the phone. The phone rang again, and I let it ring until it stopped. Jake, it wasn't a minute after that, my secretary came into my office and said there's a very angry man on the phone and, if you don't take his call, you will be dead within an hour. I picked up the phone and, before I could utter a word, he screamed and I quote, 'We own fifty percent the stock in Osterfeld Construction Company and you better listen to what I have to say.' I told him he was full of shit. Diego laughed out loud, and that's when he dropped the bomb. He said his friends in Columbia would not be happy if I refused to meet with him."

"You gotta be kidding me. Hans gave all fifty percent of the stock to the Columbians? They must have told him one hell of a bunch of crap," Jake said.

"Yes, the proposition they gave me, in short, my company is to acquire a small building in the Lind City area, purchase several small electric cement mixers, and they will make it look like a legitimate business. Jake, this would make me an accessory to a crime. I would be a major contributor to the Cartel."

"Yes, I'm afraid you're right."

"What the hell am I going to do? The Columbians will kill me if I don't comply and, if I bring local law or the Feds into this shit, I'm dead. Jake, man, you gotta help me."

"I don't know how I can help you. I have three homicides in the Lind City limits which makes it a local problem. It's a problem I've been retained to investigate. Were you involved in the other two homicides?"

"No. I had absolutely nothing to do with those homicides. I'm sure those hits were ordered by the Cartel," CO replied.

"I'm going to tell you what I think, and then we'll have to leave the park." Jake believed there was no possible way to be tactful about his next comment. "CO, when Hans approached Diego with a proposition which included half of your company, it seems to me, they could care less about a partnership with Hans. What they were more attracted to was you and your entire company."

CO jumped out of his chair and with malice in his voice said, "They'll never get my company."

"The Cartel is giving you orders. To them you're just one of their many puppets. Give me a call if you ever change your mind about getting the law evolved. Jake stood from the chair and methodically folded it. He took a few steps away from the fountain, stopped, turned around, and asked, "How did you know Hans had oversized, heavy, chains on him?"

"I saw it in the newspapers," CO replied, irritably.

"No, you didn't. The media, including the newspapers, were not given those details."

12

Jake sat patiently waiting for, Carman Cruz his opening day fishing partner, to appear from his home. The forty five minute journey to Big Bass Lake, stopping for coffee and a bagel, and reminiscing about all the big ones that got away, signaled the bass fisherman's real first day of summer. At last, Carman made his way from the garage weighed down with all the required equipment to nail the biggest bass of the day.

Carman, after placing his fishing equipment in the trunk of Jake's car, slid into the front seat. "Morning, Jake. Its dark at five thirty, and I'm right on time. The weather looks good and the bass are waiting to be caught."

"Good morning to you, Carman. You're chipper this morning."

"I left the assistant manager in charge of the hotel and, without any major problems, I'm free as a bird for the next three days."

"It sounds like a plan. I called the marina yesterday and Marvin, a new employee, answered the phone. He assured me the rental boat will be stocked with bait and ready for us at sun-up. It seemed odd at first, I mean, not talking to Gus about our rental boat," Jake remarked, as he pulled into the drive through lane of the bagel shop and placed their order. "Speaking of food. Maggie will meet us later at the cottage with some steaks to burn up on the grill and her famous potato and tossed salads.

Carman took a healthy bite from his bagel and thought this it would be a good time to let Jake know about a guest at the hotel. "Jake, I know we agreed not to talk business while we're on our fishing weekend, but then, I thought you would be interested in an oriental guest who checked into the hotel last night and had dinner in the dining room with a well-dressed Latino."

"What about them?"

"The waiter who was responsible for the table told me the Oriental guy waited for about half an hour for the Latino to show up. They had a few loud words about the Latino being late and the Oriental guy started to leave. They finally calmed down and ordered their food," Carman replied.

"What's the problem?"

"No problem, Jake. When the waiter approached the table to serve the food, he overheard the Oriental ask when the building will be available for the mixer, and the Latino said, 'CO ordered the machines and, as soon as he gets off his ass, the building will be ready.' I don't know the significance of the conversation, but when Carter Osterfeld's initials where mentioned, I thought you should know. Was I right?"

"Thanks, Carman. You did the right thing," Jake replied. He flashed the car's bright headlights as they passed the 'Welcome to the Village of Big Bass Lake' sign. "Perfect timing. It's not too dark to check in at the marina, load up the boat, and we can be on the lake at sun up."

A young man stood by the front steps of the marina office keeping an alert eye out for early customers when he noticed the two men in a black Mercedes pull into the parking lot. "Good morning, I'm Marvin. You guys are the first ones here. Are you ready to do some bass fishing?"

"Good morning," Jake replied, cheerfully. "I'm Jake Lester and yes, we're ready." Jake heard a familiar voice coming from the marina office. "Gus, is that you? We didn't think you would be here."

"Damn straight it's me. I wouldn't miss the first day of bass season for anything. The ass kicking, I got would be the last thing stopping me," Gus replied. "Did you guys register in the bass contest?"

"No, we're going catch and release and have some fun," Jake said hesitating. "Gus, we're sorry about George."

"Yup, it seems like he got screwed up with the wrong people and was in way over his head." Gus shook his head and said, "You guys didn't come here to hear about our problems." He pointed at a large flat bottom bass boat at the end of the dock and shouted, "Marvin, let's get these guys out on the lake before the big city people get here, make all kinds of noise, and scare the hell out of the fish."

"Gus, after the sun goes down, we're going to have a cookout at our cottage. I'm going to burn up some steaks and we might even have some adult beverages. There'll only be a few people and you'll know most of them. Why don't you stop by?"

"Thanks, Jake. I might take you up on that," Gus replied. "Have a good time out there. I'll push you away from the dock."

It was a couple of hours to sundown when Jake maneuvered the bass boat up to the marina dock.

"How was the fishing," Marvin asked, as he tied the boat to the dock.

"The bass were hitting today and we had one of the best catches ever," Carman replied.

"Is Gus around?" Jake asked.

"He was going to leave about noon. He said he wanted to take a nap and get cleaned up for your cookout," Marvin replied. "Then a funny thing happened. Not a ha-ha, funny. Gus was walking to his pickup truck when two men in a dark blue sedan stopped next to him. They talked with him for a few minutes and, the next thing I saw, one of the men got out of the car and opened the back door for Gus. It looked to me like Gus didn't want to get into the car. They didn't waste any time speeding away from the marina."

"Did you get a look at the two men or the license number of the car?" Jake asked.

"No, I didn't pay much attention to the men or the license number. I'm sorry I couldn't give you more information," Marvin replied.

"Well, let's hope it's nothing and Gus shows up at the cookout. Let me know if he calls you," Jake said.

"What do you think of that, Jake?" Carman asked.

"I don't know what to think. That's so unlike Gus not to greet the people coming off the lake after they've had a long day of fishing. He usually waits until the National Bass Officials weigh out the catches before he leaves the marina," Jake replied. "I'm sure we'll see him later at the cottage."

"Jake, can you drop me off at the motel I'd like to take a shower and get out of these clothes." Carman asked.

"Are you sure you want to stay at a motel? The invitation is still open. You're more than welcome to stay at our cottage."

"No thank you. You and Maggie are most gracious for asking me. I'll be fine at the motel."

Jake dropped Carman off at the motel and began to drive toward the cottage. He couldn't shake the thought about Gus reluctantly getting into a car and speeding away with two men. The fact that Gus was a witness to George Grazer's murder added more fuel to his suspicions.

When Jake arrived at the cottage, he saw Maggie's car backed up to the garage door. Her arms were full of the evening's cookout supplies. "Hi, can I give you a hand?"

"No thank you. Your timing is incredible. The car is unloaded," Maggie replied. "Where's Carman?"

"Carman, for some unknown reason, decided to stay at the motel tonight," Jake replied.

"I saw Gus leaving the village with two men in a dark blue car, and they took off like a bat out of hell. I hope he's coming to the cookout tonight. We have enough food to feed the entire village."

Jake opened the refrigerator door and pulled out a cold beer. "I'm very concerned. Gus was the only witness to George Grazer's murder, and he declined police protection. The new man at the marina stated Gus reluctantly got into the car with the men. I don't know Gus very well, and hopefully, my concern will be for nothing."

"Can you have the Lind City PD send out a BOLO for Gus and the two men in a blue car?"

"I don't have any real cause, or the authority to ask for a 'Be On the Look Out'," Jake replied.

It was eleven thirty when the last guest left Jake and Maggie's. The fire pit produced enough soft glowing embers to suggest Jake and Maggie have a nightcap and count the bright stars in the Milky Way.

Maggie broke the silence and commented, "Gus was the only person who didn't make the party. I hope he's okay."

"We have another day of fishing tomorrow. If he doesn't show up for the final tournament payout, I'll know something is wrong." Jake opened a fresh bottle of champagne. "I called the desk sergeant about a half hour ago, and there haven't been any incidences in the Lind City area all evening." Jake grinned at Maggie. "You know, I hate to let this romantic evening go to waste." Jake proceeded to topped off their glasses with the champagne.

Maggie's eyes glistened in the moonlight, "Mr. Lester, I think you have a splendid idea. I feel exceptionally amorous tonight."

Jake put his arms around Maggie's waist, and gently pulled her close to his and kissed her passionately on the lips.

It was five-thirty a.m. when Jake peeked through the cottage porch's vertical blinds and saw a light drizzle of rain falling on the lake. "Ah, a perfect day for bass fishing." He strained his eyes and focused on a dark silhouette of a person stumbling toward the cottage from the lake's shoreline. He quickly threw on some slacks and rushed out the door and, as he approached the person, it was apparent he had severely beaten. Jake didn't realize Gus was the man he helped into the cottage until he turned on a light, "Holy crap, Gus! Gus, can you hear me?" he shouted.

Gus mumbled incoherent remarks.

Maggie rushed into the room shouting, "Jake, what's going on?" She drew closer to the figure laying across the sofa. "Oh my God, it's Gus. What the hell happened?"

"I don't know. He can't talk," Jake replied.

Maggie knelt in front of Gus and wiped his face with a cloth, "Jake, get my medical bag. It looks like he has a broken jaw. I need to check his vital signs. We have to get him to a hospital."

Gus murmured, "No. No hospital. They'll kill me."

"Jake, he needs medical care right now, what should we do?"

"He doesn't have bullet or knife wounds. We don't have to report this to the police until we find out who beat the hell out of him. I'm going to take him to our friends at The Mother of Peace Convent. They have a basic emergency room in the basement of the Monastery. Honey, call Sister Mary Francis Carter, her tell what happened and I'm on my way."

"What should I tell everyone when you don't show up at the marina?"

"I don't know."

The twenty minute drive from the cottage to The Mother of Peace Convent seemed forever. The security gates were open, which was unheard of at the Cloister Convent. He looked into his rearview mirror as he sped up the quarter mile dirt driveway and saw the gates close behind him. Jake was relieved to see his friend, Mary Francis, who was obviously anticipating the possibility of someone following him.

Fr. Sullivan was a Catholic Priest during the Second World War. He was captured by the enemy, tortured on a daily basis and, by some miracle, survived the horrific ordeal, and was released. It was at that point he knew his calling was to be a steadfast friend and servant to the Cloistered Nuns. It was a more simple time when the large structure was the Monastery for several women who chose to become Cloistered Nuns, devote their lives to God, and live a life in silence and prayer. Sister Mary Francis and Jake were high school friends and remained friends throughout the years. Mary Francis tagged Jake with the nickname, Jakel, and she is the only person on earth who could call him by that name.

Jake entered the small parking lot, where Sister Francis and four other nuns, wearing blue scrubs, stood next to a gurney. The nuns worked as a team extracting Gus from the back seat of the car, and placed him on the gurney.

"Jake, I haven't seen anything like this since I was a trauma nurse in Afghanistan. My Lord, what happened to this pour soul?" Mary Francis asked.

"His name is Gus Highland and is he's my fishing partner. He staggered out of the lake early this morning. The only words he's uttered were 'they're going to kill me.' Mary Francis, this is the only place he will be safe until I figure out what happened and come up with a long term plan to keep him from whoever is trying to kill him."

"How are you going to explain why he's not fishing with you today?"

"That's a good question. I'll think of something. The fishing tournament ends at noon today. I'll get back here as soon as I can." Jake walked back to his car, turned, and nodded his head.

Mary Francis smiled, "Jakel, be careful. Whoever did this to your friend is outside talent, and they must have thought he was dead before they dumped him into the lake. Now, you better get your butt out of here."

It was three thirty Sunday afternoon when Jake returned to the Mother of Peace Convent parking lot and saw a mint condition vintage Jeep backed into the pathway. He slipped out of his car and peeked into the Jeep. The interior of the vehicle was immaculate and impossible to find a clue to identify the owner.

Mary Francis, accompanied by a woman in her fifties, walked toward Jake from the flower garden, "Jake, we're glad see you. I'd like you to meet Sister Rose Thomas. Rose is a retired surgeon who served with me in Afghanistan."

"Mary Francis," Jake said, firmly. "I'm confused, what's going on."

"Please, Jake, you know me better than to jeopardize our friend's whereabouts. It turns out his injuries were beyond our expertise. I trust Rose with my life."

"Jake, it's a pleasure to meet you. I have no reason to report this to any law enforcement agencies. When Mary Francis called me this morning and, described the man's injuries, I hustled right over here. He has several broken ribs, broken jaw, brain concussion, several contusions, and cigarette burns all over his body. The man was tortured close to death and obviously thrown into the lake and left to drown. I patched him up as much as possible and, by some miracle, he's going to live. He's sedated, needs rest and a copious amount of TLC. He may be able to converse coherently in a few days. Don't worry about him. He's in good hands here."

"Jake, you have to go about your business as if nothing happened," Mary Francis remarked.

Jake thought for a moment, "You're right. The people who threw Gus into the lake are assuming he's dead and we should keep it that way."

13

After traveling for two hours on a county highway toward the Adirondack Mountains, Jake turned his all-terrain vehicle onto a local dirt road, drove another mile, and stopped at a crushed stone driveway blocked by a manual swinging gate at the entrance. He opened the squeaky gate and continued on the dirt road until he came upon a large log cabin. Jake stood at the front door and as he raised his hand to knock, the door opened. A man in his early seventies appeared, holding the door wide open.

"Well come on in. I thought you would never get here," his father said. John Lester retired from the Lind City Police Department eight years ago, and watched his only child, Jake, as he climbed up the ranks in the same police department. He and his wife built the log cabin twenty years ago as a summer getaway.

"Dad, I came as soon as I got your text," Jake said, as he gave his father a bear hug. "We're going to have to cook our own meals. Maggie's on call and couldn't make it this time."

"I'm going to miss your wife's great good cooking, but we'll make do somehow." John looked at his watch, "its five o'clock somewhere." He reached into a cupboard, pulled out two glasses and a bottle of thirty year old single malt scotch. "We should have a sip or two before we throw the steaks on the grill." He handed Jake one of the drinks and said, "Let's sit on the back deck. I always love looking over the mountains from there."

Jake knew his father's body English from years of experience and this would be one those long conversations before the real reason for looking out over the mountains. He also knew interrupting his father's MO would not be a wise thing to do and, at this point, patience and understanding would be prudent.

"How did the fishing tournament go last week?"

"Dad, we hit it big. You know I catch and release. The thought of attending the opening day festivities of bass season is what turns me on."

John swirled the small amount of scotch at the bottom of his glass and slowly drank the glass empty. "Jake, we can't stand on one leg, let's get a refill, and throw the steaks on the grill before the sun goes down."

It was after the steak dinner, as Jake and his dad sat in rocking chairs on the back porch enjoying the peaceful sunset, that John asked, "How's the case of the young man you found in Bass Lake?"

"It's cold, as far as any real evidence. The people who did the murder where pros and knew how to cover their tracks. The Forensics team couldn't find trace evidence. I have my suspicions of who could have killed the kid but nothing solid to go on," Jake replied.

"What about that Carter Osterfeld guy? The word is he had a visit with you about his son getting murdered. Did he have an ulterior motive for the visit?"

"Yup. He blew a lot of smoke at me about his son giving the Cartel all the shares of the construction company stock his mother gave him for a piece of the action. He claims the Cartel is forcing him out of the company so they can operate a fentanyl drug mixing and distribution operation in Lind City."

"Do you think Osterfeld is full of shit and playing you for some other reason?"

"I believe the part about his son getting wacked by the Cartel; however, the part about mixing and distributing drugs out of Lind City is bullshit. Why would the Cartel openly do business in the middle of a city of any size? The answer to the question, CO is working with the Cartel and the talk about setting up shop in Lind City is a diversion. Oh, I'm sure CO's company is going to build some sort of warehouse in Lind City, but the real operation will be in some obscure remote area."

John grinned, took a healthy sip of his scotch, reached over the side of his rocking chair, and pulled up a pair of night vision binoculars. Son, do you remember the old talc mines near the "Twin Peaks?" John pointed to the North. "The mines were abandoned thirty years ago." He handed Jake the binoculars. "It's dark enough for us to use these. Take a look at the Twin Peaks and tell me what you see."

"Holy crap. It looks like ten or fifteen people sitting and eating at the opening of the mine."

"Right. Some half assed company with a phony name bought the mines about a month ago. I spotted those people with the binoculars one night while I was checking for deer poachers. They stay in the mine all day and come out at night. Scan the area about a hundred yards around base of the Twin Peaks."

Jake followed his father's suggestion and slowly moved the binoculars in a panoramic sweep. "Damn," He whispered in disbelief. There are laser trip lights all over the place. This has to be the Cartel's actual operation. I need to get a better look."

"Relax, not tonight. It's too dangerous," John said. "I know a better way to approach the talc mines. When the mines were in operation, the mining company gave the hundred, or so, miners and their families a home to live in as a perk. The miners could live there as long as the mines were in operation, and they never took the county highway to the mines because it was too far. They drove their vehicles a couple of miles up an old logging road to the mines. My bet is, these people don't even know the logging road is on the map. We'll have an early breakfast in the morning and head over to the mining town."

Jake shot down the remainder of his scotch, wiped his lips with his hand, set his glass on the table, and said, "I think I'll hit the sack."

"Hell, you say. It's nine p.m. We're just warming up." He poured some scotch, about three fingers high, into Jake's glass. "Now Son, tell me what you really think about your new career and don't spare the details."

The morning dew was burned off the grass and foliage when Jake and his father left Max's diner. The winding back road led them to the deserted mining village. The once well-kept lawns and manicured shrubs were now a scene out of a depression movie. John followed West Street, through the tiny village to where the pothole filled paved road ended and the remanence of a logging road began.

"Uh, Dad, I don't think we should try our luck on this road. It's over grown with small trees and there's a good chance we're going to get stuck in the middle of nowhere."

"Jake, have no fear. Why do you think we took this old warhorse all-wheel drive jeep out here?" John pulled a lever with a thud and, like a giant behemoth, the jeep jumps forward and started conquering the over grown foliage. He brought the jeep to a stop about a hundred yards from the talc mine. "I think this is close enough. We can hike up the road a little way to get a better look."

Jake looked at his father with admiration he had never felt before. He had never, in all the years he was growing up, had the opportunity to assist his father in anything. Yet, here he was standing next to his dad, ready to take on the unknown together.

They stopped at a point where the wild vines, trees, and thick undergrowth gave them optimum cover, and where the view was most advantageous.

Jake raised the binoculars to his eyes and, as his father mentioned, not one soul was outside the mine during the daylight hours. "Dad, there's no one outside the mine. What are we doing here?"

John pulled a small coffee thermos from his backpack. "Here, have some coffee. Jake, when you were in Afghanistan on a recon mission, you found a stealth place to observe in total silence.

Silence was the operative word, and eventually something usually happened. The difference between then and now, no one is shooting at you." John grinned, "Not yet."

Jake said, "Dad, have you forgotten there are several security devices around here, and we're ninety nine percent sure those people in the mine are members of the Cartel. We also have to assume they're heavily armed."

"Son, don't sweat the small shit. I forgot to tell you. I scoped this location well in advance of us coming here. The Cartel's property line is about fifty feet in front of us and there are no security devices in this location."

"Jake whispered, "We're doomed."

The morning watch extended into late afternoon without out a trace of a human outside the mine. The sunlight would be gone in less than two hours and traveling back to the village on the logging road in the dark would be extremely dangerous. "Dad, what do you think?"

"Let's give it another hour and, if there's no action, we'll call it a day and get back here in the morning," John replied.

The sun was close to setting behind the Twin Peaks when Jake's attention was drawn to the sound of a truck engine. A vehicle appeared inching its way to the base of the mine's entrance. "Dad," he whispered.

"Ya, I see it."

Jake held his camera over the bushes, zoomed in to the activity, and started the video recorder, "It looks like they're going to unload electrical equipment, a large spool of heavy chain, a large machine of some kind. The chain is similar to the chain that was used in the Hans Osterfeld murder. Zig stated there was a trace of talc powder inside the small boat. Hans was murdered in the mine and transported to Big Bass Lake." He focused on the people getting out of the truck and zoomed in on their faces, momentarily dropped the camera from his eyes and raised the camera back to his eyes. "There's a woman with the men. I recognize her from the 'Want and Warrants' database. Her name is Consuela Delgado, she's known as the Angel de la muerte, the Angel of Death. Dad, the only one reason she would leave Columbia."

"She's going to kill someone, right?"

"Right," Jake replied. "We better get out of here."

"Well, if these people are with the Cartel, and they're from Columbia, who the hell is that Oriental guy with them?"

"I don't know." Jake snapped several pictures of the man. "I think we have enough bars on the phone for me to send these pictures to the face recognition base. I should have an answer in a few minutes."

"Son, we're losing the sun, and people are coming out of the mine. I think we better get the hell out of here."

The paved road at the mining village was a welcome sight as they drove out of the logging road to West Street and sped down the county highway.

"Jake, I would call today a very productive day and, when we get home, I have another adult beverage we should sample."

"You mean, we should have a couple of drinks to celebrate." Jake's phone rang as a text picture appeared on the screen with a positive ID of Mùchén Yáng, a notorious drug dealer from China. "Holy crap. Why are these high level people arriving at the mine? Dad, this is going to be the major distribution center for drugs, including fentanyl, for the entire Northeast."

"What are you going to do with this information?"

"I'm going to hang on to everything we uncovered this weekend until I know who else is involved with the Cartel and China. Dad, at this point I can't trust anyone but you."

"You're going to confide in Maggie, aren't you?"

"I have to think about it. If I tell Maggie about our discovery, her life might be in danger."

"On the other hand, Jake, if you don't tell her, your life will definitely be in jeopardy, and whatever you decide, I'll have your back. Stay focused on the murder case of the young Osterfeld kid. Don't worry about the people at the mine. I'll keep my eye on them and let you know if anything significant happens," John remarked.

Maggie poured two glasses of wine and carried them out to the patio where Jake was dictating notes into his laptop about the extraordinary events of his weekend with his father. She placed a glass of wine into Jake's outreached hand and sat quietly while he completed the dictation. His purpose for coming home from the mountains a few hours early was to note everything he saw while it was fresh in his mind and to bring Maggie up to speed on the events of the trip.

"There, that's done," Jake said, as he closed the laptop. He sipped some wine and slid back into his chair and waited for Maggie's comments.

"I must say, Jake, you had one very exciting weekend with your father. Now that you have all of this intelligence information, what are you going to do with it?"

"The best way to treat the information, including the photos and videos, is not reveal what we have. The only people who know about this are my father and the two of us. I keep asking myself questions like, who can I trust. The answer keeps coming up, no one. The tentacles of the Cartel run long and deep. Who in the

Lind City PD can I trust? Again, the answer is, no one. Why were the Angel of Death, Consuela Delgado, who we couldn't ID until this weekend, and Mùchén Yáng, from China at the talc mine?" Jake paused, "There is one thing certain. Consuela Delgado didn't come here from Columbia to go bass fishing."

"I would think the FBI would be all over this. They must know about the purchase of the mine. Why don't you contact your friend John Harper? He's a Senior Special Agent, and you've always been able to confide in him." Maggie sensed Jake's innate determination not to share the information beyond the three of them and stopped her suggestions. "I ordered Chinese delivered for tonight's dinner."

Jake laughed, "Thanks for your input but, for now, we'll keep this weekend to ourselves. I think Chinese for dinner would be appropriate."

14

When Jake arrived at his office Monday morning there was a stack of messages neatly placed on his desk next to a steaming hot mug of coffee. He flipped though the stack of messages prioritizing the topics while taking a sip of coffee as he went along. Surprisingly, there were no hard copy messages warranting immediate action and no red flag messages on his computer. His train of thought was interrupted by Penney's robust voice.

"Good morning, Jake. How was your weekend?"

"Weekend was great. Thanks for the coffee," Jake replied.

Penney opened a folder and placed it in front of Jake. "I did a little homework over the weekend. I searched deeper into Anthony a.k.a. Bubba Commons background. When he was killed in his apartment, the homicide people ran a Wants and Warrants check on him and ran into an FBI sealed file. They could only see recent arrests of assaults and car thefts on the database. I was able to reach out, don't ask me how or who, to gather a more in-depth history on Bubba."

Jake glanced at the first page, "Penney, this man's rap sheet is a mile long. He's been connected to the head of the Cartel for years. It says here in the comment section, Bubba was eliminated by the Cartel because they found him to be a double agent." Jake slapped the folder down. "Damn, does anyone know you have this information?"

"The person who got the file for me, and you," Penney replied. "Jake, I knowingly went out on a limb to get this information and, being a PI, you wouldn't have to bring it to anyone's attention."

"How well do you know this person? I mean, there's a possibility the FBI is setting us up."

"No, I trust this person with my life," Penney replied." She closed the office door and sat down. "Take a look at the name of the Chief FBI agent who arrested Bubba and put him on the high level FBI Informant list."

Jake looked at the agent's name. "Okay, you have my attention." He slid the folder across the desk to Penney. "Are you still saying there are only three of us who know about this folder?"

"Well, obviously, and the person whose name is at the bottom of the FBI folder," Penney replied. She moved the folder back to Jake. "You hang on to the folder. I know I've placed you in a very precarious position and you may find yourself on the dirty end of the stick. If that happens, you know someone in a high place will have your back." Penney stood, walked to the door, turned and said, "Not even Dr. Lester."

Jake slid the file into his briefcase and pondered over the conversation he just had with his secretary. He'd never kept anything from his wife and, regardless of Penney's suggestion, didn't care to start now. The more he thought about Penney's position with the Lind City PD and the capability she had of obtaining confidential information through high sources, the more his 'trust no one' paranoia was sparked. It was obvious to him there was an effort from outside sources for him to divert his attention from the Hans Osterfeld murder to the federal narcotics case of distributing fentanyl related drugs. He ruled out the Lind City PD's narcotics department and the FBI. The Lind City PD and the FBI reach for outside help when, and only when, their investigation warrants a person capable of crossing the grey area of the law. His agreement with the Commissioner and the Mayor was to solve Hans Osterfeld's murder and, once he had met that obligation, he would be free to pursue other clients. Jake slapped his Major League Baseball cap on, "it's time to visit an old friend."

Jake drove his old pickup truck slowly through the most controversial part of Lind City the locals called 'no man's land'. Once a thriving part of the city, with small boutiques, and direct rail service to New York City, it was deemed antiquated by the city council in the mid-fifties. The terminal was partly demolished to make way for more modern services to be constructed in another part of the city. The controversy stemmed from the fact members of the city council owned the land where more modern facilities were to be built. He parked next to a partly sealed entrance to the old terminal, walked down two flights of trash filled stairs and on to a dark rail platform. He turned his flashlight on, found his way along a walkway lined with discarded rail equipment, and knocked on an office door. "Teddy, are you in there?"

"Yup, I'm here. I've been waiting for you. Come in," Teddy replied. Theodore Conway and Jake were buddies in Afghanistan. Teddy chose a life of poverty and Jake took the path of law enforcement. Through those years they remained friends. His outward appearance, tough hardened body, ruddy wrinkled face, and dirty clothes, was not indicative of his warm hearted nature. Jake relied on Teddy, from time to time, for Lind City's hard core information.

Jake swept away the cobwebs and dust from an old bench, pulled out a small bottle of bourbon, two plastic glasses from his jacket, and held the bottle in the air.

"Don't mind if I do," Teddy said. "Don't spare the contents." He took a long swig of the whiskey. "Good stuff," he said, wiping his lips with the back of his hand. "I know you didn't come here to share your booze. I knew you would be here sooner or later so I did some homework. First, tell me if I'm wrong about why you're here. I figure the big shot's kid getting himself murdered has something to do with your visit."

"The big shot meaning Carter Osterfeld. Everyone calls him CO?"

"The one and only." Teddy held out his glass for a refill and laughed. "I know you have another flask with you." He wiggled the glass in front of Jake. "Well, are you going to put some in the glass?" Teddy asked. "Jake, you know I never gave you bad information and I'm running a little shy in my wallet. "Do we have the same arrangement?"

"Yup." Jake replied. He poured the whiskey into Teddy's glass, at least four fingers high, "What do you have?" He pulled a piece of paper from his pocket and started jotting Teddy's request. One month supply of fresh veggies from the farmers' market, and one month's supply of prepared food from Saul's Deli. "How many souls do you have down here?"

"By my last count, twenty six," Teddy replied.

"Done. Let me know if you run short. Now tell me what you have."

Teddy swung his feet on top of a dust covered desk and sipped a little whiskey. "The start of this whole thing was kind of crazy. The terminal, as we call it, is very dangerous during the day and no one dares to come in here at night. It was about three weeks ago, at ten or eleven at night, a big guy, I mean big, shows up on the walkway without a flashlight. I figure this guy is dead meat because he's alone and he can't see down here without a flashlight."

"What do you mean?"

"People who belong here are able to move around without lights and someone will mug him before he can say shit. Well, I was wrong. The big guy beat the hell out of five people without working up a sweat. When the dust settled the guy..."

"Jake interrupted, "Was the big guy's name Bubba?"

"Yeah, he told us his name after the fight. Bubba asked two of the guys he beat the hell out of if they wanted to earn some easy money. He offered them five grand a piece to kill someone, get rid of the body and Bubba specified dumping him in the shallows of Big Bass Lake. I asked him how he was able to walk into the terminal at night without a flashlight. He said he was in night patrol of the 15th Marine Expeditionary Unit and 26th Marine Expeditionary Unit. You remember those guys. They were all bad asses. They used to sleep all day with blinders over their eyes and go out at night looking for bad guys. The two guys took the five grand a piece and did the job on CO's stepson."

"Have you seen the two guys after they killed Hans?"

"No, but I heard one of the guys, I think his name is Grazer, is doing odd jobs at the Big Bass Lake Marina. I haven't seen or heard from the other."

"George Grazer's dead. He was killed at the marina right after I found CO's stepson in the lake and, by the way, Bubba was murdered in his apartment a couple of days later. Do you see a pattern here?" Jake asked.

"Yeah, anyone who had anything to do with the kid's death is dead or gonna be." Teddy emptied his glass and placed it on the desk. "That's enough booze for now. I'm sure CO gave the order to have the kid whacked."

"We need solid proof for the DA. I've worked with Anne Moffitt long enough to know there's no possible way she'll go in front of the Grand Jury for an Indictment without strong evidence."

Teddy picked up his empty glass and helped himself to the remainder of the bourbon, "What kind of strong evidence?"

"I'll give you a couple of examples. If CO did the job himself, there would be traces of evidence at the murder scene, like DNA, and we can nail him. The ME team found Bubba's DNA under George's fingernails and, if Bubba was alive, the police could arrest him."

"Okay I see what you mean." Teddy sat silent for a few minutes and said, "The old man knows how to cover his tracks. Maybe he has other murder skeletons in his closet when he wasn't so careful about covering his tracks."

"You're right. Bubba had a cell phone on him when forensics went through his pockets. Maybe, Bubba recorded the conversation with CO when he ordered the hit and the entire conversation was recorded. The DA might have a chance with a sympathetic Grand Jury; however, it would be a long shot." Jake touched Zig's speed dial number. "Zig, Jake here. When you went through Bubba Commons' pockets at the crime scene, I remember you found a cell phone. I'm looking for a possible recorded conversation between Carter Osterfeld and Bubba Commons before Hans Osterfeld's murder. Is there a way you can locate and copy the conversation?"

"Yes. When we find a cell phone in a victim's possession, each individual recorded conversation is separated, labeled, and copied. If such a conversation was recorded, it would take me less than five minutes to find it and send you a copy," Zig replied.

"Teddy, I'm thirsty. You wouldn't happen to have some water, would you?"

Teddy laughed, "We have all the comforts of home here, and we even have cold bottled water. You know water will rust your pipes. I'm sure I can find some of our very best homemade single malt booze somewhere around here."

"No thanks." Jake grinned and said, "Teddy, you're the only man I know with a Master's Degree in Law Enforcement who can come up with a bottle of homemade booze in an abandoned train terminal. I know you went through more hell than the average bear in Afghanistan, but give me a shout if you ever think about a change."

"Thanks, Jake. You will be the first to know when, and if, the time comes."

Jake's phone buzzed announcing a message arrived. He sat and slowly read the incriminating transcript between Carter Osterfeld and Bubba Commons. "Holy crap the DA will have no problem taking this to the Grand Jury."

"We did good today, Jake?"

"Yup, we did very well today. Thanks for your help. I have to be on my way. Remember what I said."

Jake started the thirty minute drive back to his office prepared to share his findings with Robert and the Mayor, when he remembered Teddy telling him about city council member's involvement in condemning the old terminal and the approval of the newly constructed terminal. He needed the names of council members, the name of the construction company, and the city official who signed the construction contract. He knew it would be essential for him to have this information before he decided to release the recording. Maggie and his father are the only people he could trust.

"Jake, you're home early, and your clothes are dusty and wrinkled. Is everything okay?" Maggie asked.

"Yeah, everything is okay." He took the cell phone from his briefcase. "Honey, before I get cleaned up, I want to play a recorded conversation. Zig recovered the phone from Bubba Commons' clothes and sent the recording to me this afternoon. It's a copy of a conversation Bubba had with OC. Please listen to it while I get cleaned up." Jake turned on the conversation and left the room.

Maggie listened intently to the recorded five minute conversation. "Oh my God." She raced into their bedroom with the phone clutched in her hand. "Jake, is this what happened to George Grazer? CO ordered Bubba to kill him? Why?"

Jake, with a bath towel wrapped around him, came into the room and replied, "Yes, that's exactly what CO did and not the Cartel. Why, that's a good question, because CO ordered Bubba to have his stepson killed and Bubba hired George and another man to do the dirty work. Bubba paid the two guys five thousand a piece for doing the job. The guy, I have no name, got the hell out of town that day and George got a job at the marina. Bubba killed George and beat the hell out of Gus and left him for dead. CO killed Bubba thinking there were no more witnesses. The recording is proof CO was involved in the commission of a crime. There are two more aspects of the recording. If we can locate the other man who was involved in Hans' murder, there's a chance the DA would offer him a deal to flip on CO and be a witness for the prosecution on a murder charge. The other factor in the recording, I'm positive the council members took bribes from CO's construction company to condemn the old terminal."

"Jake, number one, the man is still out there and, number two, you're being paid by the city," Maggie said, apprehensively.

"You're right about number one. Maybe with Teddy's help I can find him. If I'm right about the bribes, either old or present council members, whatever the city does with that portion of the recording, is their business."

"Honey, who else knows about the recording?"

"The only people who know about the recording are you and Teddy."

"You mean the Teddy who lives in the old terminal?"

"Yes, that Teddy, and I need to let my father know about this. He knew all the people who were on the city council when the old terminal was condemned and he personally knows all the present city council members. I'm sure some of the present council members where on the council back in the day, or some of them may be related to the present council members."

"The recording will establish, with reasonable doubt, CO's guilt in the commission of two crimes. I want to have witnesses when I snag CO admitting he killed Bubba and ordered the execution of George and the other man, which will establish his guilt without reasonable doubt." Jake knew the consequences related to the information in the recording and his plan to establish CO's guilt. "I will have solved the murder I was commissioned to investigate. I also know there's a good possibility I will be out of a job but I will have a PI license. I'll cross the job bridge when I come to it."

Maggie sighed, "Jake, these people are dangerous. You're nothing but a bump in the road to them and they will snuff you out with no problem. I thought Gus was witness to George's murder at the marina."

"Gus claims he didn't see who hit him in the head and killed George. He's with Sister Mary Francis recuperating from a beating he got from loan sharks, not the Cartel."

Maggie sat on the edge of the bed with a concerned look in her eyes. "You have a plan B, don't you?"

"The top priority at the present time is to put Carter Osterfeld in jail. I'll think about a plan B after you and I enjoy some time on our new boat."

15

Jake stopped at the employee's coffee bar, poured a mug of black coffee, grabbed a Danish pastry, and headed for his office. He surfed through the morning reports and stopped when he noticed a red flag next to one of the reports which indicated high priority. The report, filed by a night patrol officer stated, the man's name is, Paulo Espinoza, five foot eight, male, and wearing expensive clothes, and jewelry. He was a victim of a hit and run at two a.m. The man was rushed to Lind City's General Hospital emergency room where he remains in grave condition. Jake nibbled a piece of the pastry and sipped some coffee and thought, why is this man high priority?

"Good morning, Penney. Can you please come into my office?"

Penney entered Jake's office and asked, "You want to know why there's a red flag next to a hit and run victim's report, right?"

"Right, and why should it concern me?"

"Well, as you know, the red flag is a priority and in this case it's a very high priority. The man was a guest of Mr. and Mrs. Comfort for dinner last night at the Lind City Hotel. They were in the hotel's lounge for drinks until closing time."

"I suppose you know the man's name," Jake said, sarcastically. "Why was the Mayor and his wife with this guy?"

"I don't know why he was with the Mayor and his wife, and his name is, Paulo Espinoza. He is a partner in a large out of state construction company," Penney replied.

"If the man is staying at the hotel, why was he walking in the street at two a.m.? Penney, how did you know the man had dinner with the Comforts?"

Penney smiled, "I know a guy."

When Jake drove into the hospital driveway he noticed Joan Fetter's blue compact car in the parking place, close to the front door, which meant she was at the hospital early this morning. He drove through the rest of the parking lot specifically looking for other recognizable vehicles and there were none, not even the Mayor's car. He made his way to the Emergency Room nurse's desk and asked, "Could you please tell me the room number for Mr. Paulo Espinoza?"

The nurse politely replied, "Mr. Espinoza is only allowed relatives. Are you a relative, Sir?"

"No, but I'm a private detective working for the Lind City Police Department," Jake replied.

"Sir, you're not a relative. If you have a seat in the waiting room down the hall, I'll see if I can get permission to let you in the room."

Jake entered the white painted, sterile looking waiting room, and found Joan curled up, sound asleep on a fake leather sofa. He quietly sat in a chair next to the door and patiently waited for permission to see Mr. Espinoza. Jake counted ceiling panels for about thirty minutes when the nurse entered the room.

"Sir, the patient is out of surgery and the doctor said you can spend a few minutes with him. The nurse was nearly out of the room, turned, and said, "The doctor stressed a few minutes."

Joan jumped from her fetal position and loudly said, "Jake, I didn't know you're here. I've been here since three this morning. I want to see him too."

"Okay. How did you get in here at three this morning?"

"I have a Lind City Times police scanner in my apartment. When the call came out about a hit and run accident, I thought I would check it out," Joan replied. "Jake, I didn't know it was Paulo Espinoza until I asked the police at the emergency room entrance if they had the victim's ID. Can I have the lead story on this case?"

"Joan, you're with the press and you can do whatever you have to do," Jake replied. "I'm going to run a want and warrants on this guy to see if this was an accident or a planned hit and run. I'm going to give you a heads up before you send your story to your editor. Espinoza is an owner of an out of state construction company and was a dinner guest of the Mayor and his wife. They closed the hotel's lounge about midnight. Let's go to Espinoza's room and see if we can get something. You might want to hold your story for a while."

A female hospital security guard and two of Espinoza's personal bodyguards stood in front of Espinoza's door. Jake and Joan were patted for weapons before they entered the room.

Espinoza was laying on his back with one of his legs in a plaster cast placed in a metal sling anchored from above the bed. His face was almost entirely wrapped in white gauze, leaving openings for his eyes and mouth. There were several wires attached to his body leading to monitoring devices.

Jake moved close to Espinoza's ear and softly asked, "Mr. Espinoza, I'm Jake Lester and I'm a private investigator working for the Lind City Police Department. Can you hear me?"

Jake waited for a minute and was about to repeat his statement when he saw Espinoza's eyes blink twice. "You can hear me but you can't talk. Can you give me two blinks for yes and one blink for no?"

Espinoza blinked twice then raised his finger toward Joan.

"Mr. Espinoza, I'm Joan Fetter and I'm a Lind City Times reporter. Do you mind if I stay in the room and listen to your conversation?"

He blinked is eyes once and became agitated.

Jake walked with Joan to the far end of the room and whispered, "Joan, I think he wants you to leave. I'll fill you in when I'm through."

Joan willfully left the room and Jake continued his questioning. Espinoza seamed to realize the gravity of his condition and answered several personal and incriminating questions, including OC's involvement in a phony construction company, and ordering his stepson's murder. When the nurse ordered Jake out of the room, he turned off the video- audio recorder and pondered whether or not to share his entire dying man's conversation with Joan. He had been at the hospital from early morning and was tired and hungry. He walked to the waiting room where Joan had been patiently waiting to hear about Jake's conversation with Espinoza. "Joan, would you like to have breakfast? I'm hungry and headed for the diner."

"Sure, I'm starved. We can talk while we eat."

It was late morning when they arrived at the almost empty diner. Jake found a corner booth away from the few customers who were left over from the early morning rush and, after ordering two large breakfasts including a pitcher of black coffee, they started recounting the early morning hit and run case.

"Joan, before we get into the meat of things, would you mind if we were off the record for a few minutes?"

Joan hesitated, then replied, "If you think it's necessary."

"The hit and run this morning was an attempt on Espinoza life. We know he had a late dinner with the Mayor and the Mayor's wife. After dinner he received a call on his cell phone from one of his partners to meet him on the corner next to the hotel."

"It wasn't an accident?" Joan tried to calm herself. "The man was minding his own business, went out for a walk to meet a friend, after dinner with the Mayor and his wife, and was mowed down. Why?"

"I couldn't get all the answers because he's in such terrible condition. I had to suggest everything in our conversation in a yes or no context. I asked him if he was discussing a business deal while he was having dinner with the Mayor. He blinked his eyes twice, indicating a yes. I also asked him if he had a part in killing CO's stepson, Hans Osterfeld. He blinked twice again. Espinoza knew he was incriminating himself and the audio visual recording of his deathbed conversation would be admissible in a court of law."

"Why do you want this part of our conversation to be off the record?"

Jake nervously looked around the diner for eavesdroppers and replied, "If CO wanted Espinoza dead and he reads a news headline stating we had a dying man's confession, we could be dead too."

"What should we do?"

Jake replied, "Let's see. How does this sound? You can scoop the other reporters with a headline saying, 'A prominent partner in an out of state construction company was struck early this morning by a hit and run driver. The victim remains in grave condition at the Lind City Hospital,' you can fill in the rest of the story, but don't mention my conversation with Espinoza."

"Jake, when CO learns Espinoza isn't dead, he'll never let the man leave the hospital alive, and then he'll come after us."

"Exactly, that's why we're going to have undercover officers guarding Espinoza twenty four-seven. I'm sure CO won't kill Espinoza himself. When we catch the person in the act of committing a murder, we'll squeeze that person until we get the information we want. I promise, you will have the breaking story."

"Jake, if it leaks out you were alone in Espinoza's room for several minutes, you and Maggie will be in a very precarious position."

Jake's cell phone rings, "Zig, what's going on?"

"A patrol unit found the vehicle used in the hit and run this morning. It's at the south end of town under the river bridge. We're going to be here about another hour and, as soon as we complete our investigation at the scene, we'll haul the vehicle to our garage. Jake, first blush for fingerprints inside the car, we came up negative. I checked with the stolen vehicle division and they have a report of this car being stolen yesterday afternoon. This was no accident. It was a deliberate hit and run, and it was done by a pro."

"Thanks, Zig. I'll meet you at your garage."

Joan tapped her lips with the napkin, "Jake I'm going to run. I want to get the leading story into the evening issue. I'll give the public just enough information for them to salivate on what's coming next, and I promise discretion in every sentence."

Jake planned to stop at Maggie's office on his way to the forensics' garage. It is essential for her to be cognizant of the day's events. There is always the possibility, however remote, she could be in danger. He was positive CO directed the order to end Espinoza's life, and had to connect the dots from all the murders to CO. The irony of the bungled first attempt on Espinoza's life, catching the same perp in the act of a second attempt, which would be the means of connecting CO to all the murders.

Jake peeked through the plate glass window of the autopsy room as Maggie conducted a post mortem examination. He caught Maggie's attention by softly tapping on the window with his car keys. Maggie gave him a two finger wave, which meant she would be through with the deceased in two minutes.

Maggie, with her wild hair askew, barged into her office prepared to hear why Jake made an unexpected stop at her office, only to see her lovable husband sound asleep in a chair. She gently brushed her hand across Jake's shoulder and whispered his name, "Jake, wake up."

Jake woke up, sleepily stared at Maggie, rubbed his eyes, and proceeded to fill her in on the events of the day.

"My God, the man obviously knows he's in grave danger, is there anything I can do on my end to keep him safe?"

"The doctor said he doubted if the patient would make the next forty–eight hours, and will keep him sedated until the very end."

"Honey, it's not Espinoza I'm concerned about. I'm afraid for your life. I think you should take a sabbatical until I get CO behind bars."

Maggie swiftly slipped out of her white smock, tossed it on a chair, sat next to Jake, and held his hand. "I know we've been married only a short time and you're concerned about your bride, nevertheless know this; whatever you do, we do it together. I'm not going to run and hide from a piece of crap like Carter Osterfeld. You, at this point, can't trust the Mayor or anyone inside the police department."

"Maggie, CO would try to eliminate you first. He and the Cartel would have no qualms about killing family members…" Jake's cell phone rang. "Yes, this Jake Lester."

"This is the charge nurse for the Intensive Care Unit at Lind Memorial. You left instructions for me to call you if there were any changes in Mr. Espinoza's condition. I'm afraid he passed away a few minutes ago. Is there a next of kin we can notify?"

Jake had to think fast. It was imperative the notice of his death not be released. "Nurse, I'm going to have the ME take charge of the deceased for an autopsy and, until the ME arrives, no one is to move the body."

"Jake, what's going on?" Maggie asked.

"Espinoza died a few minutes ago. We have to keep this quiet, "Would it be difficult to justify moving the body to the morgue?"

"This is a murder case now and having the ME involved wouldn't be difficult at all. I'll meet you there, I'm out of here. I should be able to have the body here in about two hours."

"I'm going to call Joan Fetter. I know she'll be able to post a story about Espinoza's condition improving. That should bring out CO's hit man and when he tries to kill the person in Espinoza's hospital bed, we'll arrest him and squeeze the hell out of him. Trust me, we'll have CO by the short hairs."

"Who's going to be the person in the bed?"

Jake replied, "Honey, I'll be the person in the bed with a very formidable authority posing as a doctor nearby."

"Maggie gave Jake a kiss on the forehead, "Well just in case, make sure you're armed."

Jake hurried to the hospital, made his way to the back entrance, and, to avoid the elevators, scaled the stairs to the ICU floor. He stopped at the Charge Nurses desk, arranged to have a room and number changed to match Espinoza's room. His cell phone rang, "Hi Joan."

"Jake, I did exactly what you said. The story will be on the five o'clock channel nine news and in time for our early morning edition."

"The timing couldn't be better. Espinoza passed away a few minutes ago, and now this is a murder case. Maggie was able to have the body transferred to the morgue. I'm at the hospital making arrangements to set a trap for the hit man. I'm sure CO will take the bait as soon as he sees your story on TV."

"Jake, will there be plain clothes police nearby?"

"No, I don't want the police involved in this yet." He replied. "We don't know the final cause of death. I'm assuming blunt force trauma to the head. I'll give you a shout after we nail the hit man."

Jake sat at the edge of the hospital bed mentally walking through the steps to be taken to catch the hit man and ensure CO's apprehension. His thought process was interrupted by Maggie's caller ID on his phone.

"Jake, I know you're busy, but you need to know before Espinoza was hit by the car, he was on Fentanyl. The man was a health freak. I couldn't find any damage to his major organs and no signs of any drugs, not even over the counter drugs. I don't think he knowingly took the Fentanyl. Honey, be careful. I hope you have expert back up."

"I have the best of the best, thanks."

111

Jake checked his three fifty seven magnum, slipped it under the bed sheets, and attached the wires leading from the monitor to a mechanical sensor under the sheets. The monitor immediately started producing beeps and rhythmic lines on the screen. Jake carefully slipped into the bed and plugged a wireless transmitter into his ear, "Check, check,"

A man's voice whispered, "Check, check. Read you five by five."

The trap is set. Jake looked at the wall clock, ten p.m., and postured himself on the bed to enable a quick response. The time slowly slipped into the early morning hours with an unusual eerie silence. He started to wonder if his plan was useless. The wall clock now read four a.m. He would give his plan another hour.

"Jake, a female doctor just came out of the stairway door and headed down your way. She has long black hair, wearing diamond earrings and all the buttons on her smock are buttoned. The woman looks Hispanic.

"She's not a doctor. I think she's Consuela Delgado, the Angel of Death, and she's the deadliest person on this planet."

A voice in Jake's earpiece whispered, "She's about seventy five feet from your room and she's opening the buttons of her smock."

"Okay, I made the adjustment. I'm ready," Jake responded.

Jake's hospital room door swung wide open slamming against the wall and, in the doorway stood Consuela Delgado 'the Angel of Death' with her Glock nine mil, a silencer attached to the barrel, pointed directly at the person in the bed. She stepped closer to the target and released the safety on the pistol. In a split second her body was catapulted across the room. The pistol slid across the floor and rested under the hospital bed. She could smell a man's body pinning her to the floor, duct tape sealed her mouth, and the pain of her arms being pulled behind her back as metal handcuffs tightened on her wrists angered her. "Get off me you son of a bitch," Consuela mumbled.

Jake jumped from the bed, snatched the pistol from the floor, and ejected the magazine from the weapon. "Holy shit Teddy, what took you so long?"

"I wanted to make sure I had the right person," Teddy chuckled. "I have my pickup parked out back with a couple of people waiting for me. I'll have her in my office in fifteen minutes. I have a lot of volunteers waiting to guard her for as long as it takes to have her behind bars. How are you going to get CO into the terminal?"

"Have you ever heard about rats eating each other in desperation? Well, the first person we're going to contact is Pablo Ramirez, El Capo's top leader. Ramirez isn't going to like CO getting Consuela Delgado captured and nowhere to be found. You can color CO toast and begging to be saved."

16

It was five a.m. when Jake drove into his driveway and waited while the overhead garage door opened. He eased his car into the garage and turned off the engine. He took a long tired breath, and sat quietly for a few minutes before getting out of the car. It was a long, dangerous night and the task of sending CO to prison without tipping his hand to others in the law enforcement circle would be a monumental task.

Maggie stood next to the car. "Are you going to come into the house?" she asked. "Come on Jake, I made some fresh coffee and, if you want to talk about why you were out all night, I'd be happy to listen."

Jake eased himself from the car and followed Maggie into the kitchen. The aroma of fresh brewed coffee filled the air. "Coffee smells good." He wrapped his hands around the mug of coffee and stared at the steam coming from the freshly poured coffee. "We have Consuela Delgado."

"Jake, what do you mean we have Consuela Delgado? Who's we? And where do we have her?"

"I lured Delgado into the ICU of the hospital where Paulo Espinoza was supposed to be recuperating from his hit and run injuries. Joan Fetter posted a news alert saying Espinoza was conscious and willing to cooperate with authorities. When Consuela came to the ICU room, where she thought Espinoza was resting, she pulled out a pistol with a silencer and aimed it point blank at the head of a black haired mannequin and, before she could pull the trigger, Teddy jumped Consuela and subdued her."

"Wait a minute. Jake, you mean Teddy Conway? The guy who lives in the old underground terminal?"

"Yes, that Teddy. He is the only person physically tough enough who could help me in this situation and keep his mouth shut about Espinoza."

"So, what about Espinoza?"

"He's lying dead in the ICU. I'm surprised you didn't get a call."

"How did you manage to keep the monitor's vital signs on?"

"That was the tricky part. Teddy switched rooms with another person in the ICU." Jake sipped some coffee, placed his elbows on the table, and cupped his hands around his face. "The shit's going to hit the fan when I contact Carter Osterfeld and tell him we have the Angel of Death. We're also going to tell him she's fingering him as the person who contracted all the murders associated with the Cartel. Diego Garcia, the head of the US Cartel, isn't going to take the news lightly."

"When the Cartel finds out CO has been double dipping, so to speak, he's a goner," Maggie commented.

"Exactly, and when CO finds out the Cartel is on to him, he will name names of local people connected with the Cartel. The minute we have those names it's a matter of following the money trail to everyone in the community who's involved in the drugs."

"Jake, if there's anything I can do to help, you know I'm here for you. We need to get these people out of our community. I had a young boy, seventeen years old, on my table last night, who over dosed on candy mixed with Fentanyl. Can you believe the Cartel have people called mixers who mix Fentanyl and other drugs into something resembling candy? The boy ate what he thought was candy, never did drugs in his life, and his parents had to identify him. After the parents left my lab, I couldn't stop crying."

"I don't think the Cartel is in local production yet. When Dad and I went to the talc mine entrance, we observed their activity and it appeared they were close to production." Jake sat back in the chair and rubbed his eyes. "I need to get some sleep. I haven't slept for twenty four hours."

Jake's cell phone rang, with Robert Marshal's name on the caller ID. "Jake, we've been concerned about you and, when I read the morning paper and saw the news on TV, I found out you identified a contract killer who was about to kill Paulo Espinoza. I'm about ten minutes away from your home. We need to talk."

Jake turned off the phone, "So much for sleep. Robert's on his way over here."

115

"Honey, don't you think it's time you confided in your boss, Robert, who has also been your close friend for thirty years?" Maggie asked.

"Yeah, I guess you're right," Jake replied. He refilled his mug with coffee, sat at the kitchen table thinking how to diplomatically fill Robert in on the evening's events, why he didn't inform Robert of his plans to use Teddy Conway to apprehend Consuela Delgado, and preferred not involve the Lind City PD. Whatever he tells Robert, he will not mention the reconnaissance he and his Father had at the talc mine. He knew Robert would have a difficult time recognizing last night's decision as the appropriate decision. Jake was brought out of his thought process by the rhythmic sound of the front door chimes.

Maggie placed a mug of coffee on the kitchen table in front of Robert, and left the room. She found a comfortable place in an adjoining room and stayed within listening range of the conversation about to unfold.

Robert, while in deep thought, slowly pulled the coffee mug toward him in an effort to stall for a few seconds of time. He didn't relish the thought of giving Jake, an independent PI, a chewing out.

Jake broke the eerie sound of silence, "Robert, I know I owe you an apology and, before you give me a royal ass kicking, I want to recap the last twenty four hours events." Jake proceeded to chronically relive the entire evening starting with the call of a hit and run accident involving Paulo Espinoza, a partner in a phony construction company, who had a late night dinner with the Mayor and his wife. Joan Fetter, a Lind City Times reporter, who was at the hospital before Jake arrived and was ready to release a story involving the Mayor's association with Espinoza. Joan Fetter was persuaded to release a news bulletin indicating Espinoza was alive and in critical condition in the Lind City

Hospital's ICU, when he was actually pronounced dead a few minutes after the bulletin was released. My friend Teddy Conway assisted me through most of the evening."

"Jake, you're telling me you were involved in a bogus news bulletin to induce a killer's response to eliminate Espinoza? Why did you call your friend Teddy and not our PD?"

Jake replied, "Robert, put yourself in my shoes. A partner in a phony construction company was purposely run down in an attempt to shut him up before he could go any farther with the Mayor. I didn't know the Mayor's involvement, but I knew the phony construction company was the brain child of Carter Osterfeld. CO had a lot to gain if he could get the Mayor to approve a construction site for the phony construction company. The Cartel would have the Mayor in their pocket. Robert, remember this was all speculation on my part and at three o'clock in the morning I didn't know who I could trust. The man I trusted with my life in Afghanistan came to mind. If it wasn't for Teddy's brave move early this morning, I wouldn't be sitting at his table having coffee with you."

"Jake, I came here to kick your butt and to fire you. Now that I know the stress and pressure you were under, and you knowing Espinoza was dead, I would have probably done exactly what you did. Okay Jake, what do we do next?"

"I don't think you want to know," Jake replied, with a smile. "It's going to get messy before I'm through. There is one thing, you can keep everything I told you this morning to yourself."

"Where is Delgado?" Robert asked.

Jake hesitated and reluctantly replied, "We have Consuela Delgado hidden in a safe place, and she'll stay there until I can put all the suspects together. At that point, I will call you to bring your most trusted officers to that location to make the arrests. If I

117

told you where we have her and, someone was to ask you about her whereabouts, you would have to lie on the record." Jake paused. "It isn't a matter of trust. It's a matter of keeping you clean. If anyone gets dirty from this it will be me. If I lose my PI licenses I can survive. On the other hand, you could lose your hard earned pension."

"Okay, I understand. I'm going to head for my office, and you try to get some sleep. Hopefully, we can keep the Fentanyl overdoses away from our kids."

It was eight o' clock in the morning when Jake finally crashed into bed. The adrenaline hadn't stopped pumping through his body and his brain refused to turn off. He couldn't stop thinking about the conversation he had moments ago with Robert. It may be nothing, however, why did Robert ask where Delgado was? Jake sat up in bed and whispered, 'something's wrong with this picture. I never said anything about Delgado, and yet Robert knew the Angel de la muerte was involved in the attempt to shoot Paulo Espinoza while he lay dead, and I didn't say anything about Espinoza being dead in the ICU.'

The bedroom door opened and Maggie started to tiptoe into the room until she saw Jake sitting up in the bed. "Jake, you're awake. Why aren't you getting some rest?"

"Maggie, what time was the young boy who overdosed on Fentanyl admitted to your lab?"

"It was ten- thirty-seven last night. Why?"

"I was curious," Jake replied.

"Honey, he isn't the only young person overdosing on Fentanyl. The average for Fentanyl overdose in our community is two a week, and the Fentanyl is mixed with other drugs and made to look like candy. Thank God most of the overdose cases, with immediate emergency response, survive." Maggie walked toward

Joseph DeMark   THE MIXER

the bedroom door, turned off the lights, and whispered, "Get some rest."

17

It was mid-afternoon when Jake returned to his office. He started his usual routine of reviewing the messages Penney had placed on his desk earlier in the day. There were no handwritten messages of real importance and it was certainly premature to expect correspondence from CO. He turned on his laptop and downloaded emails accumulated from yesterday and the current day's messages. The current emails that reflected the news of Paulo Espinoza's murder and questions from all levels of law enforcement, filled Jake's laptop screen. It was understandable that there were no emails from Robert's office. Jake assumed the Mayor was attempting to downplay his late night dinner with a high ranking member of the Cartel, who was also a partner of a fictitious construction company. He decided to let Robert's chips fall where they may and continued to the next subject on his to do list. He took his personal cell phone from his pocket and speed dialed Teddy.

"Jake, I was wondering when you were going to call."

"Sorry about that. How's our guest doing?"

Teddy answered, "The guest is doing fine. We have her in a cubicle with Mable."

"Who's Mable?"

"Mable is one of our more gifted dwellers. Her past experience was with the state correction departments. She's on the ninth step, brotherly-love, of her twelve step program and has a degree in Nursing. She has our guest well in hand. How's it going with you?"

119

"Nothing yet," Jake replied. "I think Joan Fetter should be awarded a Pulitzer Prize for headline news. The headlines were perfect and, when the people read between the lines of the subject matter, the results will be exactly what we're looking for. The people who will be implicated in a legal scandal will be scrambling out of the woodwork."

"Jake, if what you predicted happens, you know you might be out of a job with the city, or worse," Teddy said.

"Yes, it's certainly a possibility. Teddy, Penney has a call for me. Talk to you later."

"Hey Jake, John here. Can you talk?"

"Hey John, tonight's meatloaf night. Stop by the house around six?" Jake replied. Jake turned off his cell phone and slid it into his pocket. The conversation he just had with his best law enforcement friend, John Harper, Senior Special Agent with the FBI, wasn't about a meatloaf dinner at Jake's home. Although John never refused a good home cooked meal, it was how John communicated with Jake on an unsecured phone line. John would never contact him for an impromptu meeting unless it was extremely important.

The afternoon flew by and the contact from CO Jake was anticipating, although down deep he knew any contact from CO or his people would be premature, didn't happen. Jake liked to play an occasional game of chess and knew that the time waiting for your opponent to make his move is necessary to determine your next three moves.

"I better call Maggie and let her know we're going to have a dinner guest and I'm going to stop at the Wine Shop on my way home," Jake mumbled to himself. He drew his pistol from his shoulder holster, placed it into the glove compartment, to eliminate the screaming metal detector when he entered the store, and locked the compartment. He felt a little undressed without his Smith and Wesson equalizer in the holster, but it is what it is.

"Hey Jake, what can I do for you today," The Wine Shop owner asked.

Hey, Tom, I'm going to need some of our usual red wine for dinner tonight. You might as well give me some extra for the weekend," Jake replied.

"Are you going bass fishing this weekend?" Tom placed a box of wine on the counter. "Can I carry that out for you?"

"No thank you. I don't think we're going fishing this weekend, Jake replied. "This will be enough wine for a while," Jake said, with a grin. He picked up the box of wine, and left the store with both hands grasping the box. As he approached his car, a black van sped into the parking lot and stopped next to him. The van's side door forcefully slammed open and two men wearing hoods and masks jumped from the vehicle, and slid a canvas hood over Jake's head and face. Jake dropped the case of wine, reached into his empty shoulder holster, and was completely overpowered by one of the men. The men threw him into the van, and handcuffed him to a metal bar on the floor as the van sped out of the parking lot. The entire snatching took less than a minute and was executed with the expertise of a Special Ops team.

"Where the hell are you guys taking me? "Jake shouted, as he tried frantically to pull out of the handcuffs.

There was no response from the men.

Jake started counting the vehicle's turns and any unusual sounds he could identify. "Where are we going?" he repeated, with a calm voice. "You might as well tell me. I'm going know to when I get to wherever we're going."

There was no reply.

The journey continued without a spoken word as the driver navigated the van through numerous turns and an occasional U-turn. The vehicle slowed to a crawl, bounced over a small curb, entered a dark building, and came to a stop. The two men, who were sitting with Jake in the back seat, scrambled out of the van dragging their prisoner with them. They sat him on a metal folding chair and stepped away.

Jake heard the ominous sound of a pistol's hammer clicking into place before firing. He held his breath through seconds of agonizing anticipation, "Shit." He was dumfounded by the pistol's hammer slamming into the metal breach and he was alive. He shook his head in an attempt to rid the pearls of sweat dripping over his eyelids. "What the hell do you people want?" He shouted. Jake could hear the sound of men's dress shoes walking toward him on the concrete floor.

A man with a Latino accent said, "Mr. Jake, you are starting to annoy us with your stupidity. You are not the police, you are a little private detective with a big mouth. In our country we would kill for less."

"Who are you?" Jake asked. "I don't know what you want from me."

"For your life today, we want you to be our inside man with the police. All you have to do is let us know when they're planning to do us harm, and for that we will take you back to the Wine Shop. You can go home like nothing happened."

Jake thought, they're not negotiating Consuela Delgado's release. They're unaware of her situation. If they had any knowledge of her captivity and, if they knew about Paulo Espinoza's murder, I would have been dead in my tracks at The Wine Shop parking lot." Jake replied, "I don't have access to high level police information."

"Who the hell do you think you're talking to? You think I'm some nobody. I'm Diego Garcia one of the "Patrons" I'm boss of the Cartel in this country. My source tells me you are friends with the Police Commissioner," he shouted, as he brutally pushed Jake to the floor. He reached out his hand to one of the men standing next to him, and screamed, "Give me your gun. I'll put this son of a bitch out right now."

Jake was stunned from banging his head on the floor, his legs were in pain and folded under the chair. As he desperately struggled to move his legs from underneath the half folded chair, he felt two large hands wrap around each side of his ribs pick him up and place him upright on the chair. He sat motionless, for what felt like hours, not knowing what was going to happen to him. Jake flashed back to his military training and his rotation in Afghanistan. In the event of capture by the enemy, take charge of your mindset, neutralize your thoughts, and turn panic into peace.

Diego shouted, "We know you have Consuela Delgado. Where are you hiding her?"

Jake thought, "Shit, he knows about Consuela." With his head down and leaning forward, Jake replied, "I don't know what you're talking about." His sentence wasn't complete when he felt a crushing blow to his face. "I don't know what you're talking about."

"You say you don't know what I'm talking about, when my source tells me you captured Consuela in the hospital." Diego pulled off his short leather jacket and gave it to one of his men. "You bastardo. You think I am stupid. He swung another damaging blow to Jake's face, causing blood to spew from his mouth.

"I don't know what you're talking about," Jake repeated. He dropped his head and fell unconscious.

One of the men said, "Patron, he will not give us the information we need. Let's take him out into the country, finish him off, and leave him dead on the roadside like an animal."

The driving rain on Jake's face brought him to a semi consciousness state. He was covered with mud and lying in a ditch. He could feel a sharp pain in his right shoulder and gently touched the wound. For some reason, it was only a minor flesh wound. 'Why didn't they kill me?' He managed to get to his feet and tried to regain his composure. Through the heavy rain and darkness, he looked for civilization. There was nothing in sight. Jake's mind was fuzzy, at best, however, the words adapt, overcome, and improvise ran through his mind. He stumbled forward until complete exhaustion dropped him to his knees. The driving rain turned into a light drizzle and visibility improved. He looked up from his low kneeling position and saw the silhouette of a horse barn about a hundred feet away. "Thank God," he whispered.

The barn seemed like a luxury hotel when Jake entered the doorway. There were bales of hay stacked neatly around the inside of the barn with a huge nest of hay in the center of the building. Jake collapsed, covering himself with layers of hay, and passed out.

The sun shining into the barn and the sound of horse whinnying woke Jake out of a sound sleep. It seemed like very bone in his body was racked with pain, and the wound in his arm stopped bleeding. He saw a long wooden handled shovel leaning against the wall next to him. He grabbed the handle and tried to raise himself up, but the pain was excruciating and he fell back to his knees with a thump. "Somebody please help me," he screamed. "Shit I can't stay here forever. Surely Maggie's got people out looking for me and, if John came to the house last night, he must be looking for me too." Jake started to get dizzy. His consciousness was short lived.

Jake's eyes were blurry and itchy when he started to regain consciousness. He could feel a soft pillow beneath his bandaged head and soft warm sheets spread across his body. There were silhouettes of people sitting in the room. "Where am I?" Jake asked, as he tried to lift his head.

"Maggie, wake up, your husband is conscious," Robert said.

Jake strained his eyes, "Maggie, where are you? Where are you? I can't see you."

"I'm right here, next to your bed," Maggie replied. She leaned over Jake and gently kissed him on the lips.

"How long have I been here?" Jake whispered.

"Jake, this is Robert. You've been here three days. A farmer found you in his horse barn and called the local EMS. When they arrived, they found you badly beaten and unconscious. When they checked your PI ID, they brought you here and the Chief of Staff of the hospital called me."

"So, someone thinks I'm dead," Jake mumbled. "I need to find a more secure place. The people who did this will eventually know I'm alive and find me here. I gotta get out of here now or they'll finish the job."

A short middle aged nurse, wearing a white smock, stethoscope around her neck and carrying a small laptop computer in her hand entered the room. She was obviously a person of authority and probably had a military background. She loudly commanded, "I need all of you to immediately leave the room. This patient needs rest and we have to run more tests on him. You can wait in the family waiting room down the hall. The nurse waited for the room to empty out before she closed the door. "Okay Mr. Lester, my name is Mable. Teddy sent me here to get you to our place safely. Don't worry Maggie, knows what we're doing."

125

"How did you get through security and the Charge Nurse?" Jake asked.

"You don't want to know," Mable replied. "Now I'll help you get dressed and roll you out of here. We'll have you in our VIP Suite before you know it."

"What about Maggie?" Jake asked, anxiously. "She can't stay at our home. These people would have no problem torturing her to find me."

Mable gently slid Jake out of the bed, helped him into the wheelchair and, with the strength of a construction worker, pushed the chair with one hand, and rolled the monitoring equipment with the other. "Mr. Lester, you look concerned. No worries, I was a front line combat soldier in Afghanistan and was transformed into a front line nurse."

Jake sat in his wheelchair looking out the rear window of the large van thinking of Maggie and what a terrifying experience it was for her. "Mable, you didn't answer my question. Where is Maggie?"

"Teddy said something about a Nun in a Monastery," Mable replied. "The head Nun and a guy named Gus would take good care of her." Mable glanced at Jake's pale white face, concerned about his chance for survival. She calmly said, "We're almost there, Mr. Lester."

"Mable, please call me Jake." He started to see familiar places and knew it wouldn't be long before they reached their destination. The early morning wakeup and the strain of the ride drew his stamina level to zero and he passed out.

Mable shouted to the driver, "You better step on it he's going to need serious attention soon."

Teddy was at front door of the old terminal waiting for Jake's arrival when he saw one of the terminal people driving a commandeered hospital vehicle, Mable riding shotgun next to him, and heading straight for him. Teddy jumped out of the way as the vehicle screeched to a stop.

Teddy sat at Jake's bedside in the purposely dimly lit VIP room for Jake's comfort. The well-equipped VIP room was funded by Teddy and people who graduated from the 'Terminal' into successful lives.

Jake opened his eyes and saw Teddy's somber face, "Teddy, thank you."

"Don't thank me. Thank the person who gave the flesh wound and not a bullet in the head. Someone was on your side."

18

The noise of New York City was muffled and became a muted when it found its way to the thirty fourth floor's office suite in the Osterfeld Building in downtown Manhattan. The building donning his name was built prior to CO and his stepson's affiliation with the Cartel, and a product of an excellent quality construction company.

Carter Osterfeld's office suite was lavishly decorated with the finest oils, sculptures, and rugs, money could buy, and a large mahogany table set with construction memorabilia. CO sat contentedly behind his desk in an overstuffed desk chair, smoking a fat Cuban cigar, his feet propped up on his credenza, and looking out the window at New York's skyline. The contented gaze on his face was erased when his secretary announced Pablo Ramirez, El Capo called and wanted CO to call him immediately on a secured phone. CO dropped his feet from the credenza, stuffed the cigar into an ashtray, and pulled out a prepaid cell phone from his desk drawer, "Pablo, you called me. What can I do for you?"

Pablo replied forcefully in broken English, "Where is Consuela? What did you do to Consuela?"

"I don't know what you're talking about," CO replied. He sat on the side of his desk anxiously waiting for Pablo's next word. Pablo had never called him before. The line of communication was always through the head of the US Cartel, Diego Garcia, or one of his lieutenants.

"Consuela was sent to accomplish an important job for me and now she's gone. What the hell did you do with her? You better find her now and she better be alive. If I don't hear from you, that means you screwed up and she's dead. If that is so, you're dead. I'll find you no matter where you are, and I'll kill you."

CO shouted into the phone, "Pablo, Pablo, shit he hung up."

CO slouched in his chair staring at the carpet designs on the floor, and contemplating his next move. His fear was that Consuela was dead, and regardless who killed her, Pablo would have him eliminated. He went to the bar, poured some brandy into a crystal brandy snifter, and pounded it down with a gulp. He stood motionless, poured another brandy, walked to the window, placed the glass on the windowsill, and started to walk toward the bar for some water. His concentration was interrupted by the distinct sound of crystal shattering. CO instinctively threw himself to the floor and crawled under his desk. Pearls of sweat streamed from his forehead and down his face as he anxiously awaited another bullet to come through the heavy glass window. He remained on the floor until he believed it was safe. Gradually, he stood and examined the small hole in the window, made by the piercing bullet, and found safety in his private restroom. The many years of dealing with the New York City underworld and the Columbian Cartel told him the bullet wasn't meant to kill. It was a strong message informing him he could be reached anytime and anywhere.

The New York City lights were shining brightly when CO scurried from the office building's front door and into his waiting limousine. The limo sped away to his luxurious home in Noho, one of the most expensive neighborhoods in the City and, upon arriving, he proceeded directly to his self-contained safe room. The options floating through his brain as he paced the floor for hours, were useless. It was well-known in the drug world that, if you were tagged by the Cartel, you were a venomous snake to everyone. CO stopped pacing, took a full bottle of brandy from his bar, and set upon the task of making certain the bottle would be empty before morning.

The sharp screech of CO's cell phone shocked him out of a hangover. His watch read six a.m. with an unknown caller on the phone. CO groaned, "Hello."

"CO don't hang up. This is Teddy. Do you remember me?"

CO rubbed his eyes, cleared his throat, and replied, "Yeah, I remember you. You're the guy who lives in the old terminal. How did you get this number?"

"Don't worry about that," Teddy replied. "Look, we need to talk about something very important. Can you come to the terminal tonight?"

"I'm not leaving my home for a while. What do you want to talk about?"

"Yeah, the world heard about your visit by a small guest through your office window. I have something you need to get your ass out of the sling it's in."

"Shit, the world knows I'm marked?" CO laughed loudly "Yeah, right, you're going to save me from Pablo Ramirez. He told me to find Consuela Delgado, bring her to him, and if I don't, I'll be dead. If I brought her to him right now, I'd still be dead."

"You have zero options on the table, don't you?" Teddy asked, sharply. "Smarten up. I'm trying to help you this one time. If you don't want my gift, so be it."

CO replied, "People are going to be following my every move. If I go to your terminal, we'll both be marked."

"You're a clever man, you'll find a way. I'll see you here at eight p.m. tonight, and come alone."

CO turned off the phone and thought, "This Teddy guy must think I'm some kind a fool. He thinks I'm going to fall into his trap so he can knock me off for killing one of his people. He cautiously stepped out of the safe room and climbed a flight of stairs leading into his home office. The landline phone message light was blinking with three dubious messages. "Only a few of my close friends have this number. Pablo Ramirez's people are checking to see if I'm out of my safe room." He scurried through every room in the house closing the drapes as he went along.

The brain has a strange mechanism deeply implanted, in the brain called amygdala. It's responsible for processing strong emotions, such as fear and paranoia. It was one o'clock in the afternoon when CO left his home disguised as an old man, holding a walking stick. He decided to rent a compact vehicle and, in an attempt to lose any would be follower, took unnecessary turns, and side streets before taking the five and a half hour drive on the Interstate to the old terminal building in Lind City. The compact car took its toll on CO's back and kidneys. He decided to stop for a restroom and coffee refill at the next fast food restaurant. The GPS indicated an easy in and out burger restaurant five miles farther on the Interstate. "Damn, I can't wait another five miles." He turned off the highway at the next exit. He looked for the first secluded dirt road to relieve his bladder, opened the front and back doors of the vehicle, and started the urgently needed relief.

A tall husky well-groomed Deputy Sheriff asked in a deep voice, "Sir, what are you doing?"

CO instantly zipped up his trouser fly and, with eyes wide open replied, "I had an emergency stop, Officer."

"No, Sir. I have you as an indecent exposure suspect. May I have your driver's license and registration?" The Sheriff stepped closer to the car with his right hand on the handle of his holstered pistol. "Step out of your vehicle and keep your hands where I can see them." He maintained a frown and a sharp eye on CO's every move. "I've seen people like you who come out of the city and think they can break the law with no consequences. Where are you headed?"

"I'm going to Lind City." CO followed the procedure and handed the information to the officer. "Officer, I swear it was an emergency. I've never done this before. I saw this dirt road and…"

"It's not a dirt road, it's someone's driveway." The Sheriff completed a wants and warrants using his mobile computer. "It looks like you have a clean record and your license and registration are in order. Mr. Osterfeld, I'm going to let you go with a warning. The warning is, don't piss on my driveway again."

CO thanked the Sheriff, climbed into his car, made three attempts at a U turn, ran into a small ditch, and proceeded on his route to Lind City. CO laughed out loud, "That dumb Sheriff didn't do his job right. He didn't check the trunk or under the hood. If he did, he would have me in jail now."

The Sheriff watched the vehicle drive away, shook his head, slipped his personal cell phone from his pocket, and tapped a speed dial number. "It's me. The package is on its way, disguised like an old man, and he's alone. I didn't have to stop him. He stopped himself. This guy's dumber than shit."

CO drove north for five hours and decided he should take his disguise off and rest before he reached the terminal. He spotted a small welcome area located a few hundred feet past the Lind City line. The grounds were dimly lit with two cheap single light fixtures, mounted on wooden poles, and a weathered picnic table next to the poles. He parked under one of the lights, turned off the engine, and pulled on the hood release. He opened the hood, reached under the air filter compartment, and yanked off the duct tape holding a pistol and two fully loaded magazines. The thought of walking into a meeting unarmed with people he screwed, or tried to kill, would be ludicrous.

It was five minutes to eight when CO stepped out of the shadows of the building across from the terminal, He turned his head from side to side, and cautiously walked to the front door.

Teddy opened the door and, with an outstretched hand, said, "Please come in, we've been waiting for you. It's warm in the tunnel, can I take your jacket?"

"No. If it gets too warm, I'll take it off," CO replied. He knew Teddy would feel the weight of the pistol and loaded magazines in his jacket and, even if it was warm, he didn't want to have Teddy's people annihilate him before the meeting started. "Teddy, this place is filthy. Why do you live like this?" He reached into his jacket pocket, touched the pistol, and curled his finger around the trigger. "I don't like this, Teddy. I don't like this at all."

"CO, don't worry, no one's going to get hurt, especially when everyone knows you have a gun pointed at my back. Watch your step when we pass through that metal fire door you see ahead of us." Teddy slid the old rusty door sideways and let it slam behind them. They walked into a pitch dark room, once used as a passenger vestibule, and stood for a few seconds as their eyes became used to the darkness.

"What the hell's going on? I'll shoot your ass right now," CO screamed. He pressed the pistol handle with his right hand, his trigger finger in the ready to shoot position, "I'm not shitting you."

Teddy calmly replied, "Wait a second. This is our security room. Teddy grabbed the metal handle of an electrical circuit breaker and slammed it up the side of the metal box. The modern light fixtures came on displaying a clean, well maintained room, with conservative furniture. "It's not the Carter Osterfeld Building, nevertheless it works for us. The bedrooms are down each one of the four halls, and our meeting room is right in front of us. Let's go in and get started. Oh, no one is armed in this community as long as they're in the confines of the terminal. One of our people will relieve you of your weapon, for safety reasons, and return it to you as soon as you leave the building. I'd like to give you a full tour of our home but the people here are persnickety about their privacy."

CO looked at a closed wooden door with no windows, "What's in that room?"

Teddy pointed at a closed door, "That room is our infirmary," He opened the meeting room door and paused, "The infirmary, for obvious reasons, is very private."

"I have to say I'm impressed. The façade at the front of this place sends the message of poverty. It must have cost a ton of money to refurbish this underground." CO noticed an area away from the residential quarters with an extra wide double door and combination locks. He decided not to ask any questions about that particular room. "Where did the funds come from to do all this shit?" CO asked.

133

"We have some very generous people who made their way back into society after spending as much time in here as they needed to get their act together. Some donations came from people who know, that from the grace of God they could be here," Teddy replied.

"Okay. I'm here. How do you think you're going to save my ass?" CO with the tenacity of a raging bull said, "This better be damn good or I'm outta here."

"CO, before I give you your ass back, I need to ask you some questions. If you don't care to answer them, we can shake hands and you can leave." Teddy placed a recorder on the table.

CO exploded, "You're full of shit if you think I'm going to let you record this meeting. If it gets out, I had a sit down with you, I'll be dead before I leave this town. Who the hell do you think you are?"

"Whether you let me record this meeting or not, Pablo Ramirez's people will kill you the minute you leave this place." Teddy turned off the recorder stood, and coolly said, "This meeting is over. I'll have someone show you the front door, and don't forget your weapon, you will definitely need it."

The room went ominously silent. Teddy picked up the recorder, stepped away from the table, and thought, now would be the moment he might be forced to play his trump card.

CO cleared his throat, "If I agree to let you record our conversation, will you guarantee my safety when I walk out of here?"

"You know as well as I do, there are no guarantees in life. The minute you leave here, one day or one year, the Cartel will get you and your legacy will be that of a lawless criminal. If I let you stay here, the terminal will no longer be effective for the people who need it the most. No...you can't stay here," Teddy replied.

There was no doubt in Teddy's mind CO was on the brink of imploding.

CO threw up his hands and said, "Okay, okay, you can turn the recorder on. I'll make it easy and tell you I was there when my stepson was killed. I even helped put him in the cans filled with cement. I personally killed anyone who was a witness to me pulling the trigger…"

"So, you're admitting to killing your stepson?"

"Yeah, and I killed George Grazer at the marina office and Bubba Commons in his apartment. I ordered Paulo Espinoza's hit and run."

Teddy looked at CO dumbfounded by the ease at which the man in front of him was confessing to multiple murders. There were no signs of remorse in his voice as he described the details of each and every victim. "CO, we've been here almost three hours without a break. Would you like something to eat or drink?"

"No thanks," CO replied. He rubbed his eyes, "I think I've covered everything I did over the last six months."

"Did you have Jake Lester killed?"

"Yeah, I ordered the hit and I was there, but I didn't pull the trigger. Lester was getting too close to our real money maker so I had to do it."

"Who pulled the trigger, and who's the real money maker?" Teddy asked.

"I don't know their names. The Cartel sent these guys to me and I went with them for the hit. When the Cartel sends their own people for a hit, and you're in on it, you're theirs forever. That's where the real money comes from. They own everything I have, and paid me a lot of money to be a figurehead."

"Who ordered the hit on Consuela Delgado?"

"Shit, I'm a dead man anyway so I'll let you record this too. Ramirez sent Consuela to kill someone very important. I don't know who. She didn't do it, so he ordered her hit. It wasn't me."

Teddy said, "I need some water. Would you like a beverage?"

"Yeah, water." CO watched Teddy leave the room with the recorder running. He leaned over the recorder and noticed a few wires coming from the recorder and into a little gadget with blinking lights on it. He heard Teddy coming back and sat back in his chair. Where the hell were those wires going?

When Teddy returned to the meeting room, Consuela was walking behind him, carrying the water, and swearing in Spanish. "You stupid son of a bitch. You were ordered to kill me," Consuela broke out laughing, "The laugh is on both of us. Ramirez ordered me to get rid of you. He has people all over this country and he'll send an army after us if we don't show up dead."

CO's mouth dropped. "I don't believe you. You're trying to get away from something. Tell me how he would know if I'm here or in my home in New York?"

Consuela sneered, "You are a big shot and think you know everything. You actually are very naïve to think the head of the Columbian Cartel doesn't know your every move. I ask you this, did a Sheriff stop you while you were on your way here?" She glared at CO, "A Sheriff stopped you, and he didn't search you or the car...right?"

CO glanced at Consuela and pleaded, "Teddy, can you get us out of here?"

"No," Teddy replied and turned off the recorder.

"You were recording everything CO and I said?" Consuela pointed her finger at Teddy. "You got nothing in this place. You're a phony. You take the money and, with it, you live a high life off the grid. She screamed at CO, "You see what this son of a bitch has done."

"Yes, I recorded every word you two have said, but I don't think it will be used against you in a court of law," Teddy replied. "CO, to answer your question, I told you earlier I can't jeopardize the generous assistance we receive to keep this place running. Consuela, you accused me of being a fraud. If you'll be patient, I'll prove to both of you I'm not cheating anyone. I'll be right back." Teddy hurriedly left the room, closed the door behind him and returned a few minutes later. "Now I'll show you one of our accomplishments." He stepped away from the doorway.

"This is bullshit," CO screamed. "This is bullshit. You were dead. I told Diego Garcia in New York I was certain you were dead, and I know he told Ramirez the same thing."

Consuela was astonished, "Oh my God, you're not dead."

"Yeah, right. You both thought I was dead," Jake said. He took a few steps closer to CO, "Now I'll be happy to escort you and Consuela out the front door."

"Teddy, Teddy, you can't let him do this to us. Do something," CO begged.

Teddy shook his head, "No CO, I can't help you guys. Jake will show you the front door, and don't come back."

The short walk from Teddy's inner sanctum to the front door was actually a death march for CO and Consuela. When they reached the front door, Jake unlocked it, watched them step into the alley, and closed the door, "There go two extremely dangerous people," he said, locking the door.

CO and Consuela started to walk away from the Old Terminal Building when a black SUV came speeding at them with a back window open. They instinctively started to run away from the vehicle. A man holding an automatic weapon, opened fire sending a hail of bullets through their bodies. They were left for dead on the pavement.

Jake heard the unforgettable sound of automatic reports from a high caliber weapon. He quickly unlocked the door and rushed to the two fallen bodies. His first scan of the scene was CO's face blown away and Consuela lying next to CO's body bleeding profusely from a bullet wound to her chest. Jake noticed she was still breathing and trying to say something. He knelt closer to her lips, lowered his ear close to her mouth, and whispered, "What?"

Consuela closed her eyes, and murmured her dying words, "Trust no one…Cartel is everywhere."

Jake was still kneeling when Teddy came running up to the carnage. "Jake, what the hell happened?"

"It was an obvious hit by the Cartel. A black SUV came down the alley, headed straight for them and let loose with an automatic weapon. They didn't have a chance," Jake replied, sorrowfully.

"Jake, don't feel sorry for these two. They were in the business of killing people. You know the saying, "they lived by the sword and died by the sword." Teddy waited for a comment from Jake which never came. "Were they able to say anything before they died?"

Jake thought about Consuela's dying words. He wanted to protect Teddy from any repercussions from the Cartel and replied, "No, they were dead before they hit the ground."

"Jake, I gotta get the hell outta here before the cops get here. You know how to reach me if you need anything."

"Welcome back, Jake. You were missed around here. Can I get you a mug of coffee?" Penney asked. She pulled the vertical blinds open. "It's a beautiful sunshiny day. Isn't this better?"

Jake replied, "Penney, I've been away for three weeks not three years. Yes, I would love a mug of coffee." He reached for the thin rope controlling the gap between the blinds, and grimaced. "I guess I need a little help closing the verticals."

"Here, I'll do that. Why do you want to close the blinds on such a beautiful day?" Robert asked.

Jake was startled. "Yeah, I heard that from Penney. Robert, I didn't know you were in the office."

"I'll leave you two alone," Penney said. She was halfway out the door. "I'll be back in a few minutes with the coffee."

"I have to say I was surprised when the desk Sargent told me you were here early this morning. Jake, you had a hell of an experience. You completed the work you were hired for by solving the murder of the young Osterfeld boy. You took down Consuela Delgado, the Cartel's top killer, Carter Osterfeld, a killer and Cartel puppet, and got shot and busted up for your effort. The Mayor was duped into thinking Paulo Espinoza was legit and ready to sign a construction contract with a bogus construction company. You got the Mayor's chestnuts out of the fire and saved the city millions of dollars. Someday, when you're up to it, you can tell me how you accomplished an almost impossible task. Now you and Maggie need to take some time off and get yourselves rested. I see you're packing your belongings."

"Yeah, I thought you might need this office space for someone else."

Jake, the Mayor is on an unscheduled sabbatical and, before he left, he asked me to say you will always have the Lind City PD as a client."

Penney stepped in and placed the mug of coffee on Jake's desk. "Black. Let me know if you need anything else." She smiled at Robert and left the office.

"Is she always this happy?" Robert asked.

"Yeah, always." Jake paused. Robert was the first person who asked him, in a half assed way, to reveal his experiences and wondered why now? "I know, you're right. Maggie's been through a lot of hell too. We're going to our place in Bass Lake, get on the boat, drop a line in the water, and let the world go by. I just need to tidy up here a little before I leave."

As soon as Robert left Jake's office, he disconnected the desktop computer. He lifted the computer loaded with the information he had stored for nine months and packed it into the box. He looked around the office to make certain he wasn't leaving anything behind, and sealed the box.

He understood what he was about to do would propel him into an extremely dangerous world. The world of the Cartel, drugs, and murder.

19

Jake and Maggie were up early and on the highway toward their cabin in Bass Lake. The sun was in the process of burning off the low lying fog as they drove into their driveway and parked next to a black, four door sedan. "You would think the government would be more imaginative when they chose a color for the FBI fleet," Maggie snickered.

Jake saw John Harper and a stranger standing on the cabin porch. "I don't mind the color of John's vehicle, except I don't know the guy standing next to John," Jake remarked.

John saw the expressions on his friends' faces and hurried to their car. Hey Jake, Maggie, let me help you get your things into the cabin and I can explain what's going on."

"We'll unload the car later. Let's get inside our cabin." Jake started walking toward the cabin. "John, you know why Maggie and I are here," He whispered.

The stranger walked down the stairs and met Jake and Maggie with his right hand held out. Jake, Maggie, I deeply apologize for being here without asking you first. My name is Marshal Dunkin and I can't even start to imagine what's going through your minds.

"Okay, I don't think it's a good idea for us to talk out here. Let's get inside the cabin and you both can tell us what this is all about," Maggie ordered.

In an effort to break the cold silence as they found a place to sit in the living room, John said, "I took the liberty of making extra coffee when we got up this morning. I hope you don't mind."

Jake observed John, a high ranking officer of the FBI, frantically trying to impress Marshal Dunkin, who most likely was someone higher up the pecking order than John. "I think I can speak for Maggie as well when I say our shock wave is over. John, thanks for making the extra coffee, and it's just the way we like it."

John took the queue when Jake stopped talking and said, "Jake, Maggie, the FBI has been in Lind City, undercover, from the time you started the Hans Osterfeld murder investigation right up to the night Consuela Delgado and Carter Osterfeld were gunned down in the alley next to the old terminal. We don't know why you were there at that particular time and we don't want to know. After the evening of the drive by shooting our intelligence people were informed of the possibility of a major increase in the Cartel's activities in the Upstate New York distribution of drugs."

"John, we didn't need your intelligence people to tell us a big move was underway. It's a well-known fact on the streets," Jake said.

"Jake, Maggie, forgive me for not introducing you to Marshal Dunkin's title. Marshal is Deputy Director of the FBI," John said.

Marshal took the lead with the proper attitude of a British Royal and said, "I guess we got the proverbial cart before the horse, and I apologize for that. I'll come right to the point. The Cartel is very big in our country and growing. They're growing to the extent they can't produce the drugs fast enough for the demand, and especially the high demand for drugs mixed with Fentanyl. The Cartel is out of mixing and distribution space inside the metro areas of big cities like New York, Boston, and Philadelphia. The area around Lind City is a perfect solution to their problem. Jake, we have a few highly qualified Independent Contractors who assist the FBI in our investigations, and you have all the credentials for in an Independent Contractor with the FBI. I would like to know if you would be interested in such a position. This is a great opportunity for you to further your career. Take some time, but not too much, to think about it. I have to leave for DC now; however, you can give John your decision."

Jake's eye contact with Marshal was piercing, "Are you asking me to be your CI, a Confidential Informant?"

"Yes, well yes, if you put it that way," Marshal replied.

Jake walked Marshal to the door, "I'll have an answer for you by the end of the day." He returned to the living room to his favorite recliner, and said, "John."

John tried desperately to think of an explanation in which Marshal insulted Jake. Now would be a good time for the truth. "Jake, I honestly didn't know Marshal was going to offer you a forty dollar an hour CI position. Please believe me. He told me he was authorized to offer you a major position with the FBI. He wouldn't give me any specifics."

Jake considered John a close and trusted friend. Their dangerous rotation together in Afghanistan led to years of an impeccable friendship, and he had no reason to think John was a part of the arrogant manner in which Marshal proposed, a low stature 'snitch,' and financially unrewarding position. However, the words etched in his mind, 'trust no one,' reflected reasonable doubt. He had no desire to burn bridges with John and opted to low key the situation. "John, I know you're a good friend and I'm sure you were not in the loop with Marshal. Why don't we forget about the whole thing? I'll give Marshal my answer this afternoon. The bass are biting. Why don't you stay the night and wet a line with us tomorrow morning?"

John replied, "I'd love to go fishing with you and Maggie, except I have to leave immediately for a meeting in Washington. I don't know what your plans are for the future. Whatever they are, please give me a shout if I can be of any help."

Jake thought now was a good time to get this over with. He fumbled through his wallet, found Marshal's card and dialed his cell phone number. "I might as well do this now."

"Jake, I didn't think you would get to me this soon. I hope it's good news."

"Marshal, I appreciate the offer and, as good as it sounds, I'm going to decline."

"I'm sorry to hear that. I think you're making a huge mistake. I'm extremely disappointed. An offer like this from the FBI comes once in a lifetime."

The dial tone sounded before Jake could reply. "Well Maggie, I guess Marshal is pissed off at me for rejecting, what he called, an offer of a lifetime from the FBI, and hung up."

"Their loss. Jake, think of the offer as a lesson learned. The FBI isn't your cup of tea."

Jake and Maggie sat on their patio enjoying a glass of wine while watching a spectacular sunset, and communicated without saying a word.

Maggie sipped the last of her red wine, reached for the wine bottle sitting on the table, and, with a sigh, said, "I must say, I could get very used to this kind of life."

"I could tell from our conversations over the last couple of months you were disenchanted with your ME position. Are you thinking of leaving the ME's job?"

Maggie paused for a few seconds, "Yeah, I'm thinking about it. After all, you're going to need some help kicking the Cartel's butt out of Lind City. What do you think?"

"I think the sun's gone down and it's starting to get chilly out here. It's five minutes to eight. Let's get something to eat from the deli, bring the food home, open another bottle of wine, hit the remote on the gas fireplace, and make mad passionate love."

"Jake, you dickens. Sounds like a great plan. We've had a couple glasses of wine, it's not very far to the deli, let's walk."

The locals have called Momma's Deli, 'the deli' for the last five years. The food was excellent, great service, exceptionally clean, and it was the only deli in the Village of Bass Lake. The actual owner of the deli, Minna Hurwitz, with slightly graying hair, a touch on the heavy side, and a cheerful personality, is a fifty year old entrepreneur who started the business for that very reason. There wasn't a deli within forty miles of the village. She was also a member of the Bass Lake Volunteer Fire Department. The police and fire department scanner was turned on the entire day. It was common for business owners to have a scanner on their premises. The customers who had been frequenting the deli for several years didn't seem to mind the scanner's constant crackling as long as they weren't the subject of an emergency call.

The bells hanging over the front door of the deli rang a loud jingle when Jake and Maggie entered the store. "Hey, you guys, how's it going?" Minna asked, cheerfully. She wiped the perspiration from her forehead, "Please excuse my appearance. I've been cleaning the ovens."

Jake replied, we're doing just fine. You know we've been coming here for about ten years, and you always have a genuine welcome in your voice. What's your secret?"

Maggie laughed, "Jake, I'm hungry. I'm gonna look at the food. You can talk with Minna."

"Well Jake, the good Lord has been good to me in many ways and that's the secret. What can I do for you?"

The scanner started blaring an emergency call for the Police and Fire Departments to respond to an explosion at 216 Main Street, all services respond. The call repeated several times.

Maggie shouted frantically, "Oh my God, Jake, that's our house."

Jake ran out the door, "Holy shit."

Jake and Maggie arrived at the scene as the volunteers were connecting the large fire hoses to the water hydrants and stood in disbelief. The entire structure was leveled to the ground. Their once beautiful cottage was a mass of burning rubble. The fire department volunteers were pouring hundreds of gallons of water on the rubble and extinguishing several small pieces of burning debris hanging from trees and shrubs.

Maggie stood next to Jake sobbing, "How did this happen?"

Jake replied, sternly, "It had to be a bomb. This was no accident."

145

Minna gently stepped next to the distraught couple, "I'm so sorry. You're welcome to stay with me as long as you'd like."

Maggie said with tears in her eyes, "Thank you, Minna. It looks like the volunteers saved our car. We'll be able to drive home." She cuddled up to Jake, "Honey, we've been here for hours watching the Fire Marshal and Zig's team. Maybe we should go home and try to get some sleep and come back in the morning."

"I want to talk with Janis Dalton for a minute."

A large crowd had formed on the sidewalk across from the fire, taking amateur pictures and videos with their cell phones and commenting on the disaster. Among the crowd was one professional photographer and village historian, Janis Dalton. She was snapping photos, capturing the activities including the crowd around her, with a very expensive camera.

Jake made his way to Janis and asked, "Could I please have copies of your work? I'll pay whatever you need."

Janis replied, without hesitation, "Jake, you can have every bit of my work at no cost."

"C'mon, Honey, let's go home," Maggie pleaded.

"Wait just another minute. Zig and the Fire Marshal are coming our way." Jake hurried toward Zig. "What do you have?"

Zig had a small, mutilated piece of metal with two wires dangling from it, one red, and one yellow, in his hand. He pushed the two wires aside, and held it in front of Jake, "This is the detonator. Does it look familiar?"

"Yes, that's a sophisticated military detonator. I saw those in Afghanistan," Jake replied. He took the detonator in his hand, turned it in several positions and said, "This could have been set off with a cell phone from anywhere in the country."

146

The Fire Marshal opened a large plastic evidence bag, "Drop it in, and I'll hold it until you're ready to leave. We might be able to find more parts to this thing."

"Jake, it's obvious someone is out to kill you. What's going on?"

"It's the Cartel. I brought down two of their major players. Let me know if you find any physical evidence that would link this bombing to them," Jake replied.

"Maggie, let's go home."

The sun was three hours away from rising over the willow tree in front of Jake and Maggie's home, when Jake stopped the car a hundred feet short of entering the driveway, pushed the button on the garage door opener, waited until the door was completely open, pushed the button again, and watched the door close. He remained in the street with the car's engine running and reopened the door and cautiously drove into the garage. They keyed in the house security code on the doorway wall and, without turning on any lights, walked into the kitchen. Their uninhibited life, as they once knew it, changed when he took Consuela Delgado and Carter Osterfeld out of the Cartel's equation.

They fell into bed, too exhausted and traumatized to sleep. They tossed and turned as the hours passed and, the once unnoticeable house noises, which most homes have, were now suspicious sounds. The first signs of daylight dimly lit the room and the sunrise soon followed.

Maggie rolled close to Jake and broke the silence, "Honey, as much as we loved our cottage, it was brick and mortar. We're alive, we have each other, and we can rebuild another cottage."

"Yes, I know the cottage can be rebuilt, and we will start as soon as the Fire Marshal clears the site. My concern isn't the cottage. My concern is the Cartel, if it was the Cartel, blowing up our home and killing us. I look at it in terms of, hypothetically speaking, blowing them up first. I know it would be impossible for me to shut down the flow of Cartel drugs in our country, but I'm sure as hell going to try and kick their ass out of Lind City.

Maggie loudly said, "What do mean, you're are going to try and kick their ass out of Lind City? We're going to kick their ass out of Lind City. I have enough time to retire from the ME position, and I know enough about the law to get my PI license. Would that work for you?"

Jake grinned and kissed Maggie, "That would be just fine, Maggie. Just fine."

20

The sign painted on the full length, glass office door read, "Lester and Lester Private Investigators," on the first floor of a century old brick building, close to the Lind City Police Department, and within walking distance to the Police Forensics building. The phone system, upscale computer system, not yet connected to all the law enforcement investigation tools, and a major part of the newly formed detective agency will prove to be the most beneficial monetary investment the couple could make. The decor, and the two private offices, were mainly a façade for the purpose of a walk in client who actually required their services.

Jake swiped his building security card, and entered the hundred year old office building. He looked at the names on the office door and smiled the first smile after the bombing of their cottage. He stepped into a room of stacks of boxes and mumbled, "This will be the waiting room, once we get the boxes out of the way."

A woman in her late fifties looked through the open door, "Mr. Lester, it's six a.m., you're the first one in the building this morning." She placed her broom against the freshly painted wall, and stood in the office doorway. "You and your wife have been working like beavers since you moved in two weeks ago. Can I help you with anything?"

"Good morning, Bonnie. Come in, if you can find your way through the maze of boxes," Jake replied.

The hardwood floors creaked as Bonnie sidestepped her slender frame through the open path to where Jake was standing. She pushed back her baseball cap, and swiped the dust off one of the boxes, "I think you need help with all these boxes."

"Yeah right: It's gonna take weeks to get the stuff into the right file cabinets, and have this place organized and running like it should. Tomorrow is Saturday. Maggie and I will be getting our computers completely programmed before we can tackle that job."

"Mr. Lester, like I said, you're going to need help with all these boxes. I'm a retired businesswoman, I live alone, and have nothing but time on my hands. You and the Misses seem like nice people. I'd be happy to file or scan the information in these boxes."

Jake replied, "Bonnie, it's very nice of you to offer your services. We have a very low budget and I'm sure we couldn't afford your salary."

"Maggie appeared wearing sneakers, dressed in blue jeans, and carrying dust cloths and a broom. "Good morning. I could hear you guys all the way down the hall. What's going on?"

"Bonnie and I were discussing the possibility of her helping us through the settling process of the office," Jake replied.

"Mr. and Mrs. Lester, before we continue this conversation, I'd like to say, I'm volunteering my services. I would be very happy to help you, and you'd be helping me. I do nothing but sit around my apartment every Saturday and Sunday watching TV."

"Oh, by the way, Bonnie, what is your last name?" Maggie asked.

"Goodwin, it's Bonnie Goodwin. You can look me up on any computer search site. I'm sure you'll see I am for real. Whatta say?"

Jake and Maggie knew by their eye contact they were on the same page. Jake replied, enthusiastically, "Bonnie, I don't know how we could refuse your offer. We'll be here early tomorrow morning and you can get here anytime you can."

"Maggie, how long will it take you to link our computers with the law enforcement agencies?"

"Our programs are compatible with theirs, and it's a matter of securing a safe internet. We should be up and running in about an hour. The very first task will be vetting Bonnie Goodwin. She's only going to be with us a couple of days, but we shouldn't take any chances."

"Hello in there. It's me," Zig shouted.

"Hey Zig, come in. Good to see you. Please excuse the boxes," Jake said.

"I'm behind the last stack of boxes, and Maggie is working on our computers in one of the offices. I'll be there in a second." Jake wiped the perspiration from his face and met Zig at the door. "How you doing?"

"I'm doing fine. I saw your car parked in front of the building and I thought you would like an update on that timing mechanism."

"Absolutely." Jake shuffled two chairs from a nearby closet and wiped them clean of the carpenter's dust. "We've been doing a little refurbishing."

"No problem." Zig opened a manila folder and placed it on top of one of the boxes. "Jake, whoever synchronized this device is not only a pro, he knew exactly where your family room was located and your habits. The bomb was situated under the family room. The bomber made a mistake and assumed you and Maggie would be in for the night." Zig fished two photos from the folder, pointed to one of them, and said, "This is the latest bomb the Afghans used in the war." He gave the second photo to Jake. "Here's a photo of the mechanism the bomber used. The first photo doesn't have a switch on it." He pointed at a small toggle switch in the second photo. "You see this little switch? The bomber added a switch to the mechanism so it could be detonated by a cell phone or a timing device."

Jake said, "So the bomber used a timing device instead of the cell phone because…"

They simultaneously said, "Because the bomber is local and didn't want to take a chance the cell number would be traced."

"What's all the racket out here? Hi Zig. What are you guys up to?" Maggie asked.

"Honey, Zig's research told us, among other things, the bomber knows us and our habits. He assumed we would be in the cottage for the evening. If we didn't go to the deli together, one of us would have died in the explosion. The bomber knew it was my last week at the police department and we wouldn't be at the cottage until the weekend. Whoever placed the bomb had almost a week to set the timing device."

Maggie hugged Jake, "It wasn't our time." She looked at Zig. "How can we thank you?"

"No need for thanks. Glad to be of help. You can keep these photos. I have to run. Give me a shout if I can be of any help with your new endeavor."

"Honey, I have a suggestion. With Bonnie's help, I can get the office organized. You need to stay focused on your goals."

"Yeah, you're right," Jake said.

Maggie reminded herself Jake had been traumatized twice in two months and she was sure, after the bombing, his retirement and PI goals have dramatically changed. "Jake, I know you're pissed off at the Cartel and hold them responsible for trying to kill us. There's no possible way we can stop the Cartel's activities. What's our plan of attack?"

"It's funny you asked me that question. You're right, I had a lot of time while I was laying in the hospital bed to think about what we should do to achieve maximum damage to the Cartel. We can't bring down the entire Cartel. We should concentrate on making it extremely difficult for them to operate in Lind City and the surrounding area, including Big Base Lake."

"And how do we accomplish what you're suggesting without getting ourselves killed?" Maggie asked.

"We know the Cartel is trying to establish our city as a point of assembling and mixing all the drugs into a single compound, and distributing from somewhere in this area. The most important part of the equation is the mixer."

Maggie said, "So, we never allow that person, or persons, to perform their job."

"Yes, you're right. After the bombing, our rules of engagement have escalated, and we will use every possible means, legal or not, at our disposal to accomplish our goal." Jake slipped the photos into the manila folder. "Tomorrow morning I'm going back to survey the cleanup of our cottage, check our boat at the marina and, while I'm in town, see if Janis Dalton took some clear pictures of the curiosity seekers. History tells us that ninety percent of the time an arsonist or bomber will return to the scene of the crime and try to blend into the crowd."

"Jake, be very careful while you're checking out the boat. It is very possible it is also booby trapped."

"Yeah, I know. That crossed my mind too." Jake's experience with roadside bombs in Afghanistan may give him a slight edge when he inspects their boat, however, having a real pyrotechnics specialist with him would certainly give him a true comfort level. "I'll call Teddy. He's the bomb expert."

Maggie let out a sigh of relief, "Good idea. Why don't you invite Teddy for dinner, and ask him to stay overnight? It would give you a good start in the morning."

It was early dawn when the two men drove West with the sun rising at their backs. They had made the trip to Bass Lake numerous times for a relaxing day of fishing. This trip was unexpected and not for fun. This will be the first time Jake will see the cottage debris empty from the site, and the foundation of the new rustic chalet in its place. The minimal Sunday morning traffic decreased their travel time by twenty minutes, and the trip actually became a pleasant forty minute ride to Big Bass Lake, with an occasional, 'slow for deer,' sign as evidence of nearby civilization.

Jake stopped the car in front of the chalet construction site and marveled at the amount of equipment staged and ready for a scheduled Monday morning start up time. He left Teddy in the car, walked up to one of the red flagged construction stakes, briefly looked around, and went back to the car.

153

Teddy noticed his friend's face wrinkled with a discouraging grimace. "Jake, you and Maggie are strong people. You have each other to cope with the business transition, and the construction of a beautiful year-round home. You were in deeper shit than this when you were in Afghanistan and you came through it with your mind and body intact. Let's find this Janis Dalton and see what she has to offer. Who knows, with her town history background, we might find out more about this town than you think possible."

"Right, but first I want to check out the boat." Jake put the car into forward gear, drove to the marina, and parked adjacent to his boat. The majority of boat owners can recognize with quick a glance if anything is disturbed, however, with the professionalism of the bomber, this warranted closer scrutiny. "Teddy, before you board the boat, I'm going to see if there's evidence of the boat being moved or any signs of extraordinary activity around the boat lines or dock cleats. You can take it from there." Jake, with his eyes fixed on the boat, slowly got out of the car and walked the length of the hull looking for signs of the notorious boat loving marina spiders who build their webs across mooring lines and shady crevices. He was unusually delighted with the attendance of several spider webs in the usual places. Their presence indicated the boat had not been moved or boarded for quite some time. "It's all yours, my friend."

Teddy emerged from the cabin, locked the door, joined Jake topside, and placed the bomb detecting equipment into its case, "This place is clean."

Janis pushed her bifocals into place, and adjusted her floppy hat, "Hey, you two. I thought I saw you guys pull into the marina. I brought you these pictures to you, you know, the ones I took the day of the bombing," She was carrying a briefcase in one hand, and a camera in the other as she tried to maneuver past the loose boat lines lying on the dock. "Some of these weekend boat people don't know how to secure their boat lines properly," she muttered, and returned to shore. "I'll wait here for you guys to finish whatever it is you're doing. Are you going to be very long?" She took a half-eaten doughnut from her pocket, took a bite from it, and stuffed it back into her pocket.

"Hi Janis, we're through here. We'll be right there," Jake replied.

Janis looked at Teddy, and said, "I don't know this handsome guy."

"I'm, Teddy. I'm here for the ride."

"Well, anyway Jake, I figured you might be here sometime soon looking for my photos. There's one hundred and ten of them." Janis passed the briefcase to Jake. "I went through every one of them and most of the people in the pictures are local people. There are a few people I didn't recognize. Jake, the photos, and the camera chip are yours to keep and I hope you catch the son of a bitch who did this to you and Maggie."

"Thank you so much, Janis," Jake said. He hugged her, "These will be a big help."

"You guys going to hang around for a while?"

"No, Janis, we have to get back home. Maybe another time," Jake replied.

Janis winked at Teddy, "And make sure you bring this guy with you."

Jake and Teddy watched Janis as she turned and briskly walked away. "Janis is one of a kind, and Maggie and I love her dearly," Jake remarked.

"What now, Jake?"

"I'm taking these pictures home, look at them through a magnifying glass, and hope we find something."

"No, I mean what's in the future?"

"In the near future Maggie and I are going to finish settling the office, get a project manager to oversee the construction of our second home, take our laptops to my Dad's place in the Adirondacks, and try to sort things out for a few months. In that order."

"Wow. If there's anything I can do for you while you're gone, you know how to reach me,"

Jake's plans, as he described them to Teddy, were not totally accurate. The part about going to his Dad's place was true, however, he and Maggie weren't planning to sit and watch the world go by. On the contrary, their plans were to aggressively find the local Cartel members and keep them out of Lind City.

21

The wooden sign above the entrance to John Lester's lodge, and the two hundred acres of pine trees was named Whistling Pines by his late wife Wilma. The lodge was planned and constructed six years ago with bulletproof floor to ceiling windows on the East and West sides of the building, and was completed a few months before Wilma's passing. It was Wilma's suggestion to have bullet proof windows in the event a hunter's stray bullet penetrate ordinary glass windows. After Wilma's passing, John decided to permanently reside at Whistling Pines.

It was six a.m. when John pressed the 'open' button on a remote pad, activating a noiseless electric motor. The drapes slowly drew neatly into place and, just before the usual spectacular sunrise, the Eastside of Whistling Pines seemed to enter into the open floor plan of the living room. The beeping the coffee maker caught John's attention. He filled a mug full of black coffee, grabbed his high powered binoculars, and sat on the porch steps scanning the woods for his animal friends. "Life doesn't get any better than this. I think I'll sit out here and enjoy the morning air until Jake and Maggie show up."

"Jake, I'm glad we decided to stop at that new diner, said Maggie. "The food was delicious."

"Yeah, and the Saturday morning gossip was interesting. What wasn't gossiped was especially interesting"

"What was that?"

"We're about an hour away from Dad's place and not one word about activity at the talc mine. Maggie, you'd think people living within a hundred miles of the old mine would be chattering about any activity there, especially in a diner." Jake activated his right turn signal, and turned onto a county road. "We're about thirty minutes away to peace and quiet."

Maggie stared out the window, mesmerized by the serenity of the mountains, as they cruised along the quiet road. "I hope you're right about the peace and quiet part of the trip. We need a little of that, at least for a few days." She pointed to a dirt road, "There's Dad's driveway."

Jake turned onto the dirt road, stopped at a steel-bar gate, and looked at the facial recognition scanner. The gate jumped and clattered into motion, and opened wide enough for a large truck to pass through with a minimum amount of effort. "Maggie, smile we're on camera. Dad had this elaborate security system installed right after I asked him if we could visit for a while. I think it was for his safety as well as ours."

"That was very thoughtful of him. What does Dad do in the middle of winter when it snows three feet a day?"

"I don't know, but Dad's a pretty resourceful guy."

Maggie looked into the mirror attached to the sun visor and brushed her hair back a few times, "I want to look nice."

Jake looked at Maggie and snickered, "Honey, we're going to be in the mountains with no one around us for miles."

Maggie gave Jake a "humph."

John saw one of the red lights flashing on his newly installed security board and a video of Jake's vehicle passing through one of the check points on the property. 'This should impress the hell out of my son.'

Jake and Maggie saw a doe fifty yards away, heading straight for the car. Jake slowed the car down, and watched the animal nonchalantly trot past them. Maggie remarked, "What a beautiful sight. If there wasn't a clearing in the woods, we wouldn't have seen her coming."

John grinned and shouted, "Hey, it's good to see you guys. Jake, after you unload your car, you can park it the barn but first, give your Dad a hug." When he gave Jake a hug, he felt a noticeable bulge in Jake's down vest. "Son, you won't need that piece here." He smiled at Maggie, "Thanks for keeping Jake..." Tears filled his eyes, "Let's go in the house, and get you settled in."

Maggie stood in the center of the living room, "Dad, I can never get enough of the panoramic view from this window. I can almost see where a doe crossed in front of the car."

"Yeah, the window was Wilma's idea, and it was my idea to have a security perimeter around the lodge. The perimeter is basically to keep the hunters, who ignore my 'no hunting' signs around the property, from shooing in this direction."

"And it also gives the perimeter security cameras a clear view." Jake quickly changed the subject to something more enjoyable. He looked at the kitchen clock, "Dad, it's four in the afternoon, but I know it's five o'clock somewhere. We brought some single malt scotch and some very nice wine with us. Are you ready?"

John laughed, "Good idea son. I'm ready for the single malt, how about you Maggie?"

"I'm in the mood for the single malt," Maggie replied.

"Good, single malt for you, Jake?" He walked to the bar where Jake deposited a case of beverages when they arrived. "Oh, by the way, I picked up some nice steaks at the market and I have them ready for tonight's dinner."

The afternoon blended into the evening and, the three Lesters completed a scrumptious dinner. They then settled down on the enclosed screen porch and listened to the evening music of the Adirondack Mountains.

Maggie knew it was time for some dad and son talk, and she broke the silence, "I'm out of gas, and I'm going to get ready for bed." She sipped the last of her drink. "It's been a long day, Honey. Don't keep Dad up too long."

"Jake, I want you to know, it's a pleasure having you and Maggie here. You can stay here as long as you want." He picked up his empty glass and asked, "Are you ready for a night cap?"

"Sure."

John slowly walked to the refrigerator as he thought about the best way to approach his son's ordeals. He dropped a few ice cubes into each glass, poured a generous amount of scotch, twizzled his drink with his index finger, and handed Jake the other glass. He was about to pose the question, when Jake interrupted his thoughts.

"Dad, I know you're wondering about the dangerous episodes Maggie and I went through the last few months." He sipped some of his drink.

"Yeah, my scanner couldn't reach Big Bass Lake. I saw some of it on the news and, as a matter of fact, I was about to ask how the hell you and Maggie survived such horrendous times." John abruptly stopped and changed his approach. "Son, you and Maggie are going to be with me for a while. You must be very tired. Why don't we save it for another time?"

"I am tired, and maybe tomorrow Maggie and I can fill you in on everything. But I would like to say, when we drove up the driveway, we noticed you had several remote controlled security cameras stationed at several obscure points, a fifty yard clear perimeter around the lodge, motion detector lights, and I thank you for that."

"I thought you might be impressed with the high tech equipment around here. I'll tell you what. How about tomorrow morning the three of us go trout fishing. We can pack a lunch, and make a day of it. Whatta yah think?"

"I know Maggie would love it, and so would I. But not too early in the morning. Good night, Dad:"

The aroma of bacon and coffee wafted into the guest bedroom and drew Jake out of a sound sleep. He threw his arm over to the other side of the bed, and found an empty mattress. He threw on a pair of sweat pants and headed into the kitchen. "Coffee."

"And a good morning to you, your highness," Maggie laughed. "Pull up a chair. Dad's getting fishing tackle ready and he'll be in shortly for some breakfast. Don't I get a kiss?"

"Oh, yeah. Coffee first."

John entered the kitchen and walked straight to the coffee maker, "Good morning, Jake. Did you sleep well?"

Jake nodded, yes, while he was swallowing a mouthful of coffee. "Yes, I slept like a log."

"After we're through with breakfast, we'll take one of the All-Terrain Vehicles to the best fishing hole in the county."

Maggie said, "I'll throw a couple of beach towels into the ATV. You never know, I might want to go for a swim."

John drove the ATV up and down a mountain road for about five miles, dodging tree branches and boulders along the way. He saw a female bear and two cubs, came to a slow stop, turned off the vehicle's engine, and whispered, "Be quiet and don't move."

Maggie, not thinking about John's instructions, slowly moved her cell phone into a strategic position and snapped a few tender pictures of the bears as they waddled cross the road. "Now that's worth the trip through the woods."

"The bears are pretty docile around here unless you antagonize them. Hold on, we're going to go over a small wooden bridge over the stream, and to your right is my favorite fishing spot. I added a picnic table, Adirondack chairs, and a brick fireplace for times like this."

"So that's why you told me to pack a bottle of wine and no food. Great idea, Dad." Jake jumped from the ATV headed down to the stream. "Fresh trout for lunch."

Maggie opened the three creels and, with a big smile, said, "Dad, now I know why you didn't want me to pack food. Can someone open the wine while I clean these beautiful trout?"

"You can rinse the fish out at the creek and put the fish innards in a plastic bag. The animals can smell blood from miles away."

Maggie carried the dressed fish to a five foot deep calm area of clear blue water. She started to rinse the fish when she saw what appeared to be a doll in the water, wedged under a broken maple tree branch. Her curiosity drew her closer to the edge of the creek bed for a better view. "Oh my God, there a baby's body here, she shrieked" Without care for her safety, she plunged into the creek, submerging herself under the water. She pushed the large tree branch aside and, with her last breath of air, she pulled the baby into her arms.

The two men came running to the water's edge. They saw Maggie standing chest deep in the water, panting, and holding a small baby in her arms. The men, for a split moment, were motionless. The sight before them, Maggie holding a dead baby, eclipsed anything they had ever encountered.

"Jake, help Maggie. I'll call the Sheriff." John ran to the ATV and jerked the cell phone from its stand, "Hello, this is John Lester. We found a deceased baby in the creek, about two miles northeast of my lodge.

Jake helped Maggie to dry land, gently placed the baby on the ground, and wrapped Maggie in one of the beach towels. Maggie, is that what I think it is?"

"Yes, the umbilical cord is still attached to the baby. Someone gave birth to this little girl and threw her into the creek. How cruel. She didn't ask to be born into this world and someone with no conscious threw her away like garbage."

John returned to the creek, "The Sheriff and his deputies will be here in a few minutes. I can't imagine how deplorable a person would be to kill a newborn baby."

"The County ME will have to determine how long the baby has been in the water and the actual cause of death," Maggie remarked. "Dad, do you know the name of the Wilson County ME?"

"Well, at present, I believe there is no full time Wilson County Coroner or ME. Sheriff Ronny   Plank can fill us in on all that," John replied. He saw three ATVs, Ronny, and six deputies speeding their way to the fishing site.

"Hey Ronny," John called out, and waved his hand, "The deceased is over here."

Ronny approached John, "Hey John," he looked at the covered body lying on the ground, squatted, and looked under the picnic blanket, "Man, oh man. Who would do such a thing?"

"Ronny, you remember my son Jake and his wife, Maggie. We'll let you and your men do what you need to do. We're going to be at the lodge when you're done here."

Jake and his father were silent in their rocking chairs on the lodge's back porch sipping coffee while trying to surmise what possible motive a mother, or mother and father, would have to dispose of their newborn baby girl.

"Dad."

"Yeah, Jake, I know what you're thinking. We should find out what the hell's going on at the mine. I've been over that way a few times and I noticed large trucks covered with tarps, and, other times, I saw minivans, sometimes two or three a day, leaving the place. Do you remember the time you and I looked at the mine entrance with our night vision binoculars?"

"Sure, I do. There were men hanging around the place in the middle of the night and the next day, when we went to the abandon mining town, there was no one to be seen."

Maggie stepped onto the porch holding a large mug of coffee. Her hair was wrapped up in a towel and she was barefoot. "What are you two gabbing about," she asked. "No sign of Ronny?"

"No. Things move a little slower in Wilson County," John replied. "Ronny's hurting for help with this one. You might want to think about offering Ronny   a hand with your ME expertise. Just a suggestion."

Maggie took a chair pad from the porch's storage room, and sat in one of the handmade wicker chairs, "I'd be glad to lend John a hand, that is, if he wants my help. I don't want to offend him, so I think it might be better if I wait for him to ask." She covered her face with her hands, and started to cry, "Whoever killed that poor baby could have dropped her off at the Fire Department. Someone would have loved to have a little girl. Jake, we have to catch this piece of crap."

The roar of ATVs speeding up to John's porch broke their concentration. Ronny jumped off his vehicle, stood at the bottom of the steps, and looked at his boots, "Hang on a second." He reached down and rubbed off some of the dirt from his boots, "Oh hell," he said, in frustration.

"Ronny, never mind your boots. Come on up here and relax." John slid a chair in front of Ronny. "Here, set your butt down. Did you find anything?"

"No. My deputies and I searched all the way up to the talc mine property. The new owners have private property signs strung all the way to the mine. I'll have to 'show probable cause' or get a court order to search their property. It's important we determine where the baby was born, when it was born and was she alive when she was thrown into the creek. I need a Medical Examiner to help us. We don't have a full time ME and we don't have a Coroner on the payroll."

Jake handed Ronny a mug of coffee, "Ah, Sheriff, I think I can be of help. I've been known to trespass. I don't need a court order and, if someone calls the Sheriff, it might take a day or two for a deputy to respond."

Maggie thought the Sheriff, in his own, way gave her an opportunity to respond to his dilemma, "Ronny, I'm a Medical Examiner, and I can double as a Coroner. Whatta ya think?"

Ronny slipped his Sheriff's cap off, smoothed his grey hair back, and shouted to his deputies, "Why don't you guy's head home. We'll get a fresh start in the morning." He watched his deputies' scoot down John's driveway and, he put his cap back on. "John, it's close enough to five o'clock, and I'm powerful thirsty. You wouldn't happen to have any of your single malt Scotch hanging around?"

"I certainly do, and I'd be happy to pour," John replied. "Jake, come help me with the ice."

"Maggie, it was kind for John and your husband to give us a few minutes. Thank you for your offer to help out. I would be a fool not to accept, but the Wilson County budget is pretty low. I wouldn't be able to compensate you what you're used to."

"Lonny, before you say any more, I would do this pro bono. I don't want anything. I just want to catch the bastard who killed and threw that little baby into the creek. Do we have a deal?"

"Absolutely." Lonny swiveled his butt in the chair and looked through the screen door, "Okay you guys, Maggie, and I are thirsty, and you guys can come out now."

165

22

The Wilson County Courthouse was located in the quaint village of Marilyn, New York, boasting a population of three thousand. The Sheriff's Department, jail, and the morgue, shared the basement floor of the late century Medina Stone building. The landscaping was meticulously maintained by village volunteers. Marilyn, New York was, until now, the epitome of peace and tranquility.

It was seven a.m., forty-five minutes before her appointment with Ronny, when Maggie drove into the center of Marilyn, searching for the local diner. She spotted a small stainless steel building, resembling a railroad dining car, with a small neon sign on top of the building. It flashed the word, 'Eat.' She circled the unpaved, and almost full, parking lot until she found a place to park. "This will have to do for now. A coffee to go and I'm out of here."

The partly covered sign 'reading, 'seat yourself' was a few feet in front of a long counter with red covered stools spaced evenly apart. There were a few booths along the window side of the diner, which seemed to be the extent of the greeting area. A woman behind the counter shouted, "There's more seating in the back room if you're not in a hurry. Oh, you must be Dr. Lester, the Medical Examiner. Ma'am, this is a small village, everyone knows everyone, and yah can't fart without everyone knowing about it."

Maggie smiled, "Could I have a large black coffee no sugar, please?"

"Sure, Sheriff Ronny was in here about an hour ago. I overheard him and the Mayor talking about an ME coming into Marilyn for a few days." She turned around, stood in front of a battery of filled coffee pots on an electric warmer, poured the coffee into a plastic container and, in one single motion, swung around holding the coffee in front of Maggie. "Oh, by the way, my name is Heidi."

Maggie, without a security check, freely searched the basement for the Sheriff's office, saw an open door at the end of the hall, and heard Ronny talking with another man. She tapped on the open door, "Sheriff."

"Maggie, please come in. We were just talking about you. Please, meet the Village Mayor, Gilford Sloan. Everyone calls him, Gil."

The Mayor took off his floppy fishing hat and softly shook Maggie's hand. "It's a pleasure. If you need anything, please let us know." He twisted his hat back on. "I'm goin to leave you two so you can get to work."

Sheriff Ronny escorted Maggie down a flight of stairs into the subbasement of the building, through a short metal tunnel. He stopped at a double glass door and flipped on three switches. The large room was lined with five refrigerated drawers, a glass cubical, with the basic technical equipment for performing autopsies. Lonny remarked, "I don't know why the founding fathers put this place in the bowels of the building. Anyway, here it is, it's all yours." He pointed to an overhead garage door, "That's the door leading to the back parking lot."

Maggie went directly to the bank of refrigerated drawers, and saw drawer number one with a tag marked "Baby Doe." She tugged at the stainless steel handle, slowly drew the retractable table half way out of the refrigerated compartment, and waited a short and agonizing time before unzipping the tiny plastic body bag. Maggie struggled to keep her composure while she confirmed the body as the baby she hauled out of the creek.

Lonny whispered, "I'll close the drawer while you check out your office."

"I'm going to need an assistant to perform the lab duties." Maggie blotted her tears away, "and a video and sound recorder in the examination room."

"I'll see to it right away."

Maggie removed a few stacks of papers from the midcentury oak desk, and found an official Coroner's register with dates and details of previous autopsies. She thumbed through the empty pages until she found the handwritten, one page, autopsy report performed on a Hispanic immigrant, as a result of a fentanyl overdose, single motor vehicle accident, on November fourth, two thousand, twenty-two, in Windsor County. She thought, "That was four months ago." Why was an autopsy performed here for an incident in Windsor County? She licked her index finger, and flipped to the previous autopsy dated July fourth, two thousand seventeen. The autopsy was performed as a result of a DWI, single vehicle accident?

Sheriff Ronny entered the office, "I requested assistance from a retired local nurse I know. She has experience in this sort of thing. She'll be here within the hour, and I also ordered the video and sound equipment you need from our local dealer. He knew exactly what you wanted, and he promised me he would have the stuff here in a few minutes."

"That's awesome." She picked up the Coroner's Register from the desk, and showed Sheriff Lonny the opened page, "This says an autopsy was performed in Windsor County, on a Hispanic immigrant, four months ago. His death was a result of an overdose of fentanyl."

"Yeah, we have reciprocity with the people in Windsor County, because they don't have a morgue, and lack the equipment to perform an autopsy."

"Maggie asked, "Windsor County, where is it?"

The Sheriff laughed, "It's a four square mile piece of land, etched out of the side of a mountain. It was purchased by a group of high-end New York lawyers, so they could have their private hunting area. It's located, in part, next to John's property."

"Hello," A middle aged woman, wearing shorts, blue golf shirt, and sneakers, stood at the office doorway, "Hi Sheriff."

"Hi Mary, thanks for coming with such short notice. I'd like you to meet Dr. Maggie Lester. Mary Vincent's the nurse I asked to assist you with the autopsy.

"Welcome, Mary. The Sheriff spoke very highly of you, and he said you have the experience we need in a cutting room. I found some scrubs and surgical masks in the closet. If you're ready we can get started."

Maggie entered the autopsy suite, turned on a bank of switches labeled ceiling lights, and negative ventilating system. Negative ventilating systems are used to contain airborne contaminants within a room. She pressed the 'on' buttons of the recording equipment, stepped up to the adjustable stainless steel table, and waited for Mary to gently place Baby Doe on the table. The battery of high intensity lights were in perfect position to start the external examination. Mary, with dignity and respect, placed the machine over the baby and stepped away from the table. The brief purr from the x-ray machine indicated the x-rays were taken, and the process was soon over. Maggie said a short prayer and proceeded with the internal examination by making a Y shaped incision into the baby's chest.

Sheriff Ronny watched the entire examination from Maggie's office, and when the three hour autopsy was concluded, he poured three mugs of coffee, sat on a high office stool, and patiently waited for Maggie's preliminary report.

Maggie pulled off the sweat soaked surgery cap, "Ronny, I have to say, that was most sensitive autopsy I have ever conducted." She dropped the surgical gown into a metal container, placed her hand on Mary's shoulder, "Mary is a real pro, and she's welcome to assist me anytime." Maggie gulped some of the black coffee, "Ronny, you know how to really treat a lady, hot black coffee." The room fell quiet for a few minutes. Maggie cleared a few empty boxes from a small sofa, found a comfortable spot to sit and said, "Sheriff, for the record, I can give you a preliminary autopsy report with more detailed and conclusive findings to follow. Baby Doe is of Hispanic descent, about two to three hours old and, from my experience, her mother was a drug addict, possibly fentanyl. She was deceased when she entered the water. We're sending blood samples to a lab and requesting a DNA report. The DNA report, hopefully, will ID the parents. There was foliage debris lodged in her mouth. The foliage might indicate where the child was dropped into the creek. I wish I could be more elaborate but, for now, that's all we have."

"Actually, I didn't think we would have that much information," Ronny said.

Maggie finished her coffee and parked her empty mug on a nearby table, "Ronny, are there any migrant work camps around Wilson County?"

"Not that I'm aware of, "Ronny replied. "We're not an agricultural community, and there's no requirement for seasonal labor. In fact, I've never seen any Hispanics in our town."

"I have. It was about a week ago when I saw a man who was Spanish purchasing some over the counter meds in Harry's Drugs," Mary stated.

"Did you happen to see what the man was driving," the Sheriff asked.

"Yes, it was an extra-long black van. You know, the type that can handle ten or twelve passengers," Mary replied. She neatly folded her soiled scrubs, and dropped them into the metal container. "I could probably identify that van if I see it again."

Maggie asked, "Ronny, are you thinking what I'm thinking?"

"Yes, I am. I'm going to stop by John's place, talk with him, and your husband. I'm going to need all the help I can muster."

"Dr. Lester, if you don't need me, I'm going to check out," Mary said.

Maggie waited for Mary to leave the room, "Ronny, we're going to burn up some steaks on the grill tonight, would you like to join us?"

"Thank you, but I don't want to impose. I'm sure, after the day you've had here, you would like to get comfortable and let your hair down with adult beverages."

"It's absolutely no imposition however; while you're sipping some of that adult beverage, you can talk to Jake about the possibility of a recon mission. He and his father can snoop around the place without a 'show cause' order."

It was late in the afternoon, the day Maggie performed the autopsy on Baby Doe, when she received a call on her car phone from the Hospital Lab Technician. "Dr. Lester, the results of the DNA test indicated no match on record to ID the mother of the child. The test also confirms your assumption that the baby had a

171

high level of Fentanyl in her system, and she died of an overdose. Is there anything more we can do for you?"

"No thank you," Maggie replied. She looked up the road and saw John turning into the driveway with his pickup truck with Jake sitting in the passenger seat looking at a map. "Humph, they hardly stopped at the Whistling Pines gate. I wonder what those guys have been up to."

The two men climbed out of the truck, gave Maggie a short wave, and watched her parked next to them, "Hi Maggie." John noticed a grim look on her face. "Jake, something's up."

"I received the lab report from the hospital on Baby Doe. They found no match to the DNA, in addition they found a high level of Fentanyl in her blood." In a moment of grief, she covered her face, "That little baby died from an overdose."

Jake put his arms around Maggie, and held her tight. "We're going to get the bastards."

23

The warm July light drizzle of rain hindered the usual scenic sunrise at the Whispering Pines Lodge. Jake and his father stood on the back porch reviewing their immediate plans to reconnoiter the area around the talc mine. The object of the trip, find a strategic location to place two remote, night vision cameras, and return to the lodge without being detected.

Jake checked his watch, "It's six thirty. It's about a four mile hike through the thick part of the woods. We better leave now."

"I agree," John said. He flipped the hood of his rain jacket over his head, and started down the stairs. "This rain will help keep our movement quiet while he walked through the underbrush."

"It took a few drinks and a steak dinner last night to convince Ronny we could work better without being deputized," Jake remarked.

"I think you're right, but I have this funny feeling he has our backs as we speak." John slowed their pace down, held his hand out, stopped, and whispered, "Listen."

The two men stood motionless, straining their ears to ascertain what the strange reverberating sound is and where it was coming from. They carefully crouched behind a large pine tree and recorded the strange sound for several minutes until it stopped. John shook his head and whispered, "Let's move on. We don't have much farther to go."

The rain had stopped before they reached the area, about twenty five yards from the mine, where they wanted to place the cameras. Jake shimmied up a short tree, started to anchor one of the cameras to the crotch of the tree, when he saw two men standing by the mine gate. He instantly hugged the main stem of the tree, pushed a small branch from his face, remained motionless, and listened to the men talk as they puffed on their stinking cigars. His Spanish was a little rusty; nevertheless, he remembered enough of the language to catch the gist of the conversation. The two men neatly placed their partly used cigars on a wall leading to the entrance and left the scene. Jake slid down the tree, and found his father waiting behind a wild berry bush.

"Dad, let's get outta here."

"Hold on a minute. I'm getting some of these berries for your wife."

It was late afternoon when the two men came walking down the path leading to the lodge. They saw Ronny's personal car parked in the driveway and Ronny on the back porch resting in John's favorite rocking chair. John shouted, "Hey Ronny, is your life insurance paid up?"

"Sorry, John, I couldn't resist. That's one hell of a rocking chair," Ronny laughed out loud. "I know you guys had a heck of a day in the woods."

"Yeah, we did," Jake replied. He took off his knapsack and set it on the porch steps. "We were able to get up close to the mine and caught some conversation from two of the workers."

Ronny reached into a brown paper bag and said, "Why don't we talk about it while we taste some of this twelve year old, single malt scotch."

"I've got some berries for Maggie. I'll take them in and I'll be back with some glasses," John said.

Jake and his father had known Lonny long enough to know that Ronny had a purpose for the scotch, other than a social meeting and, as soon as John came out of the lodge with the glasses, Lonny would pour the scotch, and wait for one of them to volunteer their accomplishments for the entire day.

John came out of the lodge the carrying glasses and Maggie was right behind him with a charcuterie board loaded with cheese and crackers.

Jake took a chunk of cheese from the tray, leaned his butt against the porch railing, and took a sip of scotch. "Lonny, we were setting up our cameras close to the mine's entrance, and when I was mounting a camera in a tree, I overheard two heavily armed men talking in Spanish. They said, 'We got more bitches coming tomorrow night. That makes two hundred this week.' Lonny, they're not pushing Fentanyl from the mine, they're human trafficking from that location."

"You're sure of that?" Ronny asked, anxiously.

"We are absolutely sure," John replied. "The camera Jake positioned in the tree will provide us with live action."

Jake remarked, "Ronny, you can position your people around the perimeter of the mine entrance, catch the bad guys when they try to escape and, with a little bit of luck, we might catch a big fish."

"Jake, it's one in the morning, fifty of my people have been out here for three hours, and there's no sign of trucks or any kind of vehicles. I think we should scrub the operation. Whatta ya think?" Lonny   asked.

"I know, Lonny. I don't understand why there's no activity. The night is perfect, no moon, no rain, and the temperature is balmy. I think we should give it another hour." Jake replied. "Hold on. I think I hear something like truck engines." He looked through the night vision binoculars and saw an eighteen wheeler inching its way through the crater size pot holes in the makeshift road. "Lonny, this is it."

Lonny   whispered into a handheld radio, "Listen up, people. We have company in an eighteen wheeler approaching the entrance to the mine. The suspects will be heavily armed and dangerous. When the truck gets to the mining office building, where we believe the captives are being held, I will give the signal to move in."

"That's a pretty big truck for ten people." Jake jacked a round into the chamber of his thirty-thirty rifle, and looked intently at the large truck as it stopped at the gate. He whispered, "Ronny, I see four men getting out of the truck's cab, and three men and a woman jumping out of the trailer."

"Yeah, I see them, and they all have automatic, long barrel weapons."

The truck continued in the direction of the mining office building and stopped when the truck's tailgate pulled even with the building's double doors. The driver turned off the engine and jumped out of the cab. One of the guards reached up to the trailer doors, shoved the door lever to one side, rammed into the open position, and swung the doors wide open.

"Lonny, check it out. We have five, maybe six men coming out of the mine shaft shack. Shit, they're armed." Jake inched forward for a better look. "We have women climbing out of the trailer."

"Yeah, some of them look to be about twelve years old. I've seen enough." Ronny shouted into his mic, "Go, go, go. They're armed, they're armed."

Jake sprinted to the gate and knocked the gate guard on his ass. His front line stint in Afghanistan flashed through his mind, remembering assault procedures, and he brought his weapon up to strong point position. He glanced around and saw a large contingent of law enforcement officers running a few feet to his right and left. "Let's get these bastards." When they stormed the office building, one of the guards pointed his weapon at a Deputy Sheriff and, before he could fire his weapon, the Deputy smacked him in the chin with his rifle butt. The skirmish was over before it got started.

Ronny declared, "We have control. Now, where are the women and children?"

Jake noticed all the guards constantly glimpsing in the direction of a man with a big cigar in his mouth. He recognized the man from the day he and his dad were positioning cameras. "You speak English?"

The man slipped the cigar from his wet lips, "Sure, I speak English," he replied, in broken English. He stuck the cigar back into his mouth and slurred, "So what?"

"I'm going to ask this question once, and only once. Where are the women and children, you're getting ready to sell?"

"You must think I'm a fool. Do you see those cameras? He pointed to three cameras, each one was mounted on tall wooden poles and focused on the enclosure. My boss is watching us right now." He cackled, "Amigo, if I tell you what you want to know, I'm dead."

"I really don't care if you live or die." Jake stepped close to the man, "What's your name?"

"José. Why do you want to know?"

"José." Jake put his arm around José's rotund shoulder. "Walk with me, away from the cameras, while we talk." José tried to pull away from Jake. Jake squeezed José's trapezius muscle, the neck and shoulder muscle, rendering him helpless. "Listen you fat shit. We're going to walk together for a few minutes and, in those few minutes, you're going to tell me where you're hiding those people."

"Whatta ya goin to do to me? You think you can scare me? I'm not telling you shit."

Jake released his grip on José, stepped away from him, shook his hand, looked up at the cameras, and smiled, "Thank you for your help."

"They're going to kill me," José shouted.

"No, they won't kill you, the Sheriff will." Jake stepped behind Ronny, "I don't want to get any of your blood and brain matter on me."

Ronny pulled a large caliber, long barrel pistol, from his ankle holster, placed the barrel against   José's temple, "One, two." When he pulled the hammer back, it made a distinctive clicking sound. three."

José screamed, "Don shoot…don shoot. They're in the mine, second level. We have people here, and some drugs. You gotta protect me. Please, you gotta protect me from those people."

"Who do you work for?" Jake asked.

"I don't know. I don't see him. He's in the city. He's the boss…he sells people and drugs," José replied.

"What city?" Jake asked

"Lind City. Now please, put the handcuffs on me."

"Where in Lind City?" Jake asked.

"I donno."

Lonny ordered his Deputies, "Get the women and children from that mine, make them comfortable, and tell the volunteers to come in with food and blankets."

"Ronny, were you really going to shoot that guy?" Jake asked.

Lonny smirked, "Nah, the weapon was empty. By the way, you didn't believe his story about not knowing his boss?"

"No, I didn't believe what he said. It's what he didn't say tells me his boss, who sells people and drugs, is well known."

24

It was late evening when Jake and Maggie drove onto their neighborhood street and, the minute they saw their home, a sense of great relief came over them. Jake drove into their driveway, where they sat for a few seconds, thought how fortunate they came from good homes, with understanding parents and no worries. The priority in their lives will focus on finding the head of the snake and cut it off. The task would not be easy, their mission will not falter, and, through it all, their family values would not be altered.

Maggie checked all the messages on the phone and found one significant message left by John Harper. It was dated this afternoon. "Jake, contact me as soon as possible."

"Jake, did you hear the message? Maggie asked. "I'm exhausted, I'm going to get comfortable."

"I wonder why he didn't call on my cell." Jake picked up the phone, raised it to his ear, and put it back down. It's too late. I'll call him in the morning. Besides, after what went down a few weeks ago with him and his boss, I don't know if I should return his call."

"I'd like to see how our place at the lake is coming along." Maggie appeared in a fluffy bathrobe. "I don't think he has any control over what his boss does. Maybe you can call him on the way to the lake."

"I'm going to have a glass of wine and watch the news for a little while." Jake turned on the TV, took a of sip wine and shouted, "Holy crap. Maggie, you gotta see the headlines on TV." He turned up the sound.

"What's going on?" Oh my God." Maggie sat on the sofa and listened intently.

The news anchorman described how a large drug and human trafficking ring was successfully raided in Wilson County. The raid was spearheaded by Private Investigator, Jake Spencer. The statement was released by Sheriff Ronny Plank, of the Wilson County Sheriff's Department. The raid took place yesterday in the early morning hours. An estimated two hundred women and young girls were set free from what is called the largest single raid in this area.

Jake lowered the TV volume, "Ronny gave me all the credit. That's not right." His cell phone rang and the CID red Ronny Plank. "Hello, Ronny."

"Jake, did you and Maggie see the news on TV? I didn't think you would mind if I gave you the credit for the bust. After all, you did all the work, and your father agreed with me. Jake, I gotta run. Wilson County thanks you. You've been up for twenty-four hours. Get some sleep."

Jake looked bewildered. "Maggie."

"I know. The notoriety carries a double edge sword. We could use the business, then again, at what cost? She touched the 'do not disturb numbers' on the landline. "That should take care of the people we don't know. We better screen our cell phone calls, at least for now."

"John's message on the phone must be…" Jake slipped off his shoes and socks, turned off his cell phone, leaned back in his recliner, and fell into a deep sleep.

Jake rubbed his eyes and looked around the family room. He realized he had slept the night away in the recliner and tried to maneuver his body into a sitting position. He could smell the aroma of brewing coffee wafting from the kitchen, and heard the hot water nob squeak in the master bedroom shower, as Maggie turned the water off. He sighed, "Coffee." He wandered into the kitchen, filled a mug to brim with black coffee, and looked at the wall clock. "Maggie, it's five a.m... I need some coffee and nourishment."

Maggie shouted from the bedroom, "I received a text last night from John Harper. He said it's very important, and he needs to talk with us in person. I didn't think we should see him at our office. He will be here early this morning."

"Humph."

"Jake, I didn't hear you. What did you say?"

Jake turned on the TV as the three anchor news people, two men and one woman, started commenting on the morning news cycle. It was the same narrative as last night's late news cycle covering the human trafficking raid. "I better shower and get dressed."

Jake stepped into the shower and adjusted the water temperature. He started to ask himself questions and strategize while he stood under the warm flow of water. This morning's shower was going to be a real think tank. He remembered Consuela Delgado's dying words, "Trust no one…Cartel is everywhere." Why did Bonnie Goodwin, a building janitor, walk in from nowhere and volunteer to help us settle the office. Is Bonnie really who she says she is? Why is it a high priority with the FBI to send John Harper, a Senior Special FBI Agent, to talk with me and Maggie? It seems odd for a politician, like Sheriff Ronny Plank, to give me all the credit for the Cartel's Human Trafficking bust. Jake turned off the water and scratched his chest. The Cartel knows I'm going after their drug business in Lind City. The Cartel thought they had me dead once. Why haven't they tried to kill me again?

"Jake, are you in the shower thinking again? John will be here in a few minutes."

 Jake refilled his mug with coffee. "I'm going to take my coffee out on the patio. When he shows up, I'm sure the media will be all over him for a statement. Bring him to the patio."

"John's a big man. He can handle the media," Maggie commented.

"I don't know why John wanted to meet with us. Whatever it is, I think it will be less formal on the patio." Jake sat in his lounge chair and started to take in the clear warm sunny morning, when he heard John's voice in the living room. "John, I'm on the patio."

"I pulled John away from the media before they had a chance to accost him," Maggie said.

"Hi Jake, it's good to see you. I think I spotted a drone circling your house a few minutes ago," John declared.

"Good to see you too. With all the trees in our yard, the drones will have a difficult time getting videos."

"Jake, I know we left each other on a sour note. I apologize for what went down that day. I'd like to get right to the point. But first, would it be possible for you and I to speak alone?"

Jake's face became flush, and his solemn stare was armor piercing, "That was strike two, John. Whatever you have to say, you can say it in front of Maggie."

"If you insist. I'm going to take you back to the night when you were beaten and dropped in a ditch. A person walked up to you, pointed a pistol at you and, instead of killing you, left you lying there with a superficial wound. The superficial wound was no mistake. The person who shot you was a marksman with all hand guns and long barrel weapons."

"Was... a marksman?" Jake asked. "You mean the person who saved my life is dead."

"You don't know the person and you will never know the person's identity. Suffice it to say, the person was a paid informant, performing a job by shadowing a person of interest, much like the job Marshal Dunkin offered you. The mission was to infiltrate the Cartel's operating groups, specifically the drug producers, suppliers, and distributors."

"You keep referring to the paid informant or, should I say Independent Contractor, as a person. Was the IC a male or female?" Jake asked.

"Female," John replied.

"Why are you sharing this information with us?" Maggie asked.

John hesitated, "It's a well-known fact your interest in life, or mission, if you will, is to bring down the Cartel's drug business in Lind City. She was in the process of gaining their trust as a member of their local crew when they somehow discovered she was an IC for the Feds. The Cartel wasted no time. She was off the grid before anyone missed her. Marshal sent me as his spokesman to, first, apologize for his behavior and second, ask you if you would consider working with the FBI as an Independent Consultant Investigator, ICI, with no interference from the FBI. You will report directly to Marshal. If you accept the position, he would, within reason, approve your compensation and expenses."

"John, you and I go back to the days in Afghanistan. You're blowing smoke up my ass. Why has Marshal changed his mind and opened the federal purse strings? Why haven't you answered Maggie's question. Why are you sharing the information with us?" Jake asked, brazenly.

"Jake, I'm not blowing smoke up your ass, and I don't know why Marshal changed his point of view. I can tell you there was a high-level meeting in the Director's office with 'a need to know' security level and I wasn't in the loop. When Marshal came back from the meeting, he gave me a directive to see you ASAP."

"Jake stood, walked to the edge of the patio, turned, and looked John straight in the eye. "When does your boss need an answer?"

"He would like me to leave here with an answer today. It's nine a.m. I can wait a few hours."

"Maggie and I are a team, and will be compensated accordingly. Is that a problem?"

"No problem," John replied, without hesitation.

"We'll have an answer for you today."

Jake watched John push his way through the media crowd, climb into a black SUV, and speed away. "Maggie, I'm leaning toward accepting Marshal's offer, what do you think?"

"You sound apprehensive. I know when something's bothering you. I could tell by your body language. When John said he wasn't in the loop, you got that strange look on your face."

"Right, John is a Senior Special Agent, a step away from a Deputy Director, and he wasn't in the loop. Why are we reporting to Marshal instead of John?"

"Yeah, I understand what you're saying, and it does seem odd. Then again, let's face facts, we need the money. We can work from our own office, build our client list and, if things turn South, we can bail out without any ramifications."

"That sounds like a vote for yes, and I agree. I'll give John a call, let him know we have an agreement, and we can start immediately."

"Wait, don't call him yet. There's been something on my mind ever since Lonny mentioned there was a part time opening for an ME in Wilson County…"

Jake interrupted, "And you want to continue your profession as a part time ME, am I right?"

"Right, I have a PI license, with very little experience, and I would be holding you back. If Ronny calls me for a case, I'm sure your Dad would let me stay overnight at his place." Jake smiled, "I was wondering when you would bring the conversation up. I saw your eyes light up when Lonny mentioned the opening was available. You are a master at your profession and there's no way I would stand in your way. You'll be home most of the time and, when I need your expertise, I can literally reach out and touch you."

"There's something very puzzling on my mind. When I looked out the window this morning and saw all the major media people standing around waiting for a statement from you, I didn't see Joan Fetter among them. You would think Joan would have personally called you. After all, you did promise her a lead story when something big happened."

"Yeah, your right. I wonder what happened."

25

John Harper pushed the elevator button for the twenty third floor of the FBI Headquarters located at twenty six, Federal Plaza, in New York City. The elevator bell rang, the door slid open he switched his briefcase to his other hand and stepped into the elevator car. He seemed oblivious to the people who packed the elevator with him as he shuffled sideways to allow the last person standing in the hall to enter. He placed the heavy briefcase on the floor next to a similar briefcase and waited for the elevator to reach his floor. The new elevator system deposited him at the twenty third floor within a few seconds where the people rushed out of the elevator, into the hall, and went on their way to the FBI offices. John reached down, pick up a briefcase, and scurried on his way to his office.

"Good morning, John" his secretary said, with enthusiasm.

"Good morning."

"Director Marshal asked me to tell you he wanted to meet with you in the conference room as soon as you came in this morning."

"Did he give you an agenda?"

"No Sir, but he seemed a bit concerned."

John continued into his office, entered the combination to the lock, flopped the briefcase on the desk, quickly unzipped the top compartment, and looked at the contents. "Good."

When John entered the conference room, he was surprised to see two people waiting for him including Marshal. He found an open seat, and sat down. The room was silent for several minutes before Marshal started a whispered conversation with the man next to him. John didn't know or recognize the man. Marshal whispered for a few seconds and looked at John.

"John, we notice you have a small scar on your face. You must have been out with a wild lady last night," Marshal laughed. He passed a manila folder to John.

"I had a tough night with my cat last night, and I got the worst of the deal. Now that we're all looking at each other, what's in the folder? "

"Okay, sure, go ahead and open it. You might be surprised, "Marshal said.

"I can't stand the suspense," John, uttered. He briefly looked at the two men and noticed the grim faces staring at him. He opened the manila folder and saw a title page labeled, 'Project C.' "What's 'Project C'?" He flipped open the first page and recognized the format of FBI transfer form with his name typed at the top of the page. "What's this?"

"The Director wants you to act as the FBI Liaison with your Mexican counterpart. You will be located off the grid in a small Texas town called Salineno, Texas. The population is two hundred and three. The town is so insignificant, the Cartel has no problem smuggling drugs across the border. There's no law enforcement within two hundred miles," Marshal replied.

"There are two hundred and two citizens in this town, an army of Cartel members sliding through town loaded with, most likely, Fentanyl, and I'm supposed to…" John paused. And, what did I do to deserve this great honor?" he asked, sarcastically.

Marshal remained silent, gave John a frown, picked up the interoffice phone line, and asked, "Can you please bring John's briefcase into the conference room?" He placed the phone back in the cradle, and slipped back a few inches away from the table. John's secretary rapped on the door, entered the room, placed he briefcase in front of Marshal, and left the room as quickly as she entered. He keyed in the briefcase combination and, with a testier cat smile, opened the brief. His eyes widened with disgust and said, "Shit."

John knew exactly why Marshal performed a surprise briefcase inspection. The Deputy Directors have the combination to all their subordinates' briefcases and are allowed to surprise inspect the contents. "What's the problem?" John asked.

Marshal slammed the cover down, and slid the briefcase over to John, "No problem."

John perused the transfer orders and noticed the date of transfer section of the document was blank. "Who is my liaison, and when am I supposed to start my new assignment?"

"You will leave New York City tomorrow morning, via an FBI jet, and you'll meet your liaison when the jet lands. John, as always, this is top secret. If knowledge of 'Project C' leaked out, the operation would have to be aborted, millions of tax dollars would go down the drain and, not to mention, the Cartel would change their MO. Do you have any questions?"

John replied, "Yes, I have one question. Who the hell is the man sitting next to you, and why is he in a Top Secret meeting?"

"Well alleluia, I was wondering when you were going to ask that question, "Marshal replied, mockingly. He passed another manila folder in front of John. "Meet Terrance Cantrell. Take a look at his dossier. You can read it now. I want it back before you leave this conference room."

John started reading the type written ambiguous paperwork, flipped a few pages of the folder's contents, not computer produced, absent of the FBI embossed emblem on the letterhead, looked at them for a few minutes, and closed the file. "So, Terrance Cantrell is a contract hit man, aka Terry, slash bodyguard who's a Mexican with a gringo name. Why do I need a man with such talent babysitting me?"

"Don't be a wise ass," Marshal shouted.

Terry said, "Marshal, maybe I can explain the assignment. John, the town of Salineno, Texas, might be a small jerk town to you however, the Cartel view this place as a logistics heaven, and will kill anyone who might and I repeat, might, interfere with the movement of thousands of pounds of bulk drugs distend for mixing in the U.S."

Marshal chimed in, "Although you're not of Mexican descent; your dark skin color, facial features, and your ability to speak fluent Spanish will keep you alive longer than the average bear. Terry here, as you see by his dossier, is the best of the best at his trade. He will never be more than a few feet away from you at all times, yes, even when you're sleeping. Your mission will be, blend in with the locals, and report every movement the Cartel makes through the town. They move freely around Salineno without difficulty and don't give a shit about killing anyone who gets in their way."

"Right, it's a small town and everyone knows everybody, even the Cartel. How am I supposed to show up in the town and blend in?" John asked.

Marshal replied, "You'll be staying with Marta Spinoza. You're her stepbrother who's been living in Venezuela, and you are visiting for her a while after the death of your wife. We'll fill in the blanks before you land in Mexico. You have less than twenty four hours before your plane leaves New York City. If I were you, I would take the time to tie up whatever loose ends you have in your private life, because your private life ends the minute you walk out this door. Don't pack any clothes. You will receive a complete wardrobe befitting the local dress when you get on the plane. Once you're on the plane, change into those clothes. When you report your findings to my office, and only to my office, you will use the FBI code words using the Spanish language."

John stood, picked up his briefcase, backed way form the conference table, and started to walk toward the door.

"John, you'll have no use for your briefcase, leave it here. Give me your cell phone." Marshal handed John a miniature cell phone. "Use this phone, and only this phone. This is a top secret line directly to me, and use it when you are in dire situations."

John's immediate thought process, Marshal was paving the way for him to have a one way trip to Mexico. If the Cartel doesn't off him, Terry Cantrell will. He continued toward the conference room door and, like an intricate starting mechanism, Terry was on his feet and standing next to him. "Where do you stand when I have to relieve myself in a men's restroom?"

"Consider me a part of your back, and watching everything behind you. If you're using a stall to take a dump, I'll be standing there with my back to the stall door. Like Marshal said, I'll never be more than a few feet away from you."

"What happens when you…?"

"You read my dossier. Don't worry about me," Terry replied. "There's an FBI plane waiting to take us to Mexico. We'll leave from the back door to our parking garage. When we get to the car, you'll get in the back seat with me. There will be a change of appropriate clothes on the plane."

"I assume all my friends and contacts will get some explanation of my whereabouts?"

"Yes, that's all been taken care of."

John sat quietly in his window seat thinking of the possible ways his demise would come about. He viewed the colorful clothes he was wearing as the epitome of stupidity by the FBI to fabricate some kind of accident while he was in this undercover costume. He glanced at Terry, who was sitting in the seat next to him, with his hand wrapped around a glass of orange juice, and reading last years' Time Magazine. My God, even his fingers have muscles. He leaned his head against the plane's window and slipped into a deep sleep. He was rudely awakened from what seemed like a few minutes nap by a nudge in the shoulder from Terry.

"Wake up. The captain has the seat belt sign on. We're about to land in a Government Airport about fifty miles from Salineno, Texas. The rest of the trip will be by Range Rover." Terry handed John a semi-automatic long barrel weapon. "We're headed into Cartel territory. Hang on to this and don't use it unless I tell you."

"Is it that bad here?" John asked, with a smirk.

Terry didn't answer John's question. "When we deplane, run right to the vehicle. Don't even stop to fart. Jump in and buckle up. The driver's priority is to, get us in to the open desert as fast as possible before we get popped off by some Cartel sniper wannabe. There could be Cartel snipers waiting for us as we deplane. Do you understand the gravity of this situation?"

"Yes. If this area is so dangerous, why isn't my weapon loaded? I used a weapon similar to this in Afghanistan before you graduated from high school."

"I'll explain when we get into the desert. The plane is coming to a stop, stay close to me and, as soon as the door opens, run for the Range Rover."

John and Terry were in the Range Rover and on their way into the desert without a shot being fired. Terry said, "Now relax, we have about an hour drive to the safe house."

John sat back, pushed the air conditioner vent toward his chest, and looked out the window. As he gazed at the scenery, he marveled at the large shadows on the sand from the Saguaros cactus. His keen sense of direction revealed the shadows were in the wrong position for their destination. He thought, 'shit we're headed in the wrong direction.' The facts were falling into place. The secret and expedited deployment to an obscure location on the map, a small boarder town, a top secret cell phone, and an empty firearm. 'They found out I'm working for the Cartel. They're going to make me disappear somewhere in the desert, and blame it on the bad guys.' He looked at Terry, the best of the best in his field, sitting next to him sound asleep. The driver was completely preoccupied with navigating on a half assed desert road and time was of the essence. He swiftly reached across the seat, anchored Terry's head with his right hand, drew his left hand under Terry's chin, and, with one powerful jerk, snapped his victim's neck. The sweat from the action streamed down his face and onto his shirt. The driver was unaware of the split second act of violence which took place behind him and continued to press on to the obscure destination. John needed the vehicle to escape and, somehow, he had to disable the driver without damaging the Range Rover. The element of surprise was on his side. He grabbed Terry's pistol from the leather holster, "Driver, I gotta pee." When the driver stopped the vehicle, he jumped from the back seat, pulled open the driver's door, threw the driver to the ground, and pumped one nine millimeter round into the driver's head. He returned to the back seat where Terry lay dead. He quickly changed into Terry's clothes, reached into the blue jean's pocket, and retrieved a civilian cell phone with enough cell bars to make contact. "It's me, and I'm in deep shit. They're on to me. Check this phone's GPS for my location, and get me the hell out of here. I'll explain everything when I see you." He thought, 'I gotta get rid of this vehicle. The GPS in the car will give my location to the FBI.'

"You're in Arizona, about fifty miles South of Interstate four, and West of Scottsdale."

John screamed into the phone, "What the hell do you mean I'm in Arizona?"

John sped from the scene, looked into the rearview mirror, saw the two dead men laying in the hot desert sun, and mumbled, "buzzard meat." He drove the fifty miles to Scottsdale, dumped the vehicle at a truck stop, and disappeared into a nearby park.

Marshal was walking to a meeting with two other Deputy Directors in the main hall of the FBI building when he was approached by one of his aides. "Sir, excuse me, I have a message from our man in the Arizona office."

"Not now. Can't you see I'm on my way to a meeting?" Marshal asked, angrily.

"Sir, it's of Top Secret importance. He needs to speak with you immediately."

"Shit, okay." Marshal retrieved his cell phone from his vest pocket and touched the Arizona hotline key. "It's me. This better be dammed good," he growled.

"The subject is in the wind and two agents are dead. One of the agents was found nude. The subject traded clothes and shoes with one of the deceased. We have no active commutation or tracking devices on the subject."

"Son of a bitch, he knows we were going to eliminate him, and now he's a dangerous rogue on the loose. He's smart enough to know all the rules of engagement when it comes to tracking someone. Hell, he wrote the training procedures. We need to keep a lid on this."

"Sir, it's too late. One of the news agencies picked it up on a local police frequency."

"Okay, okay, I'll think of something. Don't do shit until I get back to you, and absolutely no comments when the media catches up to you."

26

Maggie stepped from the front door of their Lind City residence, picked up the morning paper, and read the large black print headline, which covered the entire front page, 'Two Undercover Special FBI Agents Brutally Murdered by the Mexican Cartel in the Arizona Desert.' She stood in the doorway scanning the smaller print desperately looking for the agent's names. "Jake," she shouted, as she rushed back into the house. "Jake, you have to see this. There's no mention of the agents' names."

Jake read the headlines, nonchalantly tossed the newspaper onto the kitchen counter, and remarked, "No names mean a cover up. The FBI knows where every one of their agents are at all times, even the undercover people. I hope none of my friends were involved. Which reminds me, at his request, I have to touch base with Marshal on a video call. I assume after the call I'll be independent and able to work from our office."

"Have you thought of asking Bonnie Goodwin about the possibility of joining our PI firm?"

"Yes, she's a perfect fit for us. I did a background check on her, and her credentials make me wonder why she's a custodian in an office building. She has five years experience in a small town Sheriff's Department, a degree in Psychology, and is an expert in telephone line transmission. I'll ask her today at the office."

"I'm leaving for the Wilson County Sheriff's office. I received a text from Ronny this morning. There was, what they think, a DWI fatality in Wilson County. I'll be back after I'm through with the autopsy, and my statement to the Wilson County AG. When you have a chance, let me know how your video meeting with Marshal went." She gave Jake a kiss, and went out the door.

At precisely nine a.m., Jake's new FBI laptop lit up with an alert of an incoming video meeting. The entire screen was covered with a picture of the FBI Shield, Marshal's full name and position across the middle of the shield, and, within seconds, the shield disappeared and Marshal, sitting at his desk, appeared. "Jake, can you see me?"

"Yes, your reception is very clear. Good morning."

"Good morning, I'll come right to the point. First, this may be the one and only time we meet by teleview. As we agreed, you will be on your own to search out and find the people responsible for the mixing, distribution of drugs in your area, and report your findings to me. How you accomplish this task is entirely at your discretion. Do you understand, you are in no way a member of the FBI?"

"Yes, I understand."

"Jake, there's one more thing, and this is Top Secret. You've likely read the morning newspaper or seen it on TV about the two undercover FBI agents found murdered by the Mexican Cartel in the Arizona desert. The report was given by the head of our FBI Public Relations Department. The real report by our people in Phoenix, and censored by the Director of the FBI, himself,…a rogue FBI agent actually murdered those agents. The rogue agent is John Harper. The two murdered agents were Terrance Cantrell, John's bodyguard, and the driver, Phillipe Gargonza."

Jake was crushed by the news and temporarily without words, but managed to retain a stoic facial expression. One of his friends, who he served with in Afghanistan, and longtime personal friend, is accused of being a rogue agent and murderer. He knew there had to be more to the story than Marshal was telling him and, for the time being, he had to roll with Marshal's statement. Jake replied, "It is what it is."

The session was over and the screen went blank. Jake turned off the laptop and stored it in the broom closet. He knew, without a doubt and his sense of paranoia, the laptop would never be turned off. The timing of the media's story was two days past the actual alleged crime. If John was responsible for the two agent's death, why did he resort to murder when he could have just as easily left them in the desert? John must have been in very deep shit.

Jake wanted to talk with Teddy Conway about John's possible involvement in the murder of the two agents. He was certain all his phones including the new office phones, were tapped by the FBI. He went into his home office, took out one of the burn phones from the safe, and went out to the patio, "Teddy, I'm on a burn phone, and our conversation can't be repeated. Did you hear about the two FBI agents getting murdered in the desert by a rogue agent?"

"I don't repeat anything. Yeah, I heard. Do we know the rogue agent?"

"John Harper!"

"John Harper? Jake, that guy is as straight as an arrow. Who told you it was Harper?"

"The Deputy Director of the FBI, Marshal Dunkin. He's the guy who hired me to do some contract investigating for the FBI. Teddy, if the FBI finds him, they won't apprehend him, they will kill him, and call it a 'Rightful Shoot'. The real story will never be told."

"What do you suggest we do? "Teddy asked.

"I don't know. There was a short pause in the conversation. "I wanted to give you a heads up. We can't do anything until he contacts one of us. I've got to run. Let's keep in touch."

It was almost noon when Jake arrived at his new office and found Bonnie putting the finishing touches on a contact file. He glanced around the two room office and thought this place is way too neat. "Hi Bonnie, I'm glad to see you here. The place looks great."

"I wanted to make the place as orderly as possible just in case we get a walk in client. I hope you don't mind."

"I don't mind at all. There is one thing I'd like to talk about. Maggie and I read your profile online and we were impressed with your accomplishments. Would you consider an Office Manager's position with us?"

"Well, I've been retired for a while and life is boring. I would be honored to work for a startup detective agency. When would you like me to start?"

"Aren't you going to ask me about a salary?"

"No, I should pay you for getting me out of my apartment," Bonnie replied, with a smile. "Oh, while I think of it, there were two men here this morning working on the building telephone lines. I think they were legit. They showed me their telephone employee badges. I looked out the window and saw a telephone company van parked in front of the building."

"Did they do anything to our phones?"

"No. They were here about ten minutes. They attached a couple of wires with alligator clips to the incoming phone lines, looked at a portable meter, and left the office. I watched them leave the building hop into the van, and motor away."

"That's interesting. We didn't receive a notice from the phone company about a problem with the phone lines. Would you remember the men's faces if you saw them again?"

"Maybe. I don't remember faces very well, and they were only here for ten minutes. However, I did manage to get videos of them with my laptop camera." Bonnie grinned, "Will that do?"

Jake shook his head, "Yes that will do just fine." He gave Bonnie a hand gesture to meet him in the building lobby.

Jake took the elevator, made it to the lobby before Bonnie, ordered two coffees at the coffee bar and waited for her arrival. He was startled by Bonnie's voice behind him.

"Hi, I took the stairs. Thanks for the coffee. I'm sure there was a good reason for meeting in the lobby instead of talking in the office."

"Until I'm certain those two men were telephone company employees, we should discuss the new client we have out of the bugs hearing range. We have an Independent Consultant's agreement with the FBI and, if my instincts are correct, those two guys who came into the office this morning, are FBI people."

"So, they weren't checking phone lines, they were actually planting bugs," Bonnie surmised.

"Right, so until I know one way or the other, we will remember Big Brothers' in the office."

"Jake, I already love this job."

27

A man was on his knees meticulously measuring each cinder block of a planned vegetable garden. He looked around to see if he was being watched, and placed another row of blocks on the garden wall. He tapped the blocks with a rubber mallet making certain they were precisely the length of the body he was going to place into the four foot deep garden. He stood looked around, pulled the back of his blue jeans up, moved another block to the end of the wall, and, with extreme care, measured the width of the structure. He picked up a shovel, slammed it into the dirt pile, bent down, removed some of the pebbles under the blocks, poured the shovelful of dirt under a block, and placed a metal level on the top row. He continued the process until the dimensions of his garden were perfect. The site became the start of a gruesome graveyard for an undercover FBI Agent. His concentration was interrupted by his neighbor's voice.

"Sam, what the hell are you going to grow in that big ass garden? You know nothing grows out here in the middle of nowhere. Hell, the desert mice will eat everything you plant before it grows."

Sam thought, 'What a jerk ass neighbor,' and replied with a grin, "Yeah, I know. I brought in some cinderblocks, high grade top soil, and some wire mesh for the top. I'm going to pour some concrete for the base so the mice can't get under my veggies." He growled under his breath, 'maybe I should plant that shit head with the agent.'

It was Monday night, eight p.m., when Sam saw the bright sign off the highway, Scottsdale Truck Stop, and parked next to the restaurant entrance door. The hour drive from his off the grid home, through the steaming hot desert to his rendezvous point with John, gave him a powerful thirst for a shot of bourbon and a beer chaser. He made his way to the nearest barstool and ordered exactly what he had in mind. The shot of Jack bourbon went down with a little bight until he sipped some of the draught beer. He never met John Harper and had to rely on the description sent to him in a text message. The large mirror behind the bar was perfect for him to size up the other patrons and look for Harper.

After scanning the room with the aid of the mirror, he saw several young truck drivers sitting at the bar and a sun drenched old man, who obviously was drunk. He decided to finish his drink and wait for John in the car. He slid off the barstool and started to walk toward the door, when he saw the old man approach him. "John?"

"Yeah, let's get the hell out to your car. I need to get out of these dirty clothes. Did you bring some fresh clothes for me?"

"Yeah, they're in the back seat," Sam replied.

"Good, I'll get in the back seat, and change out of these rags." He slipped behind Sam and unfolded the fresh clean clothes, "That's better."

The ride out of town and into the desert was fast and quiet. The moonless night was dark and perfect for what Sam was ordered to accomplish. He knew a spot in the desert where there would be no witnesses. "John, you're quiet. Are you okay?"

"Nah, pull over I gotta pee," John commanded.

Sam carefully brought the vehicle to a stop, without getting stuck in the loose roadside sand and said, "Make it quick."

John swiftly leaned forward, clamped his left arm around Sam's neck, and, with the palm of his right hand, violently drove Sam's chin back, snapping the second and third vertebrae. John dragged the limp body from the front seat, and dumped it into the truck. The vehicle's GPS easily gave him the directions to Sam's home where he could plan his next move.

When John drove into Sam's garage, a slight dawning of morning was overtaking the pitch black darkness of a few hours ago. There wasn't enough time, or means, before daylight to dispose of the body without being discovered. John knew it would only be a matter of time before another assassin would be dispatched to make him disappear. He chose, for the moment, to rest, make a pot of coffee and contemplate how to stay alive. The aroma of hazelnut coffee took him away from thinking what his prognoses would be if he were to stay at Sam's house. He poured a mug full of coffee, stood at the kitchen sink, looked out the window and noticed what he thought were two unfinished garden boxes. "That's interesting." He stepped out the back door and into the backyard and, with a closer look, realized one of the unfinished garden boxes was for him. The hole inside the box was about four feet deep and a large bag of 'quick dry' cement was propped up against the cinder block wall. He smirked as he visualized Sam laying under a garden of vegetables for an infinity amount of time. His trance was interrupted by the sound of a man's voice shouting from next door. 'Damn, leave it to Sam to build a house in the middle of nowhere and have some idiot move in next to him.'

"Hey neighbor, where's Sam?"

What a dumb shit… John replied, "He had an emergency up North and asked me to finish his garden," He turned around and hustled into the house before the idiot neighbor came over and started asking questions.

It was early Sunday, almost a week after John buried Sam's body in the box garden, when he realized something was wrong. He had no communications from anyone, there was nothing on the TV stations about a wanted rogue FBI agent, and his instincts told him Marshal, and the Cartel had separate elaborate master plans in motion to eliminate him. He's a sore in the FBI's side and, because of him, the Cartel's Southwest Fentanyl traffic was in jeopardy. It was time for him to call on some old friends and disappear.

28

Jake was on a step ladder holding telephone wires as he tried to find the origin of the new wires. "Just what I thought."

"What did you find?" Bonnie asked.

Jake climbed off the ladder, and replied, "The two men who were supposed to be telephone company employees and said they were here checking our phone lines. Well, actually, our suspicions were right. They were FBI people placing a bug in the lines to monitor all our phone conversations and text messages. I checked our offices for listening devices and there are none. I'm positive their orders came from Marshal. Now we have the advantage over Marshal."

"Yeah, you have a good point. What more can they do to monitor our business?"

Jake replied, "There is one more concern. Cell phone records, otherwise known by the FBI as "Call Detail Records," indicates the caller's phone number, duration of call, start and end time of the call, and the cell phone tower connection. Bonnie, welcome to the world of the FBI."

Their conversation was interrupted by the loud ring of the office phone. Bonnie answered, "Lester and Lester Detective Agency."

"Good morning, this is Dr. Dan Zigerfield. May I please speak with Jake?"

"Good morning Zig, how you doing?" Jake asked.

"I'm doing great. I'm on my way to a multiple vehicle accident on County Route four with at least two fatalities. The new ME, Dr. Sam Springs, and I were contacted by the Sheriff's Department a few minutes ago. The Deputy at the scene alleges the accident was caused by drugs and alcohol. It might be unrelated to what you're working on but I thought you might like to meet us there."

"Yes, thanks Zig. I'm on my way."

Jake slowly approached the yellow police tape stretched across the county route about fifty yards from the accident, and stopped short of touching the tape with his SUV.

A Deputy Sheriff recognized Jake, "Hey Jake, good to see you. I wish it wasn't under these circumstances. Zig and the new Medical Examiner got here a few minutes ago. Jake, I've seen bad accidents before, but this one is beyond bad."

Jake started walking toward the accident scene and, twenty yards before the actual impact, he noticed car debris scattered across both sides of the road and over the highway guardrails. "Holy crap." He saw Zig standing next to one of the smoking vehicles. "Hey Zig." He shook his head. "Pretty bad."

"Yeah." He pointed to a red sports car, "I figure this vehicle, by the marks in the road and debris, and was going about a hundred miles an hour without braking at impact. There were three vehicles involved in this mess, and they were headed north toward Lind City. The ME is in the shrubs next to the big oak tree working on a victim. It's going to take a while to figure out who belongs to which. My team's first observation, there were at least two empty vodka bottles in the red vehicle and a bag of drugs. We noticed the drugs have the same characteristics of the Fentanyl crap that hit the streets last week. I'm waiting for the fire department to open the truck with the 'jaws of life'. We have an army of EMS people here, but I don't know if we're going to need them. Ah, here comes the ME."

A man in his forties, wearing a white jumpsuit and holding a black medical bag, stumbled over a highway guardrail, walked up to Jake, "Hi." He pushed his red horn rimmed glasses up his nose, set his medical bag on the pavement, and removed his floppy fishing hat, "You must be Jake Lester, and I'm Sam Springs. Most people me call Dr. Sam. I've heard a lot about you and your wife. All good things of course."

"Hi, you're right, I'm Jake Lester. It looks pretty bad here."

"That's an understatement. I've just begun the preliminaries with the first body…" Dr. Sam was interrupted.

A sheriff's deputy came running up to the road's guardrail, waving his arms in the air, and frantically shouting, "We found another person about a hundred feet off the road, imbedded into the muddy marsh, and she's alive."

Dr. Sam grabbed his medical bag, bolted across the road and, with his short muscular legs, vaulted over the guardrail, and disappeared into the marsh, shouting, "I'm gonna need some help."

Jake sprinted into the marsh, followed by five of the EMS Technicians, beating the wild tree branches and high brown cattails aside, until he came upon Dr. Sam. He was laying on his stomach in several inches of black mud, trying desperately to reach the young lady trapped under the demolished vehicle. Her outstretched arms were inches away from his grasp. It was obvious his attempts were futile and time was running out.

Jake shouted to the EMS men, "We don't have time to wait for a tow truck. We need to lift this sucker high and long enough for Dr. Sam to pull that lady out of there."

The men gripped their hands on whatever part of the wreckage would yield the best leverage and with heavy grunts, lifted the side of the car up high enough for Dr. Sam to gently pull the young lady from beneath the car. The EMS group placed her on a gurney, then labored to slide the gurney up the mud filled incline and into the ambulance.

"Where are you taking her," Jake asked.

"Lind City General," the EMS person replied.

Jake surveyed the area around the scene looking for possible clues to explain why this vehicle ended up in the marsh, while the other two vehicles remained on the highway. Where is the driver of this vehicle?

Zig called out, "Jake, the fire rescue people were able to crack open the trunk of one of the cars and found it loaded with uncut Fentanyl. It's got to be worth millions on the street."

"Damn, what about the other cars?" Jake asked.

"They're working on getting the other cars open, Zig replied. "Jake, we have a witness to the accident. He was riding his bicycle on the road because there's never any traffic on it."

"Thanks, I'll be right there. I need to talk with the deputy in charge of the scene before I ask the witness any questions." Jake made it onto the road, brushed off some of the mud from his shirt, and looked around for the deputy in charge. He saw Deputy Barry Farquhar standing next to one of the vehicles involved in the accident. He and Barry were friends and Barry always cooperated. "Hey Barry, tough looking scene."

Barry pushed his white Stetson hat back, took off his shades and said, "Tough isn't the word for it. We got three fatalities and a young lady on her way to the hospital. I suppose you want talk with the witness?" He pulled his trousers up and adjusted his sidearm, "Just so you know, I was called by my boss, who told me, as soon as Dr. Sam reported the Fentanyl in one of the cars, and I gotta be nice to you. Shit Jake, I'm always nice to you, even when you're a pain in the ass, right?"

"Do you mind if I talk to the witness?"

Barry laughed, "I gotta hand it to you, and you're always polite. Sure, help yourself. His name is Harry Cantrell."

Jake stepped over the mangled car parts until he found a young man wearing cycling shorts, sitting on a fire truck bumper, sipping orange juice from a large plastic container, seemingly in a daze.

204

"Excuse me, Mr. Cantrell, I'm Detective Jake Lester. I work with the FBI when Fentanyl drugs are involved. I understand you witnessed the accident. Can you tell me about it?"

Cantrell replied, timidly, "Yeah, I already told the sheriff what I saw but, now that I'm more relaxed, I can elaborate much better. As I told the sheriff, I ride my bike on this road because there is very little traffic and it's extremely peaceful. Well, today I started about five miles back, going at my regular pace, with my music playing a little loud. I have the new high end ear buds, well that doesn't matter, I could hear the roar of car engines coming behind me. The cars were about a half mile away, coming right at me. I jumped off my bike and flew over the guardrail. I'm sure they were going at least a hundred miles an hour when they went by me."

"Were they racing?" Jake asked.

"No, at least they didn't seem to be racing. I'll say this, they were bumper to bumper when they went by me, and then it happened."

"What happened? Did one of the cars blow a tire?"

"No, Mr. Jake, the lead car slammed on the brakes, making a terrible screeching sound, when it hit two deer standing in the road, and the other two cars banged into the first car. The next thing I knew car parts were flying all over the place. It scared the shit out of me."

"It looks like, from the body count, there were three people involved, including the car in the marsh."

"No, Mr. Jake. There was a driver and a female passenger in the lead car."

"Hold on a minute, did you see where she went?"

"No."

Jake looked around, caught Deputy Farquhar's eye, waved to him, and shouted, "Barry, there's another victim somewhere around here. The impact could have tossed her into the deep part of the marsh."

"Thanks, Jake. I'll get some men from the diving squad out here. Maybe they can find what's left of her. Hey, if you were planning to talk with that woman the EMS guys took to the hospital, you're too late. She never regained consciousness."

Jake stood in the middle of the road attempting to digest the sudden chain reaction impact of three cars going a hundred miles an hour, and analyze the amount of energy sent to the lead car. He noticed the lead vehicle was crumpled and disintegrated all over the scene. There was something wrong. He called out to Zig who was standing a few feet away. "Zig, do you have a minute. I think there's something we might be missing."

"Take a good look at the lead vehicle. Do you see anything wrong with this picture?"

"Sure, my team hasn't gotten to that vehicle yet." Zig surveyed the heap of metal in front of him. Yeah, a couple of things. There're no deer parts on the front of the vehicle but, there's car parts all over the road. Shit, this car wasn't the lead vehicle."

"Right, there was a fourth car involved. When this vehicle hit the rear of the front vehicle the inertia sent the front vehicle careening forward and away from the impact of the three cars behind it. The witness said he got the shit scared out of him and jumped over the guardrail. He didn't see the entire accident."

"So, where is the fourth vehicle," Barry asked. "Yeah, I've been listening to you guys and it makes sense to me. They couldn't have gotten very far with a severely damaged car, or whatever kind of vehicle it was. I'll get a BOLO out right now."

"Jake, I didn't know you were a physics major," Zig said.

"I'm not, a friend of mine was a physics professor, and some of his knowledge trickled on to me." Jake walked to his car, pulled out a roll of paper toweling, and rubbed some mud from his shoes. "Zig, you know what's bothering about this accident? When the Cartel drivers have a load of drugs in their vehicles, they obey every law on the books to avoid getting stopped. Why were these people going so fast and what was their destination?"

29

The sound of an engine on the large green standup lawn mower startled Jake as sat on his patio enjoying one of his favorite beers. It was the first time he'd been without Maggie drinking a cold beer on a hot summer evening since they tied the knot five years ago. The height of his night was watching a middle aged man wearing a floppy hat, long hair, facial growth to match the length of his hair, while sitting on a lawnmower performing wheelies without digging the wheels into the turf. The first day of an assignment from the FBI turned out to be, not only puzzling and traumatic, but he found himself without Maggie, his best sounding board at the scene. They say, whoever **they** are, it's not good to drink alone. Jake stood, waved his hand at the man, and shouted, "Come and have a cold one with me."

The man shut the engine down, jumped off the lawnmower, swiped the loose grass from his blue jeans, and stepped onto the patio. "Well sir, thank you. My name is Lonny, Lonny Donavan. I'm Desk Sargent Michael Donavan's son. A cold beer sounds great."

Jake popped open a bottle of beer, "Would you like a mug?"

"No thank you."

Jake saw no resemblance of Sargent Donavan. "I haven't seen you here before. Are you new with the company?"

"Yes, I started yesterday." He took a couple of gulps of beer. "I know what you're wondering. Why do I look Hispanic with a name like Donavan?" he laughed. "My mother is Columbian and my father is Irish."

Jake was well aware of Lonny's heritage, and was satisfied with Lonny's explanation. He saw a tattoo of a red heart with silver a sword piercing the heart, on Lonny's forearm. "I noticed your tattoo. Were you in the military?"

"Yeah, Marines, I was a bomb expert. I did two tours in Afghanistan." He raised his pant legs and pointed to the two metal prostheses. "I didn't quite make it through the last test." He put the bottle up to his lips, popped a few pills into his mouth, and, before he took a drink said, "I don't mind. I helped a lot of GIs before this happened. Yeah, I know drugs and alcohol don't mix, but these are a special mix. They have a little Fentanyl in them. They're cheap and it helps fight the pain."

"You don't have a prescription?"

"Nah, I get them from a local buddy who was in the Marines with me." He looked at his watch, "I better get going. Thanks for the cold one."

Jake watched Lonny as he finished mowing the lawn and went on his way. He thought, that was too easy. Why a man would have one beer with a complete stranger, divulge his drug habit and the source of his supply, is inconceivable. Jake picked up his cell phone and touched the speed dial number for his lawn mowing company. "Hello, this is Jake Lester. I wonder if you have an employee named, Lonny Donavan."

"Lonny Donavan, never heard of him, Mr. Lester."

"Well, a man who calls himself Lonny Donavan just mowed my lawn, and said he worked for you."

"No sir, don't know him."

Jake turned off the phone, "Shit, he was a bomb expert in the Marines."

The street lights were lighting Jake's office building parking lot when he pulled into his parking spot. He showed a high degree of concern when he saw his second floor office brightly lit and a person's shadow behind the drapes. He chose the stairs instead of the elevator in an effort to lessen the amount of noise. He slowly approached his office door, stopped to listen for noise coming from inside the office, and gave a sigh of relief when he realized it was Bonnie humming a tune from the seventies. "Bonnie, you scared the heck out of me. Why are you here this early?"

"And good morning to you too, Jake. I wanted to finish the last of the files we were purging through the shredder so we could hit the floor running his morning." She pushed her hair back and looked at Jake. "You look a bit frazzled, is everything okay?"

"A man showed up at my house last night posing as an employee of the company that takes care of our lawn. The name he gave was Lonny Donavan. Through our conversation over a beer, he told me he was a bomb expert in the Marines and he was in Afghanistan. His story seemed kind of suspicious. After he left the house, I called the owner of the company to verify it. The owner said he didn't know the man. I took this as some kind of message, especially after our summer home was bombed about four months ago."

"Jake, I didn't know your summer home was bombed. I can see why you were concerned about the lights turned on in the office early this morning. What do you want to do?"

"I'd like you to check out Lonny Donavan's name on the FBI database. It's probably an alias. He had a tattoo on his forearm of a red heart with a silver sword piercing the heart. It could be a tattoo of his Marine unit."

"I'm on it," Bonnie replied.

Jake went into his office, closed the door, and went to the walk in bank vault. The vault was left in place by the regional bank when it moved to a more modern building. When Jake took the office, he thought the vault would be a pain in the ass. He carefully moved the rotary in different directions until he heard a loud metal click and swung the heavy door wide open. The safe contained a few built in file drawers and a small metal table. He opened one of the file drawers and removed an electronic tablet. The tablet contained the names and detailed information, including unsavory information never entered into their military records, of the men he commanded while he was in Afghanistan. It also included when they were discharged. The unsavory section, might possibly shed some light on the character he met last night.

Bonnie tapped on Jake's door and walked in, "Jake, so far, the FBI databank shows three people with our man's name, all of which are deceased. However, the tattoo you described is for real and it was the emblem of the bomb experts in Afghanistan. The commander of the unit was Colonel John Harper."

"Oh shit." Jake blurted out.

"I take it you know the man."

"I do, and this conversation never happened." Jake was taken by surprise. He was certain it was John's way of trying to contact him. The thought of even trying to help John, a fugitive, would be certain jail time.

"Jake, you know this man and you look troubled. Is there anything I can do?" Bonnie asked.

"No, thank you. If I do anything, I will have to do it alone."

Jake knew John would never try to contact him unless he was desperate, and the story in the media was skewed and directed by

Marshal Dunkin himself. On the other hand, what if all this was one of Marshal's schemes to see if Jake knew where John was hiding.

It was well after six p.m. when Jake left his office and headed home by way of his favorite deli. A large deli hero and a cold beer on the patio seemed fit after a long and stressful day. The thought of John Harper's dilemma lay heavy on his mind. After finding out who Lonny Donavan is, he had a long talk with himself and decided not to make any changes in his routine.

Jake was relaxing on his patio after devouring the deli hero, drinking a frosty cold beer, and watching the humming birds fill their beaks up with simple syrup. Jake methodically places syrup in the feeder every morning before leaving for work. He was particularly fascinated this evening by the simple life of an insect sized bird hovering over the feeder for his turn to plunge his exceptionally long tongue into the sweet fluid. The pecking order was obvious. The larger birds took the first fill, the second largest followed, and so on. The interesting part of the bird watching; there was always a bigger bird around to take the place of the first large bird. Jake began to apply this act of survival to a Cartel organization chart. Through the process of elimination, starting with Diego Garcia, the head of the U.S. Cartel, and concentrating on the mixing and distribution of drugs on a state level. The chart had a major transformation when Consuela Delgado, Paulo Espinoza, Hans Osterfeld and Carter Osterfeld, were murdered. He knew he had to focus on discovering the logical replacements of the hypothetical organization chart in order of influence. His original thought of not changing his routine seemed, for the time being, to still be the best approach. Now that the original drug movers were gone, the proverbial pecking order theory should begin to surface.

Jakes concentration was interrupted by Maggie's cheerful voice, "Hi handsome, you come here often? Would you happen to have the brother to the bottle you're hanging onto?"

"Maggie, you're home. What a nice surprise." Jake opened a bottle of cold beer and poured it into a frosty mug. "How's that?"

"Great. I was able complete the autopsy and file a DWI statement against the driver who caused the accident this morning. Dr. Sam called me and asked for some assistance on the highway fatality victims. He said you were instrumental in pulling one of the victims from underneath the wreckage."

"Yeah I, and several EMS people, were able pull to the woman from under a mangled car." He sipped the last of his beer, paused, and asked, "Did you hear about John Harper?"

"Yeah, the whole world is looking for him. Do you really think he's capable of doing all those alleged crimes?"

Jake replied, "No, at least I don't think so. I know John. He wouldn't hurt a fly unless the fly was trying to kill him." Jake placed the empty glass on a table and looked at the sunset disappearing behind their shed, "That sunset is one of my favorite sights. That reminds me, I'm going to check the shed to make sure the door is locked."

Jake unlocked the garage sized door, entered the reinforced steel shed, switched on an overhead light, looked around the walls and ceiling, and saw a spider weaving a web on one of the metal joists. He muttered, "I hate spiders." He found a can of bug spray on a shelf and doused the daddy long legs. He turned off the light and went into the house.

"Jake, what were you doing in the shed? I thought I heard you talking."

"I saw a daddy long leg spider and I sprayed the hell out of it."

Maggie laughed loudly, "the last of the big game hunters."

30

The temperature in Bogotá, Columbia topped the thermometer at forty one degrees Celsius. The mountain dew in the air made it difficult for the boss of the US Cartel, Diego Garcia, as he waited for his driver in front of the El Dorado International Airport. He was summoned by Pablo Ramirez, El Capo's top man, for a meeting at the headquarters of the Cartel located high in the Andes Mountain range. He took a monogramed handkerchief from his white slacks, wiped the perspiration from his forehead, rolled the handkerchief into a tight ball, and clutched it in his hand. The perspiration wasn't totally from the heat and humidity. This would be the first time he had been summoned to the mansion by his boss, and his driver hadn't arrived. He took the last puff from his cigarette, dropped it on the ground, and mashed it with his alligator boot. The possibility of his return to the U.S. was questionable.

A camouflage colored six seat jeep came to a sliding stop in front of him. The two armed men who were sitting in the back seats jumped from the vehicle and stood at attention in front of Diego. A third man carrying a side arm and dressed in a military uniform, slipped his slender frame from the middle seat, asking, "Diego Garcia?"

"Yes," Diego replied.

The two armed men escorted Diego into the jeep and, before they were seated, the jeep was speeding onto the highway. The long speedy ride ended at the foothills of the Andres Mountains to a place the locals call "Nudo de Amaguer," where the mountain range splits in two. The driver gunned the engine and drove the jeep onto a steep rock filled narrow dirt road.

"What the hell, why didn't Ramirez send a helicopter for me?" Diego shouted, as he bounced around on his seat.

"If you should see El Chapo, I would not ask what he does."

"What do you mean, if I should see El Chapo?" Diego asked.

"You were summoned by Pablo Ramirez, yes?"

The message was quite clear. El Chapo would not be present at the meeting and Ramirez would be conducting the meeting. In the Cartel world, this could very well be his last day alive. Diego sat back on his seat and remained silent for the remainder of the two hour ride.

El Chapo's mansion was high on the mountain top with perfectly designed landscaping for beauty and security, reaching a hundred yards in all direction from the mansion. Diego had, on a few occasions, visited the mansion for more pleasant reasons, but was never summoned.

Ramirez was sitting on an enormous, overstuffed sofa when Diego entered the luxurious living room. One of the three bodyguards who was watching over Ramirez, stopped Diego in his tracks and patted him down for weapons. Diego politely commented, "This was done at the airport. Why would I even think of bringing a weapon to our meeting? We are all friends here, yes?"

Ramirez replied, "Certainly. I apologize. Please, have a seat. Would you like a beverage?"

"Water, please."

"Diego, I must come to the point of this meeting. We've been friends for many years and made our way up the ranks together the hard way. And all through those years, business always came first. Am I right?"

"Certainly," Diego replied, He sipping water. "That has always been the way and, even today, business is first."

Ramirez motioned the guards to leave the room. When the guards were out of the room and the double doors were closed, Ramirez said, "We have a big problem and see no reason for the guards to hear what we are going to say."

Diego assumed, "Oh shit, he's the one who's going to kill me".... "What are we going to talk about? I thought I was summoned for a favorable reason."

"This is favorable for you. El Chapo wanted me to permanently eliminate you."

"You mean kill me."

"Yes, that's true. I reasoned with Geraldo because you're loyal and to this point, you've made a lot of money for us without mistakes. It has been a month since we lost hundreds of millions of dollars in that car accident in New York, and we've lost hundreds of millions of dollars in sales after the accident. This detective, what the hell's his name, Lester? He's been knocking the hell out of our distribution and sales. Every time we bring a load of stuff from New York City, Chicago, or any other city, he finds out where it is and the FBI confiscates it. We have everything ready to start mixing in that shitty little place in Northern New York and nothing's happening. What the hell happened to our contacts in the FBI? Why aren't they doing what we're paying them for? Hell, they don't even know how to get rid of one of their own people without screwing it up. Is that FBI guy dead or not?"

"I don't know, and neither our contacts at the FBI. If he died in the desert, the animals will take care of him. The FBI thinks he's alive and, as they say in the FBI, he's ghost." Diego replied.

"Bullshit. If the man's alive, he has to eat and sleep somewhere. We really don't care about him. I want Lester dead."

Diego saw the anger in Ramirez's eyes, "Amigo, wouldn't it be better if we get his wife and keep her somewhere. That way Lester will have to stop his battle against us."

Ramirez commented, "You suggest we take her alive and keep her at our place in the jungle." He took a small puff from his Columbian cigar, blew the smoke into the air, looked out the window at the wild jungle below, and said, "He will have to cooperate with us as long as she's alive." He saw a cockroach at his feet scurrying across the floor. He raised his foot and, with a lightning strike move, crushed the bug. "And if Lester doesn't cooperate, we'll crush him and his wife like that cockroach."

Diego looked at the mashed bug on the floor and grasped the clear message. If this plan didn't work, he would be the one like a cockroach on the floor. "Would you like me to leave immediately for New York?"

"No, not yet. El Chapo would like you to have dinner with us this evening. I think he will remind you it was your idea to take the U S Northeast operation to a small town."

Diego said, "I will be prepared to present my thoughts." He remembered the officer in the jeep telling him not to count on seeing El Chapo. Why would he say such a thing?

"Maybe you should listen to El Chapo first. Remember we lost Consuela Delgado and Paulo Espinoza only because you told us they were working with Lester." Ramirez doused his half used cigar into a glass of water, nonchalantly swiped a small cigar ash from his white shirt and said, "Little ashes annoy me. We have a lot of time between now and dinner, so let's quench our thirst."

Diego knew the innuendos, crushing the cockroach and getting rid of the small cigar ash from his pristine white shirt, were meant for him. He glanced out the mansion window and saw the backdrop of mountain wilderness at the top of the mountain and the swampy jungle below. The construction of the mansion at the top of the mountain was not by mistake, it was meant to keep people out, and make it impossible to escape the mansion complex. In the next few hours, he will know if he will live or die. "Yes, I think a thirst quencher would be most appropriate."

It was promptly six p.m. as Diego and Ramirez walked into the mansion's massive dining room for dinner with Geraldo Quostona, El Chapo. The riches of the Cartel's drug business were throughout the dining room with sculptures by renowned artists and century old oil paintings, large and small, adorned enormous walls highlighted by soft lighting above each painting.

The high wooden double doors swung wide and four, supposedly unarmed, guards entered the room and stood at attention.

Geraldo Quostona, El Chapo, dressed in blue jeans, brightly colored shirt, and sneakers, arrived with little fanfare. "Diego, Pablo, please relax. My associates, as I like to call them, insist they enter the room first as a precautionary measure. Only a fool would think of harming my family and me in my own home. Please let's sit and talk before we eat. My chef has a fantastic dinner planned. We should take the time to eat and enjoy our food, not talk business. Let's have some wine."

El Chapo's custom made, high profile, cushioned sneakers squeaked on the ornate Spanish tile floor as he proceeded to his favorite high back chair. El Chapo wasted no time, "So Diego, we followed your advice and spent millions of dollars, lost two of my top people, Consuela Delgado, and Paulo Espinoza and several other people in the organization, and we're not in operation. Because of you, our connections at the FBI are drying up and they are afraid to help because of Jake Lester who knows too much." He pulled a revolver from is blue jeans, pulled the double action hammer back and pointed it at Diego's head. "Tell me why I shouldn't put your brains all over my rug."

Diego's eyes widened, perspiration rolled down his face, and his mouth went dry. When he reached for his water glass to quench his thirst, the four guards drew their weapons.

"No, let him drink," El Chapo shouted. "He will not try to harm me."

Diego remembered the earlier conversation with Pablo, "I will take Lester's wife out of the equation. A man will always protect his wife before himself. We will take her away from him for a few weeks to show him we can get him and his wife anytime we want."

"Why don't we kill Lester? Why do you think Lester will stop if you kidnap his wife?" Geraldo asked.

"I'm El Chapo and, if I were killed, someone would take my place because of the riches I have. If you take Lester's wife, you will anger Jake Lester and he will never stop his hunt. If you kill Lester, no one will take his place because he has nothing." He took the gun away from Diego's head, placed it on the table, and said, "You had Jake Lester once and he got away. I want you to kill Lester, and I don't care how you do it. Stop this bullshit, and get the operation going. This is your last chance. Do you understand?"

"Yes."

"If I know this type of person, when he knows there is a price on his head, he'll come after you and whoever thinks they can make two million dollars. El Chapo stood, tugged his blue jeans up, and said, "Let's eat."

31

Jake's burn phone rang. It's the first time the untraceable phone was used, and it was only to be used in an emergency. He waited for the four security rings and answered, "Yes."

"Jake, it's me. I still have friends in high places, and they're telling me there's a price on your head. I'm talking two million dollars. There was a big meeting in Columbia with El Chapo himself, and he personally gave the order. He was ready to off Diego Garcia because he hasn't stopped you from interrupting his business." Pause… "Jake, did you hear me?"

"Yes, I hear you. Is the price on me and Maggie?"

"Jake, two million on you, and they want you dead yesterday. Jake, you should get Maggie out of town. These people don't give a shit if there's collateral damage."

"Thanks for the heads up. Be safe."

"Who was that, Jake?"

"Nothing, Maggie. Go back to sleep." He flipped the bed covers across the bed, walked to the window, and peeked through the drapes. The street was empty of parked cars. He sat on the side of the bed and rubbed his hands through his hair. "Damn."

Maggie looked at the Big Ben digital clock on the nightstand. "Jake, it's two in the morning. Now I'm awake and worried. No one calls on the burn phone unless there's something drastically wrong. Please tell me what's going on." She pushed the bedding from her, slipped across the bed, and sat next to Jake. "Ok, I'm starting to get pissed."

"Let's go down to the basement game room and put on a pot of coffee. Trust me, let's just do it. Don't turn on any light on the way down there. I'll explain in a minute."

"Okay, we made it down here in the dark without breaking a leg, and the coffee pot is on. Now, can you tell me what the hell is going on?"

"It looks like all the work we did for the last month, confiscating raw drugs before the Cartel could mix the bulk product, made El Chapo very angry at me, and he told Diego Garcia, his top US man, to kill me. There is a two million dollar price on my head. Thank God the contract is not on you. They will only kill you if you get in their way. We need to get you out of Lind City, like now."

"What do you mean thank God they're not looking for me? I'm staying right here with you."

"Maggie, there is no other way to do this. I'll call my Dad and tell him what's going on. I'm sure he will understand. You have a full wardrobe at Whispering Pines. We can leave right now."

"But Jake, I don't want to leave you alone."

"I won't be alone and, when this is over, we'll have a big cookout, and invite our friends to our new place on the lake."

It was slightly before sunrise when Jake and Maggie were a hundred feet from the Whispering Pines entrance; the gate was in the process of opening. Jake read his father like a book and grinned, "It looks like Dad saw us coming up the road." He parked his pickup inside the barn and turned off the engine. "Honey, you'll be out of harm's way here. They won't touch you as long as you stay here and, if something comes up, Sheriff Plank is only a few minutes away."

Maggie took a deep breath and hugged Jake, "Honey, I have a bad feeling about this. I know I'm being paranoid, but the Cartel is everywhere, maybe people we know, and trust."

Jake's father came running up to the pickup truck and called out, "Jake, Maggie, let's get into the house. Did you have breakfast?"

"Dad, I don't have much time. I need to get back home before anyone knows I've been gone. I need contact some old friends and get my plans into action. A mug of coffee to go would be great."

Maggie repeated her concern, "Honey, be careful. You're not as young as you were when you were in Afghanistan, and you don't have the same backup." She watched Jake as he drove away, put her arms around John, let out a deep sigh, and, with tears in her eyes, said, "Dad, I'm afraid Jake is crashing right into hell's kitchen."

"Maggie, don't worry. I know Jake will be fine."

Jake returned home about mid-morning, showered, put some work clothes on, and went to a sectioned off part of the basement. The red light on the security camera above a solid metal door was blinking, which indicated the room was secure. He placed his thumb on the security pad and, with a loud clank, the steel door was unlocked. He yanked the heavy reinforced double doors open, and an arsenal of weapons and ammunition appeared. The weapons were clean, oiled, and neatly placed into sponge formed slots. He opened a drawer located below the weapons and pulled out an address and phone number book which listed the people he could trust. The information in the notebook was secret and independent of his computer. He brushed off some of the dust from the cover and flipped the pages to Lonny Donavan's name. Jake knew there was a camaraderie between John Harper and Lonny Donavan when John gave Lonny an excellent review, and he knew it was no accident Lonny Donavan was mowing his lawn.

Jake stepped out of the vault and, using his burn phone, entered Lonny Donavan's phone number, "This is Jake. Our lawn looks bad and needs mowing."

"I heard about the situation you're in and I was about to call you. I'll be there in less than an hour."

Jake learned from his experience in the military, the best defense was a good offense, and he was about to embark on an unheard-of offense to prevent the distribution of drugs from entering Lind City. If Lonny is as good with explosives as John says he is, there will be a multitude of ways to keep Lonny busy and keep the Cartel on the defense.

Jake's front doorbell rang. He saw Lonny standing in front of the doorbell camera, raced up the basement stairs, and opened the door, "Come in, Lonny."

"Good to see you, Jake. John contacted me yesterday and said you were in a bit of trouble."

"Yes. Let's go to the basement. I have an extra apartment size room in the basement I call my man cave. We can talk there. Why don't you put your umbrella next to the front door?"

"I don't mind holding onto my umbrella," Lonny replied.

Jake opened the apartment door and said, "After you. You can sit anywhere you like."

"Pretty nice digs down here, Jake. I'll bet you spend a lot of time down here; however, I'm sure you didn't ask me to come here to chitchat. How can I help?"

"You mentioned John contacted you. Do you know where he's located?"

"I'm not positive, but I have a good idea where he might be hiding. Jake, I'm sure you're good at what you do, but you would never make a great interrogator," Lonny smirked. "John, you can come out now."

John appeared from the laundry room and chuckled, "Lonny, when in the hell did you start wearing a wig? A blond one at that."

Jake let out a sigh of relief. If John took Lonny into his confidence to the extent of sharing the secret hiding place, and the safety of his life, he could trust Lonny with his plans against the Cartel. "Okay, this is what we're up against. You know there's a price tag on me for two million dollars, which means there's going to be a lot of professional bounty hunters out there looking to get rich. Our objectives, hit them in the money, where it hurts the most, and detour any wannabe millionaires from killing me. I know where three small worksites are going to be located and are under construction. Here is the biggest problem, I can't get a handle on the location of the major mix and distribution site presently in operation. I'm supposed to send my findings to the FBI. However, John, since you're not there, I don't know who trust."

John said, "I know of a few people who are loyal to the FBI. I can make the connection for you."

"Lonny, the three buildings I'm referring to are concrete structures, in an off the grid location, and away from people. You shouldn't have any difficulty doing your thing," Jake said, reassuring Lonny.

Lonny set his umbrella next to the chair, stood, bumped his head on the overhead light, leaned over a table, pulled a sheet of paper from his pocket, and started to draw a rough schematic of a typical concrete building. He carefully marked the possible weak points in the structure, stepped away from the drawing, and bumped his head on the hanging light. "Damn, that hurt. Now if I'm correct, a smidgen of urea nitrate at each of the areas I've pointed out on the schematic should implode the buildings without collateral damage. These are basic concrete buildings, with very few support beams, making it effortless for the implosion. I must add, the materials are easy to purchase."

"Lonny, don't you think it might be a challenge to place the explosives?" John asked.

"Not really. Maybe I could act as a subcontractor who mows the lawn next to the construction site. When the coast is clear, I'll be able to place the explosives and, by using a cell phone, blow the place up about two in the morning," Lonny replied.

"Lonny, this might sound a little crazy. I don't want to blow up all these places. Do you remember when we were in Afghanistan and we wanted to scare the hell out of the workers so they wouldn't come to work?" Jake asked.

"Sure. We'd put fake bombs in the building to let them know we could blow the place up anytime we wanted," Lonny replied.

"I'd like you to position fake explosive materials where construction workers can easily find them, and I want to do it over period of a few weeks. That will give us time to review the effects of your work, and maybe scare the hell out of the people so they never return to the construction site," Jake said.

"Yeah, I can do it as frequently as you would like. I'll make the materials large enough to scare the hell out of them. They'll get our message loud and clear," Lonny said, grinning "Just tell me when to start."

"Jake, how many of our friends have contacted you?" John asked.

"No one. Just you two guys. I can't say I blame them. The Cartel have me colored dead and they'll kill anyone with me. I guess I made a point for you guys to take off."

"Nah, I'm on the FBI's short list, dead or alive," John replied.

"I haven't had this much fun in a hell of a long time," Lonny replied.

"Thank you... I can work from my downtown office and here. I'm sure the FBI has the upstairs bugged, so I can't change my routine. John, you can stay in the basement as long as you see fit. There will be a time when we can address an FBI fugitive in my home. Lonny, don't change your habits. You know the drill. Any questions?"

Lonny replied, "It sounds to me like we're facing a double whammy. The FBI is playing a cat and mouse game with Jake, and the Cartel is trying their best to kill him and anyone helping him.

Now, with John's expertise, duping the FBI will be a walk in the park. The question is, will the plan we just discussed keep the Cartel out of Lind City."

"Lonny, while you're setting things up at the buildings, I'll make it my sole purpose in life to prevent the Cartel, from the top down, from coming into Lind City." Jake leisurely walked to the open vault, closed the doors, and said, "I have an ace in the hole. An employee of the federal government, Bill Stutz, the FAA agent at the airport, is going to inform me of every aircraft scheduled to arrive at our airport from Columbia and New York City. He didn't ask me why I needed the information. He's going to do it because he enjoys the life he has in Lind City. I don't think there will be much time before Diego Garcia shows up to micromanage my demise and, when he arrives, he'll wish the hell he never he came our city." Jake watched Lonny climb the basement stairs with one hand on the wooden railing and the other hand swinging his umbrella. "John, do you know what the umbrella's all about?"

John laughed, "I don't have a clue, but he had that ragged ass umbrella with him all the way through his hitch in Afghanistan. He might think it's his good luck charm."

Jake let out a belly laugh, "We all had our lucky charms when we went after the Taliban."

"Jake, you never asked me about all the shit that happened in Arizona. This might be a good time to tell you."

Jake interrupted John and said, "You told me it was a legal shoot and that's good enough for me."

32

The whining sound of a small aircraft's jet engines hampered the conversation between Jake and Bill Stutz as it taxied for takeoff at Lind City Municipal Airport.

Bill loosened his tie, took off his horn rimmed glasses and with his baritone voice bellowed, "Jake, let's get into my office. It's quieter there and the coffee isn't bad either."

"Bill, you're right. It is quieter in here. I want to thank you for helping me out with this whole crazy thing with the Cartel. I'm sure you have your neck stuck out a mile."

Bill handed Jake a mug of coffee. The dated Strategic Air Command emblem on the mug signified Bill's time in the Air Force. "I use hazelnut coffee. I hope you like it."

"This is my favorite, and I recognize the emblem on your mugs. Afghanistan?"

"Yes. I know you and your guys went through a lot of hell before you got out of that rat whole. To answer your concern about me getting into trouble over helping you, the information I'm going to provide you is open to the public. If you need any more help, I mean outside my duties here, let me know." Bill pulled a printed list of arriving aircraft from his desk drawer, took a gulp of his coffee, put on his glasses, and placed the printout on his desk. "Take a look at the arrivals from New York City and Columbia. I highlighted the second one from the top. That one might interest you the most. The others are questionable."

Jake moved closer to the desk, "Yes, I see what you mean. What does the asterisk by the aircrafts ID number mean?"

"It means the passenger, or passengers, in the aircraft have Diplomatic Immunity. If the passenger is who I think he is, the immunity doesn't mean squat to him. He is a high ranking individual in the Cartel and the Cartel certainly does not enjoy Diplomatic Immunity. Regardless of what he may think, he has to go through customs. You know Jake, we don't have a resident customs agent here, and sometimes it takes about thirty minutes to get an agent here. The law says the passengers cannot leave the terminal until they pass through customs, and a lot of things could happen before the agent gets here. I understand, by rumor of course, the passengers are detained for days if they become unruly. The person in question goes by the name of Diego Garcia."

"Yes, I know the name, and I have good reason to believe he's here to kill me or have someone do it for him." Jake had a curious look on his face.

"Jake, I know you're thinking why I am I getting involved. I have seen firsthand the Cartel's invasion of drugs does, especially Fentanyl, to a community. I lost a brother from an overdose of Fentanyl when the Cartel started pushing their poison in a small town in Kansas. He was one of the many people in that town who died from the drugs and if I will do anything to stop it from happening in Lind City. The aircraft is scheduled to arrive in about ten minutes. What can I do to help?"

"Bill, you're doing it right now. Everything is in place and all you have to do is go about your business as usual. I have a man waiting in a van outside the airport gate. Thank you so much for your help."

The ten minute wait seemed to last an hour. Jake checked with John in the van, "John, are you good to go?"

"Yes."

Jake scoured the morning sky for the approaching aircraft's landing lights. He squinted when he noticed the FAA mandatory bright wing lights on an approaching aircraft. "John, the aircraft is in sight."

"Roger."

Jake scurried into the terminal and disappeared into the maintenance shop. He partially closed the door and waited for the coming events to begin. The silent wait in a small room was reminiscent of the times he was serving in the Marines in Afghanistan and waiting for the enemy to walk into an ambush. He could hear the reverse thrust of the powerful jet's engines as the pilot maneuvered the plane down the runway into a slow taxi and coming to a stop in front of the terminal. Jake could hear Bill talking politely to one man, "Sir, you have to wait for a customs agent."

The man shouted loudly in Spanish, "What do you mean I have to wait for a customs agent? I'm Diego Garcia. I'm a diplomat from Columbia and I have Diplomatic Immunity. The hell with customs."

"Bill politely replied, "Sir, you must comply or I may have to detain you."

Diego replied in English, "Bullshit." He dropped his briefcase, placed his hands on Bill's chest, and shoved Bill backward. He knew he had just broken a US Federal Law. He put his hands on a Federal Official in a violent manner. He backed away from Bill and looked defiantly at him in an attempt to intimidate the man he accosted.

Bill tilted his head to one side, looked at Diego, smirked and, within ten seconds, the altercation was over. Diego was slightly bruised, handcuffed behind his back, and standing in a glass holding room.

Diego pleaded, "I didn't mean to touch you. I have Diplomatic Immunity."

Bill kept his silence, left the room, and vanished.

Diego thought, "What a stupid Gringo, He didn't lock the door. I can leave here anytime I want."

The sight of Diego standing alone in a room with no bodyguards present was the perfect queue for Jake to execute his plan. He dashed into the holding room, dropped a burlap bag over Diego's head and grabbed one of his arms. He hastily pushed him out the terminal's rear door, shoved his quarry into the waiting van, and sped away.

"Diego screamed, "You people are crazy. Do you know who I am? You'll be dead in less than twenty four hours."

Jake turned on the police scanner and sat quietly in the van as John maneuvered the vehicle in a high speed zig zag fashion a few times. The maneuvering caused Diego to bounce from wall to wall until he landed on the floor. John took several evasive moves through the countryside in an effort to confuse Diego's memory of the amount of stops and turns over a period of thirty minutes. The van came to a slow stop, waited for an overhead building door to open and proceeded into a small dark warehouse, then stopped.

When John slid open the van's side door, Jake tugged at Diego's arm, to pull him out of the van. He turned on the light switch at the outside of the room, grabbed the bag from Diego's head, and shoved him into the room. H bolted the steel door.

Diego screamed, "You bastards are going to pay for this. I'm gonna see you die in such pain you never felt in your lives. My people will find me and I will personally kill the both of you."

"Do you know who I am?" Jake asked, calmly.

"I don't give a shit who you are," Diego said, sternly. He glared at Jake. "I know you. I don't know the man with you, but my people will find him too."

"You shouldn't worry about the man with me. You should know me. You have people hunting me down for two million dollars. After the people hear you have disappeared, and there's no money, the hunt for me will cease. Your family will never see you again. The Cartel, well that's something different. They will think you betrayed them, put a price on your head, and replace you with a new and smarter person."

"Hah, if you shoot me or hang me your government will put you in jail for murder, and I will have the last laugh."

"I'm not going to touch you. I'm going to see how long you can live in the dark with no food, lights, and water. It will take a long time for your body to fade away to nothing and, when you're dead, I will stuff your legs into five gallon buckets full of concrete, and drop you into a lake, like you did to Carter Osterfeld's son, Hans Osterfeld."

"You will not get away with this. Someone will find me before I die."

"No one will find you. The room is soundproof, there are no windows and no heat or air conditioning. No more talk. I'm done here. I might stop by in a few weeks." Jake walked out of the room, and locked the steel door. Jake grinned when he saw John, who heard every word of Jake's presentation, "What do you think?"

"Well, you scared the shit out of me. How long do you think it will be before he breaks?"

"When we caught one of the Taliban, we took the T-Man into a room, similar to this room, and fed them the same type of story. It took about four or five days for the T-Man to break. We better get going. Lonny's going to need his van for this evening and we have to get you out of sight."

"Jake, one thing, how do you know no one will find him in this storage warehouse?"

"When I retired from the police department, Maggie and I took some of the money we saved for retirement and invested it into this old building. We're in the process of refurbishing it into a modern storage facility. The contractor finished up the last of the storage rooms and, until we start renting them, no one will be in the place. I can check on him without his knowledge every day."

John put the van in gear and looked at Jake, "Man, you're scary."

33

Lonny carefully wiped the sweat from his forehead with a western style neckerchief and, without disturbing his long haired wig, sponged the back of his neck. He folded the neckerchief, blotted the sweat form beneath the fake beard, and continued riding his lawn mower in a vacant lot close to the evening's target. It took thirty minutes to mow the high grass in a crisscross pattern and, with his experience in demolition and using a crisscross pattern, he was able to calculate where to place the fake explosive. The first impression to an employee's eyes of seeing the word 'explosives' usually is the best scare factor. He would return to the site in the early hours of the next morning and strategically place the phony charges.

"Jake, it's me. I have a mental schematic of the interior of the target. Are we good to go?"

"Yes, we're good to go. Would you like me to be there?"

"No, thanks. The target is not boarded or locked, no construction safety lights, and there are no CCTV cameras in the area. I'll layer my van with black advertising adhesive cover, and blackout my license plate."

"It sounds like you have everything covered. Be safe. When you get there, and you feel even the littlest suspicion, drive away."

"Roger that. I'll get back to you when I'm done," Lonny replied.

A black van drove by a partially constructed cinder block building at the speed limit, with a clean shaven, short blond driver behind the wheel. The first drive by was essential for reconnoiter of the target to establish the safety of his mission. Lonny could feel the rush of the mission he was to undertake. He did his homework and knew he could accomplish his objective without difficulty. It was precisely two a.m. when Lonny entered the building and, with the use of night vision glasses, placed the first three of the plainly marked containers at the building's entrance. He was in the process of placing a few more of the phony containers when he saw vehicle headlights approaching his van. He stopped, his heart raced as he stood motionless, while he watched the vehicle come to a stop next to the van. He could see two young men in the front seat of the four door sedan. Lonny had not planned the basic ingredient of entering a building; an escape route. He watched the two men quickly climb out of their vehicle and run to the van. "Shit, those are kids trying to steal my tires." He rushed to the open front door, lit the fuse on one of the fake explosives, and threw it at them.

One of the boys shouted, "Holy shit, let's get outta here, someone threw a stick of dynamite at us."

Lonny completed his task and left the area. "Jake, it's me. It's done."

"That's great. Did you have any problems?"

"One little hiccup. A couple of kids tried to steal my tires while I was in the building. I shocked the hell out of them with a stick of the fake stuff. They ran like hell, and I remembered to pick up the fake stick before I left the scene."

"Good job," Jake remarked.

"How are we ever going to know if our plan was effective?" Lonny asked.

"I think we'll know when the workers show up at the construction site and see your handy work. I'm counting on two things: one, the snakes will start to come out from under their rocks and, two, when Diego Garcia doesn't show up in Lind City, the Cartel will start to have reservations about him. Then we start the divide and conquer phase."

"When would you like me to plant the stuff at the next building site?"

"Lonny, that's a good question. Let's see what occurs after the Cartel gets the news about tonight. In the meantime, go about your business."

Jake's next step in the series of events was to contact Joan Fetter and get the Lind City Times reporter involved.

"Joan, Jake Lester, how are you."

"I'm fine, Jake. Long time no see. I've heard about some of your life changing issues. I remember the day we met on your boat. It was fine until we found twenty nine year old Hans Osterfeld dead and tangled in your anchor line."

"Yes, that was quite a day, and I also remember telling you, if I ever had a story, you would be the first person in the media I would call."

"You gave me first right of refusal when Gus Highland was fighting for his life in the hospital, and that got me lots of atta girls' from the Times. Frankly, I thought you were very generous for giving me that opportunity."

"I have a situation now where I think you could be a great help and would further your standing at Lind City Times. Would you be able to meet with me soon? My new office is across from the Times building and the city park. I really don't want to talk about it on the phone."

"Soon? How about now."

Joseph DeMark   THE MIXER

"Now is good. I'll see you by the fountain at the park."

Jake popped into Bonnie's office and, cognizant of Marshal Dunkin's false telephone repairmen claiming an issue with the telephone service said, "Bonnie, I'm going to lunch. If I get any calls take a message. Please don't call me on my cell unless it's an emergency."

Bonnie nodded, "Sure, Jake," and continued working a non-government account. She watched Jake from her office window as he crossed the street, waited a few minutes, went down the hall to a public Ladies restroom, and called Jake on her burn phone, "Jake, you have someone following you. He's tall, wearing a black suit, and walks like a, Government type."

"Thanks Bonnie. Yeah, I saw him standing in our building like a sore thumb. I'll shake him off before I get to my meeting."

Jake entered the park through the back entrance, walked the perimeter twice, found a bench with a full view of the park, close to the fountain, and settled back on the bench. The lilac bush next to him provided some camouflage. He was surprised when he saw Joan entered the park with a Golden Lab puppy on a leash. He waived, "Joan, over here."

Joan approached Jake with a wide grin and the tail wagging Lab, "Hi Jake, what do you think of my new mascot?"

"She's beautiful."

"She's in training to be a Search and Rescue dog. I have her for eight weeks for some basic training. What's going on with you?"

"I'm trying to steer up a hornet's nest. Joan, as usual, what I'm going to say is a protected and confidential news source."

"I agree. My God, Jake, tell me what the hell is going on."

"I'll give you the following headline. 'Information from a very reliable anonymous source reports the notorious Diego Garcia, leader of the US Cartel, using the cover of Carter Osterfeld Construction Company, based in New York City, entered the United States through the Lind City Municipal Airport claiming Diplomatic Immunity. He was last seen leaving the airport two days ago with two suspected US government agents, without handcuffs or other restraining equipment, and is now reported missing.' How's that for a lead off headline?"

"Jake, I'm going to ask you again, what the hell is going on?"

"Diego Garcia was ordered to Columbia for a sit down with Cartel leader, Geraldo Quostona. His message to Diego was to kill me at any cost because of my continuing harassment and disruption of their drug sales. And, to accomplish his goal, Diego placed a two million dollar bounty on my head. Joan, my mission in life is to stop the mixing and distribution Fentanyl and other drugs in Lind City. I have set in motion a plan to do just that."

"You know once I headline this story, the Cartel will up the bounty on you." Joan looked at the Lab, pet her a few times, and rubbed her jowls, "I can elaborate the story from here. Jake, tell me you don't have Diego Garcia hidden somewhere nearby."

"Okay, I won't. Off the record. I repeat, off the record. I have Diego hidden in a place where no one will ever find him and, one more thing, when the construction workers show up for work at one of the Cartel's building sites, they will see several cases clearly marked 'high explosives' placed around the building. When they find out the cases are fake, they'll realize we have the capability to blow them up anytime. There are two other buildings under construction, and we'll do the same to those buildings."

"Who's we?"

"Sometime soon I will be able to divulge that information; however, for now, I promised to keep their names out of this.

"Okay, I understand. I hope you have Maggie well hidden somewhere far away."

"Maggie is my first concern, and I would do nothing to jeopardize her life," Jake replied. He quickly changed the subject. "How old is the dog?"

"She's eight months old and she's been in training with me from day one. She's ahead of her program and is proficient in tracking a human subject. I'm going to hate giving her up, but that's really not your reason for the question. I still have time to post the story for tomorrow morning's edition. Jake, you know the media will be all over this when the story breaks in the newspaper, are you ready for that?" Joan stood, wrapped her hand around the dog's leash, "Be careful."

Jake gave the dog a pat on the head and, with a grin, said, "Sure, your information came from a highly dependable anonymous source. What better insurance could I have?"

Jake watched Joan and the dog disappear through the park gate. The serenity of the park allowed Jake to contemplate the many possible scenarios, good or bad, when the news breaks in the morning paper. He and his two friends are well past the point of no return. His thought process was interrupted by the vibration from his burn phone.

"Jake, it's me."

"Hey Bonnie, what's up?"

"Bill Stutz, from the airport called. He said to tell you there are three more people coming from Bogotá, Columbia. Their flight plan indicates arriving at midnight tonight as Diplomats. Jake, he sounded extremely concerned," Bonnie replied.

"Okay, it's only twenty minutes to the airport. Please let him know I'm on my way over to see him."

Jake tapped John's burn phone numbers. "John, we have three more guests arriving tonight. Do you have any plans?"

John replied, "Your plans are my plans. I think we're going to need more help."

"I think we can handle everyone without additional help. I have a plan. I tell you about it later."

"Yeah, I know, you have a guy."

"Yes, I have a guy. By the way, the Lind City Times will break our story tomorrow morning. I have to contact my guy."

"John Swift, how the hell are you?"

"I'm fine Jake, I haven't heard from you in a long time, what's up?"

"If you're presently a NARCO Detective, I have a tip for you."

"I got promoted to Chief of the NARCO Division. I'm all ears."

"I have a reliable source telling me there are three people arriving at the Lind City Municipal Airport. They're posing as Columbian diplomats claiming Diplomatic Immunity. Actually, they are believed to be heavily armed hired assassins, and may have drugs hidden aboard the aircraft."

"These assassins with drugs, might they be after you?"

"That is a possibility," Jake replied. He waited patiently for John's answer. The pause was deafening, and Jake decided he should elaborate the cause for John's involvement. "John, these people are in the process of constructing buildings in the vicinity of Lind City with the intention of turning our city into a major drug mixing and distribution center."

"You have my attention. When are these so called Diplomats arriving?"

"They're scheduled to arrive at midnight tonight and, if you approve, I would like to be involved."

"No problem. I'll see you at eleven tonight."

The bright moonlit night cast shadows between the Lind City Municipal Airport hangers and the terminal. Jake sat inside one of the hangers watching and listening to John debrief his NARCO Squad. The atmosphere among the men and women of the squad was calm, professional, and alert to the possibility of more than three people arriving at midnight. Jake had a strange feeling the Cartel may have set an ambush, and the aircraft would be empty.

Jake waited until John completed the debriefing, "John, can have a word."

"Sure, what's up?"

I have a strange feeling we might be walking into a trap and your people are going to get ambushed."

John grinned and laugh quietly, "Jake, I stationed snipers around the perimeter of the airport with night vision head gear since sundown, and I gave my people the order to deploy to their assigned positions. Thanks for your concern."

Jake watched the sleek Lear jet land and taxi to the terminal on time. The fuselage door unfolded to the tarmac four, not three, shabbily dressed people wearing long, out of season, coats deplaned and waited for their luggage to be unloaded by the pilot and an airport employee. The procedure seemed orderly, and so far, without incident. The atmosphere changed when the Customs Agent ordered the passengers through a Custom's inspection. The four men pulled automatic weapons from beneath their long coats. Jake watched in awe as four men dropped to the ground from NARCO Sniper fire. The precision of the sniper gunfire left the four people wounded and helpless on the tarmac. It was then that loud gunfire could be heard at one point of the perimeter. Jake overheard John's conversation on the command phone with an officer stationed on the perimeter, "Sir, we have one subject of interest who is wounded, not mortally, and ready for the EMS crew."

"Jake, I owe you one. We have four definitely assassin types and one sniper guy in custody. This was a great night. Let me know whenever you need us."

34

Jake pulled the morning newspaper from its plastic bag, and flopped it open to the front page. He requested an unforgettable front page and was astounded by the full page cover, large print, and editorial byline Joan Fetter produced. He placed a coffee mug next to the coffeemaker, filled the mug to the brim, and sat at the kitchen table. Joan managed to fill the entire front page and a quarter of page three without divulging her sources. He gulped some coffee and took the paper to the basement.

"John, I heard noises down here and knew you were awake. You have to see the excellent work Joan did for us."

John read the front page and said, "Jake, this is Pulitzer level journalism. If this doesn't get the Cartel's attention nothing will." After reading the entire editorial, he shook his head. "We have a freaking Cartel war on our hands. What's our plan of action?"

Jake gave John an update on the early morning action at the airport. "We have four would be assassins in custody, thanks to John Swift and his NARCO team." Their conversation was interrupted by a call on Jake's burn phone.

"Jake, Joan Fetter."

"Hold on, I'll put you on speaker."

"I thought I should touch base with you. The head of the local construction union informed me this morning his men walked off a construction site because the inside perimeter of a building they were working on was loaded with wooden cases marked 'high explosives'. The foreman of the construction site called the bomb squad, "she giggled. "After the bomb squad inspected the boxes, they announced the boxes were a hoax. The men refused to return to the site ever again."

"Imagine that," Jake jested. "I read your story in the morning paper and, I was told by a reliable source, it is Pulitzer quality."

"Thank you. I heard there was quite a stir at the airport last night. You've been a busy man. Thanks for the material you sent me. I'll keep in touch."

"John, I think we have the Cartel's attention now. I know that's a double edged sword. They will start sending the assassins to Lind City with vehicles in an attempt to kill me."

"I agree. I know you have a plan. Would you like to let Lonny and me in on it?"

"Lonny will be here this morning to trim my shrubs and, when he gets here, we'll sit down and cover our next plan of attack. Until then, I have to shower and make a few phone calls"

Jake, after an invigorating and solo- brain storming shower, sat on the edge of a bedroom dressing chair, stared intently at the empty bed, and thought of Maggie. They hadn't communicated for several days for fear of divulging her location. The temptation to call her using the burn phone was overruled by his steadfast safety discipline. He knew his cell phone and landline were bugged by order of Marshal Dunkin. The FBI was noted for oversight of their Contract Investigators, and he thought now would not be an advantageous time to change his routine phone contacts. There are two major highway links to Lind City from New York City airports and Deputy Sheriff, Barry Farquhar, covers one of them like white on rice.

"Barry, Jake here."

"Hey Jake, how's it going?"

"Making a wave when I can."

"Yeah, I heard you had somewhat of a scuffle up your way. That airport will never be the same." Barry was absolutely certain Jake's phone was bugged, and Jake was instrumental in the operation. "I heard the NARCO folks had a shootout and a big bust. Well, if those Cartel shitheads come up my highway I'll have a big surprise for them, and you can bet on it."

"Yeah, I know you will. Be safe, Barry."

Jake covered exactly what he set out to accomplish without saying a word. Barry Farquhar is one of those individuals who comes into your life and will give you all the help you need. The last time he was in Barry's county, Barry showed off his three drug sniffing K-9 units. The precision of the K-9s was impeccable. He felt comfortable with Barry minding the main highway to Lind City.

Jake heard the rumble of a lawnmower engine in his backyard. He finished dressing, walked onto the patio, and waved at Lonny.

Lonny mowed a few more swipes of the lawn, stopped at the patio, pulled his umbrella from the tool compartment, eased off the lawnmower, and brushed off some grass clippings, "Good morning, Jake."

"You look pretty warm. Let's go into the house and get something cool for you to drink." Jake led the way to the basement, pulled two bottles of cold water from the refrigerator, and handed one to Lonny and the other to John.

"It looks like the first phase of our plan is working. The construction union members are rejecting any further construction contracts with Osterfeld Company. The Cartel has found the local airport is not an option for them and, as of a few minutes ago, the main highways will be out of their realm of use. We all know the Cartel will keep looking for Diego Garcia until they decide they can do without him and that brings us to our next phase. Lonny, keep mowing lawns next to the two remaining construction sites, and when you feel comfortable, repeat your tasks about two weeks apart. We don't want the Cartel to think the first building was the last. One thing we should stress, let's not get into a predictable routine."

"I gotcha, Jake," Lonny said. "I better get out to the lawnmower." He started up the basement stairs, stopped, turned around, and pointed his umbrella at Jake. "I have an idea. What if I placed a couple of those phony cases of explosives around your home and let the Cartel guess what the hell is going on?"

John commented, "Lonny might have a point, Jake."

"Right, Lonny might have a great idea. I'll have to let my family in on the hoax, but it might just work. It wouldn't hurt to confuse El Chapo. Let me think about it." Jake thought it appropriate for him to mention Bonnie's name. "Lonny, hold up for a minute. I would like to run something by you guys. Bonnie Goodwin works with me in the downtown office. One of her many attributes is that she's an expert with telephone line transmission, and I know she can be trusted. We need to free ourselves of the constant FBI communication surveillance, and I'm sure she would jump at the chance to dupe the FBI. I think she can improvise the lines to produce static whenever they're listening. What do you think?"

"Jake, it's your ballgame and, if you trust Bonnie, I'm in," John replied.

"Do it to it," Lonny replied. He continued climbing the stairs with his umbrella tucked into his belt while holding onto the wooden railing. He hooted, "It's easier going down than climbing."

"I've known Lonny forever. He carries the umbrella wherever he goes, but never uses it. He relies on the full control of his metal leg prostheses and will never accept help," John remarked.

"Yeah, I hear ya." Jake touched his office number on the burn phone, "Bonnie, Jake. Can you meet me for lunch at the usual place?"

"Sure. What time?"

Jake checked his watch, "It's eleven thirty, how about noon?"

When Jake backed out of his driveway, he noticed a panel truck, with a rug cleaning company logo painted across the body. The homes in Jake's subdivision are approximately two hundred feet apart. The panel truck happened to be parked in front of his neighbor's home. The owners told Jake they were going to be out of town on vacation. Jake surmised the FBI, had his house under surveillance. He pulled the car back into his driveway, went into the house, poured a decanter full of coffee, and took it out to the van. He banged on the van's back door and waited. The door slowly opened and a clean shaven, young man wearing a black suit appeared. Jake handed the coffee and plastic cups to the young man, "I thought you might enjoy some coffee before you clean rugs in that elegant black suit. You can leave the empty decanter on my front porch." He walked across the street, slid into his car, and drove away.

Bonnie was sitting in her compact vehicle at a one of the less popular diners reading the morning newspaper when she heard a soft knock on her window. Jake was standing next to the car with a big smile on his face."

"Are you ready?" he asked.

"Sure," Bonnie replied. She got out of the car carrying a large cloth shopping bag.

Jake found a booth next to a window with the purpose of observing the arriving customers. He noticed Bonnie's large bag was at a bulging point and thought he would wait to ask her about it.

"Well, Jake, we ordered our food, we did the small talk, and now you can tell me why we're here. I know it's not for the wonderfully prepared gourmet food in this establishment."

Jake replied, "I noticed you were reading the morning newspaper while you were waiting for me. Did you happen to read the front and third pages?" He glanced at the bulging bag on the seat next to her and decided to continue holding off asking her the question.

"Yes, I read the entire article. I assume you were the culprit behind the scene who caused the commotion, and Joan Fetter created a remarkable byline. How am I doing so far?"

"You're doing great and, now that you have summarized part of the situation, I mean the action at the airport, I can tell you why we're here." Jake dabbed his mouth with the paper napkin, "Here's the situation. You know the FBI has our office bugged to the point of absurdity with security in mind, so they say. I know you have the expertise in telephone line transmission and cell phone software."

"Yes, that's true," Bonnie said.

"Well, with that in mind, I would like to know if you would like to join me and a couple of men with the purpose of eradicating the Cartel from Lind City. Now please, I will understand if you don't want continue this conversation."

"Can you tell me the names of the two men?"

"Bonnie, I would need your firm commitment before I divulge their names."

Bonnie glanced around the almost empty diner, reached into the large bag, pulled out several pieces of tan sheets of paper in numerical sequence, and stacked them on the table. "I thought you would never ask me to get involved in your work. I anticipated the subject of our luncheon, and brought these with me. These are the first blush schematics of the phone service in your office and home, and how I can program cell phones in the rest of our group. The

242

person monitoring the phones will hear a static screech and never your conversation. I can complete this and debug our office and your home in about two days and, when it's complete, no one, and I mean no one, will know how it's been accomplished." She meticulously slipped the schematics back into the bag.

"I'm speechless. I assume your answer to my question is yes."

"Yes….So, who is in the small, but dangerous group?"

"Come to my home about seven tonight and you can personally meet them. I want to impress on you there is a certain amount of danger to our work. The Cartel is trying their best to eliminate me and anyone who gets in the way. It's important we keep a low profile and you go about your usual daily routine."

"Jake, Cartel drugs killed my kid brother, and I will do anything to keep them out of our city. I know danger comes with the territory. I'll be there tonight."

"When you come to my home tonight, make sure you're carrying a briefcase. Now, I need to get home ASAP. See you later."

Jake looked around the parking lot for suspicious vehicles, and proceeded home by way of Diego Garcia's holding room. "Diego, I stopped by to see if you are alive."

"Go to hell," Diego screamed.

"We'll let you out in a couple of weeks, but not before the newspaper announces your heartfelt cooperation with our authorities."

Jake laughed to himself when he drove onto the street where his house is located. The obvious so called rug cleaning company van was missing and a hovering drone was in its place. He stepped away from his car, waved vigorously at the drone, and entered his house through the front door. He tossed his jacket on a kitchen chair, and proceeded to the basement.

"Hey Jake, is Bonnie on board with us?" John asked.

"Yes. Not only is she on board, she showed me some schematics she drew which will help her disable the bugs in the house and block the FBI from listening in on our phone calls. I asked Bonnie to join us tonight. Lonny will be providing lessons for the people piloting the drone on how to trim shrubs, after which he will join us here." Jake grabbed two bottles of water from the refrigerator, and placed one in front of John. Jake commented, "John, you must be getting stir crazy in the basement. Is there anything I can do?"

"Don't worry about me. I'm fine, Jake."

"Do you have any close friend in the Bureau you can really trust?" Jake asked.

"Yeah, I have a few people who know I was set up by someone in the Bureau. I was in the Arizona desert, just after my so called bodyguard, Terrance Cantrell, was supposed to kill me. I made it to the house, you know, where the box gardens were being built. It was then I received a call from one of those close friends. She told me it was a big set up by someone high in the FBI chain of command because I knew too much."

"Too much about what?" Jake asked.

"Good question. I was assigned to investigate the Cartel's drug distribution. Jake, I didn't know any more than all the other agents."

"Yeah, you must have unknowingly stumbled across someone's golden egg and you were going to be the scapegoat. That person, he or she, is the ticket to your independence, and the key to helping us shut down the Cartel's operation in Lind City."

Jake's cell phone vibrated signaling someone was at the front door. He turned on the photo app and saw Bonnie standing on the porch with a briefcase and large bag labeled Ron's Deli. "Come in Bonnie and find your way to the basement."

John focused on Bonnie holding the deli bag and said, "I like already like the lady."

Bonnie grinned, "You must be John Harper. I'm sorry to disappoint you." She opened the bag, wiggled out a handful of schematics, and placed them on the table. "I brought food for thought. I noticed a man outside wearing a floppy hat, ragged jeans, with an umbrella attached to his belt, and a mile long beard. I assume that to be Lonny Donavan."

"You assumed correctly," Jake said.

"I'm sure Lonny knows he has company circling over his head," John said.

"Lonny has a gift of knowing exactly what is happening around him at all times. He will be joining us in a few minutes," Jake said.

"Jake, after I left you at the diner, I immediately went back to the office, debugged the office, and rerouted the landlines. I hope you don't mind."

"You did all that this afternoon?" Jake asked.

"Yeah. Whatta, you think Jake? Did I do the right thing?" Bonnie asked.

"You certainly did the right thing," Jake replied.

The basement door closed, and the sound of feet stomping down the steps was heard. "You must be Bonnie," Lonny said, as he held his hand out and pulled off the long hair wig and facial hair.

"Yes, I'm Bonnie."

Jake, eager to start the meeting, said, "This will be the last time we meet together. From now on, thanks to Bonnie's talent, it will be much safer to communicate on a secure tellaview." He proceeded to outline the remainder of his simple, but aggressive, plan to harass the Cartel. I will contact you if situations change. We'll adjust and move on."

35

The Wednesday morning newspaper headlines were of a major drug bust by Chief Detective John Swift of the Lind City Police, NARCO Division. The byline by Joan Fetter went on to say the successful drug raid was the result of the arrests achieved earlier this week at the Lind City Airport.

Bonnie stepped into Jake's office, "Jake, I see you're reading the morning paper's headlines. Were we a part of the arrests at the airport?"

"Yes, we were, and I'm sure the Cartel knows it too."

"I have to tell you, I already have a great feeling about our mission. It's twelve thirty. I'm going to the deli for lunch. Would you like something?"

"No thank you." Jake picked up the newspaper and started reading. "Hold on a minute, maybe I will get a sub." Jake's cell phone vibrated. "Excuse me, I have a call coming in from Maggie."

"Hi, I didn't think we were going to call each other unless it was an emergency."

"Jake...Jake," Maggie shouted frantically. Your father didn't show up for his weekly Wednesday lunch with Sheriff Marty. They've been having lunch together every Wednesday for twenty years and your dad was always sitting in the diner at precisely noon. The Sheriff sent word out to his deputies to check the route from your dad's home to the restaurant. They found your dad's pickup parked at the side of the highway, and there was no sign of your father. Marty sent a Forensics team and a K-nine unit to the pickup. I'm at your dads' home waiting for Marty to call."

"Maggie, stay where you are. Tell Sheriff Plank I'm on my way."

"Jake, what's up?" Bonnie asked.

"I think my father was abducted. I'm on my way to Wilson County."

The thought of his dad being abducted sent chills down Jake's spine. The Cartel's MO is ruthless, and kidnapping his father would not be out of the question. As he sped past several sheriff and state trooper vehicles on the way to his dad's home, it was quite evident Marty sent the word out to his law enforcement agencies, he was going to be going fast. Jake made it to the Whispering Pines gate where he was met by two Sheriff's Deputies.

"Jake, Sheriff Plank has a command post in your dad's home and your wife is with him," the Deputy said.

Maggie rushed to Jake, put her arms around him, and started to sob, "Jake, I'm so sorry. Someone took him."

Jake embraced Maggie for a few seconds. "We're going to find him and bring him home."

Sheriff Plank shook Jake's hand, "We have a 'Be On the Look Out' bulletin everywhere in the Northeast. Hopefully, the BOLO will get some results. Also, we have a team of Crime Scene Investigators going over every inch of your father's pickup and the surrounding woods in the area."

"Sheriff, I have good idea of what's going on. I'm in the middle of an investigation with the FBI which involves the Cartel's operation. This has to be the work of the Cartel."

"I heard the bastards were doing their best to operate out of Lind City, and you're doing your best to keep them the hell out of there. I've heard about them going after family but why are they going after your father?"

"That's a good question." Jake replied. He sat at the kitchen table with his head cupped in his hands. He looked up at Maggie as she placed a mug of coffee in front of him. "Maggie, are you thinking what I'm thinking?"

"Yeah, we might have a rat within our group."

"Let's assume we have an adversary among us. Sheriff, how long did it take for your people to arrive at my father's pickup?"

"Let's see, I waited ten minutes for your father to show up at the diner. I dispatched a unit to follow the route your dad would take to the diner. The deputy found your dad's empty truck right away. I'd say a total of fifteen minutes." The Sheriff paused. "Shit, I know what you're thinking. It had to take them at least five minutes to find you father on the highway, another three or four minutes to get him pulled over and, if I know John Lester, he tried like hell to kick their ass before they subdued him. Jake, they must have him within three or four miles from here. You don't think they're stupid enough to take him to the talc mine?"

"Yes, I think they are. Let's not rush to the mine with a lot of people. If they are at the mine, we don't want to panic them into doing harm to my father. Sheriff, remember when we were chasing down the human traffickers, there was a hidden back way to the mine."

"Right, I remember, and I'm sure whoever these people are they don't know it's there."

"Can you have maybe two or three of your snipers follow us to the mine? If we bring your new 'Ground Penetrating Radar' with us, we should be able to locate their position, weapons, and the amount of resistance they have. We still have a lot of daylight."

Jake led the way through the thickets, brush, and dense prick bushes until they reached a small summit behind the entrance of the mine. He rested his high-powered rifle in the crutch of his left arm and removed the cover from the Martini five x scope."

The Sheriff received a message through his earpiece from the snipers, "We're in place." He placed the GPR on the ground with the lens pointing down and started to scan the mine tunnels. The radar waves began to span the mint-colored screen with intricate measurement numbers. "Nothing on the first level," Sheriff Plank whispered. He adjusted the GPR and concentrated on the entrance to the second level tunnel, "Maybe we'll get better results on the second level." He repositioned the instrument several times and stopped. "Jake, we have two images on the second level. One of the men is standing and the other man is sitting against a wall. "Let's see if I can get a better view." He focused on the man standing and leaning against the wall. "The man leaning against the wall is armed with a long weapon of some sort." He focused the GPR on the person sitting on the ground. "The man on the ground looks like he has something over his head." Sheriff Plank stepped away from the scanner. "Take a look, Jake."

"The guy sitting with his left leg propped up, has to be my father. He injured his knee several years ago and has never been able to totally bend his left knee." Jake looked way from the scope. "Sheriff, there's something wrong with this. It would be impossible for one person to manhandle my father into a mine shaft. There has to be more guards around there. How deep will the scope penetrate the ground?"

"In this case, with open shafts, with talc material in the way, we might be able to see a hundred feet, plus or minus," Sheriff Plank replied. He moved the GPR's scope to a forty-five-degree slant. "Nothing on the third level."

Jake knew there was more than one guard watching over his father. They would have to be in close proximity of the second level entrance. "Sheriff, is the scope capable of scanning farther into the second level shaft?"

"I don't know. I'll give it a try," Sheriff Plank replied. He adjusted the scope, pressed two buttons, and the screen went blank. "Shit. Let me try something different." He turned the GPR's EM pulse to fifteen hundred MHz, "Jake, take a look at this. There're images about a hundred feet inside the second level shaft.

"Yeah, I see them," Jake replied. He pressed his face tight against the scope, "They're big, heavily armed, and we're waiting for us to step off the elevator. The minute we enter the shaft they will ambush us. We would be bunched together and wouldn't have a chance. I know we don't have much time, but let's think about this. There has to be a safety exit with an emergency escape stairwell, about a hundred fifty feet from every shaft elevator. If we use the escape stairwell, instead of the elevator, to access the second level, we can come from behind and surprise all five of the guards before they have a chance to retaliate."

"That's a great idea, Jake. I'll coordinate my deputies' movements with the GPR while they descend to the second level. I'll join them on the second level before they implement the incursion. This could get nasty, so I would like you to stay above ground until the exercise is over."

"Yeah, right. Shit, Sheriff, you know I'm not going to stand here while my father's in the middle of all this. I'm going to be the man in front of your team, take care of the guy guarding father and if any other shit head Cartel people get in my way, they're toast. Whatta think of that?"

Sheriff Plank replied, "Hmm, I didn't' think you would stay behind."

Jake, Sheriff Plank, and fifteen deputies quietly descended down the dark, dirty, and cobwebbed stairwell to the second level safety exit. They checked their weapons, and waited for the Sheriff's command to rush into the mine. An eerie sound of silence came over the group of deputies. They all were all well trained in assault tactics, and had their assigned tasks when they rushed into the mine. Many of deputies were men and women who have served in Afghanistan, and were familiar with waiting for an assault command, however, it was never easy.

Sheriff Plank whispered into his head mic, "People, on my count of three. One…two…three."

Jake was in front of the deputies when the door to the mine shaft blew open with a loud detonation. He raced to the section of the mine where his father was sitting, and the surprised guard who was leaning against the mine's wall.

The guard brought up his weapon, pointed it at Jake, and before he could fire off a shot, Jake bashed his rifle butt against the guard's jaw, tugged the weapon from his grasp, and slammed his adversary to the ground where he laid unconscious. "Don't screw with my family," Jake shouted. He knelt beside his father, pulled the cover from his head, tightly hugged him, and whispered, "Dad, I love you. Everything's okay. Sheriff Plank is rounding up the other guards, you're safe."

Jake's father stood, and calmly said, "Jake, I knew you would show up and their asses. Thank you."

The quick action by the sheriff and his deputies brought, a speedy end to the skirmish with the scantly armed and ill prepared Cartel guards. Sheriff Ronny Plank stood tall with his deputies, for this was the largest achievement in Wilson County history.

Jake and is father found Sheriff Plank and his team located in front of the mine with the captives handcuffed and siting on the ground.

"Good catch, Marty. What took you guys so long?" John asked, jokingly.

Sheriff Plank replied, "Lester, I never thought I would be so happy to see your sorry self. It's great to see you unharmed. You know this will cost you a few glasses of your twelve-year-old scotch."

"Sheriff, I have a suggestion. When we were running through the mine, I noticed there was no prepared food or food supplies and they haven't eaten anything. These people have to eat and I'll wager food has to be brought here by other Cartel members. We can question these guys, find out where they came from, wait for the people to deliver the food, and arrest them as well. I think it's important to find out were these people based."

"You might have a point, Jake, but don't you report to the FBI?" Sheriff Plank asked.

"I do…I'll claim this is your jurisdiction and your operation. You and your deputies were responsible for finding and arresting these people. Sheriff, sometime tonight you're going to be successful in the apprehension of more Cartel members, and I was here because my father was being held captive," Jake replied.

"Jake's right, Marty. You and your people deserve the adda boys for this successful operation. Marty, I've known you since high school and you never have taken credit when it wasn't due, well now is the time you took credit for this."

"Yeah, I guess you guys are right. Now let's get ready for the people who are going to deliver the food. Jake, we can take it from here. It's still daylight and if you need to get back to Lind City, we would understand," Sheriff Plank said.

"I'll take you up on that. I can drop Maggie and my dad off on my way back home."

Jake looked into the rearview mirror as he drove away from his father home, and saw Maggie standing in the driveway waving. "Damn, I hate to leave without her."

Jake started processing the events of the last few days, from the time his dad was kidnapped to a few minutes ago when he left Maggie standing in the driveway. There were questions bouncing around in his head. Like, where did the kidnappers come from, where were they hiding before they kidnapped his father, where did the food come from to feed the guards? How did the kidnappers know his father met with Sheriff Plank every Wednesday for lunch? It was too well organized to be a hit and miss operation. Furthermore, if the Cartel wanted to prove a point and stop his investigation, they would have viciously killed his father and sent the body parts to him in Lind City.

It was late evening when Jake drove into his driveway. He made his usual stop before he pushed the button on the garage door opener, started to proceed forward, and to his dismay, a shiny, brand new all-terrain vehicle was parked in the garage. "What the hell is this?" He quickly pushed the button on the remote pad, and the garage door closed with a thud. He went into the house through the front door and rushed down to the basement, where John was sleeping with the TV on.

Jake nudged John, "Wake up, wake up."

"Hey, Jake, Good you're back. Is everything ok?"

"Who owns that all-terrain vehicle in my garage?" Jake asked, critically.

"What the hell are you talking about? Some guy came buy and said you bought the vehicle and parked in the driveway. I asked for his credentials, and he showed me his ID and auto dealership card. After he left, I parked it in the garage. That's not your all-terrain?"

"No, it's not, and now I'm sure someone is giving me the same message I'm giving Cartel," Jake said.

"It's not like the Cartel to be so polite," John remarked.

36

Jake received a phone call from Robert Marshal, Lind City Police Commissioner. He arrived promptly at nine a.m., walked the three flights of stairs, stood in front of Penney Grant's desk, and said, "Penney, congratulations heard you were promoted to the Police Commissioner's secretary."

Penney pushed back her round, bifocals, smiled and said, businesslike, "Thank you, and yes. I was prompted just after you left the department. Commissioner Marshal's secretary decided to retire and here I am. The commissioner is expecting you. I'll let him know you're here."

Jake was impressed by Penney's new businesslike manner, which is a far removed from her happy outgoing personality he was used to when she was his secretary. He noticed an open folder on her desk with a red, top-secret stamp across the cover page.

"Jake, the commissioner will see you now," Penney announced. She stood from her desk, scooped up the top-secret folder, and escorted Jake into the commissioner's office.

The commissioner, asked, pleasantly, "Jake, how the hell are you? It seems like for ever since you left us. Please have a seat."

"It's good to see you too, Commissioner." Jake has known Robert Marshal for better than twenty years, and knew when his ex-boss started a conversation with a smile and a congenial voice, it was the beginning of a very serious conversation. He was certain the topic of Robert's request for this meeting was contained in the folder laying on the desk in front of him.

"Please, Jake, call me Robert when we're alone. We've had a lot of changes here, but that hasn't changed. "You're probably wondering, why, out of a clear blue sky, I asked you to meet with me this morning…Would you like some coffee, or other beverage?"

Robert seemed a little unhinged and unusually nervous. Jake replied, "No thank you." He thought maybe it's time to fast forward the meeting. "Why did you request a morning? In the past when you wanted a meeting you gave me an agenda beforehand, which would allow me to do some homework."

Robert said, "Uh, right. This came up rather quickly, like yesterday, from the mayor. I apologize for the fast-track notice. The Mayor and the Lind City Council suggested I meet with you forthwith." Robert flipped open the top-secret folder. "Jake, you've brought a lot of attention to Lind City in the last month. The overwhelming headlines of drug busts, shootings, and the disappearance of a prominent Columbian Diplomate have appeared daily in the morning newspaper. The mayor also holds you accountable for a construction crew walking off a building project on the outskirts of the city." He shuffled through the folder, drew out a sheet of paper resembling a legal form with the Lind City Mayors letterhead, and gave it to Jake.

Jake eyed at the legal form on the desk, looked at Robert, and, said, sarcastically, "The Mayor holds me responsible. What exactly does he mean?"

"Jake, the Mayor and the City Council say you're scaring business away because the violence," Robert pleaded.

Jake, said, vehemently, "You can tell the mayor and the city officials, who can't see passed their noses, if it wasn't for my efforts and some volunteers, Lind City would be a world class Cartel hub for the mixing and distribution of drugs, and the violence would be beyond the mayor and the city council's comprehension. And by the way, the so-called missing diplomat is the head of the U S Cartel... "Robert, this goes deeper than the city officials, doesn't it?"

"I'm the messenger, and my hands are tied," Robert replied.

"Robert, you can give this message to whoever is pulling your strings. The work I'm doing is authorized by the Deputy Director of the FBI, and he is extremely happy with my work."

Robert smiled, "I knew you wouldn't care what the mayor ordered." He tore the legal form in half. "I'll be happy to convey your message. Jake, this is off the record. From my vantage point, and what the NARCO people are telling me, you're doing a fantastic job. My words to you, and, I'm sure you know, follow the money. You might be surprised."

A sudden mid-day, thunderstorm appeared while Jake was driving to his office. The deluge of rain, the intimidation of thunder and lightning, forced him to park and wait out the storm in a plaza parking lot. He opened a bottle of water, and, without drinking any of the water, placed the bottle of water into the car's drink holder. Jake knew Robert was out on a limb when he went off the record and said, 'follow the money.' Following the money is an elementary grade instruction in an investigator's handbook. Why Robert would lay it on the table? The storm diminished and Jake continued on his way to his office.

"Good morning, Bonnie. Any messages?"

"Yes, you have one message at nine thirty this morning, and the person refused to leave his name. He said he would call you later. I suggested he email or text you, he became irritated and hung up. If you would like to hear is voice, I have it on the recorder."

"No, I don't need to hear a voice. I'll wait for him to call back. It's probably a crank call. Bonnie, could you search the city official's data bank and look for any illegal outside money activity by a city official, also, consolidate all the names of people we have been dealing with over the last six months and run a similar query on them."

"Do you actually mean everyone?"

"Yes, everyone. I'm looking for an obscure money trail. I mean a little-known source, but significant amounts of money."

"Do you mean someone laundering money, and living beyond their realm of legal income?" Bonnie asked.

"Yes, right, you know what I mean. How long do you think out would take to compile all that information?"

Bonnie flashed a Cheshire cat smile, "Actually I started doing exactly that a few days ago while you were away. Lind City is a small city and, we all know, everyone knows everyone's business. I started with Mayor Richard Comfort, and I'm through all the council members. If I work nonstop, I should have it completed in about a week."

"Bonnie, that's great. Can you provide me with information as you progress?"

"Sure…Jake, not for nothing, you know you're going to get a lot of people in high places pissed off at you."

"I thought about it and that's why I want to investigate obscure incomes. My goal is, uncover illegal drug activity, arrest the bad guys, and keep the Cartel out of Lind City. I'm not interested in the peripheral legal stuff." Jake paused, "Maybe I should hear the man's voice."

Bonnie turned on the phone messages, and increased the volume level, "Back off now, or the next time we'll kill your father and you wife."

"I've heard that voice somewhere. It sounds like a man's voice; however, it could very well be a woman's voice." Jake replayed the recording, "Yes, it's a woman's voice."

"This isn't an idle threat. These people aren't screwing around."

"Yes, I know. I can't back off now. I'll give my father and Sheriff Plank a heads up about this phone message. Bonnie, I know it's a long shot. Try to can get a trace on the call."

"A minute after we received the message I started working on a trace. The message came from a bourn phone which means we will never find the user. I'm working with some of my old friends at the department to see if we can find the location of the cell tower. It's going to take some time."

"It might take some time but, if we can locate the neighborhood, there's a possibility we'll be able to cross reference the location with someone we know." Jake looked at the morning paper laying on the office coffee table. "I know how we can take some of the heat off us. I'm going to talk to Joan Fetter and see if she and a Times photographer can meet me in the front of the Police Department for a photo shoot. Bonnie, can you get Joan on the phone for me while I do a little homework?"

Jake parked his van directly in front of the Lind City Police Headquarters building sign and patiently waited for Joan and a photographer to arrive. He looked into his side view mirror and saw a Times Union truck loaded with outside antennas and video transmitters stop and park behind him. "Why would I think otherwise?"

Joan popped out of the front seat of the truck and shouted, "Hi Jake, are you going to get out of the vehicle, or are you going to pose for my photographer inside the van? What's this all about anyway?"

"Like I told you on the phone, I have another scoop for you, and I want it to be a surprise. Have the photographer stand in the street where he can get a wide lens shot of the Police Headquarters sign."

Joan bobbed and weaved as she tried to sneak a peek into the van, "You're being very mysterious. Is that why the van windows are covered?"

Jake stepped to the side of the van, and, with a strong tug, slid the side door open, and announced, "I give you the head of the US Cartel, Diego Garcia." Jake took Garcia by the hand to help his new best friend out of the van. Garcia brushed Jake's hand aside, jumped out of the vehicle, and landed on his knees.

The photographer stood in the center of Main Street, stopping traffic, while he captured rapid-fire still photos and videos of Garcia kneeling in front of Police Headquarters.

"Jake, you have an uncanny way of doing things and I love it. Where the hell has Garcia been for the last three weeks?" Joan asked.

"That's top secret. Please, no pictures of me and note in your write up that Garcia was seen walking on Main Street in front the Lind City Police Department. The readers can make their own assumptions," Jake replied, with a smirk. "Will this make the evening news and tomorrow morning's paper?"

"Jake, not only will it be in all our media, it will literally be the headlines in every major media and social outlet in the world. This is huge. How can I thank you?"

"No, thank you, Joan Fetter. With your expertise, the Cartel will receive the most highly unwanted publicity than could ever be achieved."

"What about Garcia?"

Jake replied, "Garcia, I'm sure he will be apprehended by the FBI within the next few minutes."

"You covered all your bases," Joan said.

37

In was late at night when Diego Garcia slipped out of the shadows and into the pouring rain to seek help at a location where he thought to be welcoming. The rain dripped from his hat and onto his soaking wet suit. He pushed the doorbell, stepped back to be recognized, and the door opened slightly. Garcia looked into an empty doorway and said, "I need your help. Please, I need a place to stay and hide. You are my only chance to live another day," Diego Garcia pleaded.

"No," a voice said from a small speaker. You can't stay here. If I help you, they will me too. Go, get out. How stupid you are to think you could get away with cooperating with the police without suffering the consequences." The door slammed closed. Diego gradually stepped away from the closed door, bewildered, drenched from the rain, and without a place to hide from his assassins. He revealed his location to someone, he thought was a friend and, assuredly, he will be dead within twenty-four hours. He cautiously walked out of the dark alley and onto a lightly traveled side street. He noticed lights from a bright sign flashing 'Serge's Place' in the front window of a greasy spoon diner. The two raggedy dressed patrons sitting in a booth, looked intently at Diego as he flipped the rain from his hat, and sat in a corner booth.

A man dressed in shabby blue jeans, and a soiled apron asked gruffly, "What can I do you for you,"

"A large black coffee and a pastry," Diego replied. He assumed the unshaven man was Serge.

"That'll be eight bucks, before you get the coffee and pastry."

Diego reached into his wallet and placed his wallet and a twenty-dollar bill on the table. "I only have a twenty."

"Perfect."

Diego Garcia thought, yesterday he was at the top of the Cartel ladder and tonight he is sitting in a dirty diner drinking old coffee, eating stale pastry, being chased by the Cartel, and with no help in sight.

"Hey Pal, closing time. You gotta get out," Serge shouted, from the kitchen.

Diego picked up the wallet and remembered he had Jake Lester's business card. He shuffled through the wallet compartments and found Jake's wrinkled business card. His situation was dire and he could see no other option. "My last chance." He shoved the wallet into his pocket and felt the heavy snub nose revolver in a cloth holster. The weapon in his pocket posed a double-edged sword situation. He would be in trouble if he was stopped by the police as a routine stop, but, if the two men at the other end of the diner decided to mug him, he could protect himself.

The rain had not stopped when Diego left the diner. As he predicted, the two men followed him out the door. He walked toward Main Street with his right hand in his pocket, resting on the revolver, with the hammer pulled back and locked into firing position. He breathed a sigh of relief came out him when the two men crossed the alley and walked in the opposite direction.

Diego pulled a cell phone from his jacket pocket. He held Jake's business card in the light of a street light and tapped in Jake's cell phone number.

"Hello, who is this?" Jake asked.

"This is Diego Garcia, please don't hang up."

"Why are you calling me?" Jake asked, sternly.

"I need help. The Cartel, they think I gave you and the police secret information. They think I'm a traitor."

"So, why are you calling me? I can't help you."

"I need a place to hide for a while...maybe a few weeks," Garcia said.

"You're using a Cartel cell phone, right? They know, at this very moment, your location and the number you called. Turn the phone off, drop it in a trash barrel, and walk toward Police Headquarters. Do you remember where it is?"

"Yes, how could I ever forget? I was kneeling in front of the place this afternoon."

Okay, just keep walking, don't stop for any reason and don't worry, I'll find you."

Diego walked for fifteen minutes without stopping and was closing in on Police Headquarters when a black pickup truck came to a speeding stop next to him. He pulled out his revolver and waited for gunfire.

"Get in the freaking truck," Jake shouted.

Diego jumped into the truck, slammed the door, and slipped back in his seat when Jake floored the accelerator.

Jake drove a few miles and stopped the truck next to a city trash barrel. "I have a change of clothes for you. I want you to take off all your clothes and your shoes and socks. Throw them into that barrel. You can put you new clothes on while I drive."

"Why are you telling to disrobe?"

"The Sinaloa Cartel has you bugged from head to toe."

"Why would the most-powerful drug-trafficking syndicate in the world care about me?"

"Diego Garcia, you must be the naivest person on this planet. The Cartel doesn't trust anyone, including you."

"Shit...where are you taking me?"

"You'll know when we get there. Diego, if you're bullshitting me, I'll kill you myself." Jake drove for several miles making left hand turns, while constantly looking for possible followers. The sun was starting to rise and street lights started to automatically turn off. Jake pulled into the Police Department garage and parked in the NARCO Chief Detective's spot. "I don't think John Swift will complain."

"What are you doing?" Diego screamed. "Are you crazy?"

"This jail will be the safest place in the world for a Columbian Diplomat. Chief Detective Smith is a good man and, I'm sure if you answer all his questions, he will see you get back to Columbia safely."

"No, I'm not a Diplomat. I'm a Columbian citizen. I will be dead the second I set foot on Columbian soil."

"Sure, you're a Diplomat. I checked it out with the US Embassy. They told me you are definitely a Columbian Diplomat. Jake turned off the truck's engine, opened the glove compartment, and plucked out his cell phone. While we sit here and wait for Chief Detective Smith to show up for work, you can answer my questions. If your answers are correct, I'll put in a good word for you. Jake turned on his cell phone's sound and video recorder.

"I don't know anything," Garcia said.

"I didn't ask you anything."

"I know, and I'm not saying anything. You don't know what these people will do to me if I open my mouth. Do you know what a Columbian necktie is?"

Jake knew the answer. He preferred to have Garcia explain the execution procedure and, by the power of suggestion, Garcia might scare himself into unloading secret information. "No, I don't know about the Columbian necktie."

Garcia wiggled in his seat and began to perspire, and said, "Okay, when the Sinaloa Cartel Security people catch you, they will torture you beyond belief and, when you are almost dead, they cut your throat from ear to ear, pull your tongue through the hole, and take a picture of you. They send the picture to all of your family, to show them what happens when you betray the Cartel."

"You're in big trouble."

"If you guarantee my safe asylum, I will give you all the information I have."

"I can't guarantee anything. I can suggest the authorities help you. I have some questions. I would like to know the names of the Cartel assassins who are trying to kill me?"

"I don't know. They don't tell me. They send as many people as they need to do the job."

"You're the top man in the US Cartel and you're telling me you don't know?"

"That's true," Diego replied.

"That's strike one."

"There are a lot of drugs out on the streets of Lind City. Where and who is in charge of the operation?"

"I don't know!" Diego screamed.

"That's bullshit. When are they moving the big mixing and distribution operation into our city?"

"Please Jake, I don't know the answer to those questions. That's the truth. El Chapo, Geraldo Quostona, is the only person who knows and he don't say nothing to nobody."

Jake anticipated Garcia's replies and, up to now, played softball with him. He reached across the seat, opened the passenger door and shouted, "Get the hell out of my truck and get the hell out of this garage."

Diego grabbed the door handle, pushed his foot against the door hinge and screamed, "No, no, I'll tell you everything."

Jake heard John Swift's voice and stopped pushing Diego.

"What's going on here," John asked.

Jake replied, "John, Diego and I were having quite a conversation, sort of, about the Cartel's people and their operation in Lind City. He told me he would be more than happy to tell us everything he knows, except the big mixing and distribution operation coming into our city."

John said, "I think he's telling you the truth. El Chapo has PPD, a paranoid personality disorder. He   doesn't trust anyone, not even his own family, especially when it comes to any big changes in the business. The records show he had his own brother killed because he asked too many questions about the business. He had one of his men take his brother for a ride into the mountains. When they came to the highest cliffs area, the man stopped the car, dragged the brother from the car, and threw him over a cliff. The killer watched the brother land. He then made his way to the bottom of the cliff and cut the ears of the dying man because El Chapo wanted proof that his brother was dead."

"How did El Chapo know those ears belonged to his brother?"

John gave out a loud chuckle, "Yeah right, no one ever found the man who killed El Chapo's brother."

Jake shook his head in frustration, "Okay, John, he's all yours. Keep me in the loop."

"Jake, one last thing. You might want to think about a couple of security units with you twenty-four seven. We're dealing with some pretty nasty people. I wouldn't blame you if you took the offer," John suggested.

"Nah, I don't think so. Thanks anyway." Jake drove out of the police garage, turned on his headlights and windshield wipers. He mumbled, "Rain, it's a hell of a way to end a long night." His immediate priorities were to stop at his favorite all-night diner for breakfast and take a quick shower and a short power nap before going to the office.

"Good morning, Jake. I've never been your waitress at four a.m. How about your usual black coffee for starters?"

"Good morning, Tina. Late night work. Coffee sounds great with steak and eggs to finish off my cholesterol count."

"We'll have it for you in a jiffy."

Jake took off his wet jacket and placed it over the chair next to
him. His attention was drawn to the squeaky diner door opening and
the two unshaven, long haired, sloppily dressed men walking to the
counter. They hesitated for a moment and picked out two stools at
the counter. Jake wasn't overly concerned with them until he noticed
bulges under their jackets. They kept their wet jackets on. He
watched intently, without being too obvious, to see if they were
wearing law enforcement shields.

His concentration was interrupted by Tina's cheerful voice.

"Steak and eggs the way you like them."

Jake whispered, "Tina, do you know those two guys at the
counter?"

"No, never seen them before."

Jake devoured his breakfast, picked up his bill from the table and
stood next to the cash register. He glimpsed in the direction of the
two men and calmly left the diner. "Paranoia," he mumbled.

38

"Jake Lester, Sam Springs here. When I took over the ME's job
from your wife, I assumed this position would be a walk in the park.
People are dropping like flies in this city."

"What's going on Dr. Springs?"

"Call me Dr. Sam. I'm at a crime scene at the Lind City Hotel.
Carman Cruz, the Hotel Manager, called the police when he received
a complaint from a guest. The guest stated there was a lot of racket
in the room next to him and he is positive he heard two gunshots."

"Is he sure there were two shots?"

"Yup, he knew there were two gunshots because one of the bullets
came through the wall and almost hit him. I wouldn't have bothered
you, but the deceased has a Passport from China. Wait a second, I'll
turn the phone over to Dr. Zigerfield. He'll be able to fill you in on
the details."

The new ME consulted with Jake which made it evident he was not beyond cooperating with him, and he knew he had to reciprocate every chance he had.

Zig came on the phone, "Jake, the deceased is a Chinese National and he resides in New York City. By the looks of the room, there wasn't a struggle or wasted bullets. The bullet wound entered the forehead, exited the back of his head and landed on the floor. I'll run ballistics check on the bullet and I'm sure it was a hollow point projectile. The second bullet, not a hollow point, went through his head and into the adjacent room. This has the mark of another professional hit. I'll give you more information after I work on it at the lab."

"Thanks for the update, Zig. I'm on my way home. If anything looks interesting, call me anytime."

As he drove towards his home, he periodically looked in the rearview mirror to make certain the two men who were in the diner weren't following him. It was dawn when he pulled into his driveway and turned off the engine. He leaned across the seat, opened the glove compartment, pulled out his holster with a Smith & Wesson snub nose thirty eight police special, and tucked it into his jacket. As he approached his front door, he looked above the door where he had placed a small matchstick between the door and the door jamb. The matchstick was still there. He opened the door and shouted down to John, " John are you down there?"

John shouted, "Yes I'm down here. Where the hell have you been?"

Jake replied, "It's a long story. I'll tell you after I take a shower. "

It was noon when Jake woke from a much-needed nap, turned on the TV and looked for the early afternoon news. The media was not making the episode a major item that day. Jake remembered he was going to talk with John about the happenings of the night before. He passed through the kitchen on his way to the basement door and happened to looked out the window. He saw a van marked with a plumber's sign on the side of it. 'This can't be a coincidence,' referring to the evening before when someone was supposed to be working in a house across the street. The people who own the house were away on vacation and they wouldn't be back for another month. He pulled out his cell phone and took a few pictures of the van and sent them over to Bonnie to see if they could get recognition on the license plate.

"Damn Jake, it took you a while to get down here to talk with me. I thought maybe you were mad at me for something," John said, jokingly.

"No, I'm not mad at you at all. I just had a long night and now a crazy morning. I was sure someone was following me from the diner. But I'm sure my paranoia took over and that's all it was. I have to tell you about last night. A Chinese, so-called Diplomat, was murdered. He turned out to be the top sales liaison for China selling fentanyl. John, I see a pattern here: El Chapo is getting rid of his top people and a liaison. This tells me he's cleaning house and bringing in new individuals who might be more vicious than those individuals who are presently in control in the US. "

"Yeah, I think you're right, Jake. There seems to be a pattern, and that also tells me we better start buttoning things up while they're in transition."

"Maybe the time is right now. I have my thoughts about different suspects, and a plan where we might be able to bring them all together without raising any suspicions. Our new summer home is almost completed. The contractor called me yesterday and said he's putting the finishing touches on the building. We might be able to move in in about two weeks. I'd like to get Maggie's opinion before we plan a date. It would be appropriate for us to have an open house the week we move in and invite several of the people to a cookout who I think are on the short list of suspects."

"I know a couple of friends at the Bureau who would help you when you're ready to round up the bad guys. Incidentally, you might want to invite the Deputy Director of the FBI," John said.

Jake replied, "Yeah, he's on the top of my short list. I remember someone's dying words to me, "Don't trust anyone, not even your close friends."

"I hope that excludes me," John said, softly.

Jake said, "If I didn't trust you, you wouldn't be in my home. We need to get Lonny on board with our plans. Have your heard from Lonny?"

"No, I haven't heard a word from him since he placed the fake explosives at the third building, and that was last night. He told me he was going to stop by an ATM and do some grocery shopping. He might be entertaining someone. I'll reach out to him today," John replied.

Jake was still groggy from the night before and thought a nap would be in order. He wiggled his way into a comfortable position on the sofa, set his cell phone on the table next to him, closed his eyes, and started to doze off when his cell phone rang. He looked at the caller ID, saw Lonny's name, and asked. "Lonny, what's up?"

A strange, muffled voice replied, "We've got Lonny and, if you don't back off your investigation, we'll send you his body one piece at a time."

"Who is this," Jake screamed.

"Just do it."

"Jake, what the hell is going on," John asked.

"Someone's got Lonny and, if I don't back off, they're going to kill him," Jake replied. He jumped off the sofa. "Where was he when they nabbed him?" he paused, "You said he was going to stop at an ATM and go grocery shopping. We need to check all the ATM CCTV videos in his neighborhood." He touched the speed number for his office, "Bonnie, someone has kidnapped Lonny, and we think they nabbed him at an ATM, possibly near his apartment. Can you reach out to your friends and have them check the ATM videos. Lonny is easy to ID, he always has his umbrella with him."

"What can I do?" John asked.

"Stay here and wait. If Bonnie's friends come up with something, give me a shout. I'm going to his apartment. There's the possibility Lonny was nabbed there."

Jake pulled up to the apartment lot and found a visitor parking space in front of Lonny's apartment building. He looked up at the second floor window and noticed Lonny's drapes were pulled shut. The elevator squeaked as the elevator door opened. Jake cautiously stepped from the elevator, walked to Lonny's apartment, and stood next to the door. He drew is pistol from the leather holster, gently pushed the partially open door with his foot, and edged his way into the apartment. The overturned table and Lonny's umbrella lying on the floor in the center of the room, indicated Lonny had scuffled before he was subdued. Lonny was an electronic security buff and Jake had a hunch the entire abduction was recorded from an obscure position in the apartment. He rummaged through the apartment while he tried to guess where Lonny might have placed a recorder. He grumbled, "where the hell would he stash that recorder?" He stood in the center of the living room, circling in place, scanning every nook and cranny, and stopped. He focused on a metal centerpiece of an Owel holding a small mouse in its beak. It was mounted on a bookcase. It appeared one of the glassy eyes of the captured mouse was set off center. Jake pulled the mouse from the Owel's beak, turned it upside down and saw a tiny lever at the mouse's butt. Jake grinned and, when he touched the lever, a miniature video camera slipped from its mount. The camera recorded two masked and hooded men scuffling with Lonny and dragging him out the door. "Shit, now we'll have a tough time finding him."

"Bonnie, Lonny has been taken from his apartment by two men. It doesn't look good."

"Jake, one of my friends spotted Lonny at an ATM drawing money from the machine. The video picked up two Caucasian men, sitting in a black van, and watching Lonny's every move. We have a description of the men and the van's license number."

"Were you able to get an address from the license plate?"

"Yes, I'll send the information over to you. My friends know Lonny's father and they asked, off the record, if you would like some help with this."

"I'll take all the help I can get from your friends. Who am I dealing with."

"He's an off duty, off the record Sargent, just call him Joe. You'll know him when you see him."

"Ask him to meet me a block away from the address you sent me. I want to go in soft, fast and safe."

Jake cruised to a stop behind six men crammed into a SUV. He waited for someone in the SUV to make a move. He watched a man who was in the driver's seat slide out of the vehicle. Jake became overwhelmed by the sight of a man in a t shirt with multiple tattoos. "Holy shit, Joe Bensen."

"Jake you old bastard. The last time I saw you, you were in deep shit in Afghanistan. Do I have to bail your ass out again?"

"Joe, I thought you were in the Police Special Riot Unit."

"We are. All the guys in the SUV are PSRU. When Bonnie called and said you might need some help, I mean, what could we say?"

"I appreciate your help. We have at least two men holding my friend, Lonny Donavan, hostage. Lonny's helping me with a Cartel case. I think these people are tied into the Cartel and they're holding Lonny until I back away from my Cartel investigation. They promised, in no uncertain terms, if I don't back away, they'll kill Lonny."

"Is Lonny Mike Donavan's son?" Joe asked.

"Yes."

"We have a lot of fun stuff in the back of the SUV and, trust me, Lonny will be safe."

Jake knew it was his responsibility to get Lonny, unscathed, out of this mess and asked, "Do you mind if I go in with you guys?"

Joe tightened the strap on his shoulder holster, smirked, and said, "Jake, it will be like old times. Let's go in and kick some ass."

Joe and his men, wearing gas masks, cautiously approached the house. He ordered two of his men to the back of the wood frame house, two men stood at each side of the front door, while one man slid a micro camera underneath the front door.

Jake could smell the stress in the air. While the camera was manipulated inside the structure, Joe's man withdrew the camera, stepped away from the door, and whispered, "Two men and one woman. All three are sitting at a kitchen table eating a fast-food meal. There're no sign other subjects are inside the dwelling." The die was cast.

Joe whispered into his mic, "Go, go, go, now."

Jake tightened his gas mask, slammed through the front door, gun drawn, while executing a barrel roll on the floor. He saw Lonny, half unconscious, and tied to a kitchen chair with a rope. But he looked unharmed. His primary task was to get Lonny the hell out of harm's way before the real fireworks started. He pulled a jungle knife from his belt, sliced the rope into pieces, yanked Lonny by the arms, whipped him over his shoulders, and carried him out the front door. He placed him on the ground behind a vehicle, and asked, "Lonny, you ok?"

Lonny rubbed his eyes, blinked a few times and said, "What took you so long."

Joe walked up to Jake and Lonny with one of the handcuffed criminals, "Are you guys going to sit on the ground all day?" He dropped the captive to the ground and leaned over Jake, "What do you want me to do with these people?"

"They're your collar and they were going to incite a riot. Thanks for your help. I owe you one," Jake replied.

39

Lonny was sitting in Jake's basement, with John and Jake, drinking a cold ginger ale and recounting the events of the past three days. He tapped one of his metal prostheses with his umbrella, sipped the last of his ginger ale and said, "Jake, I knew, sooner or later, you would find me and pull me out of that smelly roach ridden place. I'm more than happy you found me sooner than later. While I was sitting there, blindfolded and a little groggy from the cheap sedatives, I detected a distinct pungent odor. There was something about the stench that struck me as I fell in and out of coherence. It took me back about ten years. It was the smelly body odor in the Afghan jails. Do you guys remember when we entered a hot zone, where a lot of civilians were caught in the middle of heavy fire power and were left in the road for hours in the hot sun. The air was filled with the terrible stench of dead bodies. I'm telling you guys there was at least one decaying cadaver in that place and several prisoners."

Jake asked, "Lonny, can you remember how many people were involved in your kidnapping?"

"There were two men who grabbed me at the ATM machine and a woman driving the van. I was immediately blind folded at the ATM machine. They didn't say a word all the way to the house. When we got to the house, they tied me to a wooden chair and someone, a man, got really close to me and stuck me with a needle." Lonny paused, "That's when two people on the other side of the room started speaking Spanish."

"How did you know it was a man who stuck you?" John asked.

"I knew it was a man because he was wearing cheap men's cologne. You know, the type that smells like it cost five dollars a barrel."

Jake went to the refrigerator and pulled out two beers and a bottle of ginger ale. They were thirsty and the refreshments gave him a few minutes to ponder his next question. He sat across from Lonny, "Can you tell me, approximately, how long you were sedated?"

"I know what you're thinking, Jake. I had all my faculties while I was taking mental notes. If you're going to ask me, should we go back to the house, my answer would be 'yes'. This time we get a court order to search the place and a forensic technician working with us."

"I'm not a cop anymore. We would need a strong probable cause and a law enforcement office to ask a judge to issue the warrant." Jake wiped the moisture from his glass and drank a little beer. "What's our probable cause?"

Lonny replied, "The house reeks of body odor. You know like people haven't showered in months. It's a big old house, built in the early nineteen hundreds. It has big rooms, a cellar and probably seven or eight bedrooms."

"Lonny, are you actually thinking the house is being used for human trafficking?" John asked.

Jake replied, "John, Lonny has a good point. It wasn't too long ago when we shut down the human traffic operation at the talc mine. We may have mistaken the Cartel trafficking operation by thinking it was stopped. I don't think a judge would sign a warrant based on a smelly house. First, we should find out who actually owns the place and proceed from there."

John remarked, "What you're saying, you're going to enter an old dilapidated building alone, where Lonny was with other captives, held by members of the Cartel, and you're going to do it without backup, right."

"Right." Jake punched the speed dial numbers for his office, "Bonnie, can you get me the names of the people who own the old house on second street?"

"Jake, I was just about to call you. When I heard about Lonny's ordeal, I checked out the old house where he was held captive. I know the house. The city used to own it. I'll find out the current status of ownership. I'll get on it right now," Bonnie replied.

"Jake looked at his two friends and said, "Look I know you guys want to be in on the search but, Lonny, you're still in the process of recovering from a horrific experience and, John, you know it would be hell for you if you were recognized. I hope you guys understand?"

John replied, "We totally understand. We'll be happy to stay here and hold down the fort."

Jake's cell phone vibrated, "Hi Bonnie, I'm going to put you on speaker."

"Jake, I have the information on the old house. It was easy access to the files because the City owned it for the last twenty years until a month ago. An outfit named COCO LLC purchased it for one dollar. They told the City officials they were planning to build condominiums on the property. The City was happy to get rid of the property and for the tax money the condominiums will generate. The COCO LLC is going to break ground in about six months."

"Good job, Bonnie."

"COCO, why does that ring a bell?" John asked.

"It doesn't meant shit to me," Lonny said.

Jake sat quietly trying to connect the letters to a known entity and who would profit the most from the property. He was very familiar with the parcel of land and knew there was no possible way condominiums could be constructed on the small site. The confounding question was, why are they waiting six months to break ground? He moved the glass of beer up to his lips, stopped, and set the glass on a table, "Shit."

"What's up, Jake?" John asked, startled. "What's the matter?"

"COCO LLC, think about it? Carter Osterfeld CO, COCO is owned by the Cartel. When Carter, Mary and Hans Osterfeld were alive, a large portion of the company stock was transferred to the Cartel and, when the Osterfelds were out of the picture, the Cartel bought up the remainder of the stock. They told the Lind City officials they were planning to break ground in six months on a parcel of land which, everyone but the city officials, know the parcel's too small. This tells me the Cartel is planning to be in full operation in six months and it will be somewhere in Lind City."

"So, the Cartel needs a temporary location for, possibly six months, or until they get the new mixing plant operating. Jake, I'm happy to say I'm working with a man who believes in me and knows how to get a job done," Lonny remarked, as he tapped his umbrella on the floor.

Jake drove to the old house on second street and parked in the shade of the pot holed driveway. This is the first time he'd seen the dilapidated house in five years. 'The kidnappers didn't have far to drive when they stashed Lonny in this dump,' he thought. He stepped out of his car, opened the trunk, pulled out a clipboard and tape measure. The clipboard and tape measure were strictly for props should anyone should ask why he's entering the dwelling.

He scanned the heavily overgrown weeds and bushes in the front yard, and noticed a beaten footpath leading to the front steps. He made his way up the partially rotted, unpainted steps to the front door, grabbed a pair of rubber gloves from his pocket and stretched them onto his hands. The front door was partially ajar, and the hinges squeaked when he eased the open door enough to gain entrance into the once gracious vestibule. A pungent odor from the cellar permeated the entire dwelling to the point of eye tearing and choking. Jake covered is nose and mouth with his hankie and descended to the cellar. The night of Lonny's rescue slammed into Jake's memory, and the urge to vomit came over him. Running out of this hideous place was foremost on his mind, but he managed to stand his ground. After meticulously investigating the remainder of the basement, he realized Lonny was not hallucinating. The basement was definitely a place of death and human trafficking.

A familiar man's voice shouted from the living room a above, "Who's down there?"

Jake climbed the rickety basement steps to the living area, "Damn, Zig, you scared the hell out of me. What are you doing here?"

"A little bird, named Bonnie, told me you were investigating this dump today and she thought you might need a good forensics man here to help you. So, I got a judge friend of mine, and I got a warrant to shake down his place."

"Zig, thank you. You won't have any difficulty collecting evidence. This place is a hellhole, like I never seen since Afghanistan. The evidence steps right out and hits ya hard in the gut."

"Yeah, I could detect the smell as soon as I walked through the door. Why don't you wait outside while I scrape up some body and blood matter from the basement. You might find a flask of twelve year old scotch in my overnight case. Help yourself."

Jake sat in the driver's seat of his vehicle with the door wide open. He opted for some cold water from his thermos rather than the scotch.

Zig walked up to Jake's car, after he completed a sweeping investigation of the dwelling and grounds, "Jake, we gotta get the bastards who are selling people and doing unmentionable things to women and children."

"I know, Zig. Were you able find usable court of law evidence?"

"Unfortunately for the people who were victims of this place, yes. I found a treasure trove of old blood stains and body matter. They sold a lot of people through this hell hole and they did it in a very short period of time. I don't know if it will make a difference, but I'll rush the samples through the lab for possible DNA matches." Zig leaned against the side of Jake's car, wiped the sweat from his forehead, and brushed his hand through his hair, "Man, I've seen a lot of bad things in my career but this is despicable."

"Zig, I'm thinking, from the large amount of people we rescued from the talc mine, and the small amount of traffic through here, they must be operating several locations in Lind City."

"I have to agree with you. This is a fraction of their total operation," Zig said.

40

It was early morning when Jake arrived at his office. He was wearing a suit and carrying a briefcase. "Bonnie, Marshal Dunkin called me last night and asked me to meet with him at the FBI office in New York City."

Bonnie handed Jake a mug of coffee, "Did he give you an agenda?"

"No, not really. He just said bring everything I have on the Cartel case and nothing else. I'm assuming that would be the topic of the meeting without a formal agenda," Jake replied. He walked a few steps toward his private office, and stopped, "You better take my laptop and download all the information on the smaller Bureau cases."

A Yellow Cab Company driver stopped in front of 26 Federal Plaza in New York City. Jake stepped out of the cab and was inundated with the busy, noisy, and crushing crowd on the sidewalk. He liked the Lind City life, and hated the neurotic life of a big city. He entered the monstrous first floor and followed the signs to the security desk. One of the men at the security desk asked, "Can I help you, sir?"

The man's voice reverberated like a battery operated robot. "Yes, I'm here to see Deputy Director Marshal."

After receiving a visitor's pass and being escorted to the proper elevator, Jake arrived at the 23rd floor where he was met by a young man dressed in a Brooks Brothers suit.

"Good morning, Mr. Lester," The young man said, as he shook Jake's hand.

When Jake shook the young man's hand, he could feel a small amount of sweat on the man's hand.

"Follow me, I'll take you to the meeting room. I'm sure Deputy Director Marshal will see you shortly. Would you like a beverage?"

"No thank you," Jake replied. He wandered to the large plate glass windows and stared at the people twenty-three stories below. 'Bunch of ants going nowhere fast.' He heard the door open behind him. He turned around to see Marshal entering the room holding a manila file in his left hand while holding his right hand out to shake his hand.

"Jake, it's great to see you, please have a seat. I'm going to come right to the point. Our consultant's budget has been defunded, and we can no longer can use your services. I've been authorized to pay you for one more week. I hope you understand."

Jake knew it was a crock of shit, nonetheless, he had to play the FBI game, "Sure, I understand. It is what it is, and everyone is cutting budgets. When we open our new summer home at Big Bass Lake, Maggie and I are having a cookout with some friends. It's going to be casual dress and a lot of fun. We would like you to join us."

"Jake, that's nice of you, but you know I'm single."

"No problem, you can bring one of your colleagues. I'll fill you in on all the details as soon as possible." Jake picked up his briefcase and laptop, and shook Marshal's hand.

It was raining when he left the FBI Building, and he saw a deli a few doors from the building. Jake realized he was hungry. While he sat eating a bagel and drinking his coffee, he noticed a young man dressed in a black suit sitting in a nearby by booth. 'The FBI uniforms didn't change.'

When Jake arrived home, he noticed a black government car parked about a hundred feet away. 'Marshal thinks he thought of everything, but I still have my laptop.'

Jake turned on the living room overhead light, and shouted, "John, I'm home." He waited for a response, "John, I'm home." There was no answer. He grew concerned, and rushed down the basement stairs. He knocked on John's bedroom door, paused and opened the door. A typed note on a table read, "Jake, it's getting hot around here and I don't want you to get into trouble for harboring a fugitive. I'm sure you've seen the surveillance vehicle in your neighborhood. I'll contact you when I think it's safe, John."

He stood in the middle of his basement trying to ascertain where John could be hiding and, after a few minutes, he decided John knew what he was doing and he'd found a safe haven. He decided to rest for a minute, lifted his legs up on an ottoman, reached over to the refrigerator and pulled out a cold beer. He took a couple of swigs and turned on the television. It's been a long day, he thought, and a short nap would feel good. He woke up the next morning with the TV still on and the six a. m. and the news signing in.

When he entered the office, Bonnie was standing in the center of the room with a frown on her face. "Did we get fired," she asked.

"Yes, we did," Jake replied. He placed his laptop on a nearby desk and said, "I have all the information pertaining to the Cartel case. I couldn't believe Marshal let me walk out the door without asking for a download, however, I've had some time to rationalize. Maybe he had a motive for not asking for it."

"Like what," Bonnie asked.

"After I invited him to our cookout, he seemed to change his managerial attitude and softened a little. He may have seen an opportunity to nab someone like John Harper, and have a team of agents nearby to come in and make an arrest. I know that's a small thing for a Deputy Director, but I wouldn't put it passed him. He dismissed the thought of asking for the Cartel information in exchange for bigger fish."

"You know, Jake, he could always get a court order forcing you to turn over all of the information you have on the Cartel, and other information in the laptop."

"Yeah, I know. However, at the end of the evening cookout, it may be a moot subject," Jake replied. He went into his office, closed the door, unlocked a metal file cabinet, pulled out a burner phone from a box and touched in Lonny Donavan's burner number, "Lonny, have you heard from John."

"No, is he missing?"

"When I came home last night, I found a note on a table basically saying he's turning into a ghost, because he didn't want to get me into trouble."

"I wouldn't worry too much. Remember how he handled the situation in Arizona? If you're worried about him not showing up at your shindig, trust me, he wouldn't miss that for any reason. Relax, John will be fine."

"Jake, Dr. Dan Zigerfield is on line two," Bonnie announced.

"Jake, I ran a check on the DNA I took from the old house on second Street and came up with a strange result. When I ran it through the database, we got a positive match. It matches Hans Osterfeld. His mother and father are both deceased."

"The kid wasn't his son. The paternal father is alive and owns a restaurant in the city. He moved here from Columbia and married Mary Gonzalas. Mary divorced him and married Carter Osterfeld. Either the father was the victim or he had another child. I'll run down to the restaurant and find out what the story is. Thanks for the update. "

The city street lights were flickering and ready to fully luminate, as Jake parked his car in front of Carlotta's Restaurant. He thought it would be a good idea to bring his thirty eight revolver with him. He hauled it out of the glove compartment and slid it into the, middle of his back holster. As he approached the restaurant's door, it swung open and an old man came stumbling out. He entered the restaurant and, surprisingly, the rest of the clientele were neatly dressed, sitting at tables covered with white tablecloths and enjoying dinner.

A well dressed young man greeted him at the grapevine covered archway door, "May I help you, sir?" he asked.

"Yes, I am looking for Oscar Gonzales. Is he here?"

The young man replied, "I'll see if I can find him. May I ask your name?"

"I'm Jake Lester. He'll know who I am."

"If you would like to wait for him at the bar, I'll be right back."

Jake found a small, but comfortable, booth in the bar. He noticed a group of Hispanics congregated at the bar enjoying small talk. The ambience of the restaurant was far above what he expected. He thought, 'Oscar has come a long way from the previous greasy spoon.'

"Jake Lester, welcome, how are you?" Oscar asked, jovially. He vigorously shook Jake's hand. "Would you like something to drink?"

"No thank you, I'm fine, Oscar," Jake replied. He made a gesture toward the bar and said, "You have a fine establishment here."

Oscar sat across from Jake and asked, "I haven't seen you in a long time, so what brings you here?"

"Two days ago, we were investigating an old abandon house on Second Street and, from the investigation, our forensics man found evidence of blood and body matter. He ran the results of the DNA through the database. Oscar, I'm sorry to say the DNA matches a family member."

Oscar was visibly shaken, "That's impossible. I had two sons. You know Hans died at the hands of the Cartel and Alex greeted you at the door. There must be some mistake."

"Oscar, what you tell me will not diminish your integrity. Did you have outside relationships while you were married to Mary?"

Oscar sat back in is seat, raised two fingers toward the bartender, and waited for the drinks to be delivered. He paused until the bartender left the table, and slid one of the glasses of scotch in front of Jake. "There was a time in my life when I was married to Mary, and I had a mistress, Valentina. When she got pregnant, I was given a choice, either I leave Mary and marry Valentina, or she would tell Mary about the baby. I couldn't let any of the options happen. My real love was Mary. After a long talk with Valentina, I persuaded her to have the baby. I would pay her and the baby's finances the rest of their lives. Unfortunately, Valentina died in a car crash and Marcos, when he was old enough, decided to join the Cartel. Jake, the last I heard Marcos was the champion of Cartel's mixers. If word got out, I told you this, I would be dead within the hour."

"Why would they execute one of their top mixers?" Jake asked.

"You must know, the Cartel doesn't need a reason for executing anyone on their list," Oscar replied. He drank a large amount of his scotch, "Now that you know about this, what are you planning to do?"

"I'm planning to keep this information under wraps and, only if I have to, use it discreetly," Jake replied, as he finished his drink. "If they executed Marcos with all his experience, they plan to move forward with someone who is presently an established mixer."

"Jake, my friend, be very careful. Your closest friend may be at the mercy of the Cartel and, to stay alive, they will eliminate you," Oscar said, as he stood next to the booth.

Jake remembered the same information was conveyed to him by Consuela Delgado's dying words. He finished his drink and left the restaurant. He climbed into his car, took his revolver out of the holster, pushed it into the glove compartment, and settled behind the wheel. He looked into the sideview mirror for oncoming traffic and started to pull away from the curb when he noticed the two men, he witnessed at the diner walking into Oscar's restaurant. He didn't think they were following him. If they were, they wouldn't have gone into the restaurant. 'Coincidence, maybe,' he thought.

41

"Good morning, Bonnie, any calls?" Jake asked. He hung his baseball cap on the hat rack, poured himself a mug of Bonnie's freshly made hazelnut coffee, and walked over to Bonnie's desk.

"Yes, a man, a man named Oscar, and he said you should call him right away." She handed Jake a piece of paper with Oscar's phone number written in bold letters. "Jake, he sounded very nervous."

"Oscar, Jake here. I got your message. What's going on?"

Oscar replied, shouting, "Jake, right after you left the restaurant last night, two men came in dressed in suits and told my bartender they wanted to talk to me. Jake, when I asked who they were, they just looked at me without saying a word for a few seconds. Then one of them, a big bastard, asked me questions about you in Spanish. I couldn't tell them much because I don't know much about you. They could be Cartel, but I don't know for sure. Then, all of a sudden, they walked out the door. I gotta tell you, I was scared to death."

"Why would Cartel men wear suits?"

"Sometime, Geraldo Quostona's, 'El Chapo's' men dress lavishly, drive expensive automobiles, and they make deals with people," Oscar replied.

"What kind of deals?"

"The kind, if you say no, will get you killed. Jake, if they are watching you, they're going to walk into your life, tell you what they want, and they will not take no for an answer. I know how they work from my sons' stories, and now I have two dead sons."

"Thanks for the tip, Oscar."

"And, Jake, I don't want to see or hear from you again," Oscar said, adamantly.

"What was that all about?" Bonnie asked.

"I don't know. Oscar is worried about the Cartel," Jake replied. He walked into his office and closed the door.

Jake thought about Oscar's warning and, to be on the safe side, decided to do a little homework, "Bonnie, please get me all you can on El Chapo. The usual things I can us for a meeting with people who are trying their best to intimidate me."

"Sure, boss. Who in particular are you talking about?"

"Two men who might have the speed dial numbers to El Chapo's cell phone. I don't know their names. They've been following me around for a couple of days, and Oscar told me they may want to make me a deal, a deal they don't take no for an answer. If they are El Chapo's men, I want to have enough knowledge about El Chapo's personal life, even though I won't be speaking to him in person, to carry on an intelligent conversation about his operation."

"I'll get right on it. I know some guys and, if there's anything out there on El Chapo's local operation, these guys will have it. Jake, not for nothing, you know these people don't negotiate?"

"Maybe this time they will," Jake replied. He knew there had to be a tactic to achieve the upper hand. The best way to piss them off, stop their money flow and, to accomplish this, he had to simultaneously stop their mixing and distribution operation from Lind City. It would be impossible to totally stop their operations but, if he could get the current temporary location, he knew one person who might possibly help him.

He pulled out his bourn phone, "Lonny, Jake here."

"Hi Jake, did you find John yet?"

Jake replied, "No, not yet. I'm sure he's hiding out locally," he paused "Lonny, does anyone have a handle on the Cartel's temporary location in Lind City?"

"Jake, everyone in the world is looking for it. If you could find that location, I'm sure the NARCO people would love you. I heard something about the location, wherever it is, it's under one roof and ain't temporary. Our efforts to slow them down by slipping fake bombs in those buildings worked for a short time. They seem hell bent to be located in Lind City."

"It's not temporary?" Jake asked, surprised. "Damn, if that's true we have to adapt, improvise, and overcome. I'll get back to you later."

If the Cartel is permanently imbedded somewhere in the city, it would make life more complicated. Jake knew there were a few places in the city capable of housing an entire Cartel operation. "Bonnie, I'm going out for an early lunch and, from there, I'm heading home for the day." Jake looked out his office window, and saw the two men sitting in a black luxury car parked directly across from Jake's office building. He tried desperately to read the license plate on their vehicle, with no success. He knew, whoever they were, they chose that specific parking location for a reason.

Jake stepped out of his building door, walked toward the Lind City diner, picked out a booth large enough for three people to sit in comfortably, and waited for the two men to join him. He became impatient after a half hour of slowly eating a ham sandwich and sipping a bowl pea of soup. Without the two men, he decided to pay his bill and head for home. As he left the diner, he glanced toward the place where the two men were parked and they were gone. 'What the hell is going on?' His cell phone vibrated; the caller ID indicated Bill Stutz FAA agent.

"Hey Bill, how ya doing?"

"I'm doing great, Jake. I thought I'd give you a heads up on an incoming private jet. The pilot filed a flight plan originating from Izamal, Yucatan, Mexico, and terminating in Lind City at nine p.m. tonight, with three people on board. The names on the manifest are, Rafael Rodriguez, Leonardo Rodriguez and Sebastián Rodriguez. It sounds like they might be related." Bill said, sarcastically. "They didn't mention anything about diplomates on board."

"Thanks, Bill…Where is Izamal, Yucatan, Mexico?"

"It's a small town, about an hour from Merida, Mexico. The airfield is precisely the minimum size approved by the FAA to support a private jet. I can give you a shout when they're about two hours out. One other thing, they plan to permanently domicile the aircraft at our airfield."

"Permanently domicile?" Jake asked, amazed. "Do you have a handle on where they're staying while they're here?"

"That's their plan, and no, I don't have a clue where they're staying. Jake, my gut feeling; these people are coming in with all the legal documents, including passports, without VIP status. I think they are legitimate business men."

"Thanks again, Bill." Jake hurried straight home, picked up the morning newspaper, a few superfluous ads out of the mailbox, scurried down to his basement home office, and dropped the mail and newspaper on a table. He opened his laptop, blew some dust from the keyboard, and entered the three Rodriguez names into the menu labeled, 'Known Names of the Cartel.' He sat back and waited for the results. The laptop screen transformed into a continuous highspeed blur for a few seconds and, when it stopped, their names appeared on the screen. The brief data listing indicated the three men were brothers, with the same home address, and no diplomatic credentials. 'That's it?' Jake mumbled.

"Jake, sorry to bother you on your landline. My guys have very little on El Chapo in reference to the   new location. I asked them to keep digging," Bonnie said.

"Thanks, Bonnie. This El Chapo guy covers all his tracks and, if anyone betrays him, he has them murdered. There has to be a weak link somewhere."

Jake continued for several hours researching possible key indicators which would reveal El Chapo's habits and idiosyncrasies, with negative result. In frustration, he pushed his chair away from his laptop. 'There has to be something. Everyone has idiosyncrasies.' He went to the refrigerator and shuffled John's different brands of bottled beer around until he found his favorite lager. He took a sip of his beer, picked up the advertisements, flipped through the meaningless ads, started to read the newspaper and focused on the headline and Joan Fetter's byline, "International Development Company Seeks Large Parcel of Land in Lind City."

"Jane, I just read your byline in the morning paper."

"And hello to you," Jane said, mockingly. "I thought you would never call. I received an on the record tip from an anonymous person about a possible purchase of prime real estate in this area. I knew you would call, I hoped much earlier, about the morning headline."

Jake proceeded to ask, Jane a leading question, "I know you can't reveal your source, so let me ask you, is your source from Columbia?"

"Jake, you just said you know I can't reveal my source; however, they're not from Columbia. The reason I wanted you to call me earlier, I'm having breakfast with the principals tomorrow morning. I think they will give me an exclusive on all the details, including their plans for contracting a private security company and, if they give me a green light, you will be the first person I call."

"Thank you, Jane. I appreciate it."

Jake touched the speed dial number for Carman Cruz, the Lind City Hotel manager, "Carman, Jake here."

"Hey, Jake, long time no hear. When are we going fishing?"

"Yeah, I've been pretty busy. I haven't been fishing either. I wonder if you could help me?"

"Sure, Jake, what can I do for you?"

"There are three business men coming from Mexico to Lind City tonight. Their last names are Rodriguez. I wondered if they made a reservation at your hotel?"

"Sure, they're staying here. I approved their credit," Carman replied.

"I don't understand. Why did you have to approve their credit?"

"They requested our largest, three-bedroom suite for six months and, an additional six months with a provision for a discount at the hotel rate. They are using their own names, not a company name. I asked if I could help them get acclimated to our city, and they said it wouldn't be necessary. Jake, their credit rating is the very best."

"Thanks, Carman. We're going to have a cookout at our new summer home. I'll give you a shout when we have a date. I hope you can make it." Jake mumbled, 'these people must be the characters looking for a large parcel of land Joan mentioned in her byline, or maybe not. Who are the other two men who have been following me?'

42

"Good morning, Jake. You're off to an early start, and you're wearing shorts. Can I get you a mug of coffee?" Bonnie asked.

"Yes, thank you, black, no sugar."

"I've been working with you for six months, and you always have your coffee the same way, black no sugar. Are you going fishing?"

"Last night was a late night. I watched three men get off a plane at our airport, followed them to the hotel, and nothing of interest happened. I thought I would take a little time away from the business today, and visit an Afghanistan war buddy."

"Might it be Teddy Conway?"

"Yes, how would you know Teddy?"

"I don't. A man named Teddy called early this morning, said he was a friend of yours from the Afghanistan war, and he was going to drop by about eleven a.m. He said he has some sixteen year old Irish Scotch whiskey he wanted to share with you. I was going to tell you about the call right after I brought you your coffee. Did I do a bad?"

"No, in this instance, you didn't do a bad," Jake replied. He sipped some coffee and looked at his watch. He hadn't seen or talked to Teddy since the night of the drive by shooting, in front of his shelter's front door. He knew Teddy well enough to know he wasn't coming here for a social visit. The scotch was a way of telling him he's had something revealed about the tour in Afghanistan. He slid the half full mug of coffee to one side of his desk, opened his laptop, tapped in a password, and uploaded, 'Afghanistan Names'. The screen became flooded with Company A personnel information he compiled relevant to all the good and bad incidents while he was commanding officer of Company A. With that in mind, he stepped away from his desk and, to be on the safe side, initiated the hidden video and recording system.

"Jake, Teddy Conway is here," Bonnie said.

Jake opened his office door and saw Teddy standing in the center of the office, holding a large brown paper bag. "Teddy, come in. I'm sure you've met Bonnie."

"Hey, Jake, I sure have met Bonnie, and she assured me you have proper glasses in your office to imbibe in this wonderful adult beverage," Teddy replied, with enthusiasm.

"Let's go into my office." Jake slid a comfortable chair in front of Teddy, "Have a seat."

"How about we crack open this jug of scotch and drink to old times?" Teddy asked. "Where are those nice glasses Bonnie talked about?"

Jake reached into his desk drawer, grabbed two crystal water glasses, and placed them on his desk. "It's a little early in the day, Teddy."

"We never said that while we were fighting Ali Baba," Teddy remarked.

"Ali Baba, damn Teddy, I haven't heard that since I left Afghanistan. What made you think of the Afghan nickname?"

Teddy picked up the bottle of scotch, placed two fingers around one of the glasses, and asked, "Two or three fingers?"

"Two fingers high, for now," Jake replied. He drew the scotch, toward him, and watched Teddy fill his glass close to the top. "I hope you're not planning to drive home."

Teddy raised his glass and said, "To old time friends."

Jake repeated, "To old time friends." He saw Teddy's face change to red and, remembered, Teddy's face would always turn red when he was with his commanding officer and had to report a major problem. "I know you didn't leave the terminal to come and shoot the shit with me, what's going on?"

Teddy took a solid gulp of scotch, "You're half right. I came here to have a drink with you, and I also came here as a friend and to give you some advice. I come in contact with people of all kind and from all places. Some of the people stop at the center for food, clothes, a place to sleep for the night, and some people stay for a while to get away from something or someone. The people who are in the category of just getting away are the intimidating people. They're not staying at my shelter for lack of food or shelter, in fact, many are very well financially set."

Jake knew the answer to the question he was about to ask, "So, how long do the intimidating people stay with you, and why do they stay with you?"

Teddy swallowed another copious amount of scotch, and said, "I never ask, and they never tell me."

"Teddy, the scotch is starting to put your brain into neutral. If what you're telling me is true, you are accomplishing your goal of helping needy people."

"There is one thing; I can observe and listen to the pulse of Lind City from a crime filled perspective, which no one else in this city can. Jake, I'm telling you to rethink your aggressive approach toward the Cartel. Cooking the drugs can be accomplished in a small tank over an open fire, make no mistake they will, with or without you, have a formidable hold in Lind City, and it will become a large mixing and distribution factor in the U S."

Jake knew there was an aggressive effort by the Cartel to establish their operation in Lind City. The operation would require many people, and it would be to his advantage if he had the name of the mixer. "You've got my attention. If there is an attempt to gain a formidable hold, as you put it, can you give me some names?"

Teddy laughed out loud and slurred, "You haven't changed from the time you were my commanding officer."

There was no reason to ask any more questions, "Teddy, you've had too much to drink. You should go home and take a nap. Maggie and I are having a cookout at our new summer home. We would like you to be there. I'll remind you another time."

"Yeah, I am a little drunk. Forget everything I said."

"Bonnie, please call Teddy a cab."

"Jake, what is wrong with your friend? I could hear him from your office, and it sounded like he was getting angry."

"No, don't worry, Bonnie. That's just Teddy when he's had too much to drink."

Jake drifted through the remainder of the day struggling with Teddy's actual motive for meeting with him. 'Why today? Was the visit strategically planned with the three businessmen who arrived last night?' He looked at his watch, 'Damn, the trout will have to wait for me.' "Bonnie, 'I'm going to call it a day. If any calls of interest come in, you can reach me at home."

"Jake, it's close to five. Don't forget your dinner at six with Carman at the hotel restaurant. You have just enough time to get home, change out of those shorts and get over to the hotel," Bonnie said.

"Oh yeah, thanks for reminding me," Jake replied, as he scurried out the door.

The traffic was light, making the drive to Lind City Hotel parking place effortless. He pulled down the sun visor mirror to make sure there were no personal hygiene issues and, before he flipped the visor up into place, saw the same two men who had been following him, sitting in a car across from the hotel. 'Who are those guys.' His first impulse was to cross the street and confront them; however, there was little time for him to pursue this impulse. He proceeded into the hotel. As many times he had stood in the lobby of the hotel, he was always was impressed by its grandeur and opulent Boca do Lobo furnishings. He saw Carman standing in the center of the lobby talking with a customer, and decided to locate a comfortable chair within Carman's sight.

"Mr. Lester, would you like a beverage?" a hostess asked.

"No thank you, I'm waiting for Mr. Cruz, and I shouldn't be here very long," Jake replied. He thought after the session he had with Teddy today, there should be a timeout in the adult beverage department.

"Jake, sorry to keep you waiting," Carman said.

"No problem. I knew you were busy with a customer, and I always love sitting in this beautiful lobby. It looks like you have a full house today."

Carman led the way to a table by a window and waved to the maître d'. "I hope you're hungry. The new chef's credentials are outstanding and he proves it with a menu of tasty fish, chicken, beef and vegetable dishes."

"Carman, I would like to thank you for inviting me to the opening of your newly designed restaurant."

"Thank you, Jake. I'm sorry I invited you for dinner on such short notice, but I heard something interesting about the three men from Mexico." He glanced in the direction of three perfectly groomed and impeccably dressed men at a corner table. "See those three men, they are the men."

Jake grinned at Carman's attempt at being discrete. "Sure, I see them." His attention abruptly drew away from the three Mexicans to the two men sitting at the table next to them, "Carman, do you know those two men sitting next to the Mexicans?"

"No, I've never seen them before. Do you think they're posing a problem?"

"No, problem, my friend. My curiosity took over for a minute," Jake replied. "Carman, I know you invited me to dinner and suggested you comp my bill, and that's very kind of you; however, I insist on paying my own bill."

"As you wish, Jake, as long as I buy the beverages for our next fishing trip." Carman said.

Jake and Carman exchanged small talk for an hour while enjoying their entrées and, as Jake was about to pay his bill, he noticed the two men he had been observing throughout the entire meal, leave their table. Coincidence or not, he decided to turn the tables on the two men and follow them. "Carman, thank you for a delightful evening, but I'm afraid I have to call it a night."

Jake hurried out of the hotel, looked up and down the street, and they were nowhere in sight. "Damn." He pushed the car's key fob to unlock the doors and, in a split second, his vehicle exploded into a massive heap of debris and flames. The concussion propelled Jake into the air and slammed him onto the pavement. He laid on his back, motionless and unconscious.

The explosion immediately drew a crowd of onlookers, and people taking videos with their cell phones. The sound of police, fire engines, and EMS sirens echoed through Lind City's downtown streets. The EMS driver drove his vehicle past the mob of onlookers, and stopped next to Jake's motionless body. The EMS team jumped from their positions in the vehicle, carrying several pieces of life saving equipment, and surrounded Jake's motionless body. "We've got to get this man to a hospital STAT," the chief paramedic shouted.

"Doctor, I'm Police Commissioner, Robert Marshall, and a good friend of Jake's. How does it look?"

"Commissioner, Mr. Lester has minor body trauma and a mild brain concussion, I believe the concussion happened when he landed head first on the pavement. Now the timing is up to the patient's recovery process. He's an extremely fortunate man to be alive. If the explosion happened while he was inside the car, we would be performing an autopsy now."

"Yes, I agree. Which makes me think, if whoever placed the bomb wanted Jake dead, they would have attached the detonator to go off when the ignition chip was activated," Robert said,

"Jake could hear medical instruments making strange sounds in the distance and saw shadows of people standing next to his bed. He slowly moved his fingers, hands, then opened his eyes.

"He's awake. Get the doctor in here," a familiar voice shouted.

"Maggie?" Jake mumbled.

"Yes, I'm here. You're in the hospital," Maggie replied.

"Ma'am, please, move away from the bed," a nurse ordered. "Sir, can you hear me?" she asked with a loud voice.

"Yes, I can hear you. How long have I been here?" Jake whispered.

"Four days," the nurse, replied. "Can you remember what happened?"

"Yeah, my car exploded, and I landed on my butt." He wiggled his hips, "Oh crap, that hurt. Look, I have things to do. I need to catch the people who did this, and we have to plan a cookout," Jake uttered.

"No sir, you're confused from your concussion. You're going to stay here and get some rest," the nurse said.

"Jake, I'm going to stay home until you're feeling better," Maggie said.

"No, Maggie. It's too dangerous here. Please, you should go back to Dad's place and stay there until it's safe," Jake mumbled. He started to get agitated. "You have to stay with my father, and I'll come and get you when this is all over. Promise me."

"I will, if you insist," Maggie replied.

"Jake, this is the second attempt on your life. I'm going to have a security detail at your side, twenty four seven, until we get the bastards who did this," Robert said.

"Commissioner, thank you but, please, I don't need a security detail." Jake knew who was responsible for the explosion and had knowledge of his recent appointments, the person who is an expert in executing highly specialized pyrotechnic devices. He looked at the nurse with squinty eyes and said, "I think I need some rest."

"Okay, everyone, please leave the room," She demanded. "I'm afraid you have to leave too, Dr. Lester."

43

"Jake, it's so good to have you back in the office. Are you sure three weeks was enough time for you to recuperate?" Bonnie asked. She handed Jake his usual mug of coffee, "You know caffeine isn't good for you especially when you're under a lot of stress."

"Thank you, I'm fine, maybe a little sore around the edges but ready to get on with my work. The caffeine helps me get through the day." Jake replied.

"I didn't have a chance to tell you, the day before your incident, I took care of some easy issues, including giving Minna Hurwitz, at the Big Bass Lake Bakery, a heads up on catering the food for the cookout. I explained to Minna, you insisted on cooking the steaks on the grill yourself. She understood and it wouldn't pose a problem. Jake, you also had one crazy message, I placed it on your desk. The caller said, adapt, improvise and overcome."

Jake smirked when he asked, "I take it he didn't leave a way I could reach out to him?"

"No, he refused to give me a call back number and he said you would know him. Jake, you should be careful, some of the people you come in contact with are rather suspicious."

"We work in a suspicious business. Zig has some evidence for me to look at and he asked me to stop by his lab this morning. When I'm through at the forensic lab, I'm going up to my dad's place to spend a day with him. I'm bringing Maggie home with me. I don't think we will be in present danger. The Commissioner was adamant about giving me a security detail. If that crazy guy calls again, please tell him to call me on my burner phone."

"Jake, someone should know where you are at all times. Does Maggie know you're going up there?"

"No, I want to surprise her and, if I told her anything about me driving, she would have a fit. It's only a two and a half hour drive. I'll be fine."

When he took the short walk to Zig's forensics' lab, Jake's legs reminded him they were injured in the blast and not completely healed. He entered the Lab's garage and, by then, he was taking short steps and a slower cadence.

"Hey, Jake, if you need a few minutes, I have time to drink some coffee and chat," Zig said.

"No thanks, Zig, I'll be fine. What do you have for me?"

"I know you realize, by the way your vehicle exploded, the person who synchronized the receiver chip in your car door with the transmission from your car fob, was an expert in pyrotechnics." Zig picked up a small piece of plastic with three short wires protruding from it, "You see this?"

"Sure, it's part of a detonator receiver," Jake replied.

"Yes, you're right. However, this isn't the run of the mill receiver." Zig scrubbed the piece of plastic with his thumb, and placed it in Jake's hand, "There are a very few people on this planet who know how to program this receiver and, without a doubt, he or she would have military experience." He methodically took the piece of plastic chip from Jake, dropped it an evidence bag and set it down on a stainless steel table. "My friend, you have an enemy within."

During the two hour drive to Whispering Pines, Jake had an opportunity to think about Zig's comment. It paraphrased the message Consuela Delgado gave Jake three months ago with her dying breath, and it's the third time he'd heard it this month. He listened to Consuela's warning the night of the drive by shooting, and secretly started gathering information on a few people who would fit the Cartel's profile. The car blast didn't curb his memory. When he compiled a list of explosive experts, he refused to think one of his closest friends would be a member of the Cartel. He parked his car in front of his father home, where Maggie and his father were sitting on the porch.

"My God what are you doing here? What a great surprise. Is everything ok?" Maggie asked, as she threw her arms around Jake.

"Son, is everything all right?" John asked.

Jake replied, "I missed you both and thought I would surprise you. There's another reason for my trip. We have to start planning a cookout at the new summer home."

John opened the adult medicine cabinet and picked out his best bottle of scotch. "It's been awfully dry around here since you've been away." He poured a jigger of scotch into the three glasses. "Here we are." He gave Jake and Maggie their glasses, "Cheers, now tell us about this cookout. "

"Yes, let's all sit down and talk about what's going on," Maggie said.

Jake placed his glass on a wooden coaster and sunk into his favorite recliner. "I've been away from my sweetheart for about a month and, in that time, I've rattled some Cartel bushes, to say the least. You know Dad, I thought we were through with human trafficking when we shut their operation down in the talc mine. It seems it only slowed them down for about a day. I also thought we had slowed the flow of fentanyl too, and we have, but not to the extent I would like. Dad, remember the old house on Second Street in the city?"

"Sure, I remember it. It was a majestic home back in the day. The city has owned it for about twenty-five years, "John replied.

"The Cartel bought it from the city a month ago for a dollar and, over night, they turned it into a temporary human trafficking location until they can move into a permanent location. I tried to pursue it, but Marshal Dunkin had to discontinue our services because of a defunding issue. That doesn't worry me. It means I simply need to move my timing up a little. It's imperative I Have everyone whose been involved in the case together much sooner."

"Jake, do you think this Marshal Dunkin guy is working with the Cartel?" John asked.

"I have my doubts about him. I invited him to our cookout, and I think he will be there." Jake replied. He paused, "I suggested he bring a colleague, like FBI colleague. If he, indeed, shows up with a colleague, and a few agents, I will know he's okay. If he comes to the cookout alone, chances are he's on the take."

"Jake, it sounds like you're gambling that he's on the take and, if he is, how will you protect yourself from the Cartel," John said.

"John and a few of his trusted FBI agents will be in a nearby location. They can arrest Marshal, take him into protective isolation, and the Cartel won't know what happened. There's a little bit of a problem with John. He thought it would be better if he moved out of our cellar and got lost in the wind. He left a note indicating he didn't want me charged for harboring a fugitive. I know John and Lonny are solid, and I can trust them."

"Honey, will Bonnie still work with you, and can she be trusted?

"Yes, she is going to work on the small clients until this is over." He sipped the remainder of his scotch.

"Back to the cookout, when you said it's imperative, I have everyone together, do mean suspects in the Cartel case?" Maggie asked.

"Yes, some of the people we invite are under suspicion in the Cartel case. I think the sooner we get to Big Bass Lake to make catering arrangements with Minna Hurwitz, the easier it will be for her to have all the food ready. We can leave first thing in the morning, and get the planning completed. We might have a chance to wet a line in our new boat."

"I like the idea of wetting a line. Wait a minute, we're going to have the cookout catered, except you're not going to give up your grilling expertise to the caterer?" Maggie chuckled.

The sun was close to high noon in the small town of Big Bass Lake. The village streets looked bright and picturesque when Jake and Maggie drove past the town's welcome sign. They noticed the large flower vases and the stars and stripes flags, placed on all six corners of the town, which were proudly donated by the town's Business Association. They drove past their newly built summer home and found a parking place in front of the Big Bass Lake Deli. "We can talk with Minna about the party, pick up a sub, and head back to the house," Jake said.

"Maggie, Jake, how good to see you. Did you stop to see your new home. It's so beautiful and spacious," Minna said.

"Thank you, Minna. The contractor told me his men were extremely happy with the lunches they ordered for delivery. We're going to order a couple of sandwiches but, first, we wanted to finish the arrangements for the food," Maggie said.

"Sure, I'll be happy to take care of both items for you," Minna said, jovially.

The panoramic view of Big Bass Lake, from newly positioned porch had significantly improved from the former location beyond Jake and Maggie's expectations.

"Isn't this gorgeous," Maggie asked. She sipped her coffee. I love the way the contractor took advantage of our property frontage, and now we have a new dock, right at our back door."

"Yes, and we have a storage room for all our fishing tackle in the basement. Oh, we forgot to tell Minna what time we wanted the food delivered. I think she should also be on our guest list for the cookout." Jake said.

"Minna asked me if it would be all right to store some of the catering equipment in the storage room. I said it would be fine, and I also gave her a time to deliver the food," Maggie said. She looked out at the lake and noticed a small bass jumping out of the water to snag a large Mayfly. The Mayfly was so large, the small bass had difficulty swallowing the bug. Maggie thought for a few minutes and asked herself, was this an omen? "Jake, I know we're going to have some of our friends here in a couple of weeks for the cookout and, I also know, some of these friends, or should I say, associates, will be here as well. When you showed me the guest list, I noticed a few of those associates are high ranking FBI. Honey, are you certain you will be able to manage a high ranking agent like Marshal Dunkin?"

Jake replied, "I understand your concern. You're wondering what might happen if the shit hits the fan with a high ranking law enforcement official in attendance. You have my word, we have a solution for every scenario, from a member of the Cartel, to someone choking on the food."

"Do you really have a member of the Cartel on the list?... Whose we have a solution?" Maggie asked, sarcastically.

Jake smiled and replied, "There may be a few Cartel members and, if a ruckus starts, we'll have the best of the best ready to respond."

Maggie wrinkled her nose, "Oh my, you're kidding me."

44

"Good morning, Jake. You're up early this morning."

"Good morning, Minna. I'm stopping by to pick up six of those wonderful bagels for our breakfast this morning and to check to see if there's last minute things you might need from us for the cookout."

"I can't think of anything we need. Did Maggie have a chance to tell you about me putting some equipment in your basement storage room?"

"Yes, it would be perfectly all right. I keep my fishing gear and some boating supplies in the storage room, and I keep the outside door locked. I'll give you the key to the door when you bring your equipment to the house."

Jake took the last bite of his bagel, swallowed the remainder of his coffee, and said, "Minna makes the best bagels on this planet." He wiped his lips with a paper napkin, "I'm going to the basement for the life jackets, maybe we can get a couple hours of fishing in before our guests arrive."

"Jake, I was thinking, we have plenty of room in the store room, why don't we allocate part of the room for a wine cellar?"

"That's a great idea. I'll take some measurements while I'm getting the life jackets, and I'll leave the door unlocked for Minna."

Jake climbed onto a step ladder, wiped the cobwebs from the ceiling, and started taking the measurements for a refrigerated wine cellar. 'I'm so glad we have two entrances into the storage room. I'd hate like hell to run outside through a rain storm for a bottle of wine.' He turned on his flashlight and ran the light beam across the wooden joist, 'I'll be, someone thought of everything,' and scribbled the final measurements on a pad.

Maggie opened the storage room's inside door, and shouted, "Honey, I think if we try to get on the lake, it might be to close our guests' arrival time."

"I think you're right. I'll be up in a few minutes with a few bottles of wine to cool in the fridge."

Maggie heard a soft knock on the front door and saw the shadow of a woman through the opaque section of the glass door. She opened the door, "Minna, hi, the storage room door is unlocked, feel free to use the space. We hope you can enjoy our gathering."

"Thank you, I will have two of my employees working the food tables and, I'm sure, I'll have time to enjoy your cookout with the rest of your friends. I have to be on my way, and thank you again for inviting me," Minna said.

Jake commented from the kitchen, "It sounds like Minna has everything under control."

Maggie stepped onto the front porch and watched Minna as she backed her car up to the storage room door, when she turned to reenter the house, she noticed a black umbrella laying across one of the porch chairs, picked it up and, shouted, "Jake, do you know who left this umbrella on the front porch?"

Jake's face erupted into a large smile, and replied, "I'll bet one of the contractors left it there by mistake. You should leave it on the chair. Maybe the owner will come back looking for it." He stepped to the kitchen window, looked toward the back of the landscaped property, and Lonny was nowhere in sight. He started stacking the wine bottles into the fridge and noticed one of the bottles of his most expensive red wine was partially used 'Hmm.' He continued to stack the wine bottles, and whispered, 'It's good to know at least two friends have my back.'

"What did you say, Jake?"

"Nothing, Maggie. I was just thinking out loud."

Maggie flipped a small notebook open and said, "Honey, I want to make sure we have all the guest cards ready when people arrive, Let's see, we have Marshal Dunkin and his Aides, Teddy Conway, Minna Hurwitz, John Swift the NARCO Detective and, I'm sure, John Harper won't make it. I hope everyone has a great time. Did I miss anyone?"

Jake replied, "I think we invited Carman Cruz from the hotel, Janis Dalton, and Gus Highland will be coming without Sister Mary Francis."

"Oh, right, we can't forget Janis, the village historian and Gus. I wish your dad could be here for all the fun."

"We should plan for the inevitable guest who will invite an extra friend or two. I think my father is past crowded gatherings. I promised him a week of fishing on the lake and he thought it was a better plan."

"Oh my God, Jake, we forgot to invite one of our closest friends, Dan Zigerfield. We've known Zig for years, and he's always been readily available when we needed him."

"We're covered; I invited Zig a couple of weeks ago. Maggie, don't worry, all our bases are covered, and we're going to have an exciting party."

"Jake, what do you mean exciting party?" Maggie asked, before she walked onto the back patio, and noticed three young ladies, dressed in black and white waitress uniforms, and listening intently to Gus's serving instructions, "Jake, did you have an arrangement with Gus to have waitresses serving our guests?"

Jake replied, "Yeah, Gus asked me if we would mind having a couple of waitresses, free of charge, to serve the appetizers. I didn't think you would mind."

It was late in the afternoon when the guests started arriving for Jake and Maggie's new summer home cookout and, surprisingly, within an hour all the guests had arrived. The weather cooperated throughout the afternoon and, as the sun started to fall behind a group of pine trees, a cooling shade covered the guest while they enjoyed the catered food and Jake's grilled steaks.

Jake glanced over the guests sitting at their tables, to ensure everyone had finished their food, he picked up a spoon, gently tapped it against a glass and, with enthusiasm, asked, "Can I please have everyone's attention? He repeated, "Could I have your attention please?"

The once noisy guests calmed down to a whisper and the sound of people clinking their glasses, "speech, speech."

"Thank you all for coming. I hope you enjoyed the food catered by the Minna Hurwitz Deli, please stand, Minna."

"Thank you, Jake," Minna said.

"When we invited everyone to our cookout, we said it was going to be an interesting event, and so it shall be." Jake waited for one of John Swift's NARCO men to position himself behind Minna, and announced, "About five months ago, we received a heads up from Janis Dalton, the local historian, about shadow abnormalities in the photos of a female intruder standing next to a basement window, while she was taking early morning photos for the Historical Society. Through the cooperation of John Swift's NARCO Department, we were able to connect the dots to Minna. "Minna's real name is Martina Huerta. Martina was placed here as a Cartel mole about six years ago. She is an explosive expert and is responsible for several explosions taking in place in and around Lind City, including our summer home and the bombing of my car two weeks ago.

Martina jumped up, and screamed, "You'll never take me alive." She pulled a handheld detonator from her pocket, placed her thumb on a red button, and shouted, "I'll take every one of you bastards with me."

The guests were in shock and disbelief. Someone hollered, "Somebody stop her."

The two NARCO agents grabbed her by the arms as she mashed her thumb down on the red button. A few seconds of complete silence fell over the party guests and, much to everyone's surprise, nothing happened. There was no explosion.

"The explosives were defused by my friend, Lonny Donavan, who is also a pyrotechnic specialist." Jake waved to Lonny who was standing in the background holding his black umbrella, "Thank you Lonny."

Jake pointed at Marshal Dunkin. "Most of you have met our distinguished guest, Marshal Dunkin. It has been my privilege to work with the Deputy Director of the FBI and, during the time I reported to Marshal, we became friends. He listened to my facts, and reviewed my evidence indicating Senior Special Agent FBI John Harper had acted in self-defense by killing two rogue FBI Agents, who were recruited by the Cartel. John Harper has been cleared of all charges."

The guests clapped and loudly cheered.

Jake paused and waited for the cheering to stop. He had to give the two men in black suits, who were ordered by John Swift to follow his every step, time to position themselves for the next announcement. He started by saying, "The time we live on this earth is precious. We meet people who make a difference in our lives, good and bad. I think everyone sitting here today knew what my goal was for this community the minute we hauled a young man's body from this very lake, a young man who was brutally murdered by members of the Cartel, I knew my goal was to keep the Cartel from expanding there mixing operations. It was late one night, six months ago, when a top Cartel member who was gunned down by a drive by assassin, gave me significant advice. Her dying words were, "Trust no one…Cartel is everywhere." I didn't realize the significance of her words at that moment. When Maggie and I started connecting the Cartel dots, we realized Consuela Delgado was handing me the mixer, the person who blends the percentage of Fentanyl with other drugs, in a location no one would ever expect, and a person no one would ever believe would do such a heinous crime. A crime where the mixers had to work in their underwear to prevent a fraction of an ounce from being sneaked out of the room, and to send a deadly message to anyone caught stealing, they are executed in front of all the other mixers. A crime that kills our children." Jake sipped some water, looked out among the guests, and focused on one person. "It is with deep regret I tell you we have located, the Cartel's mixing and distribution facilities. A crew from John Swift's NARCO Department are at the scene of the old terminal building." Jake's voice quivered, "Teddy Conway, how on earth could you live among the people of this community? The people who called you a friend, you called them your friend and, you, who I called my best friend."

The guests stared in disbelief at the person they once respected, loved and trusted.

Teddy sat in total silence with his head bowed down and uttered no words of remorse.

Jake looked at the NARCO men and, in a commanding voice said, "Get him out of our sight."

Made in the USA
Columbia, SC
02 December 2023

27594957R00170